Ghost Sickness

Mae Martin Mysteries, Volume 5

Amber Foxx

Published by Amber Foxx, 2016.

GHOST SICKNESS

First edition. August 6, 2016.

Written by Amber Foxx.

Chapter One

What in the world is wrong with Niall? And where is he going? Mae Martin had come home from a morning run on the trails above the Rio Grande to find she was out of coffee. Walking through Truth or Consequences' small, historic, and summer-sleepy downtown on her way to get a cup, she was puzzled to see her father's pickup truck at the intersection of Foch and Broadway, its bed loaded with flattened cardboard boxes as if someone were moving. Niall Kerrigan, her father's life partner, was at the wheel. He lingered at the stop sign long after the lone car on Broadway had passed, staring ahead, not seeing her.

Concerned, Mae walked up and tapped on the window.

Niall jerked to attention and rolled the window down. "Trying to give me a heart attack?" His Maine accent, indestructible after fifteen years in New Mexico, flattened the *r* out of heart, making it sound almost like *hat*.

"Sorry. You looked kinda distracted. Are you okay?"

He shook his head and looked away. "Florencia Mirabal went into hospice yesterday. She wants me to clear out her house for her."

Mae had only met Florencia, a famous artist, once, but she knew how close Niall was to her. This request had to be over-whelming for him. "I've got the day free. Let me help you." Mae wanted not only to spare him a little of the grief but a lot of the heavy lifting. In addition to smoking over a pack a day, he never exercised outside of the demands of his work. Mae knew she was probably worrying too much, but she couldn't help thinking the combined exertion and emotional strain *could* give him a heart at-tack. "Why didn't you ask me?"

"It's not like she's exactly a friend of yours."

"She's *your* friend. And I liked her when I met her."

"Did you?" Niall sounded skeptical. "I thought she was rude to you."

On being introduced to Mae, Florencia had said mockingly, "Ah. Marty's daughter. The health nut." She'd looked her up and down and then up again as if Mae's height were a marvel and said in her clipped pueblo accent, "Like the proverbial horse." It had been at an Art Hop, the night the galleries stayed open late while musicians and fire dancers performed on the streets. Florencia Mirabal had been at Rio Bravo Fine Arts, her bald head crowned with an extraordinary beaded hat, her sagging face made up, her frail body clad in a bright red dress. Incurably ill, but still holding court with Truth or Consequences' other famous artists.

Mae had felt insulted for a second, but then she'd remembered something one of her health science professors had said. *Health is a crown on a well man's head visible only to the sick.* Florencia had lost that crown. "Not *that* rude. It was okay. I kinda knew where it came from. Let me give you a hand."

Niall opened the door and slid over to the passenger seat. "Thanks. I guess you could tell, I can't even think straight to drive."

Mae got in and drove. Niall slumped and took a key from his pocket, clutching it and closing his eyes. Half a block up Foch Street, she pulled the truck over to the curb on the hill in front of the antique shop and patted his thin, ropy arm. "How about some coffee before we tackle the house? I was headed out to get some, and you look like you could use a little boost."

He didn't respond, but that was normal for him. Signs of affection from anyone but Jim Bob "Marty" Martin usually made him either cringe or freeze. Mae took his stillness as a kind of compliment.

"It's a hundred degrees out." He regarded the key in his hand, turning it over restlessly. "Can't you park any closer?"

She'd already parked as close to the coffee shop as she could get without driving around the block to face the right way on Main. "Come on. It won't kill you to walk." *Wrong choice of words.*

Niall put the key in one pocket and removed his cigarettes and lighter from another. "Fine. I'll have a smoke while we do it. Then you can tell me it *will* kill me."

Mae didn't say anything. She was sure her father mentioned the issue often enough. They climbed the hill at Niall's slow pace and turned right on Main Street. Passing the brightly colored storefronts of an artist's studio, a thrift store, and a space for rent, they reached the red door of Passion Pie Café. Niall started to give Mae money, but she told him it would be her treat and left him on the painted bench outside to finish his cigarette.

She joined the line for coffee. Misty Chino, the barista, was a young Apache woman barely out of her teens, with a long face, a prominent nose, and a lithe, fit figure. She sparkled and smiled as she took orders, her service a blend of speed and charm, as graceful as her fire dancing on Art Hop nights.

When Mae reached the counter, Misty held out her hand and displayed a diamond ring. The stone had a pinkish hue and was set in rose gold. Mae caught her breath. "Wow. That's gorgeous. Congratulations. When am I finally gonna meet him?" Mae's friendship with Misty was still developing, but the introduction seemed overdue.

"Good question. He works evenings, I work days, and he's sure as heck not going running with us. Reno's idea of a workout is a *stroll.*"

That didn't sound like a newly engaged woman, more like an old married lady putting up with her husband. Mae placed her order and asked, hoping to hear more enthusiasm, "Are you excited?"

"Relieved is more like it." Misty filled two cups. "We've been together so long it's about time, you know?"

The relationship sounded more like a habit than a romance. At a loss what to say, Mae resorted to the sugarcoated diplomacy of her Southern upbringing. "Well, he's got good taste in women and jewelry."

Misty took the compliment with a smile.

As Mae exited the café, the heat and sun of the desert summer day hit her like a wall of fire. Niall half-straightened from his slouch and mumbled his thanks, taking his coffee. Mae sat beside him, grateful that the cigarette was out.

"Misty got engaged to Reno Geronimo."

"Well, if that's not stupid, I don't know what is."

"Whoa. That's a pretty harsh judgment. You know him?"

"Ayeh." Niall's Maine affirmative came out as *yuh* with a trace of effort at the beginning, a sound that always reminded Mae of pulling out dandelions by the roots, though she couldn't say why. "Know him and his father. Orville's a successful artist, Reno's a starving artist. And I mean starving. He's a waiter who's never had a show. Not even one painting in a gallery here. I don't know what he does with his work. I never see it. And those kids are twenty years old. They need to live a little before they get tied down." He sipped his coffee. "Did you tell her you got married too young?"

"She knows, but it didn't seem like the time to remind her. That would have been a downer. She shows me her ring and I say, 'When I was your age I was planning my first divorce?' "

Niall puffed out a weak laugh. "I guess not. Maybe his father will talk some sense into them. His first marriage didn't last too long, either. In fact, Florencia is his ex. He married Reno's mother later and that lasted, but Orville and Flo got married in college when they were twenty. Two artists in Santa Fe. Seemed romantic at the time, I'm sure, even if it was a mistake."

"At least they went to college."

"You thinking about yourself, or Reno and Misty?"

"Both, I reckon." At age twenty-eight, Mae had finished her first year of college in the spring, finally getting started on the education she'd foregone with her marriages. "I'd hate to see Misty stuck where I was for so long."

"She's too bright not to go to school. Orville ought to talk with them about that, too."

They returned to the truck and Mae followed Niall's directions, driving up Foch and turning down a narrow side street to the gravel drive behind Florencia Mirabal's home.

"Get as close to the front door as you can," Niall said. "I don't have a key for the back."

Mae pulled the truck into the weedy patch of dirt that qualified as a side yard, drawing near to the porch's side steps. The front steps led to a long, winding set of stone stairs set into a steep cliff, giving the little house the feeling of a castle. On their way in, she and Niall paused on the porch, looking down at Main Street and the view of the Rio Grande and Turtleback Mountain beyond the town.

Mae said, "This is such a perfect place for an artist to live. It must have been hard for her to leave."

Niall made a grunting sound, an attempt to stifle his smoker's cough, and unlocked the door. Mae followed him into a small living room full of bright, overstuffed furniture and crammed book shelves. A collection of paintings filled every space on the walls. One of Niall's smaller scrap metal sculptures, a plumber made from pipes and wrenches, bent over in the classic posture in a corner, the crack of his pipe-elbow buttocks exposed above the metal sheath of his pants.

Niall closed the door. "She wants us to get rid of the books, the food, the dishes, the furniture—everything but the art."

Mae asked, "Are we sorting it into keep, sell, and give away? How do you want to do it?"

He shoved his hands into his pockets. His brown eyes looked large and distorted through his thick glasses as he stared at his own work. "I don't want to do it at all."

"I know." Mae squeezed his hand quickly, knowing he would only accept the touch for a moment. "It has to make you think about her dying."

"No." Niall's odd Yankee version of the word came out as a nasal, descending *daow* that bore little resemblance to anything spelled n-o. "I've seen that coming for a long time. It's the frickin' *work*. She had to know I'd hate doing this."

"It means she trusted you, though." Mae sensed he was covering deeper feelings with this complaint. "I'll do as much as I can. Tell me where to start."

He walked over to a chair and gave it a small shove. "Stuff's not bad. Jamie need anything at his place?"

"I think he does, but he painted his walls so funny not much goes with 'em. Anyway, it might bother him to get a dying person's furniture." Mae's boyfriend, a singer-songwriter who lived in Santa Fe, had a few issues with death and dying—cultural, personal, and spiritual. "I can help you load the truck for the thrift shop."

"*Daow*. Make 'em come get it. It's a good donation."

Mae looked up at a full-length portrait of a handsome blond cowboy angel in a striped shirt, a Western hat, and suggestively fitted chaps. He stood alone in a desert with distant mountains behind him, his boots planted on the hard red earth while his dusky wings spread in front of clouds that circled him like layers of stormy halos. She felt the artist must have intended the way her eyes were drawn to the cowboy's dreamy blue eyes and blue-jeaned crotch about equally.

"He's not your type," Niall said, with a hint of a dry laugh.

"He's pretty, though. Is it her work?"

"How long have you lived in T or C?" Niall turned to Mae, his head jutting out, modifying his habitual slouch into a more assertive posture. "Delmas Howe."

"The guy that does the flowers?"

Niall exhaled noisily. "And the *men*. He's a New Mexico state living treasure. This pretty cowboy is worth—jeez—thousands. *Thousands*." He scuffed into the next room. "And her whole collection—she ought to have it stored somewhere secure. Get it out of the house."

Mae lingered with the cowboy. She recognized the local artist's style now. He rendered a winged, sexy man with the same depth and light that he used in painting petals and pistils. "Any idea what she plans to do with the art?"

"No idea. That's between her and her lawyer."

Mae joined Niall in the kitchen. The small table near the window was barely adequate to accommodate a single diner. "Where's her family?"

"Acoma Pueblo, as far as I know. She doesn't speak to them." Niall opened and closed a few cabinets. Mae found something sad about all the cans and jars stocked up as if Florencia had not expected to die but to keep on cooking and eating. Niall closed a cupboard and squeezed the handle. "She said she's giving instructions at the hospice that if her brother and his family try to visit, they aren't allowed."

"And she never got remarried or had any kids?"

"No. And no kids."

The look of the house—no photographs, no signs of a social life—made Mae think Niall might be Florencia's only real friend, the only person cranky and stand-offish enough to understand her. "She's lucky she has you. It would be awful to be dying and not have anyone who cared."

Niall ran his hand over the counter and then patted it. Mae sensed he was avoiding her eyes. "You want me to start clearing out in here?" she asked. "I can get the boxes out of the truck."

"Thanks." His voice was husky. "I'll start in the living room."

She went out and collected a stack of nested cardboard boxes from the back of the pickup.

A slender, brown-skinned young man of medium height strode up the back street and into the yard, staring at the truck. He wore his long black hair in a ponytail, and his face was perfectly proportioned, with brown eyes, a straight nose, high cheekbones, and full lips. He looked familiar, someone Mae had seen around town, but she couldn't place him. "What are you doing here?" he asked.

If he had smiled, he would have been stunningly attractive, but his expression was sullen and his voice quiet and hard, as if Mae and Niall had intruded on *his* property.

"We're helping Florencia. Packing up her stuff."

"What? Who are you? Why would you do that?" His accent suggested he was a speaker of a Native language—Mae guessed Apache. Mescalero, where Misty was from, was the nearest reservation. Was this her boyfriend? "She didn't die, did she?" He seemed anxious, as if he had urgent business with Florencia.

"No." Mae set the boxes down. "She went into hospice." She reached out to shake hands. His grip was soft. "I'm Mae Martin. My daddy's partner Niall Kerrigan is a real good friend of Florencia's."

"Reno Geronimo."

"Misty's fiancé. She's told me about you. Nice to meet you." *Sort of.* Reno didn't strike Mae as particularly suited to Misty.

"How long does," he hesitated, "the woman who lived here have?"

"I have no idea. I think hospice is for when you have a few months, but Niall would know more."

"If her time is short, please don't say her name. We don't speak the names of the dead. It calls back the ghost."

"Sorry. I'll be careful. My boyfriend has a taboo like that, too." Jamie was half Aboriginal Australian, Warlpiri, on his mother's side. "I didn't know not to use it already, though." Mae picked up the boxes again. "You want to come in and talk to Niall?"

Reno slipped his hands in his pockets and rattled keys and coins, frowning. After a moment, he said, "All right."

They went around through the front and found Niall sitting on the floor beside a bookshelf, pulling things off it. Mae placed the boxes beside him and Niall began to assemble one, taping its bottom. Mae was about to explain that Reno had come to see Florencia, but the young man spoke first. "You're not doing the studio?"

That was rude. No hello? No sympathy?

"Nope. It's locked. And I don't have a key to it." Niall placed a book in the box. "She doesn't want anything taken out of it. Thinks a museum might want it, the whole studio the way she left it. Her brushes. Her easel. Her work in progress. Legacy exhibit." He looked up at Reno. "She talk to you about that?"

Reno nodded. "Yes. I just wanted to make sure. I should be going." He left without further words.

Niall resumed packing books. Mae looked down at the top of his head, with the gray hairs curling through the black. "Was that a little weird? I could swear he had no idea she'd gone into hospice, but then he started acting like he was the caretaker here."

"Something came between them. She won't say what. He might have come to try to sort it out. Too late. And it's too bad. He was her student, her friend, the only person besides me that could put up with her." He opened a book that had a bookmark in it, stroking the page. His voice cracked. "I gave her this for her last birthday."

"You okay?" Mae asked.

Niall put the bookmark back between the pages and closed the volume. "Christ. Don't know why I did that. She's never going to finish it." He dropped the book in a box and went outside.

Mae began her work in the kitchen, packing mismatched plates and utensils into boxes for the thrift store. A cast-iron frying pan sat on the stovetop as if Florencia was going to come back and cook breakfast. Mae paused as she started to pack it up. Jamie always complained about her cheap nonstick frying pan—but no, that would bother him, scavenging the dying woman's stuff. She put the pan in the box.

The contents of the refrigerator, nothing but yogurt and applesauce, suggested Florencia had reached a point where she couldn't eat solid food, but there was so much left, she'd overestimated either her appetite or her lifespan.

What would it be like to know it was the last time you'd go grocery shopping, the last time you'd do all your ordinary tasks? To have to stop and let go of your life? Mae had so many plans and goals. Everything that mattered hinged on having a *future*. What would it be like not to have one? The idea threw a blank wall in front of her mind. No matter how she tried to imagine the experience, she couldn't—unless that faceless obstacle was it.

When Niall returned, a whiff of tobacco smoke came through the door with him. It bothered Mae more than ever, provoking an image of helping her father to put all of Niall's stuff in boxes. Marty, a college track and softball coach, was fit and active. His fifty-one years looked like forty on him, while Niall, a year younger, could have passed for sixty. Mae was sure he had chronic bronchitis, and lung cancer could be next.

Soft thuds came from the living room, broken up with long pauses. Mae dropped the last expired yogurt into the trash and walked to the living room doorway. Niall was putting books in boxes, very slowly, opening pages, stopping to read passages. He coughed, sniffed, sighed. Mourning while Florencia was still alive. Reeking of smoke. Mae wanted to tear the cigarettes out of his pocket.

The urge crossed her mind again and again as the work stretched out through the day. While Mae was in the bedroom packing up the clothes Florencia had left behind, he cleaned the bathroom, with frequent smoke breaks and long pauses between bouts of activity. Mae felt the weight of those silences. He was slowed down by grief, and also by lack of breath.

The bedroom gave Mae a new impression of Florencia. A silk duvet. Satin-edged sheets. Small paintings on the wall and delicately painted pottery arrayed on the dressers. She'd cared about the beauty of her place of sleep. *I wonder if she had guests here, but not the kitchen.* Not lately, though. If she'd had a lover, Niall wouldn't have been the one she'd turned to for this final favor.

Mae went to check on one of Niall's silences and found him staring at a hairbrush. *Hair.* A reminder of when Florencia had been healthy. He glared at her. "Stop fussing over me. I need to be alone."

"Sorry."

Mae returned to work in the bedroom closet, trying to shut off an image of Niall sick and bald.

She noticed a few strands of Florencia's hair on some of the sweaters as she took them out of drawers. Sometimes it was long and dark; at other times it had been cut short and dyed fuchsia. *Fuchsia.* A lot of people cut their hair when they started chemo. Had she done that and then gone crazy with the color? Defying death? Mocking her illness? Another piece of the puzzle of this woman.

As the afternoon faded into early evening, Niall declared they'd done all they could for one day. They stepped out onto the porch and he locked the front door, a conventional lock plus a deadbolt. "We should check the back door."

On the rear of the house near the driveway, a former screened porch had been converted into a sunroom. All the blinds were drawn, as they were on most houses in the hottest months of the year. Niall tested the door knob and bent down to peer into the crack. "Both locks are on."

"Is that the studio?"

"Ayeh." He rattled the door again. "Secure as it's going to get."

As they walked to the truck, Mae said, "I'm surprised she doesn't have an alarm system with that art collection."

"Not many people know she has it. I guess you could tell she didn't have a lot of visitors. Alarm's a good idea, though. Or storage. I'll call her tomorrow when she's gotten settled."

Mae drove to Niall and Marty's adobe house on Riverside Drive. Their other vehicle wasn't in the driveway. "I guess Daddy's not back yet." He ran summer softball camps at the College of the Rio Grande campus in Las Cruces. "I'll wait with you."

"No, go home. Get some rest. I could use some time by myself."

Mae hesitated to leave. Though she understood the need to be alone, she wanted Niall to have someone within shouting distance if he changed his mind. "How about I start dinner for y'all?"

He put on a shocked look. "*You?*"

"Why not? A bad cook is better than none."

She headed for the purple front door. Niall, a few paces behind her, stopped when his cell phone rang. He answered. "Hmm?" Had to be Marty. Niall would at least say hello to someone less intimate. "Yeah. Good enough." He pocketed the phone. "He got a table for us at Dada Café."

"That was real thoughtful."

"Ayeh. I'm not in the mood for it, but he meant well."

Mae offered to drive, but Niall—though he had to be so exhausted he could hardly stand—grumbled about the wastefulness of returning in separate cars when they could walk a few blocks. She shook her head. In the morning she could hardly get him to walk a block, and now she couldn't get him to rest when he was tired. If he held still, maybe the grief would overwhelm him.

They went inside for a quick cleanup, then took Pershing Street to Broadway and turned left toward the restaurant. The blue neon sign on the flat roof of the Ellis building displayed the name of its former owner, depression-era healer Magnolia Ellis, against a sky reflecting pink from the sunset. The sidewalks in front of it bore the imprint *WPA 1939*. Like much of downtown, the building dated to the years when the town, then called Hot Springs, had been a mecca for people seeking cures and even miracles. When Mae and Niall passed the two-story brick structure, she was startled to see a realtor's sign in the downstairs window below the lettering advertising the current tenant's chiropractic practice. She stopped and made sure she'd seen it right.

"What are you doing?" Niall asked, slightly out of breath. "Need to *rest?*"

"It's for sale. I wonder if Dr. Freidan is gonna retire."

"Want me to buy it for you? Set you up as the heir to Magnolia?"

There was no way Niall could afford to purchase the historic landmark. He was successful, but not like Florencia Mirabal, and though Mae had gifts as a psychic and healer, she was no Magnolia Ellis. Niall had to be kidding about buying the place. "You buy it for me, I'm setting up a personal training studio."

"Nope. In T or C, there's more call for healers." The town had become Truth or Consequences and an arts center, but it remained a spa destination. "You want a personal training business, you'll have to do that in Cruces."

Niall crossed the Ellis building's parking lot and studied the realtor's sign in the window. Mae followed.

Maybe he hadn't been teasing her. Niall liked to invest in real estate. He owned several rental houses, including the one Mae lived in rent-free while she was in college. The Ellis building would be a great investment, though not for Mae to use. She was nowhere near ready to set up a business, especially not as a full-time healer.

In the window of the office, her tall, athletic form reflected beside Niall's. Both were five-foot-ten, but she took up more space with her curves and muscles than he did with his thinly covered bones. He coughed a few times and said, "I might look into this."

What good was it to invest in a future he might not be around for?

Niall felt for his cigarettes.

Don't do that. Please. Mae put an arm around him, interrupting the act. "You're so sweet. You'd really buy me Magnolia's building?"

"Maybe. If you want it."

She didn't, but the offer touched her, and she couldn't help wrapping Niall's hug-resistant frame in an embrace. *What I want is for you to quit smoking.*

Mae's vision shifted. It was suddenly midday. The front windows of the building revealed a full waiting room. Old-fashioned cars lined up along the street, people sitting in them with their windows rolled down. More cars filled the parking lot. Mae felt a pure life force flowing through her like the brilliant light of New Mexico, like the hot springs under the city's skin. Her mind went as clear as the sky in her vision. A deep, glowing certainty filled her. Something moved from her to Niall, some of the infinite light.

He pulled back, and she let go. The strange image and feelings cleared. It was early evening again. The crowds were gone. Had she been in an altered state for more than a minute? It had been so deep, time had ceased. As a psychic, Mae could see someone's past by touching things that person had owned, but she normally had to concentrate and use crystals to do it. This moment from the town's history had come back uninvited, complete with what felt like the healer's energy.

Was it a sign? Mae looked up at the Magnolia Ellis sign and then at the "For Sale" sign and almost laughed. *A sign*. If it was, she couldn't take it too literally. It might be a reminder to keep working as a healer, but not to have Niall buy the building.

He took a cigarette out and lit up but didn't take his usual deep drag. Frowning at it, he put it out against a brick and slid it back into the pack.

Chapter Two

Why didn't Niall smoke the cigarette? Had the healing energy made him reluctant to light up? Mae wanted to know but didn't dare ask. He hated being nagged about smoking. They walked on to Dada Café in silence.

On arrival, they found Marty waiting for them in the main dining room of the eclectically decorated restaurant. He was still dressed for work, wearing track pants and a T-shirt featuring the mascot of the College of the Rio Grande teams, the Tarantulas. His sandy brown hair, streaked with gray, was mashed from wearing a ball cap all day, and his freckled arms were slightly burned.

"Hey." He stood and gave Niall a hug. To Mae's surprise, Niall returned it and held on for a moment before they sat. Marty said, "I guess you had a day of it."

Niall picked up a menu and flipped it open. "Mae helped a lot. I'll have to finish up and meet the thrift shop truck there tomorrow."

"You want me to do that?" Mae asked. "If they're coming early, I can do it before I leave for Mescalero."

"Thanks, but they didn't give me a time yet."

"Take it easy," Marty said. "Let the truck take the furniture and whatever you've packed, and I'll help you with the rest on Saturday."

Their waiter was Reno. He appeared silently and placed a basket of bread on the table. "Can I get you any drinks?"

Niall said, "In a minute." He slid his fingers back and forth on the menu, then looked up at the waiter and spoke softly. "You left so fast this morning I didn't get to ask you this. I haven't talked to your father about Florencia yet. Have you?"

Reno took in a sharp breath. "Please, don't use her name. I'll see him tomorrow. What can I get you?"

Niall ordered a beer, and Mae and Marty ordered iced tea. When the waiter departed, Niall said, "I should have remembered that taboo, as many years as I've known Reno's father. I expect you'll meet him when you get to Mescalero."

"I will?" It would be Mae's first visit to the reservation where her friend Bernadette Pena had grown up. "I don't know if Bernadette knows him. She hasn't lived there for ages."

Niall gave her an exasperated look. "He's not as famous as Howe or Mirabal, but still ..." He shook his head. "She'll know him. They probably went to high school together. He's on the tribal council, and he helped Jamie's father get his research with the tribe started. *Everybody* knows Orville."

When Reno returned with their drinks, Niall said, "Mae's headed to Mescalero tomorrow. Maybe you two could carpool."

Startled, Mae glanced at Niall and then at Reno. What in the world had prompted that offer?

"I doubt it." The young man gave her a perfunctory smile. "Are you ready to order?"

After they placed their orders and Reno left, Mae asked Niall, "Why'd you say he could ride with me? He's about as friendly as a rock."

Niall sipped his beer. "He won't ride on Misty's Harley. Scares him. And Reno drives the turquoise Rabbit."

"Oh." The ancient car was a T or C icon of sorts. With a duct-taped back window, more dents than smooth surfaces, and a layer of bumper stickers attesting to a long history of eccentric owners, it was often presumed dead, sitting on Austin Street for weeks at a time in front of a shabby turquoise-and-white trailer like a matching accessory. Then it would appear in the parking lot at Bullocks' grocery or on Main Street in front of the coffee shop. Mae had sometimes heard other pedestrians marveling over the fact that it had moved. "Maybe I should offer again. I don't think that ol' thing could make the trip. And Misty might need a ride, too, if they're going together. I can't blame him for not wanting to get on her bike with her. I've done it once, and she's kind of a crazy driver."

When Reno returned, Mae said, "If you do end up needing a ride, I live right behind Frank and Kenny's place." Her neighbors worked in Dada Café's kitchen. "They know how to get hold of me."

Reno served their salads and refilled water glasses. "Thank you, but I have other plans." He picked up his tray and started to walk off and then paused, almost smiling. With that slight thaw, he became as beautiful as Howe's winged cowboy. "You underestimate the Rabbit."

Maybe his beauty had made Misty fall for him. He didn't strike Mae as having any other charms.

After dinner, Niall did what he always did when they ate at Dada Café: sat on the bench at the corner of Broadway and Foch and lit up. Mae's hope that he might be quitting flickered and faded. She and Marty walked a few paces away to avoid the fumes.

"Got your things all packed?" Marty asked.

"Not really, no. Just some warm stuff for after dark. I'd rather come back here at night than pay for a motel."

"That's a lot of driving. Jamie okay with that?"

"We compromised. I told him I wouldn't mind getting a motel for one or two nights. But not four. I don't like having him pay for stuff like that—I like to split things. And that's as much as I can afford. Gas for the Focus is gonna be cheaper."

Mae noticed a lack of smoke and realized that Niall was doing the same thing he'd done at the Ellis building, putting the cigarette out and sliding it back in the pack.

"Daddy—did you see that?"

Marty nodded. He strolled over to sit beside Niall with a calmness that Mae admired. He had to be thrilled and hopeful inside. After a long pause, Marty asked, "You quitting?"

Niall held out the pack of cigarettes. "I can't smoke. I just stare at the frickin' things. I even light up. And I *can't smoke.*"

Mae had made a commitment not to use her healing skills without asking first. Having made that mistake once with Jamie, she was careful now, but maybe the spirit of Magnolia Ellis had somehow sensed Mae's wishes and helped. No—if she could do that, her parking lot would be like Lourdes or Chimayo. However, the place did have a legacy of healing energy. Mae must have activated it with the intensity of her desire for Niall to quit.

All she could see of her father was the back of his head, his broad shoulders and his long lean arms spread along the back of the bench. He rubbed Niall's neck. "I can think of worse things to have happen."

Niall stood, slipping out of the public display of affection. "Next thing you know I'll be wanting to exercise."

Marty rose and met Mae's eyes, his raised eyebrow and cocked head asking if she was responsible. She shrugged and held her palms up.

They walked to the near-empty parking lot behind the restaurant.

"I'm thinking of buying the Ellis building," Niall said as they approached his pale green Beetle.

Marty's face showed surprise. "That'll cost a pretty penny."

"Good investment, though. Set Mae up."

"That's generous, but we should talk before you jump into anything." Marty unlocked the car and looked at Mae quizzically. "You thinking about starting a healing practice?"

"No. I just pointed out the sign."

"Good. Might be different if you were ready to graduate, but 'til then the only time you're free to work much is the off season for this town."

Niall grumbled, "Someone will have bought the place by the time she graduates. And who knows how long I'll be around."

That was a dismal thought. Mae and Marty exchanged glances. No words needed.

Niall took out his cigarettes and lighter and went through the ritual for the third time—lighting up, staring at the cigarette, and then putting it out against his car's rear window and tucking it back into the pack. "Christ, this is *weird*. Feels like I ought to work at it if I'm not going to smoke."

Mae took the pack from him. He didn't resist. "Maybe some part of you *is* working at it. I mean, you just said you don't know how long you'll be around. Maybe you're ..." She didn't want to say it, even though it was obvious. "With Florencia being so sick ..."

"Confronting my mortality? Planning my legacy?"

"Something like that. You want me to throw these away for you?"

Niall's lens-distorted gaze stayed on her a while. "You have anything to do with this?"

"Not on purpose." She looked down, then met his eyes again. "I was wishing you'd quit, but I didn't heal you on purpose or anything."

"You did it by *accident*?"

"Sort of."

Mae described her vision and sensations.

Niall chuffed a sound through his teeth and shook his head. "And you still don't want me to buy you that building?" He tossed her the lighter. "You have a good night." He got into the car and shut the door.

Marty said softly, "He really is confronting his mortality. Florencia's situation scares him more than he'll let on. Don't worry about him actually buying that building."

"Good. I don't want it." Mae wrapped her hand around the cigarettes and lighter. "But I'm real glad I stopped to look at it."

"I'm glad you did, too. All our years together, I've been worried about losing him early. I know he's a cranky sonofabitch, but he's the love of my life." He gave her a quick hug. "Maybe I'll get to keep him a little longer. Thank you."

Marty got in the driver's side, reached over and squeezed Niall's hand, and started the car.

With the feeling of completing some sort of ritual, Mae dropped the cigarettes in the trash can on the corner, then crossed Broadway and started down Foch in the direction of the river. Vacancy signs glowed on the spas she passed. Tourism fell off when it was ninety to a hundred degrees by day and creeping down to eighty at night. No one else was out walking except a cat scurrying into an alley. She strolled the half block of Marr to her house, looking up at the stars, brilliant above the dimly lit street. After fourteen months in the desert she still marveled at them. Tonight her sense of awe was deeper, as if her mind could float into the black spaces between the thousand blazing lights. Something extraordinary had happened, in a space where life, death, love, and time crossed threads and wove a small miracle.

A miracle by mistake. She couldn't regret it, and yet it bothered her a little to be reminded that her gift could be beyond her control.

She let herself into the pea-soup green converted trailer and took off her shoes. Niall had put in silky-smooth bamboo floors and he didn't want a grain of dirt ground into them. Mae's only additions to the décor were pictures of her twin stepdaughters from her second marriage, at all ages ranging from one year to their current seven years. Otherwise, the place reflected Niall's taste, and what he'd thought people renting a house in T or C would like: fifties "antiques"—a pointy-legged turquoise couch and arm chair set, a boomerang-shaped coffee table and end tables, and two of his sculptures, a sheep made of old springs and horseshoes and a javelin thrower made of rusted scrap metal.

Mae sat on the couch and surfed channels until she found a Red Sox game. After a day like today, she needed some downtime, and baseball soothed her mind. Except when Jamie was around. She'd tried to get him to watch a game with her once and it had brought out a grouchy restlessness in him.

Her phone rang. *Jamie.*

"Wanted to let you know I'll be a little late tomorrow. Sorry—forgot I had Dr. G." His therapist. "And then, Wendy's going overboard being a manager. Wants me to get a new van for the tour. Have some time to get used to it, make sure it's good. I thought it'd be nice to find another old Aerostar, like a reincarnation, but she doesn't. She wants to go to the dealership with me and let her approve what I get. And tomorrow's the day she's free to do it."

"Then I guess you'd better buy it tomorrow. I know you loved the Aerostar, but Wendy's right. You don't need another *old* van. I'd feel better if you had something at least new-ish."

"Mm. Yeah. Guess. Might make friends with it by the time I leave."

"Are you getting rid of the Fiesta?"

"Fuck, no." He sounded as if she'd suggested he get rid of a pet. "It's my *real* car. Y'know? The van's for touring." A rustling noise, followed by crunching. Mae pictured the ever-present bags of blue corn chips and green chile pistachios in his kitchen. He talked around whatever he was eating, and his volume rose in delight at something that had entered his mind. "Yeah—just thought—yeah—oh—*great*. Fantastic." He swallowed and spoke more clearly. "Perfect. I can use the van tomorrow. I'll have a surprise for you."

"The van?"

"Nah. You know I'm getting that. Something else." His cat meowed in the background, and Jamie spoke a few words to him. "Got to spend some time with him tonight. Poor little bloke. He'll feel abandoned. *Four days.* Wish I could bring him."

Jamie took his cat on tour. He walked his cat on a leash. Gave the animal massages and Reiki. All of that was fine—but he slept with his cat, and Gasser was huge, flatulent, and jealous. "He'll be okay with your landlady."

"Yeah. I just worry, y'know?" More crunching, and then a pause and a snort-laugh. "Jeezus. That's like saying I breathe."

Mae could tell by Jamie's shift into light fretting that he was going to talk a while, and not about anything in particular. Enjoying the ups and downs of his voice and his occasional hah-snort-hah at his own jokes, she let him ramble and responded when necessary while she watched the game. Jamie's run-on chatter was like a hug of sorts, his lively tenor voice wrapping around her, and she expected that for him her fond though half-attentive listening was a kind of embrace as well.

When she rose to get a glass of iced tea on a commercial break, Jamie broke off his monologue, making her think he was winding down to say goodbye, but he got his second wind. "Sorry, been yabbering—didn't even ask. How was your day?"

"Kinda strange. Niall's friend Florencia Mirabal went into hospice yesterday—"

"Bloody hell, I didn't know she was dying. Guess I wouldn't. I mean, it's not like I knew her. Just—y'know—she's *someone.* Sad for him. He holding up all right?"

Mae poured sweet tea and took a sip. "Packing her stuff was hard on him. But she doesn't really have any other friends except maybe Reno Geronimo—"

"Reno's in T or C? Jeezus. I still think of him as a little kid. Dunno why."

"He's been studying art with her. But I think something may have gone wrong between them, and something happened with her family, too. They don't have any contact."

"You'd think she'd want to fix all that. Dying."

"Doesn't sound like it." She stood drinking her tea, watching lizards catching moths on her window screen. "I bet my mama wouldn't speak to me if she was dying. Some people are good at grudges."

"Hospice gives her time, though. She could think about it. Is it cancer?"

"Yeah. Breast cancer spread to her bones, her liver ... I think they caught it pretty late."

"Jeezus. Awful way to go. Hate to say it, but I always think about Niall getting lung cancer and that he'll die that way."

"I've thought that, too. But he might not. He quit smoking."

"You serious? That's a fucking miracle."

"It kinda was." Mae described the events at the Ellis building and Niall's inability to smoke. She knew Jamie would understand. He had a healing gift, too, though he limited his use of it.

"That's beautiful. Weird, though. Dunno what I'd do if I suddenly *couldn't* eat this whole fucking bag of chips." Crinkling sounds. "You have a bad habit, you have a relationship with it. Deep one. If it just went away there'd be like a *hole* where the habit was."

"I think there is. He kept trying to smoke and he couldn't."

"Skinny bastard. Maybe he'll finally eat." Jamie laughed. "Don't heal me, all right? I might start to smoke."

She laughed with him, told him she loved him, and that she was going to watch baseball now. "I'll see you tomorrow. Whenever you get there."

"Yeah. Dunno what time. Meet me behind the singers near the big tipi if it's after dark. Best place to see the dances. Fucking *powerful*. Lightning will strike your bones."

"That sounds wonderful. But—will you really get there after dark? Why would you be that late?"

"Got to prepare the surprise for you. Hooroo, love. Catcha."

Chapter Three

The next morning in Passion Pie Café, Misty glared past Mae with wounded anger as she handed over her travel mug and took her money without looking at it. Mae looked around to see what might be the problem. Reno was coming in. He met the barista's eyes briefly and sank into a chair at one of the art-topped tables, drumming his fingers on the picture of a lizard in the desert. Each tabletop in the café featured the work of a local artist and was for sale. Some not currently in use hung on the walls, including Delmas Howe's image of powerful male arms in an embrace. The one where Reno sat had been there a long time without selling. He stopped tapping the lizard, propped his elbows on the table and looked down at it.

Misty gave Mae her change and put on a tense, polite smile. Mae pressed her mug's stubborn lid into place, leaning on it. A man in line behind her said, "Quite the thing—Niall not smoking."

The lid snapped down and she turned to see the speaker. He was pink-faced, white-bearded and thin, a T or C old hippie in jeans and a tie-dyed T-shirt. She didn't know his name, though she'd seen him in the coffee shop before.

The old hippie shook her hand. "I know who you are. I'm Chuck Brady. Retired."

In the small town, Mae often found that people knew who she was before she told them. "Nice to meet you."

Misty's false smile melted into a genuine one. "When he introduces himself that way, he thinks you should ask him what he retired from."

Mae took the hint. "Retired from what?"

Misty answered before Chuck could. "Retired bullshitter."

"No," he said cheerfully. "I still do plenty of that. Retired lawyer. Turned the practice over to my lovely wife. Who smokes like a goddamned chimney. Niall called her last night about doing something with Florencia's place and he mentioned what you'd done for him. He knows how badly she wants to quit."

"Is your wife Florencia's lawyer?" Mae hoped Niall had talked to her about an alarm system or storing the art collection, as well as quitting smoking.

"That she is. We wondered if you could help her the way you helped Niall. Do you have a healing practice somewhere?"

Mae shook her head

"You should. Misty, m'dear, do you *know* what this lady can do?"

"No." Misty glanced at Reno, then back at Chuck. "The usual?"

"Yes ma'am, if you please." He put his money on the counter, then turned the coins on their sides, spinning them and slapping them down. "Mae is a healer so amazing she could even make your hair stop smoking."

Misty's hair had briefly caught fire during her street performance at the last Art Hop. She rolled her eyes at Chuck, then turned away and began to pour green tea, fruit juice and ice into a blender. He continued, his resonant voice carrying in the small room. "According to Niall Kerrigan, this young woman is a psychic as well as a healer. She had a vision of Magnolia's times and felt the healing—"

"Please," Mae said softly. "That wasn't a normal thing to have happen to me. I sometimes feel like my Granma guides me—she was a healer, too—but I don't do anything like channel Magnolia. I'll be happy to try to help your wife, but it won't be like what happened with Niall. Energy healing isn't usually that dramatic."

Misty started the blender. Chuck studied the baked goods in the glass case on the counter. A group of patrons left, calling goodbye to Misty, and she hollered a reply over the blender's whir. When the machine stopped, Chuck left off examining pastries and turned to Mae. "Daphne's tried everything else but she just can't kick the habit. I don't care if you channel Magnolia, as long as you can help her quit."

"Okay. We'll have to figure out where to meet ... and what I'd charge." Mae took her business card from her purse and gave it to Chuck.

He studied it. "Personal trainer?"

"I used to do more healing and psychic work before I moved to New Mexico, but I mostly work in fitness now."

"That was backwards. Most people move here and *then* get wacky. I'll talk to my better half and see when she wants you to make her even better." He tapped on the pastry case. "Misty, darling, I crave an apricot bar instead of date today."

"Same price." She began to scrape the iced tea concoction from the blender into a glass. "Have a seat. I'll bring your stuff to you."

He took the table next to Reno's and greeted him. Reno's response was expressionless and barely audible. What had happened between him and Misty? Newly engaged and fighting? He'd lost Florencia's friendship. Maybe he was hard to get along with.

As Mae passed his table, Chuck invited her to join him.

"Thanks, but I need to head out. Have a good day. Tell your wife she can call me. I'll be in Mescalero for a few days but we can make an appointment for when I get back."

Reno stood, gazed at Misty for a moment while she continued to excavate Chuck's drink from between the blender's blades, and then opened the door for Mae and followed her out.

"Is this shit actually true?" Reno sounded more worried than hostile, in spite of his choice of words. "I get the healing part. I can believe that. But are you really psychic? Kenny said you were, but well—Kenny—nice guy, but he'd believe anything."

Mae asked, "Does it bother you?"

"No. Why should it?"

"I don't know. You came across like it did. Some folks worry that I could read their minds." She noticed his uneasy frown deepening and added, "I can't."

"So what *do* you do? Tell fortunes?"

"No. I can't see the future. Just the past and the present."

"Kind of useless, isn't it?" He gripped the metal railing that aided the less mobile in getting up the hilly hump of the sidewalk. "I'd hardly need to go to a psychic to have her tell me my own past."

"I do things like finding lost pets for people. If they bring me something like their pet's favorite toy or blanket, I can sense the pet's energy and see 'em."

He spent a moment absorbed in examining the railing. "How could you tell if it was the past or the present?"

"Sometimes I can't. Context helps, though."

"Do people ever ask you to find out someone else's past?"

"Sometimes. But they have to have a good reason for needing to know it."

Reno slid his hands into his pockets and looked past Mae's shoulder. He was a smaller man than she'd realized, about three inches shorter than her as well as delicately built. A silly image crossed her mind. *I could pick him up.*

He asked, "Why are you going to Mescalero? Are you being a tourist or what?"

"Sort of an invited tourist. Do you know Bernadette Pena?"

He squinted, then nodded. "One of her cousins is married to one of Misty's sisters."

"She's a good friend of mine. She asked me to come to the ceremonies and the powwow. And she works at the same college as my boyfriend's daddy, Stan Ellerbee—and they always go. So I got invited twice."

"Ah, the professor." Reno's warm almost-smile emerged from his inner clouds. "He's been hanging out with my father since I was five."

Stan, a New Mexico Anglo, had married in Australia and lived there for many years, then moved his family to his home town of Santa Fe fifteen years ago. He'd been doing research in Mescalero off and on during that time.

"Then you must know Jamie."

Reno paused, his posture straighter yet more relaxed. A corner of his mouth twitched. "Of course I do. He's hard to overlook." He opened the door of the café. "Excuse me. I need to talk to Misty. Have a safe trip."

Mae got in her car and headed toward 25 South, following Main Street past the red-and-white striped Brady and Brady building on the corner of Foch. Mae always thought of it as the candy-cane law office. Anywhere but T or C it might have looked odd, but many of the buildings, from spas to trailers, were brightly colored or painted with murals. Plain adobe broke up the crayon-box look and blended the town with its desert surroundings, but its overall appearance, from the water tower featuring Apaches on horseback to the enormous Delmas Howe flowers on the civic center, said *Artists live here*. Artists and eccentrics. Even the lawyers were a little offbeat. She sipped her coffee, thinking about Chuck's enthusiasm for her gift.

He'd been eager to hire her as a healer, but it was his mention of her psychic abilities that had gotten Reno's attention. The young artist had denied that her gift bothered him, but his expressions and body language said otherwise, and his questions had kept coming. It wasn't like an attempt to be friendly. He hadn't thawed or smiled until she'd mentioned Stan and Jamie. For some reason, Reno seemed troubled by her having the Sight.

After nearly a three-hour drive through empty desert, the outskirts of Las Cruces, then more empty desert and some tiny towns, the Mescalero Apache lands came as a pleasant surprise, greener than any place Mae had seen since moving out West. Though the mountains were tall and peaked rather than round and gentle, the area in some ways reminded her of her roots in Appalachian North Carolina, with small homes clinging to the steep, forested hillsides.

A dark-haired woman on a black Harley shot past her on NM Route 70 as she approached her destination, the tribe's ceremonial grounds. The rider, helmet-less like most New Mexico bikers, looked like Misty—and she was going at least eighty in a fifty-five zone. Had she left work early? Broken the speed limit all the way? The talk with Reno must not have gone well.

Following the directions Jamie had given her, Mae took a side road off 70 and started to follow the curve uphill past a blue house with a sagging porch. The Harley was parked in the old house's driveway, and Misty was having a tantrum in the yard, kicking a tree, flinging pebbles at it and screaming. "I hate him! I hate him!"

This must be Misty's parents' house, the tree a stand-in for Reno—and no one was at home to deal with the drama. They would all be at the powwow. Mae drew her car alongside the Harley and got out. "Misty? What's the matter?"

The girl stopped abruptly, her tear-streaked face blank with shock. "Mae? Shit. You *saw* me."

"Honey, you were kinda hard to miss. I heard you, too. You have a fight with Reno?"

"More than a fight." Misty peeled off her leather jacket and flung it onto the porch. She picked up a cell phone that lay at her feet, its case open and the battery out, and put the parts back together. "That stupid little jackass. He's up to something. Up to his eyeballs in some kind of I-don't-know-what. He's lying and hiding and treating me like—like I don't need to know. He won't even let me come into his place anymore. What's he got *in* there?"

"I have no idea. I hardly know him." What a mess. Reno had set Misty up to either break off with him or be unbearably frustrated and curious. "You must have asked him."

"He says it's his housekeeping—that his place is a mess. Like I'd care. I keep my bike in my living room. I leave my clothes on the floor. I have to hunt for dishes under the bed." She kicked a tuft of grass. "He's lying and he's not even a good liar. Today he said he'd be late getting here because he had a commission, a painting to finish. *Reno*—a commission? He's never had a gallery show. And he never shows me his work anymore, he hasn't for months."

"Does he show his father his work?"

"No. He doesn't want him to visit, either."

"Is Reno okay? Like is he ... I don't know ... depressed?" That might explain a lot about how he acted. "Or using drugs?"

Misty stared at Mae as if she'd seen something new and strange. "Shit. He could be *selling* drugs. I don't think he'd ever use them, but he's had more money lately—and I honestly have no idea who's buying his work. He says he sells to tourists, but there aren't that many this time of year. And a waiter in T or C sure isn't making big tips in the summer."

"Does he have a *lot* more money? Anyone who's driving the Rabbit doesn't seem to be rolling in wealth."

"Not like a ton of money, just more. He doesn't spend it on his car. He spent it on my ring." Misty trailed off, pacing, thumbs hooked in her belt loops.

"You've got to keep pushing him to explain. He should want to get closer, not keep you away, if y'all got engaged."

Misty paused in her restless ambling and regarded Mae. "You don't get it. You're spoiled. Jamie talks."

Jamie *did* talk, for sure, but Mae doubted she was spoiled by it.

Misty continued. "Like you actually know what he's thinking."

"I reckon I do." He was constantly narrating his inner processes. The last time he'd spent a weekend at Mae's house he'd delivered a rambling monologue from the bathroom, sharing something he'd heard on the radio about Japanese toilets that would wash your arse and tell you how much you weighed. While cooking, he'd commented on the eggs in her refrigerator, asking if she knew that with chickens everything came out of the same hole? *Yes, sugar, it's called a cloaca.* He'd turned that word into clucking noises, *cloaca, cloaca, cloaca,* and then wondered if maybe chickens needed Japanese toilets to wash their cloacas. Mae smiled at the recollection. "It's not always what I'd call deep thought, though."

"I'd settle for any thoughts at all. Reno's turning into a hermit." Misty lowered herself onto a porch step. "Those things Chuck Brady said about you—are those true?"

"Pretty much. I mean, I'm not a miracle worker, but basically, yes."

"I don't need a healing." The Apache girl pulled her shoulders back and took a deep breath. "I want you to find out Reno's secret. It's bad, I know, me asking you that. I shouldn't. But he won't tell me. It's like he gave me the ring to make it all okay. But it doesn't. I still need to know."

Mae sat beside Misty. "He might talk to his daddy, wouldn't he? Even if he won't tell you?"

"No. His family has no idea what's up. They're worried, too. *I* talk to them more than he does."

"I'd have to have a good reason—a *really* good reason—to do that kind of work as a psychic."

"I gave you one."

"I mean, like thinking he's in danger and there's no other way to find out what's wrong. It would bug me if my boyfriend had a secret, but ..." Reno might not be in trouble. He could be concealing something like another girlfriend. He was an attractive man in his fragile way, and a little mysterious. Women might pursue him. That wouldn't be any of Mae's business. On the surface, it seemed unlikely that he would get engaged while he had another girlfriend, but Mae knew from experience with her first husband that men who cheated did some crazy things. "I don't think I should. I'm sorry."

"Then don't you dare tell anyone I asked. Especially Reno."

"I won't. Just don't marry him until he tells you."

Misty laughed suddenly. "If we got married right away, I'd *have* to see what's in his house. We'd both live in it."

"Don't even think about it. What if he *is* selling drugs? You don't want to marry into that."

"Then you'd better think again about helping me." Misty twisted her ring. "I've been with Reno since we were kids. We're not ending it."

Mae had married the first time right out of high school. Mack had been so smart, so handsome, so charming—and unfaithful, and an alcoholic. She'd thought she could help him and straighten him out, but their marriage had been a disaster, a two-year hell. The desire to stop another woman from tying a bad knot had sucked her into some unwise psychic work before, and she could feel it tempting her again. Part of her mind and half her heart told her it would be wrong, but the other parts disagreed. Seeing Misty unhappy and yet committed at the age Mae had been while in the throes of that miserable marriage, she wanted nothing more than to stop the girl from marrying Reno. Or at least to let her know why she shouldn't. As far as Mae could see, his secretive behavior was reason enough, but Misty didn't seem to realize that. She needed the secret itself.

"Okay." Mae felt a door open inside her, a door that she wished she could close already, but it was too late. Misty looked so hopeful. Mae caught herself wrapping the fingers of her right hand around her left ring finger. Sometimes it still surprised her to find it bare.

"I'll ... I'll think about it. But you should try a few more times to find out by talking to him."

Chapter Four

Misty went into the blue house in a calmer mood, and Mae resumed her drive to the ceremonial grounds, looking forward to seeing Bernadette and finally meeting her family. There was a large sign across the road announcing the powwow, the ceremonies—and a rodeo. A rodeo, at the same time? Bernadette hadn't said anything about that, and neither had Jamie. Mae had never seen one before and it sounded exciting. She would have to get Jamie to go with her. If it was anything like what she imagined a rodeo to be, he couldn't complain that it was *boring* like baseball.

She parked her car in a rough dirt lot packed with vehicles. Tents sprouted on every spare piece of ground, even in the corners of the parking lot. As Mae began walking across the lot, a group of Apache teenage girls emerged from one of the corner tents, whispering to each other and laughing so hard they nearly fell down. They reminded her of girls at church camp back home. Mae's mama had made her go, and for Mae the best part had been the silliness and bonding with friends, not the religious instruction. She wondered if these girls took their ceremonies more seriously than she had taken Bible studies.

Despite training for an upcoming triathlon, Mae noticed the effects of higher altitude on her heart rate as she headed uphill toward the entrance to the ceremonial grounds. At the top of the path she paused, wondering how she would find Bernadette in the crowd when she went in. Then the idea struck her as funny. Bernadette would see *her*. Everyone else was Indian, and Mae was the whitest white woman on the planet, a tall redhead who stood out even in a mostly Anglo crowd. She took out her cell phone and called her friend to let her know she'd arrived.

Within a few minutes, Bernadette Pena, a slim, graceful woman with strong features and long dark hair threaded with silver, strode down a steep dirt path lined with vendors.

"I'm so happy you could make it," Bernadette said as they embraced. She let go of the hug. "Where's Jamie? His friends here have been asking about him."

"He had an appointment. And then he had to shop for a new van for his tour—and he's planning a surprise for me. He won't get here until kinda late."

"A surprise? That's a fun reason to be late." They started up the path Bernadette had come down. "There are so many people I'd like you to meet. Especially my family."

"That'll be wonderful. I've been looking forward to meeting them. Niall told me I'd probably meet Orville Geronimo, too. Do you know him?"

"I went to high school with him. We only see each other about once a year now, but we were friends back in the day."

At a window of an adobe-brown cinderblock building, Bernadette paid for Mae's admission, and Mae thanked her. Passing through the gate—an open frame, like a big empty doorway—Mae felt like she'd walked into a small Indian version of a state fair, complete with the smell of greasy food and electronic music coming from an inflated play area. Along both sides of a dirt walkway wide enough for a vehicle to drive through, vendors were selling pizza and sodas, fry bread and beans, T-shirts and hats, and art and jewelry. From somewhere beyond this stretch of bright, noisy commerce came the pounding of a drum so loud it sounded like the earth's own heart. Heading toward the sound of the drum, they passed aisles with more stalls on the right—still more jewelry, pottery, and food.

Bernadette asked, "Do you need an introduction to Orville?"

"Niall would like it if I met him—but I hope Niall or Reno has talked to him. I don't know if you knew Orville's ex-wife?"

"Not well. We were never close. But Alan told me she's dying." Alan Pacheco, Bernadette's significant other, was an art professor at Eight Northern Pueblos Tribal College, where she and Stan Eller-bee taught. "She wants Alan to be the one to write about her ... when her time comes."

"You mean, write her obituary?"

"More like a full-length article. She'll also be giving him mate-rial for a biography, and she wants him to help organize a memori-al exhibit. They weren't friends, but she said that since he's a fellow pueblo painter and an art critic, he's the right person for the job. She asked him to come to the hospice in Las Cruces and talk with her."

"That's got to feel weird."

"For him?"

"For both of them. Especially Florencia—planning how she'd like to be remembered."

Bernadette slowed the pace of their walk. "It's better not to use her name when you're talking with Apaches. We don't want to say it by accident without knowing she crossed over."

"Sorry. Reno told me. I'm trying to get used to how you do that even *before* someone dies. If it slips out, I don't mean to be disre-spectful."

"It's not so much disrespect as that the name has power. It calls the spirit that just left us, and if we don't let the dead go, we can get ghost sickness, especially people who were close to the one who died. Maybe you'd call it depression, or not 'moving on.' To us, it would be the dead who didn't move on as well as the living. I'm sure Alan and I will have some careful conversations while he's writing about her. His tribe doesn't have a taboo on naming the dead."

"He told me once that they feel real close to them."

Bernadette nodded and fell silent, perhaps a hint to stop talking about death and the dead.

Mae asked, "Is Alan here?"

"No. He's on the board of just about everything, including the Eight Northern Pueblos Art Show, which is next weekend. No free time between that and this new project." They crossed toward the last booth at the end of the main row. "I think you'll remember Orville's work from seeing some of it in my apartment."

Mae recognized the style of his paintings, but she never would have recognized the artist as Reno's father. Orville had a large nose, narrow-set eyes, slightly protruding teeth, and a bit of a pot belly. He stood behind a counter displaying T-shirts, and his paintings hung on the canvas walls of his booth. Some of the smaller ones showed an image of a bird in the sky or the mountains on the horizon in the palm of a hand. The larger pictures, reminiscent of the one Bernadette owned, portrayed the Ga'an, the mountain spirit dancers. The background of the paintings reminded Mae of a million stars, the endless New Mexico sky.

Orville conversed in Apache with an elderly man with iron-gray hair and black-framed glasses. The older man's build and features were more like Reno's—Reno aged to around eighty. They switched to English for greetings, and Bernadette introduced Mae to Orville and his uncle Lonnie Bigmouth.

The artist reached out and took Mae's hand in a strong, warm handshake. "Pleased to meet you. I've heard about you from Niall. He's a good man." His accent was stronger than Reno's, his English words so clipped he sounded as if he was using the stops that made Apache sound so unlike other languages. "How is he?"

"Good and then not so good. I mean ..." Mae hesitated, not sure how to proceed. "Have you talked to Niall in the past couple of days? Or Reno?"

"Reno called. He's still in T or C. He said he had to work this morning. But nothing about Niall."

Work? Reno had been at Passion Pie in the morning. And Dada Café didn't open until lunch time.

Orville leaned with his arms braced on his counter, his gaze moving back and forth between Mae and Bernadette. His uncle sat in one of several folding chairs and picked up a small wood carving in progress.

Mae said, "Niall quit smoking. Good in that way." This news got a pleased but startled look from Orville. "But ... I think Reno wanted to be the one to tell you ..."

Bernadette took over. "Your first wife went into hospice."

"I knew she was sick." Orville frowned. "I had no idea it was that bad, though. Reno knows this and he didn't tell me?"

How self-centered of Reno. He'd called to lie about his lateness and not bothered to share this news?

Bernadette said, "I only found out because she wants Alan to write about her." She filled Orville in on his ex-wife's condition and the various projects she wanted Alan to do.

The artist sighed, and then a sad smile tugged at one corner of his mouth. "That's so like her. In charge of her image until the end." Orville looked down for a while, then regarded Mae. "This must be hard on Niall."

"It is," Mae said. "I helped him clean out her place."

"Did Reno help you?"

"No." *He didn't even offer.*

"He should have lent you a hand." Orville straightened a stack of shirts. "Her family cut her off for marrying me, and then we didn't even last two years." He refolded one of the shirts. "She had every reason not to want to deal with a Geronimo. But she took my *second wife's* son as a student. He owed her something for that."

"They might have had an argument. She didn't even tell him about hospice."

Orville turned to Lonnie Bigmouth and said something in Apache. The old man answered in a few short words.

"What's the name of the place?" Orville asked. "My uncle and I would like to go see her."

"I don't know except that it's in Las Cruces. Niall does, though."

"I'll ask him. My first wife and I had our differences, but we had our good times." He paused. "Is her parrot still alive?"

"I didn't see a parrot, no. Niall didn't mention one."

"We got that parrot when we got married. She loved that bird. A hyacinth macaw. Gigantic bright blue thing. Huge eyes. Crazy-looking. They live to be really old. Heard of one that lived to be a hundred and twenty."

Did Reno ever think about other people? He should have told his father the parrot was gone. It had once been his pet, too. "Sorry. I reckon this one didn't."

Orville nodded. "One less thing to worry about, then. It's hard to find a home for an older bird. Parrots bond to you. We couldn't even have a custody fight over Violet. She'd chosen her person. And it wasn't me."

So someone else had loved Florencia. A bird.

As they approached a huge white canvas tipi at the entrance to the ceremonial grounds, Mae asked Bernadette, "What did Fl—his first wife's family have against Orville? He seems really kind, really nice."

"He is. It wasn't him personally. It was that she moved here with him."

"That seems kinda petty. People get married and move away all the time."

"I know. It seems more about control than love. I don't think she had a good family."

They paused beside the tipi. Its poles were freshly-cut trees whose green branches wrapped around each other at its top. The area before its entrance, which faced the dance arena, was carpeted with fragrant yucca leaves and demarcated by a row of benches. In front of the benches a group of men surrounded an enormous drum, all of them beating it in the same rhythm. The singers' voices were raw and powerful, wailing the song. Bernadette spoke close to Mae's ear but it was still hard to hear her over the music. "This is where the girls' coming of age ceremony takes place, in the big tipi. Their families are in the little ones."

To the right of the big tipi spread a long arbor covered with canvas and green branches, and beyond that stood a row of smaller tipis, their peaks echoing the crowns of the mountains.

Across the arena to the left, a small scattered audience, some holding umbrellas against the sun, sat on glaring aluminum bleachers to watch a circle of older men in fancy shirts dancing with almost no movement, shaking gourd rattles, and keeping the beat with a pulsing of their legs. With a thump of the drum, the dance ended.

"Thank you, gourd dancers," said the man on the loudspeaker. "Jingle dress dancers, get ready."

As the men dispersed, Bernadette led Mae up the middle of the bleachers to join her family, and introduced her to more people than Mae could take in at once, as much as she wanted to get to know them and make a good impression. They included Bernadette's older brother Michael, his wife and two teenaged daughters whose names Mae instantly forgot, Bernadette's cousins

Pearl Tsilnothos and Elaine Fatty, and Elaine's son Zak and his wife and children whose names Mae couldn't retain either.

The family with the odd name of Fatty was big-boned and sharp-faced, not fat except for the daughter-in-law, who was huge. Within seconds they were all talking, quizzing Mae on their names, laughing when she tried to pronounce Tsilnothos and even more when she said she hoped she'd heard right that the other last name was Fatty.

Bernadette said, "I met Mae when I was teaching at Coastal Virginia University. She was a guest once in my class on non-Western healing."

Pearl's round face looked rounder as her mouth made a little O and her eyes grew wide. "Oh—this is the girl who can *see things.* The psychic."

Mae blushed. "Reckon that's my most famous moment." She was proud of her gift and yet hesitant to share it. Too many people in the past had misunderstood or mocked her abilities, or distrusted her as Reno had appeared to. As perhaps he should.

Discomfited by the recollection of what she'd almost agreed to do for Misty, Mae sat down beside Bernadette, who gave her a quick side-hug, saying, "I told people other things about you, too."

"Like, that you're an aerobics teacher, personal trainer." Zak ogled Mae's legs for so long she wished she hadn't worn shorts. He finally looked up and gave his wife a teasing little shove. In contrast to her obesity, he was cut and hard. He wore a tight white T-shirt and close-fitting jeans, as if he wanted everyone to see that he worked out. Obsessively, Mae thought, from the kind of definition he had. He'd gone past looking fit to looking vain. Zak said to his wife, "Ought to sign up with her while she's here."

An awkward silence took over. The next powwow dance began, lively and graceful, done by women and girls in dresses decorated with silvery conical bells.

"This was a healing dance, in its origins," Elaine said to Mae. "There's a story about a girl who wanted healing for her father, and she had to go a long way to find help. That dress is like the raindrops she went through on her journey."

"That's beautiful." Mae admired the quick-footed girls and young women. The sound of their jingling dresses was soft and steady, like rain.

"It's not one of our stories," Zak said. He was about her age, with a triangular face—high cheekbones, a Roman nose, and a long chin. His small bright eyes seemed to be laughing even when he didn't smile. When he did, he showed a mouth full of large, crooked teeth. "So Mom could have it wrong." He elbowed his mother and grinned. "But all this *Indian stuff*, Mae, just think: it's all about *healing*."

"*All* about healing?" Had Bernadette mentioned that Mae was a healer, too? She couldn't tell if Zak was making fun of her, or if that was just his manner of speaking. "All the dances?"

"Healing and partying. We like to party."

His wife shook her head and rose, clasping their toddlers' hands, and announced she was taking them to the bathroom. "Don't mind him," she said under her breath as she passed Mae.

"It's a ceremony *and* a party," Elaine Fatty explained. "The families of the girls who are in the puberty ceremony cook for everyone. You can come to the feast after the powwow."

"I'd like that," Mae said. Jamie hadn't told her they could eat there. He was vegan, though, so maybe he couldn't. "Thank you."

"I'm sorry you missed the beginning this morning," Bernadette said. "It's beautiful when the big tipi goes up. The men of the families put it up. Then the girls and their godmothers do a blessing with pollen, especially for the mothers with young children."

"I should have been there." Mae still thought of herself as a mother. "I could have used that blessing."

Watching Zak's wife waddle down the bleacher steps with her little boy and girl, Mae hoped this woman had been blessed. She needed it, with that husband.

"You think it'd work on you?" Zak asked. "You've been here ten minutes and you believe in Apache religion?"

Don't mind him. Mae tried not to, but he irritated her.

"It's a strong blessing," Bernadette continued. "There's a lot of power coming into the girls now. They can heal people the last day, when they come out in the morning for the end of the ceremonies, just for that time. They become White-Painted Woman, part of our origin story."

"That's so wonderful." Mae felt a touch of envy for these girls, growing up in a culture where healing gifts were seen as special and yet *normal.* "Seems like when I turned thirteen all I got was Mama telling me to stay out of trouble."

Zak snickered. "Did you?"

He might be Bernadette's relative, but Mae had a hard time not snapping when she answered. "Mostly."

The jingle dress dance ended, the sparse audience applauded, and the emcee announced, "A veterans' honor song. All the veterans, and all the active duty service men and women, we honor you here. Indians, non-Indians, families who lost your warriors, you're all invited to dance."

Bernadette's brother ran down the steps of the bleachers to join the other dancers in the arena. The singers raised their voices, and the drummers kept a driving beat on the big drum. While some of the veterans shuffled, Michael Pena stepped high, as if he danced often and loved it. Though he had to be close to sixty, he had the slim fit body and the energy of a much younger man.

Zak rose slowly and took his time going down, but once he started dancing, he grew wild, like he was letting out a hidden storm. Michael was elegant in comparison, and Mae mentioned that she thought he was a good dancer. His older daughter said they had gone to a lot of powwows wherever they were stationed, and then asked, looking around at the rest of the family, "Zak's never been on active duty, has he? Did he join the reserves?"

Pearl and Elaine exchanged glances. "He tried the Army for a while," Elaine said finally. "He's not a war veteran or anything, though. He had ... an administrative discharge."

"What'd he do?" the other teenager asked. "I know that's not like *dishonorable*, but it's not honorable, either."

Silence. The girls looked at each other and back at Elaine, who made a low, sweeping gesture that clearly meant *we won't talk about this any further.* "Zak messed up, but he was trying to be honorable. That's all you need to know."

Mae's dislike of Zak picked up a layer of distrust as well. *His mama's trying to hide what he did.*

By the time the powwow ended and the feast was set up at tables in the center of the arena, Jamie still hadn't arrived. Mae wished he was there. He was so much better at mingling than she was, and he knew a lot of people already. Bernadette kept introducing her to more friends and relatives as they lined up at the serving table, filling paper plates and bowls from the heaping salads, steaming pots of stew, home-made pies, and platters of puffy fry bread. The talk was cheerful and joking as the family went through the line. Mae did her best to remember who they all were, but the sheer volume of names and faces was too much to keep track of. She followed the group to a long table inside the arbor and sat on the end of the bench across from Zak's wife and the couple's children.

"I'm kind of embarrassed," Mae said, "but I forgot y'all's names. I met so many people."

"Melody. And this is Dean, and Deanna." Melody took a plastic knife from Dean's small fist as he started to saw at his sister's fingers with it. Deanna made a face and stuck her fingers in ketchup, rubbed it on the place her brother had been cutting and laughed. "Twins. The terrible twos going on three."

"I got twin stepdaughters. I'm divorced from their daddy. Still see 'em, though. They were a handful at that age."

Melody, wiping Deanna's hand clean, gave no sign that she'd heard.

Mae tried again. "If you need a hand with the young'uns while I'm here, let me know. I'd enjoy it, and I'm good with two at a time."

"Zak's supposed to step up." Melody bit into a hunk of fry bread, her eyes following her children's every move. "We'll see."

During the powwow, Dean and Deanna had made a fuss when Melody stopped them from taking soda cans from her cooler and rolling them down the bleachers. Though both children were throwing tantrums, Zak had done nothing, as if they weren't even his kids. The Pena teenagers had helped out instead, taking the children off for a walk.

Mae found herself at a loss for any further small talk. Melody hadn't made eye contact and didn't speak again except for occasional words of mild discipline to her twins. Maybe Zak's pointing out Mae's fitness compared with his wife's lack of it had put up a wall between them.

When she'd almost finished her meal, Mae finally thought of a new approach. "Are you Misty Chino's sister?" There was so little resemblance between the two women, the connection hadn't occurred to Mae until now. "Reno Geronimo said her sister was married to one of Bernadette's cousins."

"That's me." Melody took a bite of stew and a sip of soda, still focused on her children. Her silence felt thick and immovable.

Mae missed Jamie even more. He could talk to anyone, though he might say something like *Jeezus, what in bloody hell's the matter with you?* She looked for Bernadette and spotted her in the middle of a noisy crowd, swallowed up by her extended family. Mae finished eating quickly and excused herself to take a walk. This wasn't her family reunion. Maybe the best thing to do was stop trying to be part of it and enjoy the event as a tourist. She could catch up with Bernadette later.

"Don't get kidnapped by wild Indians," Zak called after her, and his relatives laughed. If the joke had come from anyone else, Mae would have been amused by it, too.

She passed the big tipi and saw that Reno was at his father's booth now, with two boys of around ten and twelve—probably younger brothers—as well as Orville and his uncle. The whole group sat in folding chairs behind the counter, the adults watching passersby and the boys playing a fast-paced card game. Given their age, Mae was surprised it wasn't electronic. Lonnie and Orville rose as Mae approached.

"This lady," said the elder, "needs something warm. It gets cold here at night. We'd better sell her a sweatshirt."

After her uncomfortable time with Melody, Mae was happy to encounter someone friendly. "Thanks. I got warm stuff in my car."

Reno slipped out and went down one of the aisles of booths without acknowledging Mae or excusing himself to his family. Orville watched him go. "I don't know what's got into him."

The old man took down one of the handprint images and showed it to Mae. "You like these? This is how the medicine man sees. Holding his hand up to the sunrise."

Seeing with one's hands. It was a perfect image for how she—and other healers and seers—could access their gifts through touch. "I do. Very much."

He smiled knowingly. "I thought you would."

Did that mean he knew what she could do? Mae wasn't sure what to say, but her curiosity and confusion must have shown, because Orville said, "I called Niall to ask about my ex-wife. He told me how he quit smoking. He's pretty amazed. I never heard him sound like this. It's not like him to talk about himself. So my uncle and I have been talking about you."

The older of the two boys, who somewhat resembled Orville, looked up. "Lonnie's a retired medicine man."

"Not quite retired." Lonnie glanced back at the boy. "I still help people. I just don't do the ceremonies here anymore since I married a woman from Nambe Pueblo a couple of years ago. She's younger, still working, so we live there now."

Mae found this charming, though unexpected. Stooped, ancient Lonnie was practically a newlywed, with a wife below retirement age. Maybe he didn't feel like he was eighty or so. There was a sparkle in him. "Is she here with you?"

"No. She hates camping."

"I can't blame her. Daddy took me camping once when I was little and I loved being outside all day but the nights were awful. I didn't take to the tent too well, or not having a shower or a bathroom."

"I've got a nice little Winnebago, but she says that's still too rough for her."

Orville chuckled, "She needs a break from you, that's what it is. She just *tells* you she hates camping."

Customers came up to look at T-shirts, requiring Orville and Lonnie's attention, so Mae said goodbye and wandered down a side aisle of the vending area, idly browsing at a jewelry booth, paying little attention to what was in front of her. She'd met so many people, she needed to sort them out in her head. *Bernadette's cousin Elaine's son Zak is married to Misty's sister Melody. Reno's great-uncle is a medicine man.* Where was Orville's second wife, Reno's mother? No one mentioned her. The two younger boys were playing at the back of the booth, as if there weren't a second parent to keep an eye on them. Maybe Orville was like Mae, twice-divorced. No, Niall had said the second marriage had lasted.

As Mae lingered, the vendor behind the table smiled. "You can pick them up. Try things on."

"Thanks. They're beautiful, but I don't want to make you think I'm gonna buy anything."

The man smiled. "Nothing? A pretty lady needs jewelry."

"I'm a poor college student."

Footsteps crunched on the dirt and gravel beside her, and one of the approaching feet kicked a plastic foam cup.

"Poor college student," Zak said. "What are you studying?"

Mae picked up the cup and put it in a trash can. "Exercise Science."

"Good. So you're not an anthropologist. You're not studying us."

Was that why he'd made fun of her interest in healing? "No."

"Except for a select few." He stood too close by her side. "Eh?"

"I am sure not studying *you.*"

"Hot Native guy? Come on."

Did he think all white women wanted some trophy Indian, or was this more of his joking? "I have a boyfriend, and even if I didn't, I wouldn't be interested in a married man. Or in you at all."

"Wow." Zak grinned. "I made an impression."

"Not a good one."

"Sit down. Give me a minute." He nodded toward the benches in front of a food stand selling Navajo tacos—mutton and green chile on fry bread. With the feast going on, the booth was idle except for one person buying a cold drink. "I'm sorry if I pissed you off. I'm better than you think."

"Really?"

"Ask that old man you were talking to." Zak dropped onto the bench and propped an ankle on his thigh. He leaned back against the red-and-white-checked, plastic-coated counter, spreading his impressively defined arms along it and slouching just enough to look like a model posing—as long as he kept his mouth shut and didn't show his crooked teeth. "Lonnie Bigmouth. Ask him."

"I hardly know him. I just met him."

"And you just met me, too. What have you got against me?"

She worked in a gym. She knew his type. Conceited, arrogant men, obsessed with their perfect bodies. She couldn't say that, of course, but he'd been rude to his wife and ignored his children. "I didn't like how you told Melody to sign up with me as a trainer. I mean, you couldn't have meant it—I'm only here for four days. It was like you were nagging her in front of everybody. I think it hurt her feelings. I tried to be friendly with her later and she wouldn't say much to me."

"Oh—and that's my fault?"

"It might have been."

"I bet you nag your boyfriend."

"I try not to. If I do, he either laughs at me or bites my head off." Zak's comment about anthropologists studying him suggested he knew Stan Ellerbee. "Maybe you know him. Jamie Ellerbee."

"*He's* your boyfriend?" Zak made a face as if thinking so hard it hurt. "Seriously? That's a hard pair to put together. How long have you been seeing him?"

Without the preface, the question would have been normal and friendly. With it, Zak came across as questioning the relationship, which annoyed her even more than his flirting had. "I met him last summer. He can tell you the rest."

"Don't you want to talk about it? He didn't come here last year. Catch me up on things."

She didn't want to. Jamie had been struggling in so many ways that past summer. If he wanted Zak to know his story, he could share it. It was possible they were friends—Jamie had a strange affinity for assholes—but it was also possible they were only acquaintances. She kept the news about Jamie superficial. "We've been friends for a year or so but we've only been dating for a little over a month."

"So it's not serious yet."

Zak seemed to have migrated in her direction, though Mae hadn't seen him move. She put her hands on the bench and inched away. "Serious enough."

He said nothing, as if he hadn't heard her, his gaze directed down the aisle toward a pottery booth. The vendors, a short young Indian couple, were talking with a slim, dark-skinned woman in tight, tattered jeans, old cowgirl boots, and a Western hat atop an explosion of wavy black hair. Her skin-tight tank top revealed a firm, shapely figure and a full gallery of tattoos. A tiger, an elephant, a monkey and a snake paraded down one arm and the same menagerie climbed back up the other in reverse order.

Zak stood and tucked his shirt in snug. "I'll catch you and Baldy later."

Mae wanted to ask why in the world he'd called Jamie *Baldy*—his hair was one of his most conspicuous features—but Zak was already in motion.

He sauntered over to the tattooed cowgirl and struck up a quiet conversation. The woman's body language suggested she didn't mind. Unlike Mae, she didn't move away, but looked up into his face. As the woman turned profile, Mae saw that she was older than Zak, probably in her late thirties, with a little gold stud in the side of her nose, a decoration that suited her South Asian features. She wasn't a great beauty, with a small chin and too-large eyes and a blunt nose, giving her the look of a nocturnal animal, but she carried herself as if she felt beautiful, smiling with the confidence of a woman who feels admired. The opposite of Melody.

Zak bent down to whisper in the exotic woman's ear and she giggled, giving his arm a playful swat. Hot Native Guy didn't waste time, did he?

Mae rose, fed up with Zak. Time to go to her car for her warm clothes. A flash of color across the aisle caught her eye. The plump young woman at the pottery booth had blue streaks in her short dark hair, and her earrings, fluttering in the breeze, were made of long cobalt-blue feathers. Like the ghost of Florencia's macaw.

Chapter Five

Jamie called repeatedly, apologizing, saying everything was taking longer than he'd thought. A lot longer. Though disappointed, Mae was determined to enjoy the evening anyway. She sat with Bernadette, Michael, and his wife and their daughters, bundled in blankets in the first row of the bleachers, watching the mountain gods' dances in reverent but companionable silence, broken by occasional soft exchanges. The night grew blacker as the ceremony progressed, clouds dimming the half-moon over the mountains.

Bernadette scooted closer to Mae and whispered, "Are you understanding it?"

"Sort of." Mae wasn't sure how much an outsider was allowed to know. Earlier, Bernadette had told her a legend about two men, one blind and one crippled, who were left behind in a cave as their band was fleeing an enemy. They'd thought they might die, forgotten, when spirits appeared and did this dance, healing them and opening a path through a rock that showed them their way home. "I get the feeling of it, but not what each symbol means."

One group of the painted dancers left and another came in, followed by a procession of men who added massive logs to a fire blazing in the center of the dance arena.

"You don't have to," Bernadette assured her. "You can understand without thinking so much."

Zak strode up, talking on his cell phone. Mae had felt discourteous taking Jamie's calls during the sacred event and had jogged out to the vending area whenever her phone rang. Zak didn't seem to care. He sat on Mae's other side without acknowledging anyone. "Yeah. I'll be there." He listened, his knees jiggling, shoulders hunched in. "Okay. See you then." He ended the call and leaned his elbows on the bench behind him in his model pose, arms, chest, and abs on display. His arms had goose bumps, but apparently he thought he looked too good to put on a jacket. "Pudge stand you up? Need me to keep you company?"

First Baldy, now *Pudge*? "He should be here soon."

Zak made a clucking noise with his tongue and shook his head. "But I'm here now."

"Excuse me." Mae stood. "I'm supposed to meet him down near the music."

As she started down the steps of the bleachers, she felt Zak's eyes on her, but wouldn't give him the satisfaction of looking around to confirm the sensation.

She joined a cluster of people standing behind the singers and drummers who sat on the benches in front of the big tipi. The only thing good about meeting Zak was the contrast. He reminded her how lucky she was to have Jamie.

Trusting he would show up any minute, she focused on the dancers. Those nearest to the musicians began to smack their light-ning-painted sticks against their leather kilts. Then glorious chaos broke loose. The four groups of dancers, some painted green with yellow moons or stars on their chests and backs, others painted black with white zigzags or mountain shapes, circled the fire, their body paint streaked with sweat despite the cold. A lean, muscular man, his face masked in black fabric with glittering shells above the eye holes, began to leap side-to-side, swaying his torso in deep lat-eral bends, holding his sticks up and rattling his towering, multi-pronged headdress.

The surge of life force through him was so raw and electric, Mae felt it in her body. As the dancers passed in front of the singers, one by one, they danced as if the spirits they personified possessed them. When Jamie had tried to describe the ceremonies to her, he'd said, *Lightning will strike your bones*. It did. She was mesmerized.

The boy clowns, painted ashy white, ranged from scrawny little fellows of seven or eight to a big, fat lad of around twelve. They comically exaggerated their steps when they neared the drummers. On the edge of the crowd, two tiny children with sticks in their hands imitated the dancers, as fully absorbed as the men and boys in the ceremony.

A woman Mae could only see as a black silhouette beyond the fire circulated behind the people who sat in lawn chairs around the edge of the arena. She paused occasionally, leaning down to talk to someone. The silhouette made Mae think of the woman Zak had flirted with at the pottery booth. A huge man in a sagging chair waved his arms, gesturing directions. The woman hurried off.

Hope she's not looking for Zak. Mae pictured Melody at home with the kids, while Zak was out—not paying attention to the ceremonies, but, from the sound of his phone call, making other plans. The memory of Mae's first marriage surfaced again, those nights she'd spent angry, worried, and alone.

"Hello, love." An arm slipped around her shoulders, and a big warm body snuggled beside her. Jamie had walked up without a sound, as always. The night had gotten colder than she could have imagined, and his heat was welcome. She put her arm around him inside his jacket. Jamie moved her hand under his shirt. Her cold hand on his bare skin. "Warmer?" He kissed the side of her head.

She cuddled closer. He was both solid and soft to hold onto, fit but carrying a few extra pounds. "Yeah. Thank you, sugar."

"You having a good time?" He reached around and gently drilled his thumb between her eyebrows and then brushed them with his fingertips. She must have been frowning. "Everything all right?"

"Almost."

"Sorry I was so late—"

"It's not you. It's just—" She couldn't start their vacation with a complaint. "I'll tell you later. When we drive back to my place."

"Nah. Not doing that. Got a surprise for you, remember?"

"Sugar—you didn't get a motel—"

"Sh. Tell you in a minute."

The singers' voices rose, and Jamie sang along. He was an inch taller than Mae, with chocolate-brown skin, full lips, a broad straight nose, and thick, crinkly ash-blond hair that reached past his collar. He'd braided his dark goatee with a silver bead on the end. The pointy little beard emphasized his wide jaw and cheekbones, and also drew attention to the hint of a double chin. His huge black long-lashed eyes glowed with an inner light, and the gold tooth in his face-splitting smile caught the firelight. When they'd first met, she'd thought he looked strange, but now she found him, in his own way, beautiful. His trained tenor voice blended with the others but didn't disappear among them. Mae doubted he understood Apache, but it didn't surprise her that he had still picked up the songs.

Thunder rumbled over the mountains, and a stroke of lightning slashed the night. From the direction of the long arbor and the family tipis, a silent procession approached. The medicine men, the four young women in fringed white deerskin dresses, and their godmothers walked slowly into the big tipi behind the drummers. The beauty of the moment made Mae catch her breath. The yucca leaves that blanketed the entrance to the open tipi gave off a fresh green scent as the procession passed over them. Immediately, some of the people who had been watching the mountain gods' dance moved to peer into the entrance to the tipi, blocking Mae's view as she turned to look.

"Don't worry. They'll just sit a while," Jamie whispered.

Mae faced the Ga'an dancers again, and Jamie rejoined the song. No one else in the group behind the singers moved with the beat, but he kept a pulse in his legs like the gourd dancers had, as if he couldn't stop the music from taking him over. She let the music and the dancers and Jamie's energy carry her into an altered state, a kind of ecstatic trance. Bernadette had been right, telling her to stop thinking. In some wordless way, Mae almost understood the ceremony.

Her mind snapped back to ordinary reality when a man's voice on the loudspeaker from a booth above the bleachers reminded non-Indians to leave at midnight.

"Come on, mate, I'm indigenous *somewhere*," Jamie said, but it was a good-humored complaint.

He took Mae's hand and started around the side of the big tipi, then stopped. "Listen." Through the canvas came the medicine men's sweet, melodious song, accompanied by the rustling of rattles and the strange high note of the girls' chanting. He looked up at the stars, and then hugged Mae to his side to resume their walk, heading toward the exit. Trucks and vans were pulled up to the booths as the vendors packed up for the night. Jamie said, "Thanks for hanging in with me, standing that long. You good? Was it all right?"

"More than all right, sugar. It was amazing. Now what's my surprise?"

"Camping."

Mae's heart sank. "You spent all that time getting ready for camping?"

He grinned. "Yeah. That and the van. Jeezus. All that bloody paperwork. And then I wasn't sure what to bring and I kept repacking. Never camped with you, y'know? I almost brought Gasser, thought he'd like it better than a cat sitter but he'd stink up the tent, poor bloke. So, anyway, I got a double sleeping bag—that took time—hard to find—and I brought my stove so we can make coffee and breakfast. Hope the food's all right. Did some baking. Think I got everything we need. Lots of water. Headlamp, little flashlight. Got this great solar lantern, too, holds a charge forever, makes a good nightlight. Nah, that'll bother you won't it? Never mind. Brought a couple of my flutes, play you a lullaby if y'like."

He was so wound up and excited about this surprise, Mae didn't want to seem ungrateful, but she'd seen his tent, a tiny high-tech dome, and she couldn't imagine the two of them spending four nights in it. On top of all the other hassles of camping, Jamie was challenging to sleep with even in her house or his apartment. Though he hadn't brought the cat, and he'd already conceded on the light—two of the ways he kept her awake—he radiated so much heat in his sleep, she imagined the one-man tent becoming like a sauna. *If* he slept. He had insomnia. In a tent, he couldn't go in another room to be restless. She made an effort not to sound as dismayed as she felt.

"Where are we camping?"

"Right here."

"We're allowed to?"

"Not on the ceremonial grounds. Down below the rodeo grounds. Dad's in with Indians, y'know? He and Mum always camp there when they come for the ceremonies. Bit rough. No showers. Portapotties." He let out a soft snort-laugh. "Jeezus. Making this sound romantic, aren't I?"

"Sure are. Better than a candlelight dinner. But seriously, sugar, how do we get clean?"

He released her waist and slid his hand down to hers, swinging her arm as they walked. "Wash basin. Joking. We've got friends."

"You mean you go to people's houses and use their showers?"

"Yeah. No worries. I cook for 'em, and they let us get clean."

"What about locking our things up? Do we keep going back to our cars? You can't leave everything in a tent, can you?"

"Why not? I do. Plenty of people around. Lot of them know me and my parents." He kissed her on the temple. "Did you see Bernadette? Is her brother here?"

"Yes. I met her family. I like all of them except Zak."

"Old Zak's all right. Hot air, y'know?"

"He's not nice to his wife. And he gives me these *looks*."

"I've known Zak and Melody for fifteen years. Don't mind him. He flirts with everyone. It's like a disease, y'know? He can't help it. Don't think he really cheats on her. He's got a good heart. Just won't show it."

He sure won't. Mae suspected Jamie was too generous in his estimate of Zak, but if he liked him, she shouldn't say any more.

They paused for cars moving out of the parking lot and then walked single file through the tall grass at the side of the road, heading downhill from the ceremonial grounds to the camping area. As they got away from the parking lot lights, thousands of stars exploded into the sky. Occasionally a car would slow down and someone would lean out and talk to Jamie and drive on. He was easy to spot in the dark, with his cloud of fair hair. Mae heard some of his acquaintances address him as Baldy, the same weird nickname Zak had used.

"Why do people call you Baldy?"

"Used to shave my head when I was fourteen, fifteen. Felt weird about the—learned a word for it, did you know there's a word for this?—*neoteny*, retention of juvenile traits in adulthood. My *neotenous* hair." Aboriginal children were often blond and turned dark-haired as adults. Jamie was the one in a million who didn't. "Then I'd look like a rotten peach when the fuzz grew in. My head's perfectly round."

Mae giggled and reached up to feel his skull thorough his hair. It *was* round.

He continued, "Had a lot of nicknames. Baldy. Blondie. Pudge. Pavarotti. Used to call Zak Skinny, 'cause his name was Fatty and he wasn't. But I was. So that's why I was Pudge. Melody was ... fuck, what did we call her? Dunno. She wasn't fat back then. Pretty. Kind of wild. *Cher.* Yeah, that was it, 'cause she could sing real low like Cher. We'd sing duets and I'd take the high harmony."

"It's hard to picture Melody happy enough to sing."

"Not if you know her. She used to be fun. Being a mum took it out of her. Or something did. Dunno. Didn't come last year. Longest I've gone without seeing them."

Jamie guided Mae to a stop as they reached a triangular grass island at a Y in the road. Parked in the middle was a metallic-blue van with smoked rear windows and dealer plates. "There it is." He gazed at it a while. "You like it?"

"I do. It's nice."

"Thought the dark windows were good, y'know? Traveling with all my instruments in the back. And it was hardly even used—I lucked out. Wonder if it'll get hit. Can't figure out if it's safer here or on the side of the road. Y'think I should move it?"

Worrying. A sign that he liked the van. "I think it's safe here. You'd have to be a pretty bad driver to hit it."

"Reckon?" He studied the van a little longer. "Some people *are* bad drivers."

"Relax. Come on. Let's get—" *Get it over with*, she almost said, thinking of going into the tent for the night. "Get settled in."

He opened the lift gate. The interior still smelled new—and had her suitcase in it.

"Sugar, how'd you get my things?"

"Told your dad and Niall what I was doing. Stopped by T or C. They let me into your house. Made a long fucking trip, but I couldn't take you camping with no clean clothes and no toothbrush. Niall said you'd be pissed, me going in your drawers and everything, and that people hate surprises, but your dad thought I was being romantic."

Mae wished Marty had remembered that she hadn't liked camping—or had she been too polite to tell him when she was eight years old? She didn't think she'd ever admitted it to him. It was easy to be honest with a jerk like Zak, but hard when it would disappoint someone she loved who was trying to make her happy. Especially Jamie. She met his eyes. They were huge, dark, and vulnerable. The baby seal look. Mae looked away and picked up the suitcase. "Thanks, sugar. You were real sweet to think of this."

He took the bag from her, set it down, and wrapped her in an embrace. "Had me worried for a second. Thought Niall had been right." Jamie let out a long sigh and kissed her ear, her cheek, and then her lips. "I love you so much. I want to make you happy."

He squeezed tighter and prolonged the next kiss. Mae's doubts about camping partially dissolved as her body responded. She stroked his back and murmured against his cheek, "You do, sugar. You do."

They crossed another road and passed through an opening in a white fence, coming into a congested village of tents, camper trucks, and RVs behind a row of trees. Jamie stopped outside a little dome tent next to a larger, old-fashioned tent with poles and a peaked roof. He whispered in Mae's ear, "We're next door to the oldies. Don't scream too loud. And if *they* do, don't listen."

While he apparently found the lack of privacy funny, Mae found it potentially embarrassing.

They had to duck and crawl through the flap of Jamie's tent. Once inside, he turned on his solar lantern. Beside the sleeping bag sat a stack of plastic tubs, Jamie's backpack, and a few jugs of water. There was scarcely room for Mae's suitcase. "Cozy, isn't it?" He smiled and wrestled her onto the sleeping bag, pulling her on top of him.

Shortly after they made love she drifted off, but not for long. The heat woke her. Jamie had wrapped around her with all four limbs like a tree sloth holding onto a branch, and he was breathing strangely with long exhalations. With each inhalation, his belly released and softened against her side, bringing more heat to her, and then withdrew a little on the extended exhalations, letting air touch her skin.

"You okay, sugar?"

"Yeah, yeah. I'm good. Doing some breath work, y'know? So I can sleep. Sh. Go back to your dreams." He kissed her, cuddled her closer, and rocked her a little. "Want me to sing to you?"

"That'd be nice." Silence was all she needed for sleep, but the singing would do him good. He sang sweetly, the "Goodnight" song from the Beatles' white album, and after a verse they both slept with the bag opened to let out the heat.

After what felt like an hour or so, she woke again, this time to surreptitious rustling sounds and then the pop of a plastic food tub being opened. "Sugar, you are *not* eating cookies in this sleeping bag."

"Mm, but I already ... mmm." Chewing sounds and a smell of chocolate chip cookies. "Want one?"

"No. You should think things through. You'll want to get up and brush your teeth." She knew how his mind worked. "And then you'll have to get out and get dressed so you can go out and spit."

"I know. But, see, I woke up again, so I was doing the breathing. And then I got to thinking, y'know, that you only get but so many breaths. You'll *stop* someday. How many do I have left? It's this bloody timer ticking down each time I exhale, and someday I won't inhale again at the end."

Mae smoothed his hair, stroking a few times to calm him down. His worry was like the thoughts she'd had at Florencia's house, but more frightening. She'd hit a wall trying to imagine her own mortality. Jamie hadn't. "You can't lie there thinking about that in the middle of the night."

"But I *was.* Thinking how many nights I haven't spent with you that I could have, how many years will we get, how many breaths ... And then I could hear my heart. Fucking *hear* my *heart.* Jeezus. I'm doing this fucking relaxation exercise and it's giving me an anxiety attack." He half-laughed, half-sighed. "I didn't want to wake you up, so I got some cookies."

"Did you go to therapy today?"

"Yeah." He sighed out a cloud of chocolate breath. "Talked about some hard stuff."

"That's progress when you do that, isn't it?" She propped up on her elbow and ran a hand over his smooth, hairless chest. "Even when you have a little setback like this."

"Nah. Wasn't a setback. It was good. I'll have to tell Gorman." His psychologist. "See, I was anxious because I was *afraid* to die. I really *want to live.*" He sat up and groped along the tent floor until he found and turned on the lantern. "Not as scared of death as I am of the dentist yet, but, y'know, it's still good."

He crawled out of the bag. "Sorry about the light, got to find my toothbrush." He wriggled into his jeans, an awkward process in the little tent. "Go back to sleep. Turn off the light once I'm out. I'll come back in the dark. I think. Yeah." A flash of a smile. "I can do that."

Jamie ducked outside. Mae switched off the light. The dark was probably what had been making him anxious, making him hold her like that. She should have let him have the lantern on. There was so much to get used to in a relationship with Jamie.

He didn't come back in right away, but started talking with someone, very softly. A female voice. Probably his mother. Mae grew drowsy again and drifted off with the fading, guilty thought that much as she loved him, it was easier to sleep without him.

Chapter Six

When Jamie stepped out into the moonlight to brush his teeth, he was surprised to see a woman sitting huddled in a blanket not far from his tent. All he could see of her was her broad back and long straight black hair. Strange that she should be there, but people did all sorts of things when they couldn't sleep. Jamie finished brushing, set his cup and toothbrush down, and walked a few feet away to spit so it wouldn't land where anyone would step in it. At the sound of his expectoration, the woman jerked her head around like a frightened animal. His old friend—Melody Chino Fatty.

"You scared me," she said, just above a whisper. "You still don't make any noise when you walk."

"Only when I spit." As he drew closer, he realized she'd been crying. Her eyes were red and puffy, and she was sniffling. He sat and put his arm around her shoulders, keeping his voice low. "What's the matter?"

"Zak." She wiped her eyes. "What else?"

"What'd he do?"

"Shit. Where do I start? Tonight? All day? You should have seen him at the powwow. He was flirting with this white chick, this friend of Bernadette's, like he was comparing her and me. Her face was just average but her *body*—"

"Mel, that face isn't *average*." A fire rose in Jamie. He knew he should be listening to Melody, but he couldn't hear Mae described as less than perfect. "That's my soul mate. Most beautiful face on the planet. Nothing ordinary about her."

"*She's* your girlfriend?"

"Yeah—fucking amazing, isn't it? Me, with the likes of her."

"I didn't mean it that way."

"Feel like that sometimes, though, y'know?" Belated embarrassment over snapping at Melody pulled him down into a tight huddle, arms around his shins, making it hard to breathe. He straightened up. "Sorry 'bout the rant."

"It's okay. It was sweet. Zak wouldn't rant if someone said I was average. Or worse." Melody sniffed and glanced toward Jamie's tent. "Is she camping with you?" He nodded. She said, "Then you should get back in there with her."

"Can't leave you by yourself."

"Zak would. He couldn't care less." She sniffed more loudly, rubbing at her nose.

Jamie plucked a handful of grass and offered it to her. "Hanky? Beats swallowing your snot."

Melody's laughter exploded while she was trying to be quiet, and it came out her nostrils, expelling a string of mucus. Jamie snort-laughed, then tried to stifle the sound so as not to wake people. "Jeezus, Mel. That was like something I'd do."

She blew her nose in the wad of grass, pitched it toward the road, and gave him a little punch in the shoulder. "No, *you'd* have farted and blown your boogers out at the same time."

Jamie passed wind and they fell into another bout of silent hilarity.

Melody caught her breath. "You can fart on cue? Have you been *practicing* that?"

"Nah. Vegan diet, you spend your whole life trying *not* to fart. Especially in the tent. And yoga. Jeezus. Fucking sphincter workout."

Taken with another spell of struggling-to-be-quiet laughter, Melody curled over and Jamie flopped on his back. It was like they were kids, the same kind of jokes, as well as the same connection.

She said, "I haven't laughed like that in ages. Zak never laughs with me anymore." Her smile faded. "He laughs at me."

Jamie sat up. "He teases everyone. Don't you think he's just playing with you?"

"No. He means it now. Since I got fat and ugly."

"Don't say that. Being fat doesn't make you ugly. Just ... big." He squeezed her hand. "Anyway, you've done things that matter more than your weight." She'd put it on when she quit alcohol and drugs and then had twins. "Zak should take that into account and notice what's beautiful about you. And so should you."

"*Beautiful.*" Melody toyed with the hem of the blanket. "Remember how you felt when you were really big?"

"Bloody awful. But I was depressed. Out-of-my-fucking-mind clinically depressed. Didn't feel that bad when I was just a chubby kid." He plucked a few blades of grass and twisted them around his index finger. "You think you're getting depressed?"

"No. I'm so pissed off I could explode." Melody stared out at the road. "I had to work tonight. I'm part-time at the casino travel center now, at the convenience store. They try to schedule people who aren't Apache during the ceremonies, but one of the white girls had a sick kid, and she's a single mom, so I went in, but then one of the assistant managers took over for me after a few hours so I could go to the ceremonies. I was too tired by then, though, so I went home and the damned door was locked."

"That's weird. Thought you and Zak never locked up."

"We don't. I don't ever want family to find a closed door. Especially Misty."

"Would she have locked it?"

"She doesn't have a key. And Zak was home. I could hear voices inside but there were no extra cars in our driveway. When I unlocked the door and walked in, I heard someone go out the side, through the kitchen. And then Zak came into the living room and gave me the fakest smile, all friendly, like 'Great, you got off work early.' But I could tell he was nervous, like he was lying."

"Strange. Wonder what he's up to."

"Cheating on me."

"With the kids in the house?"

"They're with Pearl for the night. Since I had to work, and Zak—I thought—was at the ceremonies."

"Still. Person went out the kitchen door, not the bedroom window."

"You think people only do it in beds?"

Jamie had never done it anywhere but a bed until tonight in the sleeping bag. "You really think he'd fuck someone on the *kitchen floor*?"

"If you knew some of the things me and Zak have done, you wouldn't ask that. We—"

"Jeezus. I don't need to know. I get the idea."

"I asked him who'd just left and he said it was no one, that he'd opened and closed the door to put a bug outside. I said it was one big bug—I heard its footsteps. And there was beer on the counter, a whole six-pack, and one of the cans was out and open. We don't have alcohol in the house, ever. And he didn't smell like he'd been drinking—it had to be the person who left. I asked him what he thought he was doing, having some woman over, and he says how did I know there'd been a woman? And that I was supposed to be at work and he could do what he damned well pleased and that included having a beer without asking my permission or having to explain. I was so mad, I just couldn't stay there. It made me want to drink that beer."

"You should've gone to your mum's. Stayed the night."

"I was going to. But when I got in the car I was scared I'd go buy something to drink. When it hits me like that, I don't trust myself. So I grabbed this blanket off the seat and hoped you'd be up. When I didn't see a light in your tent, I just sat down and cried. I'm sorry. You've got your new girlfriend here. I'm spoiling your night with her."

"Nah. Come on." Jamie got to his feet and shifted his bad hip, trying to rock the glitch out. He offered Melody a hand. "I'll make him give me the beer. Find out what was going on, too."

"Thanks. Zak listens to you." Pulling on his arm, she nearly toppled him as she rose. "Sorry."

"No worries. Be nice and soft if I fell on you." Melody glared at him. Jamie grinned, wrapping the blanket more neatly around her. "I get to make fat jokes. Entitled. Member of the club."

As they began walking across the camping area, spiky weeds in the grass stabbed at Jamie's bare feet, and the cold hit him hard, making him shake. He considered ducking back into the tent for a shirt and shoes, but he'd woken Mae enough already and would disturb her again when he came back. Anyway, the mission shouldn't take long.

Rap music pounded inside the blue house as Jamie and Melody crossed the road and cut across the yard. The driveway was full of cars, and the windows revealed a crowd in the living room.

"Shit." She huddled into her blanket and stopped for a moment. "This is crazy. I'll kill him. I complain about *one* person and *one* six-pack, so he invites the whole damned world?"

So much for a quick and simple mission. What had gotten into Zak? He must have called everyone he could think of, and with local people as well as returning tribal members camping for the long weekend, they'd come quickly.

On a front porch that sagged at one end, a young woman sat on a glider, moving the creaking seat back and forth and holding a beer can. She looked up as Jamie and Melody climbed the steps. He recognized Melody's younger sister Misty. She frowned at Jamie. "What happened to your shirt?"

"Went to the casino."

"What?"

"Y'know—lost my shirt. What the fuck's going on?"

"What does it look like?"

Melody snapped, "And *you're* part of it?"

"No. I'm here to see you."

"Then get rid of that beer."

With a stony stare, Misty handed Jamie her drink. Melody eased down onto the glider and it creaked more loudly. "I don't want you turning out like I did."

"I'm not going to. I had half of it and that's all I wanted."

Melody said, "Take care of the party, Pudge. I've got to take care of my sister."

Fuck. Jamie hadn't seen Zak yet on this trip, and this was how they would greet each other? He emptied the beer over the railing and opened the door.

Party guests packed the dimly lit living room. Jamie recognized a few faces he couldn't put names to. He remembered Will Baca, one of Melody's former drinking buddies, a short, lean man with fine features marred by a slightly crooked nose, as if he'd broken it since the last time Jamie had seen him. Not surprising, if Will was still as wild as he'd been when he was a teenager.

Zak stood in a corner, eyes closed, rapping along with the music.

Jamie projected his voice, loud without shouting. "Wake up, Skinny. Your wife's home. And turn down the fucking music."

Zak popped out of his trance. "Can't take it, Pavarotti? Or it's not good enough for you?" He lowered the volume and shook Jamie's hand. "Good to see you, man. Sorry we didn't invite you. It was spur of the moment. And I didn't think Mae would want to come." He looked Jamie over and laughed. "What are you doing? Showing off your physique?"

"What are *you* doing? You never do crap like this."

"It's a holiday weekend. I'm having a party."

"Without asking Mel?"

"She can go to her mother's."

"She was too upset to drive. Scared she'd buy a drink."

Their eyes met, and Zak looked away.

"Come on. Talk to me." Jamie led the way into Zak and Melody's bedroom.

Zak followed and closed the door. "So, you're my wife's knight in shining ..." He snickered. "... *armor?*"

"Give me a shirt and listen."

Zak opened a drawer and tossed Jamie a T-shirt. "This is hers. Two-X. You can keep it. She wears a three-X now."

Jamie pulled the shirt over his head. "Don't give up on her just because she gained weight. Jeezus. Give her time. You're making it hard for her."

"Right. *I'm* making it hard for *her*. I can't have friends over for a beer like a normal man because my wife's scared she'll drink it. After she's sober almost *four years*? How much time do I have to give her? The rest of her life?"

"If she needs it, yeah. If you love her."

"Listen to the marriage expert. You have no idea what it's like to be with the same person this long. The same fucked-up person. I love her—you know I do. I have since we were kids. But she quits drinking and drugging and starts eating. It's just another wall, like she got fat *at* me. Mel's a mess and she's always gonna be one. I need a break sometimes."

Jamie imagined Mae talking to someone in fifteen years about having spent all those years with the same fucked-up person. *Jamie's a mess and he's always gonna be one. I need a break.* A rush of anxiety battered his guts. He took a deep breath and tried to silence the thoughts. "Mel thinks you're cheating on her."

"Because I was putting a bug out. Thanks to you." Zak sat on the bed. "Want me to start squashing them again?"

"No." Early in their friendship, Jamie had yelled at Zak, *You can't kill something just because it's ugly.* Of course, Zak had held the beetle up in Jamie's face before putting it outside, asking, *Even something this ugly?* "But was it really a bug? She said she heard someone walking out."

"That was me, walking down the steps and back up. Mel's jealous. She's imagining things."

"Then maybe you should stop doing crap that makes her jealous."

"Why is this my fault?"

Jamie dropped into the threadbare old armchair beside the bed, rolling the empty can he still held back and forth between his hands. "Mae said you were flirting with her."

"Just funning. Can't she take a compliment?"

"She doesn't know you, doesn't know how to take you. You're an acquired taste, y'know? And anyway, if you act like that in front of your wife, you're bloody well asking for her to be jealous."

"I'm just being myself."

True. Flirting was a habit. Zak thought it made him charming. And the party, in some ways, was classic Zak contrariness. He resented any hint that someone was trying to control him and would go out of his way to prove they couldn't. Cheating was out of character, though, and so was lying—but he seemed to have done it. Lied, at least. "Mel heard you talking with another person. Who was here? Why'd you have to hide it?"

Zak leaned his forearms on his thighs and ground his knuckles against each other. "It's something Mel can't know about."

"You can still tell me."

Jamie waited, but Zak said nothing. Noise from the party filled the gap. What would Zak want to hide? It came across like he was doing something illegal or immoral. Strange. Unlike Melody, Zak had always been proud of staying out of trouble. "Mate. Unload it, will you?"

Silence. Zak didn't move.

Jamie thought of the things he'd kept from Mae. He used to conceal troubles he was ashamed of, but not anymore. Now he only hid things like camping. Surprises. "Were you trying to surprise her?"

Instead of answering, Zak stood and asked, "Are we done? I have a party to go to, in case you hadn't noticed."

"Jeezus. Don't you trust me?"

"Yes, damn it, but if I tell you, you'll tell her. So forget about it. Have a drink and head back to your red-hot redhead."

"Move the party to someone else's house."

"It's a lot easier to move Melody to her mother's house. And she can take Misty, too. She's having a big whine about Reno and I don't want to listen to it. Those girls need to get out of here and let people have some fun."

As they entered the living room, Jamie imagined taking center stage and telling everyone to leave. Then he looked at Will Baca with his crooked nose and scarred knuckles and thought twice. Will was smaller than Jamie but twice as tough. And drunk. A fight would only make things worse, and no one would listen to Jamie, anyway. It wasn't his house or his party.

Jamie went out onto the porch. Melody and Misty were sharing the blanket on the glider, talking softly.

"Sorry." Jamie dug his toes into the fibers of the doormat. "Couldn't talk him out of it. He says you two should go to your mum's place."

Melody's eyes blazed. She threw off the blanket and heaved herself to her feet. "He does, huh?" She swept past Jamie, making him jump aside, and stormed into the house. The music cut off abruptly, and Melody's voice bellowed, "Everybody out. Take your liquor and your beer, every last drop of it. *Now.*"

Within seconds, the guests streamed out carrying bottles and bags, some mumbling and griping, some laughing. Melody followed them and slammed the door shut. "And don't drive drunk. Sleep in your cars if you have to. Just don't piss on my lawn."

A slow smile lit up Misty's face, and she applauded. "Go, Mel."

Jamie applauded with her.

Most of the party-goers walked toward the campground. Some, including Will, were stumbling. A few slipped into cars and drove off slowly toward 70. Jamie finally dropped the empty can into the recycling bin on the porch. It rattled among the soda cans, the only sound in the post-party quiet. Misty looked to Melody. "Is it okay if I stay here tonight? I didn't pack anything and I'll need to borrow some of your old clothes."

"Of course it's okay. It's always okay." Melody opened the door to let Misty in. "Thanks, Pudge. We'll be all right now."

"Thanks for what? Didn't do anything. You did it all."

"No." Melody hugged him. "You made me strong. I couldn't have done it without you."

Jamie walked back to his tent, shivering. His feet were like blocks of ice. Dirty ice. Awful to put those in the sleeping bag with Mae. She would understand. If a friend of hers had shown up crying, she'd have gone out of her way, too. Still, he felt guilty. He was going to bother her again.

As quietly as possible, he lifted the flap and crept in, squirmed out of his jeans, and rummaged in his backpack for socks to cover his cold, filthy feet. In the dark, everything he touched felt like a sock and yet turned out to be a sleeve. A quiet curse escaped him and Mae stirred, murmuring something so drowsy he couldn't make it out.

"Sorry." *Finally. Socks.* He put them on and crawled in beside her.

She cuddled against him. "You're wearing a shirt."

"Yeah." He was still so cold he didn't want to remove it.

"You went out to brush your teeth and came back with a shirt?"

"Yeah. Long story."

Mae slid her warm hand under the shirt and caressed his back. "Sugar, you have never told me a short one."

"Is that bad?"

"No." She kissed him lightly. "But it means it can wait 'til morning."

He felt her body soften, and her breath slowed and changed texture. Already asleep again. Jamie kissed her on the nose and lay awake, resting in the embrace.

Mae's sweet acceptance touched him. After wading into Zak and Melody's marital crap, he'd come back to shelter from a storm. More than that. He'd lain down with a fucking miracle. The longer he lay awake feeling Mae sleeping against him, the more his heart filled and swelled with something too big for him, unbearable joy tangled with a sense of precariousness, as if he'd climbed to a peak with a breathtaking view and stood on a ledge so narrow and high he couldn't be safe. Overwhelmed, heart pounding, he pulled her closer and held her tight. She stirred. He apologized for waking her again.

"It's okay, sugar," she whispered. "Relax. Everything's all right."

"I know. I mean, I should. I do. I just ..." How could he explain what had come over him? "I love you." So much it scared him.

Chapter Seven

Faint morning light filtered through the fabric of the tent. Like a bird signaled by the dawn, Mae was wide awake despite her fatigue, while Jamie lay on his back borderline snoring, finally peaceful as he usually was once it was light out. When the long weekend was over, she would need a few nights by herself to recover from four nights with him. For now, running would be the best way to refresh herself.

Having slept her fragmented sleep next to the tent wall, Mae had to crawl over Jamie to get out of the bag. She moved slowly so as not to disturb him, but as soon as she was above him, his arms shot up and wrapped around her. He pulled her down onto him with a loud, happy humming sound.

His eyes were still closed, long lashes soft against his cheeks. She kissed his eyelids, then his lips. "I was trying to let you sleep."

"Mm." He loosened his hold on her. "Mm-mm."

"I'm gonna go for a run." She looked down at the shirt he still wore. It was light brown with darker brown lettering and art that looked like the signs along the roads warning of the Mescalero fire risk level. The list of things forbidden went beyond the usual—campfires and smoking—to include burning desires, smoldering passions, and old flames. The jokes made her smile. She'd seen shirts like that for sale at the powwow. Jamie's father must have loaned it to him. "Get some rest." She ran her fingers through his hair, combing a few tangles out. She should have brushed it for him when they went to bed. That helped him sleep better than anything. "I'll wake you up when I get back."

"Love you." His hand trailed over hers as she slipped away.

"I love you, too, sugar."

She dressed and crawled out the flap.

Starting her run, Mae crossed the road through a break in the steady stream of vans and trucks. Some of the vendors had already parked to set up their wares at booths along the roadside, but most were heading up toward the ceremonial grounds. Orville Geronimo grinned and waved to her from the cab of a black pickup. His two preteen boys and Reno were packed into the seat beside him and the back of the truck was full of boxes. Reno stared ahead as they passed, either ignoring her or not seeing her.

She wondered if Misty would ask her to look into his secrets again. Perhaps being with his family for a few days would get him to open up finally and make it unnecessary.

Running along the access road parallel to Route 70, Mae heard pounding steps catching up with her and turned her head to see the last person she would ever want to run with.

Zak had sprinted, but he wasn't winded. He wore skimpy white shorts and no shirt, displaying lean, powerful legs and a sculpted torso. "You must be psychic," he said. "You knew I'd be here."

"I wasn't looking for you."

He fell in step too close beside her. "Still, be glad you found me."

Mae increased the space between them. "Where did you come from?"

He nodded toward the blue house on the curve where the road turned toward the ceremonial grounds. A boxy late-eighties AMC Eagle sat in the drive near Misty's Harley. "That's my digs."

So it wasn't Misty's parents' house, but her older sister's.

Zak drew closer again. "I'll show you the route for the race Saturday."

Mae hesitated to respond. She wanted to know more about the race, but wondered if she could endure Zak's company.

"Not too talkative, are you? Bad mood? Had some problems with Baldy this morning?"

"No. We're fine."

"What's he up to while you run?"

"Sleeping."

"Maybe you'd better call and make sure that's where he is. Did he tell you where he went last night?"

The idea that Jamie had been anywhere but with his parents startled her, but she didn't want to let Zak know. It would be exactly the reaction he was looking for. She kept her tone casual and made her answer fuzzy. "We haven't had a chance to talk much yet."

"*Ri—ight.*"

Zak's smug sarcasm cut into Mae's intention not to let him get to her. Not because she doubted Jamie, but because Zak apparently wanted her to.

"Can't tell you what he did, though." Zak picked up the pace. "Man code. How far do you run?"

What was the matter with him? He was answering questions she hadn't asked, as if he had a script in his head for how she should act. "*Man code. That is stupid.*" Jamie liked to socialize and have a few drinks, but he would never leave Mae in the middle of the night for that, and he hadn't smelled like alcohol—or felt the need to brush his teeth again. "He doesn't have anything to hide."

"*Ri—ight.* Untwist your panties. How far do you run?"

Mae clenched her jaw, then blew out her breath. Jamie would tell her whatever there was to tell. She shouldn't have engaged with Zak, shouldn't have let him trip her into playing his game. She made herself shift gears into normal conversation. "Three to five miles, usually. I'm training for a triathlon now, so I'm doing more biking and swimming."

"Cool. I do tri's. Which one?"

"Me and my daddy are gonna do the Dam It Man at Elephant Butte." The name of the race punned on the dam at Elephant Butte Lake. "It's my first—just a sprint triathlon."

"Sprints are all I have time to train for. I did that one last year. I sucked at the swimming part. But I still might do it if I'm not called out on a fire."

"Wouldn't you just schedule your time off?"

"Wildfire, not a house fire." He sounded offended, as if she'd suggested he played with toy fire trucks. Was a house fire too domestic for him? "I just got back from the Wallow Fire. That was one hell of a tough job."

Though he was boasting, she couldn't blame him. Fighting forest fires took courage. Any appreciation of his work might sound like admiration of Zak himself, though, so Mae said nothing. Now that she knew Zak's occupation, she guessed the source of the T-shirt with the fire danger jokes—and Jamie's late night absence suddenly bothered her, the way she supposed Zak wanted it to. Jamie had been at his asshole friend's house.

They ran in silence for a while, playing a maddening game of tag in which Zak kept getting in her personal space and she kept moving away from him.

He looked down at her feet. "You wear those barefoot shoes. You like 'em?"

"I do." Her Southern habits made her feel obligated to return the small talk, while she widened the gap between them again. "My ex-husband got me into using 'em." She didn't feel like saying *second* ex-husband, expecting Zak would make some snarky comment.

"Bet you miss him. Jamie sure as hell doesn't run with you."

The derogatory tone grated on Mae's nerves. "He can't—his hip's messed up. He had a lot of rock-climbing accidents."

"I know—back when he was with that other white chick. The snooty bitch." Zak grinned at her. "Ol' Pudge doesn't look like he does much climbing anymore."

Mae knew she'd let Zak yank her chain again, but she didn't like hearing him cut Jamie down. "You don't have to make it sound like he's some total slob because he's not like you." She took satisfaction in Zak's fleeting chastised look. *Got him.* "He bikes and swims and does yoga—he stays in shape. But he can't climb anymore. He messed up his hand and shoulder in another accident."

"I wondered where he got the new scars." Zak gave Mae a wicked smirk. "You should've seen him last night. *Somebody* undressed him halfway—" Zak drew his thumb and forefinger across his lips as if pulling a zipper. "Whoops. Man code."

"Will you cut the stupid *man code*? You can stop trying to pretend you didn't have a party."

"You make a party sound like a crime. Is that what you think? You know, not all Indians are a bunch of drunks."

"I didn't say that."

"*Sure* you didn't."

"You know I didn't. I swear, talking to you is like playing Twister with an octopus."

Zak laughed. "Good one, Miss Mary-Mae. You're getting the hang of this."

The hang of what? Getting into an argument about nothing for the sake of having one? The prissy nickname annoyed her, too, but if she said something about it, no doubt Zak would enjoy her objection and launch a new round of recreational hostilities. She'd already let him draw her in too many times.

He guided her at a slow jog into a parking lot in front of a plain white one-story building. A sign identified it as the tribal wellness center. "The race starts here, eight o'clock Saturday. Five K, ten K and a mile walk for the beginners. *We're* doing the ten K. Ready to see if I can beat you?"

Mae wanted to leave him in her dust, but it wasn't likely that she could. She'd seen a sign on Route 70 indicating the altitude was nearly 7,600 feet, over 3,000 feet above T or C. Not enough difference to stop her from running well, but enough to guarantee he'd be faster. "You live at this altitude and I don't. Of course you're gonna beat me."

"Then you get to look at my ass. Too bad I won't get to look at yours."

"I don't like how you flirt all the time. You're married—"

"To a porker. Come on. You can't tell me *you* don't look around."

They began with a long downhill stretch. Mae stayed in the grassy verge of the road. Not only did it feel better in her barefoot shoes, it kept the space between her and Zak. "I do *not* look around."

"I wish you would."

She took off fast and hard, not caring if she burned out before the ten kilometers. Zak caught up as if he were out for a stroll. "I'm just playing with you. I don't mean any harm. Ask Jamie. He knows me."

He'd already told her. *Old Zak's all right. Hot air, y'know?* Jamie saw something likeable in this arrogant jerk, but the patience and insight it took him to do that, or the deluded optimism, were more than Mae could muster.

Cooling down at the end of the run, they slowed from a jog to a walk near Zak's house, where she hoped to shed him. He stopped in front of his driveway. "Come in for a shower?"

The day was growing hot and she looked forward to cleaning up, but she wasn't about to get undressed anywhere near him. "No thanks."

"You think white girls' sweat don't stink?" He went straight from flirting to insulting her, all with that same edgy smile.

"Jamie's got a place for us to clean up."

"Yeah. My place."

Shit. "I'll come back later with him, then."

Instead of saying goodbye and turning off at his driveway, Zak tagged along as she crossed the street toward the camp. "More fun if you come by yourself. Just you and me."

The more she rejected him, the more he enjoyed it, so she said nothing more, though she could have pointed out that they wouldn't be alone. That he had a family—something he'd apparently forgotten.

When Mae stopped to stretch at the fence outside the camping area, he imitated everything she did, claiming he didn't know how to stretch properly and was learning. It was like something kids did to drive each other crazy. *Mama, make him stop! He's mocking me!* She finished without giving in to the outburst of annoyance he seemed to crave, and started for the bubble-like little tent. Zak strolled beside her.

She said, "You need to head on home."

He walked an inch closer. "My offer still stands. Hot shower."

"Go take a cold one."

"No. Hot." He spoke with a rhythm as if rapping, though his meter was off. "Brown sugar, when you turn up the heat, makes the sweetest treat."

"Brown sugar? Pig's arse," Jamie appeared from around the side of his parents' tent, a muffin in one hand, a mug of coffee in the other. "*Chocolate* is a fucking aphrodisiac." He handed Mae the coffee, kissed her cheek, and then gave her the muffin. "Have a good run?"

Zak answered before Mae could. "We did. She's good company. I showed her the race route."

"Great. Glad you two are getting along." Jamie beamed. Mae wanted to correct him, but that would have to wait. She sipped the coffee. Jamie nodded toward the big tent. "Grab some tucker, mate? Not fancy, but it's good."

Zak declined, saying he needed to go home and clean up before the rodeo. Mae was relieved to see him go. She swallowed a bite of muffin. "Sugar, me and Zak are *not* getting along."

"But—" Jamie frowned, sounding bewildered. "He *likes* you."

"Well, I wish he didn't."

The baby seal look, hurt and disappointed.

Mae asked, "Did you go to a party with Zak last night?"

"Fuck, no. Helped Mel break it up. Did he make you think—? That bastard. Sorry. He's got a fucked-up sense of humor."

Jamie told the story of his nighttime disappearance, starting with Melody's distress over the six-pack and the sneaking-away visitor and ending with the party.

Mae had an image of the exotic East-West cowgirl slipping away from Hot Native Guy. "Did Zak explain who was there when Melody got home the first time?"

"Nah. He acted like—dunno—like it was a little shady. Dead set on Mel not knowing."

Mae's imagination changed the picture to Reno going out the back door. "Misty says Reno's being kind of secretive. Won't let her in his place anymore. Maybe it's just a coincidence, but do you think they could be into something illegal together?"

"Hard to imagine. Especially for Zak. He was always this perfect Boy Scout, y'know? Melody was the wild one. Drugs, drinking. He was always trying to stop her. Think it was the high point of his life when she finally quit for good."

Mae had married her alcoholic boyfriend when she was eighteen, thinking she could save him. It was odd to think that Zak was like her in some way. Someone who had that need to rescue people. It was hard to imagine him deserving credit for Melody's sobriety, though. He had probably nagged her about drinking the way he did about her weight.

Jamie continued, "And he's an EMT and a firefighter—which makes him a fucking *hero* around here. Can't see him breaking the law."

The only blemish on Zak's reputation was his less-than-honorable discharge from the Army. He might have made himself into a hero now to make up for it, in which case his behavior made even less sense that Reno's did. "Can you think of anything they'd be doing that wasn't wrong but still had to be secret?"

"Nah. Doesn't mean there isn't such a thing, though. Just that we can't figure it out. Party bothers me more than the secret, anyway. Zak likes to socialize, and they have parties without any grog, but he goes out if he's having a drink. Keeps it away from her." Jamie started to open the flap to his parents' tent and paused, frowning. "Fuck. It was like—like he was trying to drive her out of the house." He stared at Mae. "Like he wanted to *make* her go to her mum's."

"Misty, too?"

"Dunno. Maybe. Mel found the door locked."

"So—he was keeping relatives out while he had his secret visitor. And then he had the party to drive Melody away."

Jamie bit his lip. His left hand massaged his right, prodding an old injury. "I don't like this. Need to talk with him. Find out what he's up to."

"You already said he wouldn't tell you."

"Not yet. But I'll keep asking. I don't let my mates fuck up."

"Let me know if you find out. Misty wanted me to do some psychic work—"

"To find out what Reno's up to? Jeezus. That's a healthy fucking relationship. Hope you told her no."

"I said I'd think about it. Reno gave her a ring, and—"

"He did?" Jamie's face lit up. "That's wonderful. They're getting married."

"Sugar. It's not wonderful. What have we just been talking about? He's into something he won't tell her about. He won't even let her into his house anymore. This isn't normal."

"Yeah—but if he loves her enough to *marry* her, they can talk. They can work things out."

"I don't know. Reno doesn't talk much. What if she marries into some big dirty secret?"

"I'll get it out of Zak. Don't like you doing psychic stuff with people I know. Feels weird. You don't just find what you're looking for, y'know? You get *leaks.*"

Mae ducked Jamie's intense gaze. He was right. She did get more information that she sought sometimes. Her psychic vision was strong, but her aim could be imperfect. "I won't do it if there's any way around it."

"Thanks." Jamie took her hand and led her around his parents' tent to an open patch of grass separating it from the neighboring tent. "Come on. Say g'day to the oldies. And Lonnie. You met Lonnie, right?"

While his parents and Lonnie exchanged greetings with Mae, Jamie passed a plastic tub of muffins around, then refilled coffee mugs. The elderly man sat in a camp chair, while Stan Ellerbee, a tall, bearded white man with glasses and silver hair, and Addie, a compact black woman with thick hair going white at the temples, sat cross-legged on the grass. Jamie offered Mae the one unoccupied chair, but she shook her head and sat on the ground. In spite of his recent yoga studies, she doubted that sitting on the ground would be comfortable for his bad hip. Jamie gave her a little Japanese bow of thanks and took the chair.

Lonnie sipped his coffee and smiled at Mae, his eyes twinkling. "So ... how are you liking camping?"

Was there some special tease-you-to-death Apache sense of humor? He was putting her on the spot when he knew darned well she disliked camping. And today she had come to like it even less. There'd been a long line for the stinking green toilet cubicles in the morning. She'd run six miles and hadn't taken a shower yet and didn't know when she would get one—and when she did, it was going to be at Zak's house. What could she say that wasn't negative? Jamie had wanted to make it a nice experience. Mae smiled back at Lonnie. "It was real cozy in that little tent."

Jamie drew his chair close to her, leaned down, and kissed her head.

Lonnie chuckled. "You're a good sport, to sleep in that thing." He gave Mae a wink. "Jamie, we need to take a walk. I'd like to talk with you."

"Minute," Jamie mumbled through a mouthful of muffin. He took a slug of coffee to wash it down. "Need to brush my teeth."

Mae tried to convey a message to Lonnie with her facial expression: *Don't tell him I don't like camping.* He made the same face back at her, lips pressed in, eyes wide under furrowed brows. "Are you all right, young lady?"

She sighed. It was funny, but it wasn't.

When they'd gone, Mae asked for water. "Jamie meant well, but after a run, coffee doesn't cut it."

Addie filled a plastic cup with water and handed it to her. "He *always* means well. Think you'll last four nights?"

Mae blushed. "Y'all could tell?"

"The minute Lonnie asked, everyone but Jamie could tell."

Stan turned his mug in his hands, looking down into it. "You can't get into the habit of being afraid to upset Jamie. Sometimes you have to tell him things he doesn't want to hear."

"But the way he *looks* at me—it's so hard."

"You think we don't know?" Addie burst out laughing. "Imagine being his mum, having to send him to his room." She had features much like Jamie's and did a perfect imitation of one of his wounded looks. "Of course it's hard. His sister never did learn not to spoil him. But he'll be all right." Addie lifted her mug and took a drink. "It's not the little stuff that breaks him. He can handle this."

"Okay. I'll talk to him. If Lonnie isn't already doing it." Mae gulped the cup of water. "I'm dying for a shower. Do we all go to Zak and Melody's house?"

"No," Stan said. "We spread ourselves around. They're Jamie's best friends here, so he's got a standing invitation, and Orville Geronimo invites Addie and me. Well, he gives us a key. He's hardly home during the ceremonies. He and his boys run that booth all day and all night."

"What about his wife? He isn't married?"

"His second wife died two years ago—cancer. It's sad, Florencia dying the same way now."

"That's got to be tough for Reno. He was close to Florencia."

Addie raised her eyebrows. "Didn't realize you knew him."

"Not well. The only time he's really talked to me, it was because he was suspicious about me being psychic."

"Dunno why he would be. Lonnie's a seer."

"It wasn't like he didn't believe I had the ability. More like he was worried what I'd do with it. Like he had a secret he thought I'd dig up."

"Can't imagine that boy having much to hide. Let Orville down when he didn't go to college, but that's the biggest issue I can think of. Reno's not what you'd call a colorful character."

"Reckon not. My neighbors work with him and they never talk about him. No complaints, no gossip, nothing. But he seems kind of ... standoffish. His girlfriend's worried about him."

"That's just how he's made." Addie stretched her legs out and rolled her shoulders. "Doesn't talk. S'pose he got even more like that after his mum died, but he never was Mr. Sunshine. Serious little bloke, even when he was five and six years old."

"Misty's afraid he might be in trouble."

"Reno? He's too boring to get in trouble."

And according to Jamie, Zak was too *good*.

Mae ruminated over this paradox while Stan and Addie recalled stories about Reno's strange, unchildlike personality growing up. He'd stayed in his father's studio and drawn pictures while other boys were out playing. Once, Orville had given Reno a dollar to bribe him to stop and go outdoors. Reno had ignored him, instead trying to copy the eye and the pyramid from the dollar. When he did go outside, he would sit and watch ants or lizards for hours.

It was hard to picture virtuous but obnoxious Zak having much in common with silent, serious Reno. They probably didn't share some dark secret. They were around ten years apart in age, and they weren't exactly next-door neighbors. Though Truth or Consequences and Mescalero sat opposite each other at the narrowest point on a loop of roads, there was no direct route through the San Andres Mountains and the White Sands Missile Range. The trip took nearly three hours. Zak and Reno both had old cars. Neither was likely to be driving that far.

Unless Misty and Melody wanted to get together. Then Zak or Reno had a reason to travel and to see each other. They did have something in common after all. The Chino sisters.

Chapter Eight

Lonnie nodded in the general direction of his camper and remained silent for a few minutes as he and Jamie walked. The request for a private conversation was unusual and made Jamie uneasy, as if he might have done something wrong, though he couldn't imagine what.

Gazing straight ahead, Lonnie finally spoke. "Can an old man give a young man some advice?"

"Dunno." *Advice.* It was another word for nagging. What would the medicine man want to advise him about? *Fuck. Dad must have told him.* About the reemergence of Jamie's unwanted spiritual gifts. Seeing souls. Healing. "I'm not ready to deal with that yet."

Lonnie cocked his head. "You knew what I was going to talk about?"

"What else? Dad told you, right?"

"Ah. That. Yes, he did. This gift that keeps coming back."

"Whether I like it or not."

They reached Lonnie's camper and went inside. Lonnie filled the kettle, got a jar of freeze-dried coffee crystals from a cabinet, and turned on the gas stove. "You want more coffee?"

Jamie hated instant coffee almost as much as advice, but from an honored elder, he had to accept both. He sat at the tiny table, squeezing into the tight slot between it and the back of one of the short padded benches. "Yeah, thanks."

Lonnie tapped spoonfuls of the brown grit into mugs. "I heard you can help animals. Heal them."

"Once in a while."

"But that's all you do. Why don't you help *people?*"

"Too scared. Tried a couple of times. Makes me see too much. Pain, dark places ... People are complicated. Dunno if I'm ready."

"Why not?"

Jamie tipped the salt shaker back and forth. It had fingerprints, something like butter or bacon grease on it. He wiped it clean with a paper napkin and then caught himself. Lonnie might take the gesture as criticism of his housekeeping. Jamie wadded the napkin and pitched it into the trash. When he looked up at Lonnie again, he noticed fingerprints and smudges on the old man's glasses and wanted to clean those, too. Anxiety and distraction. Jamie knew what his mind was doing but it was hard to rein it in, and he had to look past Lonnie's head. "Had another bad spell this winter. Didn't end up in the hospital or anything, but ... it was bad. Still in pretty intensive therapy."

"Then you need to be careful. Being good with animals is a place to start. You might find animal spirit helpers. But someday, you're going to be ready to heal people. Who are your teachers?"

"No one, anymore. Took a workshop with an energy healer. Studied about six weeks with a shaman. But I wasn't planning on doing anything with it, y'know? Just trying to get a grip on the stuff that kept happening."

"If you have a healer's touch, you have to use it or it'll turn on you. If I tried to retire all the way, I'd get sick."

"I know. That's why I practice on my cat. Started volunteering to help cats at the shelter, too, get 'em sort of tuned up. Makes 'em easier to adopt. Might see if I can help at the parrot rescue place, too, when I get back from my tour."

"That's good, but it's not enough. Do you still do the healing music?"

"Volunteer in the hospital? Yeah." Jamie had been part of the Music in Medicine program at the UNM hospital in Albuquerque for several years.

"And the music you write? Are you recording healing music?"

"Nah. Been working on performance stuff lately. The healing albums were all studio work—got to have ten or twelve tracks of just me to get those effects. All the instruments, my voice ... What are you getting at?"

"I want to make sure that you don't waste what you've been given."

"Not wasting it. Just taking my time. I'll do another healing album eventually. Felt like writing love songs lately, though."

Lonnie smiled. The kettle whistled and he filled the mugs, delivered them to the table and sat opposite Jamie. "Mae has this gift, too. You're fortunate. It helps you understand each other and the things people ask of a healer. My first wife, she didn't understand. Why I was always on call, day and night. Why I had to go out on the mountain and think so much."

"Um ... We don't ..." Jamie felt the way he had when trying to defend his choice to stick to healing animals, but he had to be honest. "It's not like that for us. Don't have people asking for help much." Misty's request, which Mae had so far turned down, was hardly an inundation. "We know what it's like to have weird stuff happen, with spirits and all that, so we understand each other that way, but, y'know, dunno if we understand *it*. Don't really have the same gifts. Can't say either of us exactly goes out on a mountain and thinks about it, either."

Lonnie drummed his fingers on the table. "At least you're careful, maybe too careful, but that's better than not careful enough. Orville said his friend is a little confused by what Mae did for him."

Jamie took a tiny taste of the watery brew. Stale. He drank again to pretend he liked it. "He wasn't expecting it. She did it by accident."

"I'm not surprised." Lonnie stirred sugar into his coffee, tasted it, and added half a spoonful more. "Strange things can happen to people like you and Mae—gifted people without traditions. You're driving around the spirit world without a map."

"I've got maps."

"Yes, from every culture your father ever studied. But I don't think you follow any one of them, am I right?"

Jamie felt his shoulders wriggle in a right-left shrug. He juggled a few imaginary balls, watched them vanish into thin air, and looked at his empty hands. "Yeah. You're right. So what's your advice?"

"I don't teach people outside the tribe. This wasn't what I wanted to give you advice about."

Jamie jerked to attention as if someone had woken him up. "Jeezus. I thought ... Fuck. Sorry. Shoot me. I made that up, didn't I?"

"You did." Lonnie placed his hands flat on either side of his mug. "I wanted to talk to you about love."

Bloody hell. Since when was Lonnie an expert on *that*? His new wife wouldn't even come camping with him. "Don't think I need advice on that. Love is good."

"What do you think makes it good? How do you show her you love her?"

"Tell her. All the time. Call her a lot. Give her backrubs, sing to her, cook for her ... Loving her—fuck—it's one of the few things I'm good at. Really. I just love her all the time."

"So, you do things for her. Maybe ... surprise her?"

"Yeah." Jamie grinned. "Think I might get her a pet."

Lonnie looked startled. "Does she like animals?"

"Yeah. Mae even likes *bugs*. Tarantulas. Lizards."

"Don't get her any of those."

"Be scared to visit her if I did. I was thinking about a bird. They're sort of like lizards."

"A *bird*?"

"Yeah. Parrot. Teach it to talk like me so she won't miss me so much while I'm touring."

Lonnie burst out laughing. "Do you know what you're getting into? The worst pet I ever saw was that crazy parrot Orville and his first wife had. Great big hyacinth macaw."

"That kind is scary looking, but they're nice if you raise them right. I like parrots."

Lonnie's amusement subsided and he studied Jamie, no doubt taking in his parrot-print Aloha shirt. "So I see. And how do you know these parrots are nice?"

"Visit the parrot stores in Santa Fe a lot. The Exotic Aviary is near the place where I take yoga. Not as good as Feathered Friends, but it's all right. I hang out after yoga and talk with the birds. Pet 'em. I'm really good with 'em. The one I'm getting for Mae is really smart. Great personality. Says 'g'day' when he sees me."

Lonnie asked, "Are you sure you don't want this bird for yourself?"

"Can't. I travel a lot. But I made friends with the girl that works there and she lets me play with him."

Lonnie raised his eyebrows.

"What?" Jamie asked. "Is that fucked up?"

Lonnie bypassed Jamie's question—an answer of sorts—and drank his coffee.

"Shelli doesn't think I'm weird." Jamie slid his mug back and forth, fingered up the grains of spilled sugar that it ground across and brushed them off into a napkin. "You might have met her here—she and her husband are potters. They do a lot of selling at powwows and feasts."

Lonnie nodded. "They're the people who have the feather jewelry?"

"Yeah, that's them. Parrot feathers. He does the Acoma minia-tures, and she does the feather earrings and that gold-looking Po-joaque stuff."

"Micaceous pottery."

"Yeah, that."

"Did you tell Mae about the parrot?"

"Nah, like to surprise her. Getting her this nice little green Eclectus. Sweet bird. He likes to groom the other birds, preen their feathers for 'em."

Lonnie's prolonged silence reminded Jamie of his psychologist. Like Dr. Gorman's pauses, it was a silence that carried weight and purpose. Jamie felt pressured by it, obligated to produce an attempt at insight, but nothing came to him.

"This bird," Lonnie said finally, "is like you, isn't he? He does things for other birds. It's his nature. Maybe he's good at telling what they need. But then, maybe all parrots just want to have some-one preen their feathers. People, however—as you said earlier—are complicated. It's not as easy to do the right thing for them."

"What? You saying I shouldn't surprise her?"

"I thought Violet was annoying. She used to whistle the way Orville does while he's puttering around. What if this bird imitates Mae? Would she *like* this?"

"She likes me. And I'm annoying."

"This is my advice. Don't just guess what will make her happy. Ask."

"I do." *In bed*. Jamie asked a lot of questions there. He had less confidence in his skills as a lover than he did in his general loving-ness. Now Lonnie wanted him to be less confident in that area too. Jamie's soul felt small and ashy. He slugged down the rest of the disagreeable coffee, slid to the end of the bench, and stood. "I ask. And she's happy. She told me I make her happy."

"Did you like my coffee?"

Jamie realized it must have shown on his face, and he snort-laughed. "Nah. Like fucking ant piss."

Lonnie walked with Jamie to the door and clapped him on the back. "Yours is too strong. You and your mother, you make coffee that could turn me as black as you are. I like ant piss."

On his way back through the campground, Jamie pulled out his phone and looked at a picture he'd taken of Placido, the Eclectus. The bird would cost eighteen hundred dollars. Worth every penny, though. His breed lived to fifty or older, so Mae would have him for the rest of her life. Why wouldn't she like him? Mae loved strange animals. He'd seen her watch insects and reptiles as if they were the most wonderful things in the world. She'd probably think Placido's leathery gray feet were cute.

Lonnie didn't understand about surprises. Jamie knew Mae and how to make her light up. Or he thought he did. His confidence undermined by Lonnie's advice, he felt a need to reassure himself now.

He found his parents' tent empty and Mae inside his, putting on sunscreen. She'd changed her clothes and wore her visor hat with sunglasses propped up on it. Watching her hands rub the lotion onto her leg, he scooted over and ran a finger along her thigh. "Want me to do that for you?"

"You missed your chance, sugar. I'm done. You have a good talk with Lonnie?"

"Mm. Not really." Jamie rubbed a spot of excess sunscreen on her knee.

Mae waited, looking expectant.

"Talked a little about healing."

"Oh." A puzzled frown drew her eyebrows together. "Was that everything?"

"Mm. Yeah. Mostly." He didn't feel like sharing the rest. It would undermine him even more. "Wants me to do more healing music."

She looked relieved and then smiled. "You should. That was good advice. Ready to hit the rodeo?"

"*Rodeo?*" Jamie winced.

"What's wrong with that? I never saw one before. It sounds fun. And it starts at ten."

Jamie wound the end of her shoelace around his finger. There had to be an alternative to the bloody rodeo. "Where'd the oldies go?"

"To Orville's for a shower. Then your daddy's gonna see people for his research, and your mama's going shopping in Ruidoso."

"You didn't go to Zak and Mel's. Why not?"

"I'd feel weird going to their house to shower without you."

"They wouldn't mind."

"We can clean up together after we see some of the rodeo. I don't want to miss the beginning. Anything you need to do before we go?"

"Yeah. Tell you I hate fucking rodeos."

"You *hate* them?" She crawled past him to exit the tent, collecting her water bottle and her purse on her way. "I've been looking forward to it. Can't you just go with me for an hour or two?"

Jamie scrambled out after her. "You want me to watch people roping little calves by the legs and dragging 'em on the ground? And riding bulls? Jeezus. Saw that once and the bulls—they're so *angry*. They have to hate it. Zak and Mel took me my first year here—" He shuddered. "Never again."

Mae put her sunglasses on and started walking uphill toward the rodeo grounds. "I thought it sounded like fun. I like sports."

"That's not a sport. Sports are people throwing balls around."

"And you hate that, too." She sighed. "What would we do this morning instead? The powwow doesn't start 'til noon."

"Dunno. Not usually up this early." Between his sleeping difficulties and the nature of his work, Jamie normally got up between ten and noon. "Just be with you, I guess. Take a shower, get groceries, cook a nice lunch, the sort of thing Mel doesn't have time to make."

"They're at the rodeo, remember? Zak said that was where he was going. They won't be there for lunch. We're somewhere new and special to me. We should be together *doing* something."

Jamie took Mae's hand. He wished he could see her eyes. "You're getting grumpy, love. You pissed about me going with Mel last night?"

"No. That's not it. I'm ... I'm tired and ... I don't think I'm cut out for camping."

"But—you're a country girl. You *never camped*?"

"I didn't need to. I lived near woods and everything. I hunted and fished, but I didn't camp but once, and I didn't like it any better than you like rodeos. I need my own shower and a clean, decent bathroom."

"Bloody hell, you can shoot a deer or gut a fish and you're squeamish about using a porta potty?"

"Yes."

"But at least it's nice in the tent, isn't it?

"Not really. I know you tried to *make* it nice, but we're in that little bitty space and you're awful busy while you sleep. Like it's work or something."

"You don't like my *tent*?"

"I don't like sleeping in it. And don't give me that look."

"What *look*?"

She stopped walking and softly touched his cheek. "Please. What's so important about your tent?"

"Meant a lot to have you in it." Jamie took her hand and kissed it. "Slept in it when I used to go climbing and then, y'know—it's been with me through the big stuff. The hard times. It's part of me. Like it knows me. I mean, I know I sleep funny and I'll try to be quiet about it, but ... I like my tent. A lot."

Mae rubbed his back. "Thanks for explaining, sugar. Maybe I'll get the hang of camping. *Maybe*. Just don't surprise me again, okay?"

"*At all?*" She couldn't mean that. "What about presents? Or breakfast in bed?"

She kissed him. "I would love breakfast in bed. But you'd have to get up at sunrise."

"Nah. Easier to stay up 'til sunrise. Cook for you and then go to sleep."

They resumed walking hand in hand on the road to the rodeo. Jamie wasn't going in, but he wanted to go with her as far as the gate. She hadn't said surprise presents were okay. "You ever think about having a pet?"

"No. Why?"

"Dunno. Just ... you live alone, and I'll be on tour for three months. Thought you'd get lonely."

"I don't, though. I'm good alone. And anyway, I'll have my young'uns for most of August, and I've got Frank and Kenny next door, and Misty's nearby, and Niall and Daddy are just a few blocks away. I'll miss you, but I won't be lonely."

"Ever?" Jamie couldn't bear a night without a person or a cat, and he'd rather have both.

"Not really, no. When Hubert and I first separated I used to feel bad, but that was ..." She paused. "Not exactly loneliness. More like a hole in me where he oughtta be. You remember what I was like."

"Yeah. That was hard on you." She'd only been separated a few months when Jamie first met her. He slipped his arm around her waist. "But you'll never have to go through that again."

"I sure won't. Two divorces are enough."

He'd meant that she would marry him and it would last. Mae didn't seem to have heard that. She sounded confident and assertive, affirming that she'd seen the last of something disagreeable. Jamie felt a pinch of dread, a shadow squeezing him inside. "You ever think about ..." No, he couldn't ask her that. What if she said no?

"Think about what, sugar?"

He let go of her and yanked the top off a tall roadside weed in passing. It squeaked in his hands. Why had he done that? The plant might as well have said *ouch*. "Nothing. Just ..." He looked for a quick stopper to plug the gap in his broken sentence. "Thought you might like a pet."

They'd reached the top of the hill. Women in cowgirl outfits sat astride strong, gleaming horses milling about near the gate. Mae watched for a while, and then faced Jamie, her hands on his shoulders.

"Sugar, animals take time and money, and I'm in school. We've only been in this relationship since after exams. You don't know what my life is like during the school year. I'm in classes and labs and study groups, and I stay on campus to work in the fitness center. I couldn't have a pet. That poor thing is the one who'd get lonely, not me."

Jamie nodded, embarrassed and hurt by her rejection of his gift—when he hadn't even given it to her.

The announcer on the rodeo loudspeaker said, "Barrel racers, get ready."

Mae nodded toward the ticket booth. "You sure you don't want to come in? It's gonna be ladies riding horses, no animals getting hurt."

"Nah. Only event like that. Not worth the ticket."

Her eyes met his. "You didn't get me an animal, did you?"

"Nah. Thought about a parrot—" He cut himself off at her startled look. "No worries. It was just an idea."

Mae's face softened into a relieved smile.

The announcer called the name of the first woman to compete. Mae glanced toward the ring, and Jamie could feel her being pulled toward it. "Go on. Have fun." He kissed her. "Catcha."

"What will you do?"

"Take a nap. It's not noon. Shouldn't even be up yet."

Jamie returned to the campground. He needed music before he could nap. Something to put his heart back in place. To silence the voices that hammered his mind the way walking on pavement hammered his bad hip. *Stupid. Fuck-up.*

The day was growing hot, so he set a camp chair in the shady spot outside of his parents' tent and played his flutes, switching back and forth between the cedar flute and the shakuhachi. People paused in passing. Some stayed and listened for a while. An Apache man came over with a cedar flute and without talking sat in the grass and played a tune with Jamie, improvising around him. As they shared the moment, Jamie's anxiety softened.

"Thanks, mate."

The man nodded, tugged his Pirates ball cap lower over his eyes, and stood with a grunt, as if it were hard to rise, and said goodbye with his smile.

Alone, Jamie began exploring melodies that might work for a new healing music album. Lonnie's advice about giving Mae a parrot had been right. Maybe he was right about this, too. And about accepting the call to be a healer. Not that Jamie was ready. The music was enough, for now.

Chapter Nine

Mae took the first seat she found in the front row of the bleachers and tried to clear the Jamie-fog from her head. She hoped he was genuinely okay with her coming to the rodeo on her own. Part of her felt guilty for doing something he didn't want to do, even though they'd made it through the fight pretty well. The conversation about pets had thrown her off-balance. What had he been thinking? What would she have done if he'd surprised her with a *parrot*? She couldn't have accepted it, and yet she might have. Might have tried to be nice, the way she'd been about camping at first.

Jamie's passionate objections to rodeos echoed in her mind. He hadn't tried very hard to be nice about it. But then, he cared so deeply about animals. He'd been shocked that she'd hunted and fished. What would he think if she told him she still liked to fish? Couples didn't have to share *everything*, of course. If people were exactly alike and always together, they wouldn't find each other interesting, but she hoped he didn't think she was mean or heartless. Misguided surprises and all, she loved Jamie's kindness and generosity and didn't want to disappoint him. At the same time, she wanted to be herself. Catch fish. Watch sports. Including this rodeo.

In front of a backdrop of towering green mountains, the horse and rider raced against the clock, in and out through the row of barrels, finessing the turns with power and grace. The coordination between the woman and the animal was so precise they were like one being. Mae raised her phone to take a video. *Jamie would have liked this.*

Shadows passed behind her. Two pairs of blue-jeaned legs stepped over the bleacher. "All by yourself?" Zak teased as he sat beside Mae.

The East-West cowgirl who had been browsing at the pottery booth took a seat on Zak's other side. She wore a Western shirt with a bolo tie and a belt with a tarnished silver buckle, the same hat as the day before, and sunglasses. Mae put her phone down and said, "Jamie walked me up here, but he didn't care to come in."

Zak grinned. "Because he's too *sensitive*?"

"You make everything sound like a fault. He's kindhearted. There's nothing wrong with that."

"Just funning you. Lighten up. Get used to me."

I'd rather not. "Are you gonna introduce me to your friend?"

The woman leaned close to Zak and whispered, then took a camera from a shoulder bag, removed her sunglasses, and began taking pictures. Mae glanced up into the stands behind them, looking for Melody and the children. A few seats back, they sat with Bernadette, her brother, his wife and daughters, and her cousins Elaine and Pearl, all of whom could have seen what looked like an intimacy between Zak and the East-West cowgirl.

Zak said, "Letitia's a photographer." Letitia paused to acknowledge Mae with a brief little smile. Zak added, "And Mae is a psychic."

Letitia received this information with a polite nod—a lot less reaction than Mae was accustomed to getting—and returned her attention to the riders.

"Put this in the record books somewhere," she said. Her speech was musical, with an accent that sounded like she was from the West Indies. "I'm taking pictures of *women*." She bumped her knee against Zak's.

Zak and Letitia were making Mae too uncomfortable. She stood and climbed the bleachers to sit with Bernadette and her family. It felt rude to leave without a word, but Letitia didn't seem interested in company.

Melody commented on Jamie's absence, but didn't question it, saying she'd have been amazed if Mae could have dragged him to a rodeo. No further conversation followed. Melody stared at the floor.

Mae started to ask if any of them knew Letitia and then stopped. The awkward silence said all she needed to know. This should have been a family outing and Zak was hanging out with this stranger instead. Could he really be having a fling with her, though? Mack used to sneak when he cheated on Mae, not show off. But then, Zak was so inconsiderate he might not bother to hide.

Dean and Deanna ran past, jumping over the adults' feet with squeals of excitement. Melody sipped a soda and munched on curly fries, watching the children. "Don't go in front of people like that," she said, but they had already galloped into the next row of seats, barging past people again.

An amusing image came to Mae. "They should run down and see their daddy."

Melody shot her a look.

"I mean it. It'd do him good."

Melody ate another fry. "They'd mess up his game."

"I know. That'd do him good."

Was that a *smile* on Melody's face? Maybe. Almost. Mae felt as if she'd won something, though she didn't know what.

The barrel-racing winners were announced and prizes awarded. Calf roping followed. The family watched, but talked through it. Misty arrived, accompanied by a woman halfway between her age and Melody's, whom she introduced as her sister Montana. She was large-bosomed and slim-legged, built like neither the athletic Misty nor the obese Melody, and looked to be half-Indian, half-Anglo. Did the Chino sisters have three different fathers? *Their mama's been married more than I have.*

Misty squeezed between Bernadette and Mae. "So, did you decide?"

"I'm still thinking about it. But Jamie might be able to find out just by asking."

"You *told Jamie*?"

"I'm sorry. You know how it is, talking with your boyfriend. You share stuff."

Misty rolled her eyes. "In my dreams."

Mae stood and nodded toward the upper bleachers. Misty walked up the steps with her. Mae assured her, "Jamie's not gonna tell Reno. He's worried that Zak is into the same—whatever. He's gonna ask him."

"Zak and Reno." Misty stopped, hands on her hips, frowning. "*Zak* and *Reno*?"

Mae explained why she and Jamie had made the connection. Misty said, "That almost makes sense. But they don't really hang out together. When Zak and Mel come to T or C, Zak goes and does his thing, and Reno does his. Reno's usually either working or painting, and Zak goes off to the river or the lake. Runs. Fishes."

Zak does what I do. Mae pushed away the idea of having something in common with him yet again. "He comes all the way there and then doesn't spend any time with you?"

"Yeah. I think it's kind of a break for him. They leave the kids with his mom or Pearl and he gets some downtime."

As if he needed it. As far as Mae could tell, Zak was always on a break from his family. "I wonder if Reno really is painting, and if Zak really is doing what he says he does."

"I hadn't thought of that." Misty turned and looked down at her relatives. "Zak and Mel are coming to visit next weekend. Mom's band is playing at Art Hop. That's the only time we're all four together—for Art Hop. Zak says he has to see me fire dance in case he has to put my hair out. I guess he and Reno could be up to something the rest of the time."

They sat and watched the cowboys lasso calves. It looked like getting all four legs in the rope and pulling them together to make the little animal go down was the goal. Sometimes cowboys only caught one to three legs—and once in a while a calf got away completely. Mae imagined Jamie rooting for them as they ran free.

I sure do love him. The feeling swelled up suddenly, big and warm like the hug she would have given him had he been there. So what if he was supersensitive and hard to sleep with, or had funny ideas about how to make her happy? He cared enough to try. Cared about little calves in the rodeo, too, and even about assholes like Zak. Such a loving heart. She was a lucky woman.

Misty and Melody, meanwhile, were putting up with unavailable men who were lying to them. Why? Was it something that ran in the family? The question crossed Mae's mind as a joke, but then she wondered if the middle sister had a bad relationship, too. She asked, "Is Montana married?"

"No." Misty turned her diamond ring back and forth. "She's been engaged forever, but I don't know if he'll ever settle down. He's in town now for the rodeo and she's all excited, but he'll be on the road to the next one by Tuesday."

"So he's a professional," Mae didn't know quite what to call the occupation, "rodeo cowboy?"

"Yep. Always traveling. Wildman Will. Trouble times ten." Misty smiled as if she were talking about some character on a TV show whose wildness entertained her, not about her sister's fiancé. "You'll see him in the next event, the bull riding. It's amazing he looks as good as he does, the way he lives."

"You mean the rodeo life or bad habits?"

"Bad habits. Drinking, smoking. Will even dips *and* smokes."

Mack had somehow looked good in spite of all his bad habits. That was how the whole sad drama worked: Bad boys with good looks and charm, and the fools who tried to change them. "If he drinks a lot, Montana shouldn't marry him."

"I think it'd help him, actually. Like marrying Zak helped Mel."

"Did it? I mean, I'm sure he wanted her to get clean. I wanted my first husband to quit drinking. But you can't make anyone do that. They have to have some reason of their own why they quit."

"Oh, yeah. Kids. She wanted kids. And Zak wouldn't consider it unless she'd been sober a year. So she did it. She gained a ton of weight, but she straightened out. Tana *could* help Will, too, if he'd slow down and let her, but the way things are going I bet I'll be married before she is."

To a different kind of messed-up guy. "Have you and Reno set a date?"

"August. We haven't decided which day. We're just doing a civil service, nothing fancy, so we don't have to do a lot of planning."

"That's really soon." Too soon. The girl was clueless about healthy relationships. Mae was hardly an expert herself, with her history, but even she could see Misty's and Montana's mistakes. And try to prevent at least one of them. "Tell you what. I just decided. If Jamie doesn't get an answer from Zak this weekend, I promise I'll use the Sight for you."

When bull riding was announced as the next event, they rejoined the rest of the extended family. Zak was still up front with Letitia. Misty sat with Melody and Montana and the squirming twins, and Mae took her place beside Bernadette.

The whole group stopped talking as the first bull came flinging and kicking from the chute. The cowboy on its back grasped its huge body with his legs and held onto a rope that helped keep him in the saddle. His spine and his free arm whipping in balance with the bull's motion, he looked like he could be flung to the moon.

The announcer counted the seconds aloud. The rider lasted for eight, a buzzer sounded, and he sprang off, his white hat flying into the dirt a fraction of a second before he did. Over the tumultuous cheers, Bernadette explained, "Eight seconds is the goal. When you reach it, they score you on how well you rode. It's pretty hard to stay on that long. "

"No kidding," Mae said. "I'm amazed he stayed on at all."

A clown jumped from the fence, grabbed the hat, and ran in front of the bull, smacking his own bottom with the hat while the cowboy ran to safety. The clown popped back onto the fence, jammed the hat onto his head and grinned. As the next bull moved into the chute and a cowboy prepared to drop onto its back, the announcer boomed, "Coming up, from Mescalero, our own Will Baca! On Thunderstruck!"

Montana squealed and hugged Misty. Melody stood, shouting the cowboy's name. A cluster of people high in the stands began stomping their feet and whooping, and the crowd burst into applause. One person acted distressed, though, a heavyset boy of about twelve who scrambled frantically across several bleachers, rushing toward the front row. He shouted, "Zak—help—this is my dream!"

Before the boy reached him, Zak moved to the steps that led down into the ring and stopped there, poised like a wildcat ready to spring, as a thick-bodied, white-faced bull charged out with the local cowboy on his back. Thunderstruck didn't just buck, he swung his head and twisted as he kicked, tossing the rider sideways as well as up and down.

"Oh my god," Bernadette whispered. "I wonder what Ezra dreamed."

Baca slipped and righted himself by the rope. Melody hollered, "Hang on, Will!"

Thunderstruck dropped his head and swung his hindquarters high in a spin. Will slid to the side again, this time falling to be dragged under the bull's belly. When he lost his grip on the rope and landed, the bull pivoted and attacked. A collective shriek went up. Too stunned to make a sound, Mae felt a scream get stuck in her throat.

Clowns leaped to work, attempting to distract the bull, but Thunderstruck ignored them, butting and trampling his victim. Zak was already on his way around the perimeter of the arena as a crew of other EMTs rushed in. The crowd fell silent as if holding its breath. Finally one of the clowns straddled the fallen man, taking a grazing blow from one of Thunderstruck's horns, and drew the bull to chase him.

A rider on horseback herded Thunderstruck out. Will lay motionless. The emergency team surrounded him.

The announcer kept up a stream of reassurances until the paramedics had finished examining Will and carried him out on a stretcher. The cowboy lifted an arm for a brief wave, and the audience cheered. Though Mae was relieved that he'd survived, she couldn't bring herself to take part in the hurrah, not knowing how badly he was hurt or if he'd live much longer.

Montana was sobbing. Her sisters, each holding one of her arms, guided her out as if she were blind.

Ezra, the stout youth who'd run to Zak shouting about a dream, headed back up the steps, his eyes downcast. Bernadette rose and caught up with him, and they spoke briefly with a large woman and two equally large teenaged girls—probably his mother and sisters. The lights of the ambulance flashed as it started down the road outside the arena, sirens off.

With the boy trailing a few feet behind her, Bernadette sat beside Mae again. The boy remained standing, hands in the pockets of his long, baggy shorts, his chin tucked like a turtle going into its shell. Bernadette said, "Ezra is Bessie Yahnaki's grandson, and my godson." Mae had often heard Bernadette speak of this medicine woman as a teacher and friend. "It's a long way out to her place, and he's had a bad shock. I told him that you're a seer, too. I thought it might help him to talk with someone who understands. Would you take a walk with us?"

"Of course."

"You don't mind missing the rest of this? Ezra really needs to leave."

"I don't mind at all."

Mae followed Bernadette and Ezra out of the stands. Bull riding had no further appeal to her. The audience must have shared her feelings. Their reactions to the next rider were subdued. How could he dare come out? She understood the desire to win at a sport, and would push hard to do it, but not risk her life. The possibility that Will Baca could die shook her, and had to have shaken Ezra even more if he'd dreamed the accident in advance.

As they walked down the road toward the campground, the boy remained in his shy turtle posture. Mae couldn't see his face, only his brush-cut black hair, his round belly in an unflattering striped shirt, and his drooping shoulders. *He thinks he messed up.* Maybe he'd tried to prevent Will's accident and failed.

"Ezra?" He didn't look at Mae, but she sensed a shift in his attention. "Did you tell Zak your dream?"

The boy nodded. "At Boys and Girls Club a few days ago."

Bernadette said, "Zak volunteers a lot with the club."

Mae suppressed her astonishment and focused on Ezra. "Did he believe you saw what was coming?"

"He knows I can, but ..." Ezra paused as the sirens came on. The emergency vehicle was turning onto the access road at the foot of the hill. "I dreamed Will got struck by lightning. In his arm and his chest. I didn't know what it meant until I heard the bull's name."

"I've had some visions that I couldn't understand, too. And this one didn't give you much of a chance to figure it out."

Ezra sighed. "I should have found a way to get hold of Will myself. I don't know him to talk to, though, I just know who he is."

"But Zak knows him to tell him, right? You did what you could."

"But it didn't save him."

Something about Ezra reminded Mae of Jamie, though she couldn't say why, other than knowing Jamie had apparently been built like that when he was Ezra's age. Maybe it was the self-recrimination. Jamie was good at beating himself up over his mistakes. She said, "Even if you could have told Will yourself, that dream could have meant all sorts of things. And from what I've heard about Will, he might not be the kind of guy who'd listen to a warning."

"He could die."

"It's not your fault."

Ezra looked up at Mae. He had big round cheeks, a short nose, and bright dark eyes that seemed to see into her, old eyes in a baby face. He nodded and looked down at his feet again. "Sometimes I dream exactly what happens the next day, strange stuff like this big elk walking through Grandma's garden last year. I can't tell if those dreams are the future, or if they're just something weird like when I dream about going to school in my underwear. But when I have a big dream, I can tell. It's different. I'm not in it. I *know* it's going to happen. But it's like in a code or something. It seems like the scarier it is, the more it's in code. I wish I didn't even have these dreams. I hate it when I can't do anything about them."

What could Mae say to that? Ezra's foreknowledge was a big responsibility for a boy his age to handle, and she had no idea what she would have done had she been in his place. So far she hadn't been the least bit helpful and felt she was letting him down and disappointing Bernadette.

They walked in silence for a while. The boy was fast for his build, keeping up with the adults' longer legs, not as winded as Mae had expected him to be. There had been a boy clown in the ceremony who was his size and shape. That masked boy had danced for hours. Was it Ezra? She liked to think so, but the identities of the dancers struck her as sacred and private, not something she was supposed to know.

Still, the possibility that he was that clown, deeply engaged in his tribe's religion, gave her a sense of what he might need to hear. "I didn't want my gift at first, either. Especially when I was your age. But I bet Bernadette tells you what she told me when I finally got to thinking about using it—that it's your calling. You have to do it."

Bernadette rested her hand on his shoulder. The boy glanced up at her. "She does. And that I have to listen to my Grandma and the medicine men. But I still don't *like* it."

"You sound like my boyfriend. I made peace with my gift and use it, but he doesn't want much to do with his."

Ezra nodded, withdrawing again. Bernadette gave Mae a soft, discouraged look over his bowed head. Did that mean she had said the wrong thing? *I'm doing a sorry job of being the fellow seer who understands his problems.* Maybe she didn't understand twelve-year-old boys.

They reached the Y in the road where Jamie's new van sat in the grass island. Mae noticed a scratch and a shallow ding on the passenger door. She ran a finger over it. "Aw. That's too bad. Jamie was so worried someone would hit his new van and they did."

Ezra perked up. "Jamie. Jamie Ellerbee? Is he your boyfriend?"

"You know him?"

Bernadette said, "Bessie's involved in Stan's research here. Jamie's known Ezra since he was a baby."

"Jamie's my *mate*," Ezra declared. This was the first break in his gloom, and it was unexpectedly bright. "I had no idea he was a seer, too."

"Not the way you are," Mae said. "But he could be a strong healer. You want to see him? Talk with him?"

"Yes!" Ezra pumped his fists up and down in a kind of dance as if punching the sky.

Mae tried not to giggle. "We're camping here—"

The boy was already gone, tearing through the gap in the fence, making a beeline for the little dome tent.

Chapter Ten

Jamie had barely begun to relax into a nap when a voice intruded. "Ma-a-a-ate."

He had the dazed, half-awake thought that he'd taught the parrot Placido to say "mate" that way—the elongated version for special friends, as opposed to the clipped version for people you were pissed off at—and then opened his eyes to see Ezra Yahnaki peering through the flap. Jamie tried to talk, but in his drowsy state all he could manage was a mumble.

The boy's intruding moon-face creased with a frown. "You're sleeping with your toy?"

Jamie had cuddled up with the faded, balding, one-eared stuffed kangaroo that he'd owned since he was three. He set the roo aside, stretched, and sat up. "Yeah. I like him." Ezra continued staring at him. "What are you looking at?" *Stupid question.* The scars. Jamie had taken his shirt off. He reached for the discarded garment and began to cover up.

"You're getting fat again."

"Jeezus. Look who's talking. Go outside. Catcha in a minute."

Jamie finished buttoning his shirt, ran a brush through his hair and beard, and drank some water. He was glad to see Ezra, but the visit was odd. He usually ran into the kid at some big gathering. And Ezra loved the rodeo. Why wasn't he there? Jamie crawled out and caught up with the boy, who had begun to wander off toward the trees along the road.

"What's up, mate? Not watching the suffering of innocent animals?"

Instead of teasing back, Ezra began to cry.

"Jeezus." When other people wept, Jamie felt like crying with them. He managed to hold himself together as he wrapped his arms around Ezra, though the boy's feelings sank into him. This wasn't grief or ordinary sadness. It was something else. Something big. He held him until his tears stopped, mussed his hair and patted his back, and they walked side by side along the tree line.

Jamie said, "I've had days like that."

"Days when you *cry*?"

"Yeah. Hundreds of 'em. Usually for a reason. Not always. But usually."

Ezra ducked his head, watching his feet. "A bull tried to kill Will Baca. I dreamed it, but not in a way that could help him." He described his dream. "I told Zak, so he could tell him, but it didn't matter." He slowed down and looked up at Jamie. "Would it be bad if I quit?"

"Quit?" Ezra was apprenticing with one of the medicine men. He was young for it, but he'd shown signs of the calling all his life, and his family had high expectations for him. How could Jamie give an opinion on that? "Jeezus, like I know fucking anything."

"Your girlfriend said you're a seer, too. And that you don't like it."

So that was why Ezra had sought him out. Not because he was the fun bloke to hang out with, the adult who acted like a kid, but because Jamie would let him cry about the burden of his gift and perhaps reassure him it was okay to quit. But it wasn't.

"Yeah, that's half the story. I see ... like auras, I guess ... and sometimes spirits ...Weird crap. Don't like that at all. But I can do some healing, sort of. A little. That part's not so bad." *If I only heal animals.*

"Yeah? I think I felt that. When I was crying. You did something."

"I did?" That had been an accident. Maybe the healing energy still escaped when he didn't mean for it to. "Thought I'd learned to control it."

Ezra went quiet, shoe-gazing.

"Fuck. Sorry. Shoot me. Sounded like I didn't want to help you. I did. Just didn't know it would come out that way. I mean the help. Or the words. Let me try again. What I meant—I learned to control this stuff because I couldn't get rid of it. I tried, but it kept coming back. Like my hair."

Ezra snapped out of his slump and met Jamie's eyes. "Like *what*?"

"Y'know—like shaving my head. I hated my hair. But every time it grew back in it was still blond."

"Having dreams and visions isn't like having weird hair."

"Is to me." Jamie rocked Ezra's shoulders in a side-hug. "My whole head is strange."

"Stop making fun of me."

"Didn't mean to. I was making fun of myself. What I'm saying is ... I can't tell you to quit, y'know? You could stop your training, I guess, or put it off 'til you're older, but I don't think you get to decide about the dreams. They'll keep coming back."

"I hate having them, though." Ezra picked up a plastic bottle from the grass, tire-crushed litter blown in from the road. "I hate this, too. People trashing everything. Like, what do they think is sacred? The *earth* or the inside of their cars?"

Jamie steered their walk toward a trash can and began to notice all sorts of scraps at his feet. The corners torn off bags of snack food. Bottle caps. Touching litter bothered him, but now that Ezra had made him aware, he had to collect it all. The kid had made it a spiritual duty. Mae did it more like environmental housework. "My girlfriend picks up stuff like this, too. Like she's everybody's mum, cleaning up after 'em. But you said it like a spiritual teacher. That was good, mate. You made me think. Made me *see*. And you're just a kid."

They dropped their trash into the can. Ezra dusted his hands on his pants. Jamie wanted desperately to wash his. There was hand sanitizer in his tent. He aimed back in that direction.

"Sometimes I'd like to be *just a kid*," Ezra said.

Jamie started to reply with something reassuring, realized it was platitudinous crap, and stopped. Ezra didn't need *advice*. What he needed was a chance to lighten up and play, like he'd said—to be an ordinary kid. He'd probably gone to the rodeo for that. And his burden had followed him. Jamie had to think of something else fun to do. Something safe and relaxing. "You like to cook?"

"Yes." Ezra brightened. "I make really good mac and cheese. From scratch."

"Great. You can help me fix lunch at Zak and Melody's place. My recipes, though. No cheese. Teach ya something new."

They reached Jamie's tent. The flap was open and Mae was crouched inside, collecting bath gear into a small zippered bag. Jamie ducked in, located the bottle of hand sanitizer, squirted his hands, and gave her a kiss on the back of her neck. "Mind if Ezra comes to the house to cook with us?"

Mae rolled two sets of clean clothes, one for her and one for Jamie, into a tight bundle which she somehow crammed into the little bag, though the zipper didn't quite close. "Bernadette's getting her car. She's gonna take him to his granma's place."

"I'd rather come with you," Ezra said.

Mae gave Jamie a look, shaking her head. Did that mean she didn't want Ezra around? Jamie started to ask, but Mae nudged him and they crawled out of the tent. She said to Ezra, "We'd love to have you hang out with us, but Bernadette and your granma want some time with you."

"They'll want to talk about my dreams."

"Don't you think you need to?"

"I already did. With Jamie."

Adult pressure. Jamie felt it squeezing him and it wasn't even him that was being pressed. "Yeah. Man-to-man heart-to-heart. "

Bernadette's black Escort pulled up on the road near the campground. She waved to Ezra.

"I think you should go," Mae said. He didn't move. She added, "But it was good that you talked with Jamie first."

"Okay." With a heavy sigh, Ezra turned, shambling off to join Bernadette.

Jamie called after him. "Where're your manners, mate?"

The boy stopped and fidgeted, his chin tucked at an angle, as if undecided about raising his head enough to make eye contact. "'Bye."

"And?"

"It was nice to meet you, Mae."

"That's better. Hooroo, then. Catcha."

On the way to Zak and Melody's house, Jamie watched the little black car zip up the access road and turn onto 70. Maybe Mae had been right to make Ezra go, but the exchange had felt wrong to Jamie. As if she'd taken over for him. "That what it'll be like when we have kids?"

"Whoa, sugar. Can we back up a little?"

"Y'know, you being the one that knows best. Like, 'Your dad's nice but he's soft on you. Don't mind what he says.' "

Mae moved the bath bag to her other side and took hold of Jamie's hand. "Bernadette told me Ezra's training to be a medicine man. That's big. I'm not getting in the way of that. My granma died when I was ten, and she was a healer who could've taught me if she'd been around. I didn't meet Bernadette until I was twenty-six and she was the first person who ever respected my gift or tried to help me use it. That boy is *lucky*. He's already had more teaching than I have and he's only twelve—"

"*Only twelve.* Yeah. People need to give him a break."

"I bet you were taking voice lessons and flute lessons when you were his age. Didn't your folks have to push you to practice sometimes?"

"That was music, not seeing the fucking future."

"I'm talking about his family knowing what he needs. We're not making decisions like we're his mama and daddy. How did you jump to that *parents* thing?"

"You acted like a mum with all the answers. Made me see us with our kids, y'know? And you acting like that."

Mae changed her hand clasp, intertwining fingers. "I haven't got that far. Seeing us with kids."

"C'mon. You have to have thought about it."

"I really haven't. I'm still getting to know you. Getting to know how we work as a couple."

Jamie felt as if she'd stepped on him. He tried to talk himself out of it. Mae didn't mean to reject him, she just wasn't imaginative. No. She was, but she used her imagination for things like picturing how the inside of a knee joint worked. She didn't fantasize. Jamie had already ventured far into the future, but she was studying their relationship like love was science before she made plans.

"Does that mean ... you're not sure about me?"

She pulled him into a hug so suddenly the bath bag whacked him in the back. "Sugar, I am *sure* I love you." Her cheek pressed to his cheek. "And I know you love me. Let's not get ahead of ourselves on the rest, okay?"

Halfway reassured, Jamie kissed her, held her a while longer, and she broke the embrace to resume their progress toward the blue house.

When he opened the door, Jamie felt slightly sick. The living room was in even greater chaos than it had been the night before, strewn with toys, breakfast dishes, children's food-stained shirts and pants, tiny stray socks, magazines, Misty's motorcycle jacket and boots, and Zak's running shoes as well as crusted-over party dishes.

"Bloody hell. How can anyone live like this?"

"It's what happens when your young'uns start walking. You can't keep up with anything until they're old enough to help you. Especially if your husband doesn't help out. Mine did, and it was still like chasing my tail."

"Think that party had as much to do with it as the kids."

"I bet it did." Mae started gathering dishes from the coffee table. "Zak gave a party she didn't want and left it for her to clean up."

"You make him sound like a pig. He's not. I mean, he fucked up, but ..."

"But what? Am I wrong? Isn't that what he did?"

"Reckon. But he's my mate, y'know? I don't want you to hate him."

"I'll try not to. But it's kinda hard to like him."

Jamie's plans to cook a good meal for his friends faded. He couldn't picture them sitting down together to enjoy it. They probably weren't even speaking to each other. He helped Mae collect the dirty dishes and they carried them to the kitchen, where they cleared more glasses from the dining table, plastic tumblers with superhero pictures on the sides and stale traces of alcohol in the bottoms. A dinosaur sippy cup with juice in it sat in one of the chairs. Jamie put it in the fridge.

"Wonder if Will was off his face when Zak told him about Ezra's dream."

Mae filled the sink and began washing the dishes. "Would he get drunk before a rodeo?"

"He did. Saw him here last night."

"A professional athlete should know better than to compete when he's got a hangover. I'm sorry he got hurt and I hope he's okay, but if he drank a lot he was kinda asking for trouble." She scrubbed at a bowl with something stuck to it. "Misty says that's what he is. Trouble times ten."

"Yeah." Jamie explored drawers until he found a clean dish towel. "Surprised Zak even invited him."

"Really? I thought Will was a party guy."

"Yeah, but Zak doesn't like him. Can't say I blame him. Baca's a useless bastard. Think they're over their old high school drama, but they used to be the fucking Mescalero soap opera. Tana was the good kid nobody noticed, and Mel was the wild one all the blokes wanted. Will and Zak were both really into her, but Zak won. Tana was Will's rebound. She'd been hanging around waiting for him. Like someone was going to drop her a crumb."

"I swear, the Chino sisters have got the worst judgment about men. She's marrying Melody's reject?"

"Not all the sisters. Tana, yeah. Marrying Will. Jeezus. Zak hopes it never happens."

They washed and dried dishes without talking for a while, then Mae asked, "Do you think he even told Will about Ezra's dream?"

"Of course he did. Zak believes in that kind of thing."

"If he had, you'd think Will would have been more careful. Being struck by lightning is scary."

"Maybe not if you're Apache. Look at the Ga'an dancers, all the lightning imagery."

"What does it mean?"

"Dunno. Doesn't matter. Point is, Zak might not think 'struck by lightning' is bad news for Will. Could be some kind of blessing. Anyway, who in bloody hell would think it meant a bull named Thunderstruck?"

"Will. As soon as he knew which bull he was riding."

"Unless he got too drunk to remember."

"Or someone who doesn't want him for a brother-in-law didn't give him the word."

"Jeezus." Jamie stacked clean dry bowls with a clatter. "That's like saying Zak wished Will was dead."

"Sorry." Mae pulled the plug in the sink and the water began to gurgle. "But if he doesn't like him—"

"He wouldn't give him good news. But if he thought it was death, fuck, Zak's all about saving lives. I've heard him say he wishes Will was anywhere but in Mescalero or in Montana—" Jamie caught Mae's reluctant twist of a smile, like she didn't want Zak's joke to be funny when it was. "Yeah, he really said that. But he wouldn't want him dead."

"If you say so." Mae dried her hands. "Don't forget you're gonna ask Zak about the party and the secrets and everything. You've got a good opening with the fact that he invited Will."

"Jeezus." Jamie's nerves tightened. "You telling me what to say?"

"Sugar, I can hear you now. 'What in bloody hell got into you, mate? You never serve any fucking grog and then you had this bloke you don't like here drinking it.'"

Startled out of his annoyance, Jamie let out a loud snort-laugh and dropped back into a slightly sticky chair. "And you say you're still getting to know me."

*****

Instead of cooking, Mae suggested they finish cleaning up the mess. She could tell the process troubled Jamie. He grew more and more subdued, quiet except for a few unhappy observations. As they worked on the living room, he mumbled, "Jeezus. Whoever brought the kids back this morning must have thought Mel relapsed." And when they brought clothes and shoes to the bedroom, he stopped and stared at the bed. "Fuck. Looks like only one person slept in it."

Mae was affected, too, but in a different way. She didn't know Zak and Melody well enough to be as sensitive to problems in their marriage, but she worried how it was affecting the twins. Her step-daughters had noticed the tension between her and Hubert, no matter how hard they'd tried to hide it.

Bringing the children's toys to their room and collecting their clothes for the laundry filled her with unexpected longing for her girls. She didn't mention it to Jamie, though, afraid he would mis-understand.

When they'd finished and finally showered, he called Zak and left a message that he needed to talk with him. They dropped the bath bag at Jamie's tent and began walking uphill to the powwow.

Mae said, "I guess it's too soon to know anything about Will."

"Reckon. Hope he makes it. Not that I like him any better than Zak does, but still, y'know? Don't want him dead. And I'm worried for Mel and Montana. And Ezra. He'll be traumatized if Will dies."

Jamie was right. Ezra, with his stubborn guilt over failing to warn the cowboy, needed Will Baca to survive. Despite Jamie's con-fidence in Zak, Mae couldn't help suspecting he had been the one to fail Will, not Ezra.

Maybe, though he wouldn't admit it, Jamie was thinking the same thing. They passed the rest of the walk in what was for him an unusually long silence. Mae put her arm around him, and he recip-rocated, but remained under a mood cloud.

He finally brightened when they reached the vending area, steering Mae down a side aisle toward the pottery booth. "C'mon. Want you meet some friends from Santa Fe. Well, from Pojoaque and Acoma originally. Live in Santa Fe now. I think. Work there, anyway."

"They're your friends and you don't know where they live?"

"I see 'em at their day jobs. David's at Whole Foods and Shelli's at the Exotic Aviary. She would have sold me your bird. If, y'know ... if you'd wanted one."

"The lady with the parrot feather earrings?"

"Yeah. You talk to her already?"

"No. I just noticed the ones she was wearing yesterday. It was right after Orville had told me he and his first wife had a hyacinth macaw, and your friend had those long blue feathers on."

When Mae and Jamie reached the booth, the young woman with blue-streaked hair was crouched over a blanket on the ground behind the counter, cooing while she did something to a baby. The infant was hidden by her body except for two chubby brown feet kicking in the air. She dropped a diaper into a trash bag and resumed making mothering noises over the child.

An Apache woman on a shopping spree, plastic bags hanging off her arms, was talking with a short rotund young man with long, shining braids. He had deep-set eyes over a sharp nose that had a dent at the bridge as if someone had been making him from clay and pushed too hard, features that gave his face a serious look even when he smiled.

"You have more of those earrings you had yesterday?" the shopper asked.

He indicated a black velvet tray full of earrings made of tiny disks of pottery painted with delicate designs in black, white, and brown. Corn. Hummingbirds. Parrots. "This is what we have."

"No, I mean the feather ones."

His wife rose, holding a large baby in a pink dress. The child's hair stuck straight up, and she had her mother's thick furry black eyebrows in what was otherwise a baby version of her father's face. Mae found something charming about such a funny-looking infant and guessed that Jamie did, too. He was already making faces and chattering happy nonsense at the child.

"I'm sorry," the young woman said to the customer. "I don't have any left."

"You had plenty. You sold *all* of those? Those big ones were *thirty-five dollars*."

"They went fast." She offered the dissatisfied woman a discount on the pottery earrings, but the shopper left without buying. The blue-haired vendor shrugged and turned to Jamie. "Hi." She beamed at him. "You haven't met our baby. This is Star. Isn't she something? You want to hold her?"

Jamie took her, regarding her odd little face as if she were beautiful. For a moment he simply held her, then shifted her to one arm and slowly stroked her eyebrows with one gentle finger. She burst into a wild, juicy giggle. He looked at Mae, his eyes full of tenderness and awe, then fell back to absorption in the baby.

Look at him. He wants to be a daddy. Mae felt a pang of sadness for him. Didn't he realize how unready he was? His last major depressive episode was only four months ago, and his last debilitating panic attack far more recent. He still battled anxiety daily. Though he had all the love in the world to give, it might be years before he was stable enough for marriage and parenting.

"Is this your girlfriend?" the child's mother asked.

"Yeah. Sorry." Jamie looked up. "Shelli and David, this is the love of my life, Mae Martin."

Mae said, "Nice to meet you."

The Indian couple nodded, smiled, and scanned the passersby. Not interested in getting to know her? Desperate for customers? For people Jamie had made friends with while talking at their workplaces, they weren't as outgoing as Mae expected—towards her, anyway. Shelli had been delighted to see Jamie and show him her baby. He was babbling at Star again, oblivious to the lack of conversation.

Mae made an effort at small talk, saying to Shelli, "You had nice feather earrings on yesterday. I'm sorry I missed the ones that sold out. Do you get the feathers from the parrot store?"

Shelli paused before answering. "I used to collect the ones they shed. When I worked there."

"What?" Jamie looked stunned. "When'd you leave?"

Shelli and David exchanged glances. She said, "I got fired. A couple of weeks ago. Right after the last time you were in. I'm sorry."

"Why are *you* sorry? Whoever fired you should be sorry. How could they let you go? You were so good there."

"I lost a couple of birds." She straightened her golden pots into a neater row. "It was a freak accident. I had the back door open like we sometimes do when the weather's nice. You know how the shop's set up. The parrot room doesn't go directly to that door. And they stay in their room unless we bring them out. But they were out of their cages, the ones that wanted to be, and I had Placido riding around on my shoulder—I'm so sorry. Bouquet, the hyacinth, took off. I don't know what made her do that. When she went flapping through, I couldn't just grab her—that's a monster bird. And you know how Placido is, every bird's friend. He followed her. We keep the wing feathers trimmed a little so they can't get much height when they fly, so I should've be able to catch them, but when I got outside, they were gone. I don't know what happened. We put out lost and found ads and some good rewards—two hundred dollars for each bird. No one brought them back. The owner thinks I stole them when I closed up. He doesn't believe they flew away."

Neither did Mae. The story struck her as somehow implausible, though it had no apparent holes in it. Maybe that was the problem. It was too detailed, full of information Jamie didn't need, like the layout of the store. When Mack had lied to Mae about where he'd been and what he'd been doing, she could always tell because his stories were polished and rehearsed. Of course, Shelli might be telling the truth for the umpteenth time, making her sound over-prepared.

Did Jamie think she was lying? His expression was hard to read—frowning, mouth open as if stuck on words that couldn't come out.

"*Placido?*" he said finally. Wounded. Like the bird had betrayed him. "Jeezus. That's awful."

"I'm so sorry."

"It's all right. Not your fault." Jamie looked down and cuddled the baby. "You must miss the birds."

"I do," Shelli said. "You know how much I love parrots, and we never could afford one."

Couldn't afford one? A troubling thought hit Mae. She guessed that Placido had been intended for her. How expensive a pet had Jamie almost bought her? She tried to keep her tone casual. "You said the reward was two hundred dollars. What do the birds cost?"

"The medium-to-small ones are in the sixteen-to-eighteen hundred range."

Mae took a sharp in-breath. Her jaw dropped. Jamie wriggled his shoulders in a small version of his evasive right-left shrug and gave her a smile, that flash of brightness he put on when he wanted to be liked or forgiven. The smile's light didn't reach his eyes. What she saw there was sadness.

He loved that parrot. Mae didn't know how she could feel both sympathy and frustration, but she did. Jamie meant so well and yet he couldn't tell the difference between what would make him happy and what would make her happy, as if their needs and feelings were the same, and he'd been ready to spend close to two thousand dollars on that mistake.

Shelli came to his rescue. "It sounds like a lot, but they're hand reared from the day they hatch, and they live forever. It's not like a dog you'll only have eight or ten years. If Jamie gets you another parrot—and he still could, you know, the store has a couple of nice Amazons, they're about the same size, green, playful, good talkers—he's not really being extravagant. A parrot is a lifetime pet."

A lifetime pet. The deeper meaning of what Jamie had been doing with that gift swept over Mae. Without saying so or perhaps even understanding it himself, he'd been offering commitment.

Mae saw no reason to tell Shelli she didn't want any parrot at all, no matter how green, playful, or talkative, and she had a feeling Jamie would have struggled to select a replacement even if it had those qualities that had endeared Placido to him. This bird had been special to him, and he'd believed it would have been special to her. First, she'd turned it down, and now Placido's flight had distressed him. Mae almost wished she could give *him* the parrot. Or at least find out that Placido was okay.

Thinking, she turned one of David's miniature pots without lifting it off the table. Thin-walled and decorated with incredibly fine lines, it bore a woven pattern that created the illusion of texture on its smooth surface. It was beautiful, but with day jobs David and Shelli obviously didn't make a living from their art. Would Shelli have risked her parrot store job for four thousand dollars or less from selling two birds? It didn't make sense. Maybe she wasn't lying about their escape. Florencia's hyacinth was no longer around. Could that breed be prone to flying away? If Mae could get some feathers from the two lost birds, she could do a psychic search for them, and find out if Shelli's story was true as well as if Placido was safe.

David said, "That pattern is called 'weaving lightning.' It's a hard one. Makes my eyes cross. I could only work on it a couple of hours at a time."

Mae realized she must have looked like she was studying the pot. Being polite, she asked, "How many hours did it take?"

"About twenty."

She tipped it enough to read the price on the bottom next to David's signature and laid it down again a little too quickly. It was one hundred and seventy-five dollars. David gave the rejected pot a proprietary little adjustment, moving it to an invisible degree.

Embarrassed by her show of sticker shock, Mae picked up one of the smallest pots, a white cat figurine about an inch around, curled in sleep with its tail tucked, its back and forelegs painted with intricate black and white cross-hatching. It was only fifteen dollars. Then she noticed a whole cluster of the little cats, all the same shape but with different abstract patterns on their backs. They were probably made in a mold, the only hand work being the painting. She could afford one of these, and Jamie loved cats.

She could also use David's pottery to look for information about him and Shelli and the lost parrots, but parrot feathers would be better. She wanted to find the birds, not prove that Jamie's friends were thieves or liars. It would only upset him. Loyal as he was, he wouldn't even accept that Zak was an asshole.

Mae showed the figurine to Jamie. "You like this, sugar?"

He looked up from the baby. "You want it?"

"Not for me. I was gonna get it for you."

David reached for the little cat and cupped his hand around it, a soft hand with short, fat fingers that somehow did this delicate work. "I'll make one for you to give him. Paint something special on it for you. Like, if you met in a rainstorm, I could do the rain symbols. Or since he plays the flute it could be Kokopelli. You think about it."

The offer startled Mae. It was extra work, and probably no extra money. Did David think that much of Jamie—a guy who chatted with him while he was grocery shopping?

Jamie kissed Mae on the ear. "Tell him what to paint on it when I'm not listening. *Surprise* me."

How could she refuse? Mae asked David for a business card. He looked at Shelli. "Did you bring them?"

"I forgot. They must be in the van. But we have a web site now. MVP pueblo pots dot com."

"That's cute," Mae said. "Like, most valuable potters."

"We're far from that." David touched a large bowl that glowed with golden flecks. "This one is only five hundred." He winked at Mae. "Our prices are low. We're not famous yet."

She wondered what a high price for pueblo pottery would be, but didn't ask. "What's MVP stand for, then?"

"Our last names," Shelli said. "Mirabal and Viarral Pottery."

"Mirabal." Jamie glanced back and forth at the couple. "Which one is ...?"

He doesn't even know their last names.

David tapped his chest.

Jamie asked, "You related to the painter? Orville Geronimo's first wife?"

"You can say her name. We don't have that taboo."

"I know. But I do. Is she your relative?"

"Yes." David's face hardened, and his nails dug into the velvet of the display board. "My aunt."

Florencia didn't have contact with her family. How did he know she was dying? Jamie's wording could as easily have come from forgetting her first name as from avoiding it, so someone had told David about Florencia's illness. Maybe that wasn't such a coincidence. He was an artist, too, and the pueblos were small towns. It sort of fit that they'd be related, and Jamie couldn't be the first person to put Mirabal and Mirabal together.

Mae asked Shelli, "Any chance you have more of those feather earrings somewhere?" It was hard to believe she'd brought so few to a four-day event. "Some in your van, maybe? I could order them from your web site, but I'd rather get some now."

Shelli was slow to answer, watching as Star grabbed a fistful of Jamie's hair and pulled. While he tried to pry her fingers loose, her other hand seized his goatee. Shelli laughed and commented on her baby's strength, then said, "I still have some feathers. But I'll save them for David's corn dance regalia unless I can get more. If I volunteer at the parrot rescue place in Rio Rancho, maybe I'll do earrings again."

"Parrot rescue?" Mae helped Jamie free himself from the baby attack, tucking her fingers into Star's fists to give the child something new to grasp. "Like abandoned parrots?" The lost parrots—if they were really lost—could end up there.

"Sometimes people don't know how much attention parrots need, and they think it'll be like having a cat. But a parrot is like a little feathered person. They need you to talk with them and play with them or they get into trouble and act out, or they get neurotic. So people give them up. And sometimes owners die and then there's this poor bird no one wants."

"They must outlive their owners a lot." Mae sensed Jamie looking at her as she played a finger-tussle game with the baby. *Is he seeing me as wife-and-mama?* The idea made her uncomfortable. For years that had been the only role in which she saw herself—and now she didn't. She eased out of Star's grip. "Orville told me that hyacinth macaws can live to be over a hundred."

"They can," Shelli said. "But not always. Parrots can get sick if you give them the wrong food, or they can even get some respiratory stuff. So, once in a while you lose a bird young. And that's sad, because you might have had it for twenty years, and you'd be really attached. Most of them live to be old, though. If you got a young one now, an Amazon, or an Eclectus like Jamie picked out for you, the age match would be perfect. They make it to fifty or sixty so you could have him for the rest of your life."

"Thanks." *The rest of my life. With Jamie and a parrot.* "That's good to know."

Star began to fuss suddenly, waving her fists and kicking. When Jamie rocked her and made soothing sounds, she wailed and thrashed all the more. "What'd I do wrong?"

"Nothing." David reached for her. "Let me put her in the shade. I think she's hot."

Jamie surrendered the baby, passing her over David's delicate pots. She calmed quickly in her father's arms. Mae suspected Star had needed not only shade, but someone familiar. Jamie was new to her.

How well did he know these people he thought of as friends? David worked with food and Shelli with pets, two of Jamie's favorite subjects. They probably talked about these topics, or art and music. It was doubtful that he knew them well enough to know their ethics and values. The couple might be kind, good people—or they might not be.

*****

Jamie wanted to stay and talk with David and Shelli longer, but Mae struck him as eager to say goodbye and move on, though her only stated goal was to go to the Navajo taco booth for iced tea. After they placed their orders, she said, "Was that strange or what?"

He sat on the bench and slurped up half his tea while she was still tearing sugar packets into hers. "What? David being a Mirabal?"

"No—the parrots. Could they really have flown off like that?"

"Dunno." A group of children ran past. One was chasing the others with a can of foam string, spraying it on them and laughing. Mae sat close beside Jamie. He squeezed his paper cup. Tea crept up the straw and back down. Shelli couldn't have stolen the birds—she loved parrots, loved her job with them—but Placido's departure stunned him. And how could the hyacinth have gotten its four-foot wingspan out that narrow door? It was hard to picture, and yet it *had* to be what had happened.

Where could they have gone from the alley behind the shop? It was in a strip mall on San Mateo, with nothing behind it that he could remember but some dumpsters. The birds couldn't go far without their full flight feathers. He pictured Placido and the hyacinth getting run over by a garbage truck. How could Shelli not have caught them? And how could no one have noticed *parrots* on the loose in Santa Fe, blue and green against all that brown and adobe? It would be like Mae and Jamie disappearing in Mescalero.

He sighed. "Someone must have found them and kept them." A weight descended in Jamie's heart. He'd been fond of the bird. "Hope they know how to take care of parrots. Be awful if they just caged 'em, didn't let 'em out to play. Parrots need to have a life."

Mae rubbed his back. "I was leaning toward thinking she stole them, though unless she kept at least one of them, it wouldn't be worth losing her job—"

"Kept one and hid it while the police searched her place? Come on. You can't hide a parrot. They're loud."

"I thought of that, too—that she'd get caught. But there's something weird about the way she told that story. And she didn't call you when she lost Placido, even though she knew you wanted him."

"Could have felt bad. Didn't want to upset me. Thought they'd get him back. She wouldn't have stolen him, though."

Mae drank her tea in silence for a moment. "I was thinking that if I could get some of the earrings, if they were made with his feathers, I could find him. Like when you lost Gasser. It might be hard to tell exactly where he is, but I might get some idea."

Hope rose, then sank. "But she sold out."

"I don't think so. You heard the lady that wanted some. There were a lot, and some of them were kind of expensive. I bet there are more, and Shelli's saving them so she can sell 'em all for that price. It'd be a smart marketing thing. 'Oh look, I found some in the van after all. But they're all the thirty-five dollar ones.' "

"So she's a thief and a liar?"

"Sorry. I don't mean to insult your friends. But they're really more like just acquaintances."

Jamie frowned at her. He'd never thought of anyone he liked as an *acquaintance*. They were friends, even if he didn't know everything about them.

Mae said, "Anyway, if she doesn't have more earrings here, I can try to get some through her web site. Is Placido a different green than those Amazon parrots?"

"Yeah. Little..." How could he describe the bird's color and texture? "*Mossier*. The feathers on his body are like hair or fur. And he has these red and blue places under his wings, like you're supposed to see him from underneath when he's flying." This was somehow sad, given that he had flown low to whatever his fate was.

"So, if I see earrings that could be Placido's feathers, I'll buy them and look for him."

"Nah. *I'll* buy 'em." It was as close as he would get to buying her the actual parrot. "Or why not just tell Shelli what you're doing? Bet she'd give us feathers for that."

"Sometimes people don't like my being psychic—if they believe it. They think I'll find out something they want to hide."

"What? Like stealing parrots?"

"Maybe." She stood. "Come on. Let's go in and see the powwow."

Chapter Eleven

The emcee announced the Navajo Nation dancers. Mae let Jamie choose their seats, and he hurried her to the top bleacher. "Got to be up high for the eagle dance. The wings look best from here."

He was right. The view from above obscured the young dancers' human forms as the feathered sleeves of their dance regalia floated in birdlike motions. Jamie sat closer to Mae and put his arm around her. The eagle dancers hovered and crouched low to the ground, almost still, their wings softly pulsing. Mae pictured the lost parrots fluttering to the ground, their wings pulsing like the dancers' wings as they tried to lift off with their trimmed flight feathers. Could they really have gotten so far that Shelli didn't find them?

Niall had known Florencia's macaw. He could probably tell her if they were prone to escaping and how far they could go. Mae called him during a break between dances. She needed to check on how he was coping with the unexpected absence of his nicotine habit, anyway.

He answered the phone with a deep, hacking cough. Mae waited for it to stop. Jamie, sitting as close to her as a conjoined twin, gave her phone the sort of look he would give a bug. "Is that Niall? Sounds like he's turning wrong side out."

"I heard that," Niall said. "And I'm not surprised Jamie heard me. Been worse since I got *healed*."

Mae hadn't expected this. "I'm sorry you feel bad." She searched her memory for anything she knew about quitting smoking. "It could be normal, though. I'm trying to remember something from my health class. I think your cilia start waving again after you quit. They've been paralyzed. Now they're waking up."

"My *cilia*."

"Little hair cells in your bronchioles. They start sweeping stuff out."

"It hurts. They must still be half-paralyzed. I can't cough right."

What did that mean? Emphysema? "Have you been to your doctor?"

"Have I stood on my head? Done handsprings? No, I haven't been to a doctor. He wouldn't even be glad to see me anymore if he can't nag me about smoking."

Jamie began to rub Mae's thigh, watching her face. The gesture, though affectionate, was busy with anxiety. Mae rested her hand on his to make him hold still. "If the coughing doesn't clear up after a couple of weeks you should get a checkup. Actually, you should get one anyway."

"That's not why you called," Niall said. "To nag me to see a doctor. Your father does it enough. What did you call about?"

"Just checking on how you're feeling. Orville said you were still amazed. Is it bothering you, what I did?"

"It's frickin' weird. But it's not like I'm mad at you, if that's what you mean."

"There was another thing I wanted to ask, too. About your friend's hyacinth macaw. Do they fly off? Run away?"

"I have no idea. Violet had full flight but Florencia took her out on a harness."

"What happened to her, then?"

"She died," another prolonged coughing spell, "of some lung problem." Niall stopped, and Mae heard him spit. *Yuck.* He came back. "Sorry. Feel like I'm going to join her. Violet is buried at Florencia's house. I'll have to show you the memorial sometime."

"Like, a gravestone?"

Jamie interjected his amazement that such things as pet gravestones existed, followed by rumination on whether it was morbid or kind of nice. Mae turned her head, trying to focus on Niall.

"It's better than that," Niall said. "You'll have to see it. Reno did it for her. It's really something. You seen Reno? Did the Rabbit make it?"

"Yeah. He's here."

"Florencia's going downhill fast. I don't think she's got much longer. She says she does, but ... well, that's her. You might let him know. In case—I don't know—they can make things up."

"Does she want to see him?"

"*Daow.* He's on the shit list, along with her family. She won't say why. Says she doesn't want to waste her last breaths talking about him." Niall coughed. "But you might let him know she's about done. Hospice is for when you've got three months or less but I'd be surprised if she lasts three weeks."

Mae wasn't sure she could share this news with Reno. He seemed to be avoiding her. Maybe she could tell Misty or Orville.

Niall said that her father wanted to talk to her, and Marty took over the call.

"Hey, baby girl. How's camping?" She heard him speak aside to Niall, something about starting up the grill outside. A door closed.

"It's ... not my favorite thing I've ever done."

Jamie pulled his straw fedora over his eyes and slouched in a melodramatic caricature of humiliation. It was funny, but Mae was starting to feel like she was on an old-fashioned party line with a third person on the phone.

"Huh," Marty said. "I thought you liked it. Guess I misremembered."

"No. I never told you. I didn't want to hurt your feelings.

A long pause. "We still had a good time, didn't we? Just you and your daddy, fishing, hiking?"

"Of course we did. I loved all of it except that we stayed in that tent."

"Wish I'd known. I would've told Jamie. Listen—I sent Niall off because I need to tell you something, so you won't be too disappointed when you get back. I think he's started smoking again."

"He talks like he's quit."

"I know, but when we had one of those little power outages like we get, we were out of matches, and he went out to his car and came back with a lighter."

"He could've had that left over. It doesn't mean he keeps cigarettes in his car."

"I don't know. He's started building you a deck and I went over to see how it's going and there was a butt in the dirt."

"Building me a deck? Are you serious?"

"He says he's gonna put in sliding glass doors, too, so you can go from the living room out to the hot spring. But it's another way to be outside and smoke, too."

"Daddy, trash blows over the fence all the time. Every time there's a storm, I find some weird thing back there. Just ask him if he's smoking again. That butt could've come from the street."

Jamie mouthed the words *a butt from the street* and lifted his buttocks off the bleacher just enough to dance in a squatting wiggle. Mae smacked his bottom lightly. He sat again and began to fidget with his fingers, brushing the surfaces of his nails across each other like some kind of rhythm instrument. "Niall's filling the hole where the smokes were."

Of course. She asked Marty, "Could you hear Jamie? I think he's right. Niall needs to fill the space. Like Frank and Kenny doing yoga." Her neighbors, recovering drug users, were devoted to yoga as part of their sobriety. "And it's like Niall to build something."

Jamie mumbled, "Mel needs a new thing. Instead of eating so much. Like building a deck. Can't see her doing yoga."

Marty said, "I hope you're right. Maybe I'm just having a hard time believing he changed that much."

Mae wound up the call, telling Marty to give Niall her thanks for the deck in progress. Jamie gave her a soft nudge. "You worry about me relapsing?"

Her thoughts spun and stalled before she could answer. The possibility was always in the back of her mind, but she didn't like to mention it. Now he'd had asked, and he deserved an honest answer. An answer that could hurt him if she didn't word it exactly right. "I think about it as something that could happen sometime, yeah. If you had too much stress too soon. Something you weren't ready for."

The voice on the loudspeaker announced the next dancers, a group from Zuni Pueblo, and several small, athletic men in white leather kilts jogged into the arena. They formed a line and began a vigorous, high-knee dance, shaking rattles and green branches in time to a drum.

Jamie watched them, his heels following the beat. "Got a stress plan for my tour. Therapy by Skype. And I'm taking some private yoga classes before I go. Gwen's designing a practice for me to do on my own. And I'll have Gasser." He caressed Mae's thigh. "We'll talk, too—Skype every day if we can. Won't be as good as touching you every day," he drew a heart on her leg, "but we'll see each other. You're part of my stress plan." A tender little smile. "So you'll know I'm doing all right."

This wasn't the stress she'd been thinking about, but it was easier to talk about than his premature urge for commitment, and what he'd said was reassuring. "That's great, sugar." She kissed him, and he slipped his arm around her shoulders. "I'm glad you've got a plan."

"Yeah. So I won't gain fifty pounds or have a nervous breakdown." He jostled her softly. "That's what you think, isn't it?"

"I didn't say that."

"You don't worry that you'll end up with a fat crazy man? That we'll turn out like Zak and Mel—fit married to fat?"

Mae sighed. "No, I ..." He wasn't going to like this answer any better than if she said yes. "Like I told you before, it's too soon to think about how we 'end up' and 'turn out.' Let's just see how we handle this long-distance thing during your tour. And the rest of the weekend camping. That's enough to deal with for now."

"Jeezus. Thought women always wanted to know where a relationship was going."

He'd only had one girlfriend before Mae, so the generalization struck her as something he couldn't know from experience. "Your buddies tell you that?"

"Nah. Read it in a book. Relationship book."

"You've been ... *studying*?"

"Come on, love. Can't you *tell*?" He tickled her, his long fingers dancing under her shirt. "I'm considerate. I fucking *communicate*. I share my bloody fucked-up neurotic *feelings*."

Mae grabbed his wrists to stop the tickling before she shrieked, something she didn't think the Zuni dancers would appreciate. "You know why I can't tell?"

He brought his forehead up against hers, bugged his eyes out at her, and spoke in a deep, solemn voice. "Because you're *not listening* to me?"

"No—because you're always that nice. Pass the book on to Zak. Or Reno. Someone who needs it."

"Right." Jamie drew a circle in the air around her nose, tapped the tip of it, and then kissed it. "I'm passing the book on to *you*."

After the powwow, looking for a place to sit at the feast, Mae approached Bernadette's family at a table in the arbor. Melody made more room by moving Dean onto Zak's lap and Deanna onto her own and then scooted sideways toward Zak. Deanna promptly crawled onto her father's leg to poke at her brother.

Mae thanked them and squeezed in. She hoped to see Zak act like a father, but he managed instead to act as if he didn't have squirming children sitting on him, reaching around them to eat while talking with Michael Pena.

"Where's Jamie?" Melody asked, then shook her head. "Never mind. I can guess. He's walking up and down all the serving tables asking who made their frybread without lard. Who made their beans without bacon."

"He is." Mae had been too hungry to endure the process with him. "I can't believe he gets answers. Do people even know who made what?"

Melody shrugged. Though still a trifle sulky, she was friendlier tonight, perhaps because she now saw Mae as Jamie's girlfriend. "It takes him forever. But he finds out. Acts like he wants recipes."

In the pause that followed, Mae felt she should ask about Will but wasn't sure how. No one at the table was acting serious or unhappy, but they weren't talking about him, either. Did that mean no one cared, or that he was unmentionable? Mae decided to keep the Apache name taboo just in case. "What happened with that cowboy that got hurt?"

Zak answered, "He's better off than you'd think from how that looked. Bull riders wear vests that protect their chests. But his arm got stomped to pieces. Multiple fractures."

"Did you go to the hospital with him?"

"No. He needed more work than the docs could do on him here. They took him to Las Cruces. I just helped get him ready for the ride and went back. Someone had to be on call for the rest of the rodeo."

"Misty went with Montana," Melody said, watching her children, "but I had to stay here for the kids. I may go see him later."

Dean turned abruptly to look at something and whipped a hunk of fry bread across his father's face. Zak recoiled and wiped the grease off with a napkin. "You? I don't think so."

"Oh? Why not?"

"You know damned well why not. Anyway, I need the car."

"For what?"

Zak unloaded the startled children onto the bench and walked around to the end of the table. He gazed down at Melody, tossing his car keys in his hand. "I don't have to tell you everything." Jamming the keys into his pocket, he stalked away.

"Where's Daddy going?" Deanna whined. "Is he mad at us?"

Mae wanted to run after him and tell him to come back and act civil to his family, but that might only make things worse.

"He's not going anywhere." Melody sprinkled salt on an ear of corn on the cob and took a bite. "Probably just driving around. And he's not mad at you. He just wants to have the car." The children squirmed their way over to her. She set her food down, wiped her hands on a napkin, and put her arm around the two of them together. Looking into their upturned faces, she smoothed each one's hair in turn. "Eat your supper and we'll go to the bouncy house."

Jumping in the inflatable play palace after eating struck Mae as a dubious plan, but she knew what it was like to try to distract children from their parents' fights.

The twins chanted, "Bouncy house!" several times and bumped elbows. They began to squeal and bounce on the bench while eating. Their voices were deafening, but Melody was obviously used to it. She wiped Deanna's arm, which had grazed through her entire plate while stealing something from Dean's, and spoke quietly to Mae, barely audible over her children.

"Will used to be my other boyfriend when me and Zak would break up. My spare tire."

The expression made Mae laugh. *Spare tire.* "So *that's* why Zak needs the car? To keep you from seeing Will?"

"Something like that. Pretty stupid when you think about it. It's not like I'm exactly tempting anymore. Will's ridden bulls that are smaller than me."

Another line that struck Mae as funny. She couldn't let herself laugh at this one, though she suspected Jamie would have snorted. He was visible several tables away, stopping to joke and chat with people, his voice carrying across the crowd.

Melody finally shushed her children and said to Mae, "You're lucky you have Jamie."

The second Chino sister to think so. "I am. I know."

"Did he ever tell you about when me and Zak first met him?"

"No."

"We were out bicycling and we were passing this little house and there was this *voice* coming from it. We'd never heard anything like it. And it was coming out of this pudgy, baby-faced kid with a shaved head, singing opera on the steps all by himself like he was on a stage. We just stopped and stared. I could tell he saw us. He kept putting on more of a show. When he finished that song, we applauded and he took a bow, and then he *invited us in for cookies.* Tea and cookies. Zak kept giving me these looks, like, *Do you believe this?* We went in and we could hear Jamie in the kitchen talking to his mother and sister, like he was trying to be quiet but he had no idea how. 'Mum, Haley—I've got *friends.*' Like he'd never had any before in his life."

"I hadn't." Startled by a loud slurp behind her back, Mae turned to see Jamie. With his silent steps, he had glided up unnoticed, carrying two plates in one hand and a steaming paper cup of coffee in the other. He took another slurp from the cup and put his dinner on the table. Each dish held a plate-sized piece of fry bread, one loaded with beans, lettuce, and tomatoes, the other covered with honey and cinnamon. "I was too fucking peculiar."

Melody reached up and tapped the brim of his hat. "You were wonderful. You were smart and funny, and you'd been all over the world, and you didn't drink or take drugs—Zak thought you were the greatest discovery he'd made in years."

She moved into the place Zak had vacated, and Jamie sat between her and Mae. He said, "And I wasn't competition. No worries if the girlfriend hangs out with an ugly bloke."

"You weren't ugly. Just funny looking."

"Same thing. Safe, y'know?"

"Maybe. But Zak's always looked up to you."

Jamie studied Melody for a while, then began rolling the fry bread with beans and veggies into a massive wrap. "Couldn't have. I was short back then."

He might joke his way out of being admirable, but Jamie did have traits Zak could look up to—his honesty, his generosity, and even his being *too fucking peculiar*. Jamie—neuroses, eccentricities, and all—was authentic, and Zak was always putting on an act. Jamie wasn't a threat to Zak's ego, either. Not another alpha male and not trying to be. Mae suddenly saw their friendship in a new light. It was starting to make sense, what they saw in each other.

Jamie finished constructing the wrap and took a huge bite, some of its contents dribbling into his beard, and talked through the mouthful. "Saw Zak on my way—he looked sour. What'd you two do to him?"

"Nothing," Melody grumbled. "He's just being an ass."

Mae took a spoonful of chicken-and-corn stew, resisting the urge to add a few more words about Zak.

"Right." Jamie drank coffee. "I'll catch him in a bit. Since I'm so bloody fucking brilliant at knocking sense into him." Another chomp on his dinner spilled juices into his beard.

"Saving some for later?" Melody asked. Jamie laughed through chewing, making more of a mess of his face, and Melody hooted. She covered her children's eyes. "Don't learn your table manners from this man."

Good advice. Jamie's manners were hopeless. Mae had once imagined that various improvements in his life would somehow lead to improved manners, but it hadn't worked out that way. He talked through his food yet again, asking how Will was doing.

Melody told him the good news, and Jamie said, "Someone should tell Ezra Yahnaki."

Bernadette, at the far end of the family group, thanked him for thinking of the boy and let him know that she'd already done it.

The general conversation in the Pena-Fatty-Tsilnothos clan finally came around to the accident and speculation on Will Baca's recovery, with people guessing how soon he could ride again. Mae got the impression that rodeo riders dealt with injuries as a way of life, like a lot of professional athletes, and Will's fans expected him back on the bulls.

Dean crawled onto Melody's lap and picked up a stray bean Jamie had dropped on the table. The little boy held it up and made a fart noise. If Mae had been the mother in charge, she would have swallowed her laughter and told him it wasn't polite to make those sounds at the dinner table, but Melody cracked up as loudly as Jamie did, jabbing him with her elbow. "Dean's right. You'd better open your tent flaps tonight. In fact, maybe you'd better sleep on our porch."

"Nah." Jamie scrubbed his beard clean with a napkin onto which he'd poured some of Mae's water and slugged down more coffee. "Porch might be occupied. Zak could be there if he doesn't straighten out. Need to go talk to him." He glanced at Mae. "Catcha behind the drums?"

"Even if it rains?" The sky had been clouding up rapidly during the feast.

"How long have you lived in New Mexico? Nothing stops for rain." Jamie rolled up the second piece of fry bread and leaned over for a kiss, dripping honey onto her shoulder. He licked it off and then danced away to the music that seemed to be playing in his head.

"He's a good guy." Melody helped Deanna cut up a chunk of potato the child had been attacking unsuccessfully with a plastic knife. Thunder rumbled, and the wind picked up, blowing a napkin onto the child's plate. Melody peeled it off and urged the children to finish up so they could go the bounce house before the storm. Without losing her train of thought, she resumed talking to Mae. "I'm glad you like him. Most women don't go for good guys."

Except for her first husband, Mae had chosen good guys. Some had still turned out to be the wrong guys, but she had no fantasies about bad boys being more fun. "I think they do. At least some women."

"Not in my family. Misty and Montana and me have three different fathers, and Mom didn't marry any of them. She said she knew better. Now Montana's hanging on for Will, I picked Zak—and Misty's got Reno."

"You don't approve of Reno?"

"I used to. When they were in high school. But he's throwing his life away and she's throwing hers after him."

Unless Melody knew Reno's secret, which was unlikely, Mae could only think of one thing that would amount to throwing his life away—the same mistake she'd made at Reno and Misty's age. "Jamie's mama mentioned something about Reno not going to college."

Melody nodded. "He didn't get into IAIA so now he won't go anywhere. Orville taught him an awful lot about painting, but still. He needs an education."

They had finished their meals, and Mae took the paper plates to the trash can while Melody situated her children in their twin stroller over their protests, telling them they would get to the bounce house faster if she pushed them. Jamie had said nothing stopped for rain, but Melody clearly didn't want her little ones out in a storm. As they headed toward the vending area, Mae asked, "Is IAIA an important college around here? I never heard of it."

"It's the Institute of American Indian Art in Santa Fe. Famous people studied there—like Orville's first wife. Orville went there, too. That's where they met. It's the best place for a Native artist, if you can get in. I think Reno's good, but they told him he wasn't original. Didn't have a vision or a voice. Something like that. So he decided to just be an artist all on his own, no further training, straight out of high school. Like, 'I'll show them.' How stupid is that? I mean, I know T or C is a good place for art and it's cheaper than Santa Fe, but he could have gone to a different school. They still could have taught him something. Misty was going to study to be a dentist. She got into NMSU *and* UNM. There are scholarships for Indian kids who want to go into health care. But she put it off to move to T or C so *he* could paint."

"That doesn't make sense. It's not like they were living together. She could have still gone to college and seen him on weekends. Me and Jamie are doing fine living in two different places. If Reno had been in school in Santa Fe and Misty had been in Albuquerque or Cruces, they'd have had to do the weekend thing anyway."

"I told her that. But she didn't want him to feel left behind."

"Like she didn't want to be more educated than he was?" No wonder Misty never talked about any future dreams. She'd dropped them. "That doesn't sound like a healthy relationship."

"I know." The wind blew Melody's hair into her face and she pushed it back. "But they've been dating since they were born, practically. Like me and Zak. And who has a healthy relationship, anyway? You know anyone?"

"My daddy and his partner do. Sort of." It was more like Marty being healthy *in* a relationship with Niall. "And I'm working on it with Jamie. He's even reading a book on how to do it."

Melody let out a whoop of amusement. "Good for Jamie. And good luck. There's this bumper sticker Orville has on his truck. 'A normal person is just someone you don't know real well.' I think a healthy relationship is just one you don't know real well, too."

The music blaring from the bounce house made it hard to talk, so while Melody watched Dean and Deanna jumping and hollering inside it, Mae went over to Orville Geronimo's booth next door. Niall had asked her to tell Reno about Florencia's rapid decline, and Lonnie and Orville had wanted to visit her. The two men were sitting in the folding chairs behind the counter, eating dinners someone must have brought them from the feast and conversing in Apache.

Somewhat uncomfortably, Mae shared the news. The men thanked her, spoke to each other in their language, and took a silent moment, eyes downcast. Mae felt for Orville. Somehow a former spouse was always part of you, even after you chose to go separate ways.

She noticed a little card that read "Sold" on one of the small handprint paintings. Happy to find something more cheerful to talk about, she congratulated him on the sale. He nodded, finished the bite he was chewing and said, "Yep. Just sold it an hour ago. Not a big sale, but it made that lady happy. She's an artist herself. Photographer. Has a little business in Santa Fe doing calendars. I enjoyed talking with her. She knows a lot about Indian art."

A photographer. Could it have been Letitia? Zak's urgent need for his car looked different now, if this woman was still around. "Did she look like the other kind of Indian?" Orville nodded, and Mae continued. "I met her with Zak Fatty. She was taking pictures at the rodeo today."

"She didn't take pictures of that accident, did she?"

"No, I don't think she did."

"Good. That was respectful. She struck me as a nice lady."

Nice? To men, maybe. "I was trying to figure out how she knew Zak."

Lonnie said something in Apache at which both men cackled. Orville put his plate down and rose to greet a customer. Mae moved to Lonnie's end of the booth. "What did y'all say? What's so funny about Zak knowing that lady?"

"I was being naughty. I didn't want you to hear an old man acting up. Her business is called Notable Men of New Mexico. I said she could be taking Zak's picture for one of her calendars." He paused, sipped coffee. "Of course, I said a little more than that."

Mae smiled, guessing at the rest of the joke and thinking of the way Zak kept posing when he sat, as if he were a model. Letitia's whispers and hints at the rodeo might have been about her wanting him on a calendar. The other possibilities weren't funny, though. "I got the feeling they were interested in each other."

Lonnie grew serious. "No. I know Zak. He talks to pretty ladies all the time. The way some people like to look at art, he looks at women. I'm sure he looks at you. But that's all he does. He talks, and he looks."

Zak had said, *I'm better than you think. Ask that old man you were talking to.* Mae wanted to trust Lonnie's judgment—and Jamie's—but they hadn't seen Zak walk out on his family just now, or the expression on Melody's face while Zak flirted with Letitia. True, he had good character of a sort, or at least he did good deeds, but that didn't erase his flaws. It just made them seem irrational. Like he should know better.

Mae imagined Jamie confronting him in his tactless but disarming way, demanding answers, telling Zak to be a better husband and father. In spite of Jamie's lack of experience in those roles, he would know what to say. Stan was his role model, and a good one. Mae had seen and heard nothing of Zak's father, and wondered if his mother, Elaine, was like Melody's mother, never married, or if Zak's father was dead, or absent though divorce. Jamie would know the story and understand, and get through to his friend.

Mae rejoined Melody. Rain had started, thunder was growing closer, and she was calling to the children to come out of the bounce house. By the time she brought them home, maybe there would be a little peace in her family.

Chapter Twelve

Jamie detoured to his tent to brush his teeth and to grab his copy of *Golden Love: How to Get to Your Fiftieth Anniversary*, thinking he could give it to Zak if talking didn't get through to him. But when he got to the blue house, Zak's car wasn't in the driveway. Jamie gave himself a mental smack for the detour. It had made him miss his chance.

The vendors along the roadside were packing up, as they had to when it got dark. The sun was low behind the clouds and the ceremonies would be starting any minute. It was strange that Zak had gone off somewhere. His traditions meant a lot to him.

Still annoyed with himself for his bad timing, Jamie crossed the yard, taking a short cut to the road to the ceremonial grounds. He was surprised and relieved to catch sight of Zak's car behind his house, pulled up to the toolshed. Zak was leaning into the back hatch of the station wagon, shifting something into place. The toolshed door hung ajar. He slammed his car shut, took his phone from his pocket, and made a call.

Glad he hadn't taken the book back to his tent, Jamie changed direction. Zak was talking on his phone while closing up the shed and didn't seem to notice him. A roll of thunder sounded and rain began to fall. When Jamie drew close enough to overhear, Zak was saying, "Which hotel? ... Okay. I'll be there."

"What are you taking to a hotel from your toolshed?"

Zak spun, shoving the phone into his pocket. "Are you some kind of stalker? What do you think you're doing?"

"Just walked to your house, mate. Wanted to talk to you."

"You sneaked up—"

"Didn't mean to. I walk quiet."

"How long were you watching me?"

"I wasn't fucking *watching* you. Jeezus. You got roos in your paddock?"

Usually an odd bit of Aussie slang would make Zak laugh, but this time it didn't. He put a combination lock on the door of the shed, double-checked it, and took his car keys out of his pocket. "I told you last night to mind your own business."

Jamie didn't remember hearing that. "Nah. You said you thought I'd tell Mel, if you let me in on what you were doing. I won't. But *you* should tell her."

Zak glared at Jamie. "What do you mean, you won't tell her? How much do you know?"

"Fuck—nothing."

"You were eavesdropping. Watching me."

"I wasn't. Jeezus. You're paranoid."

"Says the mental hospital graduate."

"Low blow, mate. What's got into you?"

Avoiding eye contact, Zak opened his car door. "I don't want you and Mae in my house. You can take your showers somewhere else."

"What the fuck? What did we do? We cleaned the place for you—we didn't crap in it."

"*You* cleaned it? You and Mae? I thought my mom— Shit."

Zak got in in his car, closed the door, and made a call. When Jamie crossed behind the car to come around to Zak's window to talk to him, his friend started the engine and shot into reverse. Startled, Jamie jumped out of the way.

"You stupid bastard, you almost hit me!"

Zak turned the car when he reached the pavement. Carefully, Jamie noticed. No squealing tires. Without a trace of the urgency or anger that had triggered his abrupt acceleration in his yard, Zak stopped to look for traffic and then headed toward Route 70, no doubt at exactly the posted speed.

Feeling deflated, Jamie made his way to the porch and sat on the glider. He dimly wondered if he could be struck by lightning on the metal seat, but all his energy had left him. His hip hurt, his insides knotted with a mix of emotions and indigestion, and he was so thirsty he could hardly swallow. *What did I do?*

He felt somehow ashamed that he was still holding the book and turned it over in his hands. The faces of the authors, a pair of octogenarian marriage and family therapists, smiled at him in black and white above the blurbs praising their genius. *Masters of the art, the science, the mystery, and the plain hard work of successful relationships.* Love took work. Jamie knew that. He'd failed once and didn't ever want to fail again. But this friendship had been natural and effortless. How had he just fucked it up?

Fifteen years of friendship. His first summer in America, in that rented house on the edge of the reservation, he'd been happier than he'd been in years. Zak and Melody had *liked* him. They didn't seem to understand how rare it had been for an odd kid like Jamie to be so accepted. Over time he'd realized his friends were struggling as much as he was. Melody, with her drug and alcohol problems. Zak, with the loss of his father, a trucker who'd died in a blazing wreck. The three of them had balanced each other, Zak and Melody making Jamie feel normal, Melody and Jamie making Zak lighten up, Zak and Jamie keeping Melody on a halfway sober track when she was with them, insisting there was fun to be had without being high.

Ever since that summer, Jamie had stayed in touch with his first close teenaged friends. Sometimes Stan had spent winter breaks on the rez for his research, sometimes half the summer, sometimes only a week before going to Australia for the long college break, but Jamie had gotten together with Zak and Melody at least once every year. He'd had them up to Santa Fe for a week while he'd lived with his former fiancée Lisa, and she hadn't liked them, especially when

Melody drank too much at dinner—but Jamie hadn't battled with his friends over that. He'd fought with Lisa.

The past summer, with his own emotional, spiritual, and financial crises, Jamie hadn't seen Zak and Melody. And they'd fallen into a hard place in their marriage. Jamie knew it wasn't his fault and yet he felt guilty. Zak didn't get close to many people, not even his family. Who could he turn to? He was too proud to tell anyone if he wasn't happy, or if he'd screwed up.

Lightning cracked close to the house. *Struck by lightning.* Had Zak failed to warn Will after all? If Zak could think Jamie was stalking and spying on him, he could think anything of Will. What if Zak was going off the deep end? What if he had some sort of delusional disorder, and he didn't really have anything to hide? He'd made that crack about Jamie's history of hospitalizations. Was he secretly afraid of it himself?

No. Zak was too functional. He was paranoid for a reason, a real secret. Something he was taking from his toolshed and bringing to a hotel. Jamie wanted to call him, ask him to come back and talk, but Zak was the one who had persuaded Jamie never to talk on his phone while driving. He wouldn't answer.

The ceremonies should have started by now, rain and all. Mae would be waiting. This was the experience they had come to share. Jamie told himself to go but he couldn't move. His stomach hurt, his eyes burned, and his legs felt like lead. Finally his thirst grew so strong he stood and out of habit opened the front door, seeking water. *Fuck. I'm not supposed to go in.* And Zak had trusted him not to. He hadn't locked up.

*****

Deanna lay in the dirt having a tantrum, minutes after vomiting on her shoes as soon as she exited the bounce house. In the pouring rain, people without umbrellas were ducking under vendors' awnings. Dean announced to the world that he had to pee. While Melody crouched over her squalling daughter, Mae offered to take Dean to the bathroom. A huge clap of thunder sounded, he jumped, and a stream ran down his leg.

Without looking up, Melody asked, "Can you put him in the stroller while I get her?" She bent closer to Deanna. "Come on sweetheart, you have to stop. I know you don't feel good. Mom will get you home and clean you up. You'll feel better."

Deanna howled and shook off her mother's touch. Mae placed Dean in the twin stroller. His small size for his age struck her as she fastened his seatbelt. Melody and Zak were both big-boned and a little taller than average. The children were more delicately made, like Bernadette and her brother. Or like one of their grandfathers, perhaps—Zak or Melody's absent fathers.

"I peed my pants," Dean confided.

"Looked like the thunder scared you."

He nodded, with an apprehensive glance at the sky.

Melody, lifting a still-fussing Deanna, froze with a cry of pain. "My back! Take her, quick, before I drop her."

Mae took the child and put her in the stroller. To Mae's surprise, Dean clasped his sister's hand like a solemn little gentleman, and Deanna turned her volume down to sniveling. Melody was curling into an odd sideways position, as if one side of her back was in a spasm. The children were too light to cause much strain—at least Mae thought so, but then she was used to lifting. "You have a bad back?"

"Yeah. Ever since I was pregnant. Carrying my gut around doesn't help, either."

It was probably true, but Mae didn't want to agree aloud. "Does it hurt to walk? You want me to bring my car up to the gate?"

"I'll make it. It's downhill all the way. You can roll me if you have to."

Melody's phone rang while they walked through the parking lot. The children cowered with every thunderclap and lightning bolt, and Mae tried to comfort them while their mother talked. When the Apache woman ended the call, she said, "Zak has lost his mind."

"What?"

"He told me not to let you and Jamie in the house. And to make sure you hadn't taken anything when you cleaned for us. Can you believe that?"

Mae had no idea how to react. Taken something? It was such an alien idea she couldn't even be insulted at first. "I reckon Jamie didn't have much luck talking sense into him."

"I don't know if he talked to him at all."

"Is Zak at the house?"

"No. He said he's on his way out of town. No explanation."

"Zak's a really bad liar, isn't he? He has no idea how to cover up. He just stonewalls."

Melody stopped to rub her back. "I never thought about that. You're right. He's a pain in the ass, but he doesn't normally lie to me." She dug her fist into her lumbar region and grunted. "There's so damned much fat I can't get at the muscle."

Mae let the observation fall untouched. It was another uncomfortable truth about what it was like to be Melody, obese and angry with herself for becoming that way. "Do you have any idea what Zak might be hiding from you? Any guesses?"

They resumed walking. "Probably that photographer lady."

"Jamie says Zak's just a flirt. So does Lonnie Bigmouth. They say Zak's all talk with women, no action. Has he ever actually cheated on you?"

"Not as far as I know. But look at me. If I were him, I would."

Did she think her size meant she *deserved* the way Zak treated her? "Sorry, but that is just *wrong*. That is *not* what you do if your partner isn't perfect."

"You wouldn't know."

"Yes, I would. It's love, not how you look, that makes people faithful."

"You don't get it. Your situation is nowhere near the same. Jamie's gained a little weight, but he still looks good. I look like a hippopotamus."

"I wasn't thinking about me and Jamie."

Mae had been in rock-solid good shape and Mack had cheated on her. A good body didn't guarantee anything. Melody might not understand, though. In the family pictures that covered one wall of her kitchen, she had been a beauty—her body robust and curvy and her face arresting, with large, slightly almond-shaped eyes, high cheekbones, and a huge smile. She'd been the girl with so much power she'd had two young men who wanted her, and confidence that she could keep them both. That confidence must have been based on her appearance, not her self-worth. She seemed to have little sense of that.

Melody asked, "So what were you thinking about?"

Mae hesitated before answering. Her first marriage wasn't a story she liked to tell. "Being married to a cheater."

"What? A guy would be crazy to cheat on you."

Mae was about to thank her for the compliment when Melody clapped a hand over Mae's biceps muscle and squeezed. "Look at you. You could beat the shit out of him."

Somehow, the joke was better than any praise. In the drenching rain with two soiled, storm-scared children and Melody wincing with every other step, they'd crossed the line from being Jamie's girlfriend and Jamie's friend to being friends with each other.

When they reached the house, Jamie was slouched on the glider, a book lying unopened in his lap. Mae could feel the misery coming off him, an unmistakable signal like the smell of rain. *He talked to Zak. And he thinks he blew it.*

She asked him to help her carry the stroller up the steps, explaining that Melody had hurt her back. Jamie did as she asked, and she unbuckled the children. The rain hadn't washed them much under the stroller's canopy, and between Deanna's upchucking and Dean's accident, they smelled like kids who needed a bath. She asked Melody, "You want me to help you put 'em in the tub?"

Before his friend could answer, Jamie said, "We're not supposed to go in. Zak thinks—dunno what he thinks. But ..." He sighed and dropped onto the glider again. "He said to stay out."

"And that's just plain stupid," Melody said. "I could call someone in the family to come down from the ceremonies to help me, but you're right here. And Mae is good with kids." She opened the door and told the children to go in and get ready for their baths. "As long as I'm here, you're invited in."

Jamie thumbed the book, rubbed his hands over his face, and then dropped them with a mumbled "*Fuck.*"

Mae kissed him on the cheek, getting little response, and followed Melody inside. She wanted to talk with him, find out just how badly his talk with Zak had gone, but she would have to leave him to his mood for now. There was a lot of bending over involved in child care, and Melody was in no shape to do it.

After Dean and Deanna were bathed, Mae watched Melody sit on the twin beds, kiss each child and pull the sheets up around their chins, and remembered tucking her stepdaughters in. On those rare evenings during their marriage that Hubert hadn't been there to kiss his daughters goodnight—when he was sick, or staying late at his parents' farm—the girls had missed their daddy and Mae had given them an extra kiss and said it was from him. Melody and her twins acted like they were accustomed to doing without Zak. Maybe he was away a lot on wildfires, but even so, they should have noticed his absence since he was home today. They didn't ask for him, though, and she didn't mention him.

Mae helped her up from the second little bed, and Melody crossed the hall to the bathroom. "Okay, you're going to hate this—but I can't bend over to clean the tub, and those kids were dirty. Sorry. But I can't get in it until—"

"You don't have to apologize." Mae opened the cabinet under the sink and got out cleanser and a sponge. "I'm used to cleaning up after kids. I married my second husband when his young'uns were less than a year old."

"*Second* husband?"

Mae scrubbed. Somehow it was easier to say this without looking at Melody. "Yeah. First one was a drinker as well as a cheater. I left him."

"And then you were this next guy's second wife?"

"I know it sounds like a lot of marrying, but his situation was different. He knew his first marriage wasn't gonna last—he just got Edie to marry him so he could have custody, 'cause she didn't want the babies and he did. She was gonna have an abortion until he made that deal."

"Wow. You *do* choose good guys." Melody sat on the toilet lid. "What happened to that marriage?"

Mae rinsed the tub, shoving the suds and dirt toward the drain. The loss of Hubert hit her unexpectedly, a deep sadness that lingered in the dark of her where she never looked. She didn't feel that way about Mack, but Hubert had left something behind. A slender root of their marriage still drew some of her heart's blood. "We just grew apart. Didn't see eye to eye. Argued." She stood. "Mostly about living in that dead-end little town. He loves it and I didn't. I never fit in to start with, and then this gossiping old man started a rumor that I was a witch. My husband's family didn't believe it, but they didn't like it. So me and Hubert fought about my being psychic, too."

"Why, if he didn't believe that rumor?" Melody began putting her hair up in a twist, using hairpins from a basket on a small table near the tub. The little stand had a drawer in it and a low shelf below that, where a scale sat. She asked, "Did you read his mind or something?"

"No. I don't do that. I try to only use the Sight to help people, but it still bothered him. Like, if I hold someone's things that they handled a lot, I can see their past, or see where they are right now."

"Wouldn't you pick up other people, too? Like, if I do the laundry, and I gave you Zak's shirt to use, would you get stuff about him or me?"

"Both of you, probably. Sometimes I can aim really well and only get what I'm looking for, but not always."

"So it would work better if you used his shaving stuff. No one else touches that."

"You're not seriously asking me to do this, are you?"

"I might be, if he doesn't get home soon. You could find out where the hell he is tonight."

Melody took off her earrings and put them near the basket of hairpins. Mae hadn't noticed them earlier, hidden by Melody's hair. They were made from red feathers beaded at the top with tiny white rosettes. Wrong color parrot. But maybe she'd bought more than one pair.

Mae asked, "Did you get those earrings from a pueblo lady with blue hair?"

"Yeah. Misty got some for all of us." Melody began to unbutton her shirt. "You mind helping me in and out of the tub? I guess if you work in a health club you see ladies in the locker room a lot, but I'm not a pretty sight."

"Of course I won't mind. I hope you don't mind having me help." Mae closed the tub drain, squirted some bubble bath in, and turned on the water. "Did she have any green earrings?"

"I think so. Misty and Tana got some with yellow feathers."

"When did you get them? Early this afternoon, the woman that makes them said she'd sold out."

"I don't see how. We got these late last night right before she closed up. She had them in the back of the booth, off the counter, but there were a lot left. Are you sure she said she sold out?"

"Absolutely."

"I wonder if she's saving them for Indians or something. Didn't want you to have any."

"No, she told an Apache lady that there were none left, too."

Melody grimaced as she struggled out of her jeans. She stood in her bra and panties, watching the tub fill, and then poked the scale with her toes and put her hands under her belly. "Shit. I'm bigger than when I was carrying twins. I could be having triplets and not even know it. Get the scale down. I want to know what I weigh."

"You sure?"

"Yeah. We keep it there so the kids won't jump on it, and I stopped taking it down when it got too hard to bend over. Not because of my back—because of my *fat*. I need to know how bad it is."

Mae put the scale at Melody's feet. Unable to see past her belly, she foot-felt her way onto the scale. The dial spun.

"What does it say?"

A lot. "Two eighty-eight."

"Phew. I was afraid I weighed three hundred." Melody stepped off. When she finished undressing, Mae helped her into the tub. Melody moaned as she lay down but then smiled. "That feels good. So how much do you weigh?"

"One-sixty, I think." Mae kicked her shoes off and weighed herself. She'd lost a couple of pounds. Triathlon training. She would have to eat better to keep her strength up. "Close enough."

"I used to be that size. Not skinny, just in really good shape. I played basketball, rode horses with Will ... Can you believe that? I'd break a horse's back now." Melody turned off the faucet as the bubbles reached the rim of the tub. "Ask Jamie. I was pretty. I wasn't quite as fit as you because I drank too much, but I didn't look bad."

"I saw your picture. You were more than pretty. You looked great." Mae began putting her shoes back on. An impulse bubbled to the surface of her mind, one she didn't quite understand, but it felt right, although it was awkward after Zak's tactless comment the day before. She kept her eyes on her shoelaces. "I was thinking ... If you'd be interested ... I'd like to get some practice working with overweight clients. I'm still pretty new as a personal trainer, and I need to learn to do different kinds of programs. Could I practice on you? For free?" She finished tying the second shoe and dared a glance at Melody. "I know we live a few hours apart, but when you come to visit Misty..."

Melody closed her eyes. "I'll think about it."

"Thanks. Let me know what you decide." Something moved Mae to add, "I have a hot spring."

"I'll think about *that* for sure." Melody squirmed as if trying to stretch her back muscles, making a pained face. "Could you get me an ibuprofen?"

Mae opened the medicine cabinet and found herself looking at Zak's razor, shaving cream, and aftershave. His things she could use to find out his secret. A scatter of thoughts that had been nagging her snapped into place like puzzle pieces.

"When Bernadette told y'all I was psychic, how much did she say about it? Did she describe how I work?"

"No. She said you were really gifted, though, and that if you'd been Apache, you'd have been a medicine woman like Bessie Yah-naki."

"Wow. That's quite a compliment." Mae brought a pill and a cup of water to Melody. "It wouldn't make anyone think I can do exactly what I can do, though. Someone else must have told Zak. That would explain why he thinks I might have taken something of his. It's why he doesn't want me in the house."

Melody swallowed the pill. "They must have just told him. He was fine with you earlier. You think Jamie mentioned it?"

"I don't think so, but I can ask him. You mind if I go out and talk with him?"

"Tell him to come in."

"I don't think he wants to."

"Because Zak told him not to." Melody sighed. "Give me my phone before you go. It's in my back pocket."

Mae found it and gave it to her. "You calling Zak?"

"What's the point? No, I just need something to do. Check Facebook. Watch videos. So I don't fall asleep in the tub."

Mae sat close by Jamie on the glider. He was staring at a page in his book. It was full of underlining and notes. She doubted he could read it well in the weak illumination from the streetlight and the windows, but then, he seemed to have studied it thoroughly. His dedication to being a good partner touched her. She slipped her arm around him and leaned her head against his.

"I love you."

Jamie closed the book and rested his hand on her thigh. "Love ya, too."

"You seem kinda sad."

"Dunno what I did to make Zak not trust me."

"It's me, sugar. Not you. He must think I'm gonna use the Sight on him. Did you mention how I work as a psychic—needing to use people's stuff?"

Jamie fingered the sides of her kneecap and probed her patellar tendon. "Nah. Just fucked up, y'know? Made him think I was nosy. I wasn't." Jamie related what Zak had been doing and saying, and the spiral of misunderstanding that had followed. "Wasn't like a normal fight. Something wrong with it."

Mae knew what he meant about his normal fights. Jamie got into fusses and spats with everyone he was close to, especially his mother, and no one took those arguments seriously. He and Zak had taken this one very seriously, though Jamie had only been acting like Jamie—walking up without a sound, butting in on a phone conversation—and Zak had to be used to this. It was what he'd been doing when Jamie arrived that was the problem. "Sugar, I don't think any of this is your fault. You caught Zak at something, part of this business that he's hiding."

"I know. That's what I was trying to get him to talk about."

"But what if Reno told him what I can do? Reno acted worried when he found out. He might have passed it on to Zak, like—'Don't let her get hold of your things'—and Zak blew it off. Until he put two and two together and thought we'd taken something, or that we would."

"Bloody hell. He's got to be into something bad to even think about that." Jamie paced across the porch and drummed his knuckles on the railing. Rain blew in on him, moistening his shirt. "Can't believe it. *Zak.* Stuck-up bastard won't even break the fucking speed limit like a normal person. He's got to be perfect. The role model for all Apache youth. If he's doing something illegal, it's got to be scaring the crap out of him."

That would explain the intensity of his fear and suspicion when he almost got caught. *Role model for all Apache youth.* Jamie had said it with a touch of irony, but it was true in a way. Misty said Reno had extra money. If Zak's secret activity was part of the same thing, it would have to be bringing in a good amount for him to dare risk his reputation. If he got arrested, he could lose his jobs, and the kids that looked up to him would lose their hero.

Mae joined Jamie, placing her hand over one of his. "Could you see what he put in his car?"

"Nah. Too dark. Nothing big enough to block the windows."

"Melody said if he doesn't get back soon, she wants me to find out where he is and what he's doing. You didn't like the idea when Misty asked me to find out about Reno, but there could be a lot at stake. If they're headed for trouble and we can stop them—"

"Fuck." Jamie gave the base of the railing a small, futile kick. "I was supposed to get him to tell me." He looked into her eyes. "Give me another chance. When he gets home. He'll never forgive us if you do a psychic search and catch him out. He won't trust us."

"Sugar, he already doesn't trust us."

"Jeezus." Jamie gazed out at the storm. "I hate this." He looked down at their hands. "Guess you have to do it if Mel wants you to, but it feels wrong. Wish they'd just fucking talk to each other."

Chapter Thirteen

While Mae helped Melody out of the bath and into bed, she shared the essence of her talk with Jamie. Melody promised she wouldn't tell Zak about the psychic work if she could help it, but he still hadn't called or answered her texts, and she wanted to know what he was hiding.

Mae took Zak's razor from the medicine cabinet. It *did* feel wrong, even though her reasons for doing it were right. She could almost see Zak holding the razor, looking at himself in the mirror. Already, she felt she'd intruded too far on his privacy, and if her vision was off target she could intrude a lot further. It was weird to be doing a psychic journey sitting on a toilet lid, too. She might get some incredibly unwelcome information. However, if Zak showed up suddenly, she wouldn't have to explain what she was doing in the bathroom with the door closed.

She dug the pouch of crystals from her purse and chose a clear quartz point for strengthening her focus and amethyst for intuition, then took a moment to settle her energy.

When she heard the front door open, she froze, but no sound followed until a kitchen cabinet opened and water ran. The silent walking should mean Jamie. Though Zak was lighter, his steps were heavy, as carelessly thumping as a child's. Water ran again, followed shortly by the thunk of a glass on the counter and a loud, vocalized sigh of relief. Definitely Jamie. Even thirst was a minor drama. Once she heard him talking to Melody from the doorway of the bedroom, Mae relaxed and turned her mind inward.

She asked whatever force guided her to help her see what Zak was doing. Her inner vision narrowed to a tunnel, as it always did at the beginning of a vision, and then broke open in a new place. It was a quaintly old-fashioned motel room with small windows covered by frilly curtains. Letitia sat in an armchair, writing in a leather-bound notebook. Zak perched on the edge of a hard-backed chair, his elbows on the table in front of him, his thumbs tapping.

She looked up. "I'm grateful, you know. This will make a big difference." As she tucked her notebook into her purse, a subtle smile curved her full lips. "I'm sorry it has to be over. I wish there was some way to keep going."

"No." Zak frowned at her. "It *has* to be over."

"I know. All over but the money." Playing air guitar, she sang a line from an old rock and roll song about money, shaking her hair and shoulders to the beat.

"Is it ever going to sink in with you that this is serious?"

"I'm not a serious person." She batted her eyes at him. "Isn't that part of my charm?"

He didn't flirt back but hunched over the table, his eyes narrowed, his restless thumbs moving faster. "You need to take the risks seriously. Be careful."

"I will. We all will."

"You'd better." Zak stood and pressed his hands into the small of his back, provoking a cracking noise. "I should get going. One of my buddies is getting suspicious."

Letitia walked to the door with him and put her hands on his shoulders, tilting her face up to him as if asking for a kiss. "Should I leave a little lipstick on your collar?"

Zak gave her a light, quick hug and let go with a sigh. "Nice idea, but no."

Mae's vision followed Zak out into the parking lot. A *No Vacancy* sign glowed below one that displayed the name of the motel, the Alpine Lodge. Zak got in his boxy old wood-paneled station wagon and turned right onto a busy four-lane street. Where was this? Not Mescalero, but not far off.

At the same time the question weakened her vision, a knock on the door broke her concentration. She cleared her energy with snow quartz and took a second to feel present in her body again. "Yes?"

Jamie said, "Got to piss." She stood, let him know it was okay, and he barged in, flipped the seat up, unzipped, and sighed with relief. "Jeezus. Sorry to interrupt. Didn't want to do it in the yard, though, y'know? Fucking coffee. And then I drank two glasses of water and—do your kidneys react that fast? Jeezus. My piss is *yellow*. Does that mean you're dehydrated? I was dry as a dead dingo's donger."

The transition from Zak's problems to Jamie's rambling about urination was disorienting, and Mae couldn't think of anything to say. He finished his business and zipped up. "You find out anything?"

"Sort of, but not enough. He may be on his way back. Where's the Alpine Lodge?"

"Ruidoso. He's leaving already? He just had time to get there."

Mae put the razor back in the medicine cabinet. "He must have delivered something to Letitia—the lady he's been hanging out with. They were in her room. Talking about money and how this is the last of whatever he brought her."

"Good. It's finished."

Mae was about to correct him when Jamie tripped on the scale. "Bloody hell. Where'd that come from?"

"Sorry. I forgot to put it away. Melody wanted to weigh herself."

To Mae's astonishment, he stepped onto it. The last she knew, he'd made a firm decision to stop worrying about his weight. "Why are you doing that?"

"Mel showed me a video Will shot at Zak's party last night and I'm on his fucking Facebook with my shirt off. Thought people only did that crap to *celebrities*. I look *fat*."

What had Melody been thinking, showing Jamie that video? Body image anxiety was the one area of his mental health that had stopped erupting. But that was recent progress, too recent for her to know about, and she was feeling bad about her body. No doubt she'd expected—even invited—Jamie to join her. Or maybe she'd just wanted to vent about the party.

Melody called, "What's your number, Pudge?"

Jamie looked down, and his eyes opened wide. "I'll be stuffed. One ninety-nine." With a snort-laugh, he stepped off the scale. "Been marked down. I'm a bargain."

Mae hoped this meant he'd gotten over the worry already. She dreaded a new round of obsessing on his target weight of *perfect-one-seventy-five*. "I take it that's okay, then?"

Jamie answered by singing an old song about being too sexy for his shirt and dancing into the hallway, bumping hips with her on his way.

Mae took the crystals into the kitchen to rinse them in salt water before putting them away. The ritual was important for removing traces of negative energy from her journeys. It readied the crystals for the next use, and often it gave Mae a sense of closure.

Tonight it didn't. Zak and Letitia were winding down whatever they'd been doing, but money would still be coming in. Did this leave Zak at risk for getting caught?

Mae put her crystals away and headed to the bedroom. Jamie hovered in the doorway, while Melody lay in bed propped up on pillows. She held out her phone. "Want to see that video?"

"Not really." Mae slipped past Jamie and sat in the chair beside the bed. "I mean, it's not like I haven't seen Jamie with his shirt off.

I need to tell you what I learned about Zak. He might be back in half an hour or so."

Jamie came over and took the phone. "Got to watch it again. See if I look better than I thought. Now that I know, y'know?"

Shoot. He is not *over this.* "Now that you know what you weigh?"

"Yeah. I lost two pounds." He started to wipe the screen with his shirttail.

Mae touched his wrist. "Don't do that, you'll change something."

"But there are *fingerprints*." He held the phone gingerly by its sides. "Hate fucking touch screens."

"Your little keyboard has fingerprints, too. You just can't see 'em."

"I'm neurotic, all right? I don't have to make sense."

You sure don't.

While Jamie watched the video again, pacing back and forth, Mae told Melody about her vision of Zak and Letitia. "I'm pretty sure he's not having an affair with her."

"*Pretty* sure?"

Mae wished she could say she was a hundred percent sure, but she wasn't. Letitia had acted interested in Zak, and though he'd been preoccupied, her offer of a kiss hadn't appeared to trouble him. "He only stayed long enough to deliver whatever they're selling."

"So he didn't screw her tonight—that's all you actually know." Melody shifted against her pile of pillows, muttering that she couldn't get comfortable. "I wish you'd got a look at whatever he brought her."

"So do I. He sounded like he was ready to be done with it, but she said the money part wasn't over yet." Mae realized how useless her vision had been. The things that mattered most to Melody were still uncertain. "I'm sorry. That was all I got. I can try again—"

Jamie broke in. "You need to see this, love."

He perched on the chair arm, which creaked under his weight, and handed Mae the phone. She tapped the arrow to restart the video. It had been posted in the morning about an hour before the rodeo, and Will's comment on it read, *Jangarrai parteez w cowboyz n Indnz*. She disliked Will instantly, and not only for his pseudo-cool bad spelling. Jamie used Jangarrai, his Aboriginal skin name, as his stage name, and the cowboy had been capable of spelling that correctly, probably so he could get more hits on his page, more people to click "like" on Jamie looking bad.

Wild-haired, barefoot, shirtless, and carrying a beer can, he entered the living room from the hallway a few steps behind Zak. Zak headed into the kitchen, while Jamie remained in the living room, looking around in a dazed manner. Mae normally saw him as looking fit and strong, with his perfect posture and broad shoulders, but Will's unsteady video, which occasionally dipped to a view of his own knees, caught Jamie in profile at waist level. The cowboy's goal might have been to make Jamie look like a fellow drunk, focusing on the beer can in his hand, but it was no wonder he'd gotten the urge to weigh himself. The camera angle was as unflattering as it could get.

"Stop it here." Jamie leaned in shoulder to shoulder with Mae, making the chair arm creak again. "I was working on feeling better about it, seeing who in the room looks worse—Jeezus, that's fucked up, isn't it?—anyway, I'd picked the bloke in the kitchen doorway and then—*look at him.*"

Mae studied the stilled video. A large hemisphere of belly poked into the doorframe, its owner out of sight. The image reminded her of a cartoon character trying to hide behind a tree. "That's ... um ..." Mae had no idea what to say. Any comment on the man's girth—the clothing suggested male, with a blue cotton shirt tucked into belted jeans—could sound insulting to Melody, who was bigger even than this fellow. "That's a funny picture. Just his belly sticking out."

"Not the point," Jamie said. "See the braid?" An unusually long black braid had dropped across the man's shoulder onto his paunch. "It's David Mirabal."

Mae recognized the body shape and the hair now. "Is that strange? Him being there?"

"Yeah. Didn't think Zak knew him."

"I don't," Melody said. "Who is he?"

Mae answered, "His wife makes the feather earrings." She handed Melody's phone back to her. "They're potters. Friends of Jamie's from Santa Fe."

Melody placed the phone on the bedside table. "I know everyone I kicked out—and everyone else I saw in the video. He must have crashed the party and left."

"One Acoma bloke crashed a party with a bunch of Apaches?" Jamie sounded doubtful. "Nah. Had to be invited or he wouldn't have heard about it. Zak threw that party on short notice."

Something else was odd about David being out in the middle of the night. Mae hardly knew him, but the way he'd taken Star when she'd started fussing had made her think he was a good husband and father, not the kind of man to take off after midnight to go crash a party. He would have needed a serious reason to be out that late. The image of David's hand cupping the pottery cat flashed into Mae's mind. And David claiming Shelli had sold out of feather earrings. "What if David and Shelli are in on whatever Zak is doing?"

"Ya think?" Jamie frowned. "Like—Zak had *parrots in the toolshed*?"

"Where did that come from?" Melody asked. "That was random even for you, Pudge."

"Shelli got fired from the parrot store where she worked. She lost two birds. She says they escaped. Mae thinks she stole them." He gave her a dark look.

Melody started to laugh. "Does that mean Zak *did* have parrots in the toolshed? Shelli can't steal more because she got fired, and there weren't going to be any more of whatever he brought his girlfriend or whoever—"

Jamie cut in. "Stealing parrots is not funny. They're valuable—and they're sensitive—"

"I've been thinking he was mixed up in some awful crime or having an affair or both. Compared to that, it *is* funny. I hope he *did* have parrots in the shed. I'll give you the combination. You can go look for bird poop."

Mae paused to check on the twins before going outside, concerned that all the noise and conversation might have disturbed them. They were curled up in their beds, breathing softly. The soundness of small children's sleep—how could she have forgotten? Deanna clung loosely to a tousle-haired doll, and Dean had turned backwards, his feet on the pillow, stuffed toys scattered around him. Mae longed for her stepdaughters with a sudden stretching pain. *One more month.* She closed the door and caught Jamie looking at her looking at the twins. *Don't go there, sugar.*

She put a finger to her lips, as if talking would wake the children, and he nodded.

They went out the door from the kitchen, emerging under a big tree on the opposite side of the house from the road. The rain had tapered to a light drizzle. The toolshed was in shadow a few yards away, the house standing between it and the streetlight at the edge of the yard. It was a good place to hide something, especially if you didn't lock your front door. Passersby would be unlikely to notice the shed from the access road or Route 70, and though the structure was visible from the uphill road to the ceremonial grounds, any activity in it after dark would be hard to see.

Jamie held his phone up for Mae to use as a flashlight while she dialed the numbers on the padlock. She didn't expect to find feathers or bird droppings, though she was curious what she *would* find. The idea that Zak had stored stolen parrots in the shed was absurd and next to impossible. Melody seldom went in the toolshed, but she did use it and knew the combination for the lock. Parrots were noisy, and people went in and out of the house all the time. The small outbuilding would get too hot for a living creature during the day and too cold at night. But something had been in here that might have left a trace.

The lock didn't open. It was the kind with individual numbers that slid around, not the kind that required spinning a dial and feeling a click, so Mae could see that she'd lined up the right numbers. "Wasn't it two, six, one, six?"

"Yeah. Z-A-F. Zak Aaron Fatty."

Zak's combination was supposed to be the places of his initials in the alphabet.

Mae said, "We have a lock like this in the fitness center on the drawer for the keys to the closets. My boss changes the combination when there's a turnover in the staff. Zak probably changed his to something Mel wouldn't guess. And that you wouldn't. Since he—"

"Doesn't trust us. And he shouldn't. Look at us. Trying to break into his toolshed."

"Melody asked us to unlock it. That's not breaking in."

"Still. Feels shitty that we're doing it." Jamie shoved his phone into his pocket and leaned back against the shed. "Whole bloody night feels like crap. I feel like crap. This is my mate, y'know?

And we're spying on him. Playing bloody fucking detective. It's not right. He should talk to me. Talk to Mel."

"Sugar, you're going back to square one." This was the same gloomy mood he'd been in when Mae and Melody and the children had arrived. "We've already been over this."

"Jeezus. It's not a fucking math problem. It's a *feeling*, all right? We went inside and I felt like I was just hanging out with Mel, like I was just in their house like *normal*, y'know? And now I'm back out here and it's not. Their lives aren't normal, our friendship isn't normal, the whole weekend isn't what it was supposed to be. You hate camping. Placido flew off. David's in this with Zak. What in bloody hell else could go wrong? I'm upset. I'm disappointed. It ... it *hurts*." He hugged himself, massaging his forearms. "I wanted to share this great place and these great people with you and it's all falling apart. It hurts."

Mae leaned against the shed with him, close by his side. It was the only thing she could think to do. He'd put himself into an un-huggable posture, and he didn't want her to reassure him or solve a problem or talk him out of this mood. He was in it and that was that. She didn't know whether to credit his book or his therapist for how thoroughly he'd shared it.

She wondered if one of those sources had given him that phrase about a feeling not being a math problem. It didn't sound like Jamie, who had once claimed to be afraid of numbers, but she could imagine some advice book author telling male readers: *listen to your partner and her feelings, don't try to solve them. Emotions are not math problems.*

The situation was a problem, though, and no one was going to feel better until it was solved.

It might even be a math problem. There were at least three people, maybe four or five, involved in selling something they were keeping secret. The profit from selling two parrots at less than two thousand apiece wouldn't go very far five ways. Shelli could sell one of her big pots for what her share would have come to, without the hassle of hiding and lying. The money had to be big to be split several ways and still be worth her while. Worth Zak's risk to his reputation and his marriage, worth Reno's fights with Misty if he was part of it, worth Shelli's job, and worth David and Shelli dodging little sales to Mae. And worth whatever risks Letitia took. What did they have in common that would bring them all together? Zak and Reno had Misty and Melody, but there was no obvious connection for the others.

Jamie's phone rang and he answered. "Nah. He changed the combination ... Sorry." He listened awhile. "Hope you feel better. Yeah. We're going."

They started across the back of the yard to the road to the ceremonial grounds. Mae took Jamie's hand. She wanted to share her work on the puzzle, but she was concerned that it would oppress him to think about it. He was too close to it. The only way Jamie could solve such a problem would be to make Zak submit to a hug.

Where had *that* image come from?

Jamie hugging Ezra, then talking with him as they'd walked along the tree line. Ezra, who hadn't been able to open up to Mae and Bernadette, had thawed after that hug. Mae had no idea what he and Jamie had talked about, but she'd seen a difference in the boy's energy. He'd still been shy, but he'd walked closer to Jamie, looked up a little more often, and he'd talked more. She liked the idea of Jamie giving Zak that same long hard embrace until the truth poured out of him.

"What are you thinking?" Jamie asked. "You're smiling."

"I had this idea that if you could hug Zak—grab him in a big ol' bear hug—he'd talk to you, like Ezra did."

Jamie's words came out with care and reverence, his pace as delicate as the last few raindrops on her skin. "Ezra said I healed him." He walked more slowly. "Didn't mean to, but he said he felt it."

"Sugar, that's beautiful. And important. Why didn't you tell me?"

"Dunno." Jamie's shoulders rolled in his evasive wriggle of a shrug. "Can't see that happening with Zak." He paused and looked down the hill toward his friends' house. Mae followed his gaze and saw Zak's Eagle pulling into the driveway. The lights and the engine cut off. "Wish it could, though."

Zak strode to his house and up the steps. As he began to open the screen door, he let it fall shut again and picked up something from the glider.

"Fuck." Jamie smacked a fist into his thigh. "My *book*. I left my book."

Chapter Fourteen

Mae woke up early, looking forward to the race, but exhausted as usual after a night with Jamie. He'd wanted to stay at the ceremonies until midnight, and after the evening they'd had, the music and dancing had been healing. She didn't regret staying, but then Jamie had his usual sleep issues, magnified by the close quarters of the tent. He had wanted her to rouse him so he could watch her run, but he looked so peaceful she couldn't bring herself to disturb him yet, so she set an alarm on his phone, giving him a little more time to dream.

As she took an easy jog along the access road, she was surprised to see Zak's car pass her. What was he doing driving so short a distance? Then she noticed the station wagon was packed full of teenagers. Probably Boys and Girls Club kids. He must have collected them from further out on the reservation, which meant he'd gotten up even earlier than she had. If Melody had confronted him when he got in the night before, he might have slept poorly, too.

When she reached the wellness center, Mae found Zak in the parking lot with his group of teens, taking them through a military-style workout as a warm-up. The four boys and three girls didn't look like trained athletes. Several struggled, while others plowed through energetically with poor form. Zak was so focused on doing the routine himself that he didn't notice. Showing off? Or trying to motivate them? Mae gave him the benefit of the doubt. If she hadn't taken a course on how to teach exercise, she might have made the same mistake. She stayed out of their way, doing some range of motion active stretches—butt kicks, high knees, leg swings, and other dynamic moves.

One of the younger boys asked suddenly, "What's that lady doing?" and the whole group broke their pace and looked at Mae. Zak turned around, stared hard at her for moment, and then faced the kids again. "Something easier than what we're doing. Come on. Let's finish up and then stretch."

Smooth cover-up. Zak probably had no idea how to answer.

Runners of all ages began to arrive. A woman in a sundress unlocked the building, announcing that registration would be starting in a few minutes. The competitors milled around in the parking lot, joking and talking.

When Zak finished leading his group's overzealous warmup, he said, "Before you go in to sign up, listen." They held still, all eyes on him. "You're not all going to win today, but you're all going to do your best. You're not just any runners. You're Apache runners. You're not just running a race. You're running for your people. You're spiritual runners. Role models. Inspire others. Make me proud."

One by one, each kid fist-bumped or high-fived with Zak on their way to join the stream of people headed into the building. To follow the kids, Mae had to pass him, and her words came out without her thinking. "That was a good talk, coach."

He propped one heel up on the bench outside the door and stretched his leg. "*And* a good workout."

Her positive feelings toward him fizzled like a light bulb burning out. Was he daring her to criticize his warm-up? He was going to get what he asked for. "A good workout for *you*. Not right before a race, though. And definitely not for those kids."

"Bullshit. I learned it in the army. They know how to get people in shape. Not everybody has to go to college to learn how to work out."

A thick silence fell between them. He stretched his other leg, turning away from her. *The army.* Did he wish he hadn't mentioned that? Through the open door, Mae saw a long line of people waiting to sign up at a single table. Zak completed his stretch and stepped in ahead of her. "You sure you want to run this race?"

The line was hardly a deterrent. A race with a lot of runners was more exciting. Perhaps he meant the altitude. She felt that she'd adapted quickly, though, maybe because of the time she'd recently spent in Santa Fe. "Yeah, I'm sure. I'll be fine."

"Until you don't have anywhere to take a shower."

Zak got in line. Mae sank onto the bench. *Shoot.* Of course she would run. She was here, she was ready, and she wanted to beat Zak. It was going to be unpleasant afterward, though, with either a long, unwashed drive to T or C or a sticky, sweaty wait while Jamie negotiated a new place for bathing and cooking. His outpouring of things that hurt came back to her. Nothing *was* going the way he'd planned.

Ezra Yahnaki approached with his mother and sisters. He stopped when they reached the building and politely introduced Mae to his family without making eye contact, then added, "We're doing the one-mile walk together."

Mae was sure Ezra could walk more than a mile easily, but his mother and sisters were out of breath after walking from their car. She said, "That should be fun."

His mother let out a huff of air. "It *should* be. But I got diabetes and my feet are bad. We'll see." She went inside, followed by her daughters. Ezra told them he'd be in shortly and sat beside Mae.

"I had to make them do it. My grandma and me are the only people in our family that don't have diabetes. And my sisters are only fifteen and seventeen. It's bad, them having it already."

"I'm glad you got them to come out and walk."

"Yeah. I could have run the five K, but ... I don't know why I told you all that."

"Because the other kids from Boys and Girls Club are running? And you're not?"

"I'd be slow. I wouldn't win anything. It's not a big deal."

Mae doubted this. She'd seen the intense focus of the other runners in Zak's group. The event was a big deal to them, especially with the meaning Zak had given it. Ezra was the youngest, the heaviest, and no doubt the slowest. For him, this should have been the biggest deal of all—to train and to run with his friends, and with Zak. "I think it *was* a big deal."

Ezra slumped, one foot rubbing the other.

Mae continued, "And you gave it up to be with your family. I wish you'd heard what Zak told the other kids before they went in. He said you're running for your people. That you're spiritual runners. I think you're living up to that by walking."

"Zak doesn't. He told me it makes me look lazy, and that I should show the other heavier kids that they can run, too."

"He really said that?"

The grinding clatter of stroller wheels on the rocky dirt of the parking lot drew Mae's attention and stopped her from saying what she thought of Zak's insensitivity. Melody and her twins had arrived.

"Hey," Mae greeted her. "Is your back better?"

"A little." Melody looked down at Dean and Deanna, who appeared to be competing to see who could stomp on their footrest the loudest. "I took three ibuprofen."

"Be careful. That can mess up your stomach. You think you can stand long enough to watch the race? Is there a place to sit?"

"People bring chairs. But I'm not watching it. I'm running it."

"Don't you mean walking?"

"No. I'm doing the five K."

No way. Melody's knees and feet would take a beating. Her back could go into spasms again. She might have high blood pressure or be pre-diabetic. "Melody, that's really—really—" *Dangerous. Stupid.* Mae searched for a tactful way to express what she thought. "You don't have to prove yourself to anybody. Just do the walk. Ezra's going to, with his mama and his sisters. If you want to run eventually, that's great, build up to it. I told you I'd train you. But I don't want you to hurt yourself."

Melody's voice was steely. "I'm doing the five K."

Ezra asked, "Are you doing it for Zak?"

"I'm doing it *at* him." Melody spoke to Mae. "He still doesn't want you and Jamie in the house. He's mad that I let you in last night. But as far as I'm concerned, you can still come over. It's my house, too, and my shower."

Mae guessed there might be more that Melody had the sense not to say in front of Ezra—something about Letitia perhaps—but that could wait. "We don't have to make it tense for you. Jamie can sort it out with Zak eventually. We'll go back to my place today, or Jamie will know someone who'll let him trade some cooking for a place to clean up."

"Jamie had a fight with Zak?" Ezra asked.

Mae nodded, and Melody sighed a disgruntled affirmation.

The boy studied both women's faces. He spoke softly, kindly. "My grandma likes Jamie. I'll ask her if you guys can come over. I bet she'll say yes." He stood, and then looked at his shoes, back to his shy, awkward self. "I have to use my sister's phone," he mumbled. "I'm not allowed to have one yet."

"Thank you." Mae watched until the door of the wellness center closed behind him. "What a great kid. He's really special."

"Zak's mad at him for not running."

"Because he wants him to be a role model?"

"So he says. But it's really because Zak wants the credit for getting him to run. Hell, there are a ton of kids who go to Boys and Girls Club who aren't running at all. They do other stuff, like art. But Zak can't show them off to the whole tribe at once like he can the runners. His *high risk* kids being healthy."

"High risk for what?"

"Diabetes. Or drugs and drinking. Or quitting school. All sorts of stuff. Bernadette's always getting us grants and helping start prevention programs. The running group is part of it. You'd think it was all Zak's idea, though, to listen to him."

Dean and Deanna began a new game, batting each other's hands down and shrieking with each success. Mae stood and opened the door to the lobby. "Who's gonna watch the kids for you during the race?"

"I don't know. Mom's doing a float in the parade, Misty's running, and I didn't get hold of Montana. Jamie offered but they don't know him, and ... I didn't want to say this to him, but he's kind of flaky, and he gets those anxiety attacks. He wouldn't make a good babysitter."

Mae wished Melody *had* said it. It might have slowed down his daddy dreams a little, given him a reality check on his readiness.

She scanned the line of runners ahead of them, hoping to spot a relative who could talk Melody out of this. She only saw strangers. One trim young woman had a racing stroller with an infant dozing in it. The sight gave Mae a touch of nostalgia for when Brook and Stream were little and she'd pushed them around Tylerton in a double jogging stroller. If Melody had the right type of stroller, Mae could take Dean and Deanna in the race—but she didn't. "What'll you do if you don't find someone?"

"I'll do like that lady. Push the stroller."

"That's a special kind. Yours'll be hard on you and the kids. Why are you so bound and determined to do this? It can't be just because Zak won't let us in the house."

Melody lowered her voice so her words were almost masked by her children's squealing and babbling. "I told him *someone* had seen him coming out of the Alpine Lodge last night."

"I hope he didn't guess it was me."

"He wouldn't say anything about that even if he had. That would be like admitting he had a secret you could find out. I asked him what he'd been doing there, and if it was that photographer's room—and he said, 'What if it was? Maybe she needed a fire put out.' I told him he'd done it pretty damned quick if that was the case and he asked me what was the quickest we'd ever done it. We've had some fast ones in some funny places—so he might as well have told me he dipped his dipstick."

"Running isn't gonna un-dip it."

Melody gave Mae a look. As they reached the head of the line, she finally told her children to lower their voices. Melody signed up for the five K, Mae for the ten K, and the woman at the table gave them papers with large numbers printed on them, and a few tiny safety pins.

They moved aside and Melody turned her back. "Pin my number on, will you?"

Mae pinned one corner and paused. "If you have to stop, or get hurt—"

"Some EMT will have to drop out of the ten K and take care of me."

"Honey, that's not gonna make him be a better husband to you. You know that."

"It's going to make me feel great, though. Anyway, Jamie's bringing his van to a halfway spot. I can get in and get some AC if I'm dying."

"Will that count as finishing the race if you take a break like that?"

"That's if I'm literally dying. Otherwise, I'm not taking a break, even if I have to walk or crawl or waddle like a duck. I'm coming in last and the whole tribe is going to have to wait for me. They don't start the parade 'til the race is over, and I'm finishing this race."

"There's a parade?" Melody's mention of her mother doing a float finally registered.

"Jamie didn't tell you? He loves the parade. It's right after the race."

"He didn't mention it, but it sounds like fun. And we could use some of that."

Mae attached the last pin to the number on Melody's broad, soft back. She was sweating already though the morning was still cool. The bra visibly cutting into folds of her flesh wasn't a proper sports bra. Her breasts were going to bounce painfully. Her thighs were going to chafe so badly where her shorts rode up that she was likely to be in pain for a week. There was no point in warning her, though. Jamie had probably already tried to talk her out of it.

Or had he? He'd offered to take the kids and to be waiting halfway. With more empathy than common sense, he must have cheered her on.

Mae went outside while Melody took the children to the bathroom, and spotted Michael Pena and his wife among the crowd ready to start the race. Michael looked to be the oldest runner in the group, but as fit as the teenagers. Mae imagined him beating Zak. *I'm getting petty.* She made her way to Michael's side. "Melody's trying to run the five K pushing her twin stroller. Are your girls around anywhere?"

Michael looked briefly alarmed, took a cell phone from the pocket of his high-tech running shorts and made a call. "Leah. Watch the race route for Melody and grab the stroller ... I know. One of you should probably go with her ... She will? Excellent."

He smiled at Mae. "Leah and Chamiqua will take the kids, and Bernadette's going to step in beside Melody and keep an eye on her."

"Thank you. I hope Melody doesn't mind."

"Family." He said it like this was all she needed to know. The word obviously meant a lot here—to everyone but Zak. Melody, pushing the stroller, made her way into the group readying to start the race, and Michael gave the unlikely competitor a one-armed hug around her shoulders. "No matter what happens," he said, "you've already won."

Relieved, Mae mingled with the other runners, seeking her sweet spot in the ten K group, neither too far in front nor too far back, where she could keep an eye on the leaders. The Zuni fire-fighters who had come to dance in the powwow, small compact men who barely came up to her shoulder, chatted and joked with her while they waited. When the starting pistol went off, they fell silent and shot like rockets. Mae flew with them in a tight pack. She wanted to look back for Melody, but that would make her trip over a Zuni.

Past the Zuni crew she could see Zak and Michael together in the lead, with Michael's wife a few steps behind. Mae planned to catch them, but she had to pace her efforts. She shifted to the road-side grass and weeds. A few people she passed commented on her barefoot shoes. *Like your toes. Look, finger-moccasins.*

The runners began to pick up speed on the downhill route. By the time they turned down the road toward the Catholic church at the base of a hill, Zak was lagging. The fastest runners flew past him like a human truck careening down a mountain, and Mae was one of its wheels.

The turnaround point for the five K and the first water station were just past the church. She spotted Jamie's new van in the church parking lot, but no Jamie. There was another car nearby, a silver SUV with the license plate NMOFNM. Letitia's business name: Notable Men of New Mexico. No sign of her, either. Melody would be fine—she had Bernadette and a water station—but Jamie should know how important an audience was. Maybe he was learning something from Letitia. Finding out what was up with her and Zak.

Realizing her distraction was slowing her down, Mae refocused on the race. She was amazed how soon she'd gotten ahead of Zak, but between the party one night and his fight with Melody the next, he had to be exhausted. It wouldn't mean much to beat him when he was worn out.

"Come on," one of the girls from Zak's group gasped to Mae, "we gotta beat the men!"

Another girl passed her. She looked like a high school track star who actually could beat the men. Mae put on a little speed. At the turnaround up a wooded road, the leader varied from step to step.

Mae pulled ahead to run neck and neck with Michael Pena, the high school girl, and a Zuni firefighter. They stayed almost synchronized until they reached the uphill stretch approaching the church. As if on cue, all of them put out a burst of effort. Mae knew she would come in first in her age group for women whether or not she was first in the race, but she felt a thrill when she was in front for a few seconds. Her legs flew as if her body were being driven by some force outside herself, even when her heart pounded and her lungs burned.

She was pushing too hard to do more than glance aside for Jamie. He was leaning against his van side by side with Letitia, who was clutching his arm and talking to him excitedly. *Flirting* with him. How could he let her do that? It wasn't like him.

The hill got steeper, and Mae lost the sensation of effortless power in her legs. She picked the high school girl as the person to beat. It gave her energy, even if she couldn't catch her.

As the runners tore into the wellness center parking lot, an announcer called out times and numbers. The girl came in first, Michael next, the Zuni third, and Mae fourth. A boy named Walter—not one of Zak's group—was fifth, and then Michael's wife Casey Pena. Walking to cool down and catch her breath, Mae congratulated the other first finishers and looked for Zak to be next.

He was nowhere in sight.

Chapter Fifteen

Jamie emerged from his brain fog, still struggling to catch his breath. Bernadette was crouched beside him where he lay in the dirt of the church parking lot, her words a blur of concern. He tried to sit up, but she urged him to rest again.

This wasn't what was supposed to have happened. He'd planned well, and improvised well, too, but in keeping with the whole bloody weekend, things had gone wrong.

Before the race, he'd parked the van in the lot, double-checked that he had locked it, and then reopened it to make sure he'd brought the cooler full of soft drinks Melody had given him. It was there. He moved it to the shadiest place in the interior and discovered his travel mug of coffee that he'd filled for the second megadose of the morning and forgotten in the cup holder. After taking a few welcome swallows, he closed the van and touched its scratch. It hadn't stayed new for twenty-four hours.

Jamie made himself stop running his fingers over the scratch and went to sit on the church steps and finish waking up while he waited for the race to start. *Don't be so fucking gloomy*. He drank more coffee, hoping it would uplift him.

A silver SUV pulled up beside the van and a shapely brown-skinned woman in tight jeans climbed out and started toward the church, carrying a camera and a large purse. With her gold nose stud and tattooed arms, she fit Mae's description of the woman who'd been with Zak. He had to ask her what was going on, though he had no idea how. If he started talking, maybe something would come to him. Something that would finally get an honest answer out of somebody and put an end to the Chino sisters asking Mae to dig up secrets.

"G'day. Been here before?"

"Jangarrai." The slow dawning of delight on the woman's face and her use of his stage name made it clear that she was a fan. He hadn't expected this. "What are you doing here?" Her accent was faintly Caribbean. "Are you playing somewhere nearby?"

"Nah. Dad's a professor. Anthropologist. Studying Apaches. Been coming here since I was a kid."

Her eyes narrowed and her head angled slightly. "So that's how you know people here?"

"Yeah." An idea came to him—fuzzy, but possibly effective. "Know a few people in the race. Girlfriend's in it. And my mate and his wife. He doesn't know she's running, though. She's this really big sheila, trying to show him something, y'know? She thinks he's cheating, see. So she's trying to prove she's someone. Worth his admiration."

Jamie waited for a reaction. Guilt. Embarrassment. Anger. The woman showed none of them.

"That's very touching." She sounded more amused than touched, and then her manner grew teasing. "Are these *runners* in your party crowd?"

"Bloody hell—you saw that?"

She took a smartphone from her purse, sat beside him—a little too close, and showed him her Facebook page. On the sidebar listing what music she liked, there was his icon, his name in black script against a dotted background like Aboriginal art. "I go to a lot of your Santa Fe shows. And my massage therapist uses your older music a lot. The healing music. So I was a little surprised to see you in *that condition*." She went to Will's page and found the video. "Did you see this? Even with your new music, I still thought of you as a spiritual composer and performer."

She said this with a teasing smile, and yet something in her voice suggested she meant what she said. Confused, Jamie fidgeted and inched away from her. "Doesn't mean I don't have fun, drink a little. But not that cheap piss. That was my friend's little sister's beer—I took it from her. Wasn't even drinking anything that night."

"Really?" She touched the arrow to start the video.

"Jeezus. I've seen it. You don't have to show me. Wish I could get Will to take the bloody thing down. Makes me look fat. Fat and drunk. Dunno why he did that except to bring me down to his level."

The woman's eyes met Jamie's. She put her phone away, tapped a finger to her lips, and squinted in thought. "You need an image to undo it. I think I could make you look good bare-chested."

"What the fuck?"

"Wouldn't that be the thing? The right light, the right pose ..." She looked him over. "You wear those big loud shirts all the time now." The one he wore today featured flamingos, matching the pink striped band on his straw fedora. She regarded it with a shake of her head. "All anyone sees is the shirt."

"Um—that's the point."

"I'd rather see *you*."

"Jeezus." He scooted a bit further away. Was she flirting? Trying to get a commission for some sort of compensatory portrait? Will's video had been taken in dim enough light that the disturbing array of scars on Jamie's belly, shoulders and arms hadn't shown. This woman had no idea what she was asking. He changed the subject as forcefully as he could. "What are *you* doing here?"

"Seeing the church. I've heard the art is good."

"They let you take pictures?" He gave it a moment's thought. "Yeah. Guess you can. I was thinking at first, y'know, sacred places—like the ceremonies—but I guess churches are different." They stood and Jamie opened the heavy door for her. "That's not why you came to Mescalero, though."

Her eyes twinkled and dimples showed in her cheeks. "There's a lot here to photograph."

She stepped in ahead of him, and he let the door slowly shut behind them.

As always, the first thing he noticed was the smell. Bats. They'd lived in the old church for as long as he'd been coming to Mescalero. The second thing he noticed was the art. The central painting over the altar, of Jesus as an Apache medicine man, fascinated him. The beardless, brown-skinned Redeemer held up his hand the way the medicine men did at sunrise during the girls' initiation rites, seeing into the spirit world through his palm. Jamie thought of the picture as the Medicine Jesus. Below it, a painting of the Last Supper had Apache symbols on the tablecloths—stars and moons and lightning—and the black iron sconces around the room were designed with slits shaped like lightning bolts. They made him think of Ezra's dream, Will Baca being struck by lightning.

The woman held her camera, but didn't lift it, staring at the paintings.

Maybe she didn't get the imagery. Jamie offered his take on it. "Some people think it's controversial, like it's saying Apache religion has to be made Catholic to be acceptable, or Catholicism has to be made Apache to be acceptable, but I think of it as—*no lines.* Y'know? All the same mystery."

She nodded, gazed at the art for a while longer, then studied Jamie. "That picture gives me an idea for a pose for you. It would be good for the bare-chested shot—sexy but spiritual."

Bloody hell. She wanted him to pose like the Medicine Jesus? With his shirt off? "Think I'd better catch the race. Enjoy the art."

"No, wait just a minute. I've done some good work for musicians. And I specialize in studies of the male figure." She sat in a pew, withdrew a sketch pad from her large purse, and flipped it to a new page. Glancing back and forth between Jamie and the Medicine Jesus, she dashed off a rough but skilled drawing. Hatless and shirtless, his hair a wild cloud, her version of Jamie stood in the pose of the painting, like an Aboriginal version of the same image, powerful, shamanic, and yet also human and flawed. "What do you think?"

"Fuck me dead." She hadn't changed his body—she'd drawn his shape quite accurately from Will's video—but he didn't look bad in this pose for some reason.

"It would be a good cover for a new healing music album. Just sky for background, very faded jeans so you sort blend with it—"

"Nah. Can't do it." He ran a finger along the scar on his right forearm. "This is just the tip of the iceberg. I've had some accidents. Injuries. I look bad. Scare people at the pool."

"That could be interesting. Vulnerable but strong. A survivor. The wounded healer."

Fucking cliché. And no one used personal portraits on healing music albums; they used nature images or art. He'd used rocks and flute-player petroglyphs. She obviously wasn't going to give up, though. "Give me your card. I'll talk to my manager."

"I ran out of cards. But you can find me online. Letitia Westover-Brown."

"You don't look like a Letitia Westover-Brown. Where you from?"

"Santa Fe, by way of Trinidad. Grandparents from India. They call me Lakshmi—that's my Indian name."

"I spent a year in India when I was a kid. Goddess of wealth, isn't she? Lakshmi? With the gold coins and flowers?"

Letitia smiled. "Yes. I should have kept the name. It might have given me better karma with money. But it didn't sound good when I married Mr. Westover-Brown."

"You're married? Jeezus. You don't act it."

Laughter rolled out of her, low and melodious but loud. "I don't act it because I'm not." She looked down and handled her camera, suddenly serious. "I really am looking for some work. I need to expand my business. I made a very stupid divorce agreement. No alimony, just the property and the horses. It was the only way I could afford to keep my horses, but—" She put on a forced smile. "Santa Fe property taxes—phew. And animals are an expensive habit."

"Yeah, but you love 'em, right?"

Her smile became warm and real. "More than I ever loved my husband."

"Don't think my album cover will feed 'em for long, but I'll give it some thought. Might recommend you to people."

"Thanks."

Jamie started for the door and realized she'd distracted him out of asking the question he'd started the conversation for. "What's up with you and Zak Fatty?"

"I told you, I specialize in studies of the male figure."

"Does that mean *naked*? *Zak's* posing *naked*?"

Her eyes grew bright with amusement. Then she raised her camera and focused on the art over the altar.

Jeezus. Was that the secret?

Jamie went back outside. The overdose of coffee had kicked in finally, making him jittery and combining with the bat smell of the church to make him feel queasy. The fresh air came as a relief. He wished he'd come out into it sooner. The race was underway, and Mae had just passed. He could see her orange ponytail bobbing, her strong legs flying, blindingly white among all the brown ones. If only he'd been waving his hat, cheering her, making her smile as she ran. *What an amazing woman.* Joy and awe flooded him at the sight of her doing what she loved, being so fully herself. He shouted, "You're winning, love!" though she was moving too fast to hear him.

Zak was far behind her, slower than he should have been, with a pained look on his face. He slowed even more as he reached the church, glancing at Letitia's SUV and then glaring at Jamie. "What the hell are you doing here?"

Jamie was on the verge of explaining, but Melody had wanted to surprise Zak. Furthermore, runners were passing him, and Zak was a man who liked to win. "Catcha after the race. You don't want to lose."

"I'm losing anyway." He jogged over to the church steps and used them to stretch his calves. "My muscles are cramping."

Jamie hurried to his van, put his empty coffee mug inside and got his water bottle and one of Melody's diet sodas out of the cooler. He turned and called out for Zak to choose one, but his friend wasn't listening. Letitia had come out, and Zak stood face to face with her, finishing up what he'd been saying while Jamie was inside the van. The only word Jamie caught sounded like "him," the end of an angry question.

She took sunglasses from her purse and put them on. "What's the matter with you? I told him I take pictures. And maybe I took yours."

Zak stretched his calf muscles again and slapped them side to side, then began stretching his hamstrings, muttering under his breath.

Letitia strolled over to the van. "If Zak doesn't want that Diet Coke, I do."

On principle, Jamie didn't want to give her Melody's drink, though there were more in the cooler. Since he couldn't think of a way to refuse, though, he handed her the soda. She sipped it and turned to Zak. "Go on. You can still catch up."

Zak accepted Jamie's water bottle without thanking him, drank, and stretched again. "Not a chance. I've lost this one." More runners passed, a slower and more relaxed group, talking, not even trying to win. Letitia leaned against the van. "Look, the leaders from the ten K are coming." She tugged on Jamie's arm, jostling him as he tried to wave when Mae flew past. "Ooh, is that your girlfriend? The redhead? She's fast, that one. She would have beat Zak even if he hadn't quit."

Jamie eased his arm out of her grip. He wanted to snap at her for touching him like that, but she was a fan.

Zak gave her a long hard look—a warning?—and took off slowly. The water station was a few yards past the church parking lot and that was as far he got, stopping to drink several of the tiny cups and stretch his calves yet again while other runners gulped water and tossed the empties onto the ground as they passed.

Then, when Zak had finally begun to run again, Melody came jogging down the hill so slowly she was almost shuffling. Bernadette easily kept pace with her at a walk.

Jamie threw himself into a cheerleader dance. His limbs felt shaky from too much coffee, but that was nothing compared to what Melody must be feeling. Jumping in his best version of flying splits, he chanted, "Mel-o-dee! Mel-o-dee!"

She grinned and waved. Zak stopped and looked back. "What the hell? I don't believe it."

He changed directions to join her. His wife's smile vanished as she demanded, "What are you doing?"

"Running with you. You idiot. I can't believe you did this."

Bernadette let Zak take her place. Melody stopped for water and Zak handed her a cup. He stayed beside her as she moved on to the five K turnaround, and matched her speed as she began her laborious jog uphill. He nudged her with his elbow. She jabbed him back. He smacked her bottom and she grabbed his hand—and held it. Neither of them let go.

"Never thought I'd see that," Bernadette said.

"Melody running?" Jamie's words came out thin and broken. He couldn't seem to catch his breath. His legs felt weak and sweat was gathering in the roots of his hair.

"And Zak supporting her."

Letitia's voice held a trace of amusement. "I think he's covering up for his leg cramps."

Jamie wanted to defend Zak but he couldn't talk. His heart was thundering in his ears. Air was getting trapped halfway to his chest. He fell to his knees. *I'm fucking dying.*

*****

Mae stood in the wellness center parking lot with the other runners who had finished, watching the empty street for the missing competitors. When Zak and Melody came into sight, she was stunned to see the couple arrive hand in hand and lent her voice to the cheer that greeted them. Had Jamie seen them? He would love this. Where was he? He should be on his way up for the awards and the parade.

Orville Geronimo, standing on a low platform with a view of the finish line and the time clock, called out Melody's number and her time with a little chuckle in his voice. Had it been anyone else, Mae would have found his laughter mean, but she had caught onto his humor, though she still had trouble with his accent, so thick his English sounded like Apache. "Good job, Melody Chino Fatty. That's what this run is all about. Zak, my man, you're a winner for running with her."

Melody was, as she'd predicted, last. Orville hadn't even given Zak's time, obviously considering him to have sacrificed his place in the ten K to support his wife. Zak had made himself look like a hero by coming with her, but Mae wondered if he really was one. He might have preferred to quit rather than lose and found an excuse in Melody.

One of the Boys and Girls Club youths appeared beside Mae. "That was so cool. I wish my sister would run. She's big like Zak's wife, and this race is, like, a diabetes prevention awareness thing."

"Maybe she saw them. She might get inspired."

"Maybe." He kicked a pebble. "She doesn't have a husband like Zak, though. Her husband's kind of an asshole."

And Zak isn't? "She's got a brother, though."

The boy looked up, bit his lip, and nodded.

Zak and Melody approached the refreshment table. Melody high-fived with several people, laughed, grabbed an orange wedge, sucked it dry, and took another. Zak fist-bumped with the boy, exchanged a few words with him, and gave Mae a long look. Not flirting this time, and not happy.

"Where'd you leave Bernadette?" she asked.

"With Jamie." Zak twisted the cap off a bottle of water and drank. "At the church. They should have been here by now, at the rate we came up that hill. They could have beaten us—even the way Baldy walks." Zak imitated the little catch in Jamie's stride.

"Don't be mean." Melody wiped orange juice from her lips. "They wouldn't steal my thunder. And *you* can stop trying. Jamie loves the parade. They'll come up for that."

Mae asked Zak, "Was that photographer still with him?"

Zak finished the water in a few slugs and left the bottle lying sideways on the table. Without an explanation, he took off, dodging through the crowd waiting for the winners to be called.

"*She* was back there?" Melody picked up his bottle and crushed it, then pitched it into a trash bin. "I should have known that supportive husband shit was an act."

"If he's trying to stop her from talking to Jamie, he actually did put you ahead by leaving her." Melody rolled her eyes, and Mae conceded. "For a few minutes." Like any of Zak's better moments, it didn't last.

Orville Geronimo spoke through the loudspeaker. "All right. Listen up. The winners of this year's Mescalero five and ten K runs are ..." He seemed to relish the word Mescalero, saying it slowly with a kind of flourish. "First place for the ten K event, as well as first place for women under twenty, Heidi Chee."

A round of applause greeted the girl who had beaten all the men. She walked up to a table near the finish line where a woman hung a medal on a red, white, and blue ribbon around the girl's neck.

"Second place for the event and first place for men fifty and up—"

Orville announced Michael Pena's award. Mae kept looking down the road for Jamie. When her name was called, she felt conspicuous as an outsider going up for a medal, even though she got a cheer from Bernadette's relatives.

Mae rejoined Melody, and a sudden urge overcame her. She took the ribbon off her neck and hung it around Melody's. "I tried to talk you out of running, and I was wrong. You earned this."

Melody hugged her, whispering in her ear, "Damned right I did. My feet are killing me. My back is screaming. And I got blisters on my thighs all the way to my twat."

After the five K medals were given out, the runners took off their numbers and went out to the street with the spectators lining up along the parade route. While Melody visited the first aid station inside the wellness center, Mae borrowed her phone to call Jamie. "Hey, sugar. You on your way?"

"Yeah." Silence. "Be there in a minute. Mel all right?"

"In a way. She's hurting, but it was worth it to her. You sound funny."

A long pause. "Had a wobbly." Then a bright, cheery tone. "No worries, though. Wasn't a bad one. Catcha."

No worries? A "wobbly" meant a panic attack. It was a good thing that Melody had thought of that possibility and not let him watch the children. A good thing, too, that Bernadette had stopped with him. Mae trusted Jamie, but she still didn't like to think of Letitia taking care of him.

Melody emerged from the building with large adhesive bandages and a slick of antibiotic ointment on her inner thighs. As they walked to the parade route, the main road downhill through the center of the town, Mae had to slow down for Melody's tiny waddling steps. The Apache woman sighed. "How do fat people ever exercise enough to lose weight?"

"Bike. Swim. Lift weights. Just about anything's easier than running when you're heavy." Melody had to be thinking about the chafing, not just the effort or sore muscles. "Lycra pants help, too."

"I'll never hear the end of it if I get Lycra pants. They keep you from jiggling, though? Like a sports bra for your ass?"

Mae laughed, though she wasn't sure if Melody was joking or serious. "I don't know. I never thought about it."

"It'd serve Zak right. Have my big ass running around in some shiny tights. He'd be so embarrassed."

"Are you sure? He *did* finish the race with you. You don't think he'd be happy?"

"If I got in shape, yeah. But not until then." She stopped, pulling the legs of her shorts back down from where they'd ridden up between her thighs. "No. Even then, he wouldn't be happy. If I looked good, he'd just go back to being jealous."

Zak could have some insecurity under his arrogant surface, something that drove him to play the hero. And although Jamie had said Zak was over some old high school drama, he'd acted jealous when he'd refused to let Melody visit Will. "Did he used to get jealous of Will?"

"Hugely." They resumed walking. "Partly 'cause Will's dad has that nice big ranch and Zak's family has nothing. Partly on account of me. He puts up with Will now for Tana's sake, but he still likes to one-up him. Calls being a rodeo rider useless."

Jamie had called him useless, too. "I guess compared to being an EMT and a firefighter it is."

"And compared to being Michael Pena, it all is."

"Zak's jealous of Michael, too?"

"Big time. He used to want to *be* him. The way Jamie wanted to be an opera singer."

The career detour had upset Jamie deeply for a while. He was happy with his musical path now, but he hadn't always been. Zak might have struggled also, adjusting to his alternative to military service. Service which had not ended well, though Zak seemed suited to the army. He'd been competent and focused when Will got trampled, and genuinely caring with the teenaged runners, a positive authority figure. "I bet Zak would have made a good soldier. A good officer."

Melody fell silent, her face as closed as it had been when Mae first met her. *Sore spot. A bad one.*

When they reached the corner, Elaine and Pearl and most of the Pena, Fatty, and Tsilnothos families were already there, with lawn chairs for watching the parade in comfort. Pearl's husband got up and offered Melody his seat. She sank into it with a groan and thanked him. He tugged on the medal. "First place, huh? I musta been watching it backwards."

Melody grinned. "Guess you were."

Leah and Chamiqua Pena parked the napping twins' stroller in front of her and began to report on all the activities they had done during the race to wear them out.

"Where's Bernadette?" Pearl asked.

"I see her," said one of her sons. "Across the street, with that black dude."

The black dude, with his pink-and-green-banded straw fedora on his blond hair, stood out in the crowd. He and Bernadette crossed the street, Jamie with a worse-than-usual hitch in his bad hip, just before the first car of the parade came around the corner at the top of the hill. Miss Mescalero, in her white princess headdress and beaded white deerskin regalia, rode on the folded soft-top of an old convertible, waving and tossing candy.

"Fuck," Jamie muttered, rubbing his hip. He bent down and picked up a chocolate Tootsie Pop, twisted the paper off, and popped the candy in his mouth. The stick bobbed up and down as he spoke. He gave Melody an off-kilter smile. "Great race. Proud of ya."

"Great cheer." She grinned. "Mae, you should have seen him. Jumping like a cheerleader. It was the funniest thing."

His shoulders wriggled and he looked away, sucking noisily on the Tootsie Pop and rocking rapidly on his feet. Something was making him anxious. Was it something Letitia had told him? Mae excused herself and Jamie. They moved away from Bernadette's family to sit on the curb at the feet of strangers. Floats from the casino and other local businesses passed, their occupants tossing out more candy.

Jamie groaned as he descended. "Jeezus. Need a new body."

Mae rubbed his back. "I like the one you got."

"Feels like crap, though." The sucker knocked against his teeth as he talked. He had it tucked in his cheek like a squirrel carrying nuts. "Not just my hip. Did that bloody cheerleader dance and my legs turned to fucking Jell-O. Heart pounding. Sweating. Had to lie down. Wasn't as bad as usual. Didn't go blind and stop breathing, but ... I can't quite come back from it."

Mae took his hand, and they watched the parade in silence for a moment. She would need to wait to quiz him on the photographer.

Jamie snort-laughed suddenly. "Feel bad for Bernadette. Scared the bloody crap out of her. She was there in case *Mel* collapsed. And she ended up looking after *me*."

"That's not funny, sugar."

"Yeah, it is. I was practically unconscious after I did this stupid dance for *one minute*, and Mel is five times fatter than I am and she was the fucking little engine that could."

"It had nothing to do with your fitness, what happened to you. Do you know what triggered it?"

"Yeah. Stupid crap. Jumping like a frog after two tanks of coffee."

"That wasn't stupid, but ..." Jamie could go into a mini-panic just paying attention to his heart in the middle of the night. Abrupt, intense exertion and two of his enormous travel mugs cups of coffee, as strong as he brewed it, could have sent him into a tailspin. "That's a lot of coffee for you."

Jamie bit on the sucker so hard its shell cracked and began chewing. "For *me*. Jeezus. Are we done with Jamie the fucking sick person?"

Mae started to answer, but held back. He'd swung through three moods in less than ten minutes. No, four moods. Gloomy and worried, then laughing, then self-deprecating, and then angry with her. She wanted to tell him she *was* done with Jamie the sick person, but that wouldn't help. And she didn't mean it. When she'd taken the risk of this relationship, she'd known what she was getting into.

Jamie rubbed his eyes, and then pushed his fingers into his hair beneath his hat. "Sorry."

Mood number five. Mae put her arm around him. He returned the gesture and wriggled a little, making a soft, happy humming noise. *That's six. Stop counting.*

A marching band whose banner proclaimed them to be the Navajo Nation Band approached, led by a trim middle-aged woman in a short majorette skirt, twirling two batons with style and grace. Mae said, "She's amazing."

"Yeah. She's here every year. Saw her the first time when I was fourteen. Zak said she was hot, or whatever we called good-looking women back then."

"Speaking of women Zak thinks are hot, I saw you with Letitia. What'd you two talk about?"

"Meant to tell you. Forgot—wobbly, y'know? Fogged my head. Dunno where she took off to when I went down. Jeezus. She likes my music, and then she saw *that* and left—fuck." Jamie tucked the bare stick of the sucker into his shirt pocket. "Shouldn't have had that. Need to brush my teeth. Anyway, she was at the church taking pictures of the art. She sort of hinted like Zak's posing for pictures. In the nuddy."

Mae thought of Orville and Lonnie joking about Letitia's calendars. "He might be." As long as he didn't smile. "Orville met her. He said she does calendars."

Jamie leaned forward and picked up another sucker from the street. "Don't think Zak wanted me to know." He unwrapped the Tootsie Pop and sniffed it before putting it in his mouth. "Think she was trying to get me to hire her for some photography, too. Not naked, though. Only half." He frowned, and paused while the band was too close and loud for talking. As they marched further on, he said, "Wonder if she comes onto blokes with that."

"It might work. Zak likes older women."

"The Navajo baton lady. Not all older women. And Letitia's not *older*-older."

"Did you get a sense of what she feels for Zak?"

"Not really. Might have if I hadn't collapsed. Kind of killed the conversation, y'know? She's as big a flirt as he is, though. Might not mean much. Hard to tell."

"Melody would rather know he's posing for a naked calendar than think he's cheating."

"I know." Jamie sighed, exhaling a scent of grape candy. "But—not that he'd do it, but—the two things aren't ...whaddya-callit ... *mutually exclusive*, are they?"

Far from it. And there had to be something else going on between them as well. Zak wouldn't have had the calendars in his toolshed, and he'd made a visit too short for a modeling session.

A flatbed truck carrying a country band came around the corner, their music clashing with that of the Navajo marching band. A stocky Apache woman stood at an electric piano, belting out a song in a powerful contralto, while an all-male band, some white, some Indian, played guitars and drums behind her. The band's name, emblazoned on the bass drum, was Lorilee Chino and the Cowboy Indians.

"Melody's mum," Jamie said, projecting to operatic level to be heard.

Mae knew her small voice would be inaudible, but guessed Jamie could read her lips. "She's good."

"Yeah. Not bad for country. Mel can sing like that, too. Doesn't anymore, but she could."

Misty, who had run the five K and come in third, danced in the street behind the truck, carrying a large canvas bag from which she was tossing out toothbrushes and sample tubes of toothpaste. She'd put on a T-shirt from a dental clinic whose logo was on the bag as well. Miming brushing her large, very white teeth, she flashed an exaggerated smile at a child who ran out to grab candy. Maybe the future dentist hadn't totally sacrificed her dreams for Reno. Mae would have to do the work she'd agreed to, and do it soon, to make sure of it.

She picked up a toothbrush and toothpaste and handed them to Jamie. He put a hand to his heart and tucked the items into his shirt pocket beside the first sucker stick.

Waving and beckoning to someone, Misty broke off from following the float, danced over to Mae and paused in front of her. Montana pushed through the crowd toward them. When her sister was within a few feet, Misty gave her a thumbs-up and resumed dancing and tossing toothbrushes.

Montana crouched beside Mae and spoke into her ear. "Can you come with me? Will wants you to heal him."

Chapter Sixteen

"Sorry to act all secret agent-y," Montana said as she led Mae around to the rear entrance of the wellness center. "I don't think anyone could hear me over Mom's band, but I wanted to make sure. This is confidential."

When Mae left with Montana, Jamie's expression had been open and perky, more *what's up* than *what the fuck*. Mae doubted he'd overheard. She had scarcely made out Montana's words herself. "I think we're okay."

They sat on the steps overlooking a steep hill and another street. The place was quiet, shady, and deserted.

Montana slid a thin gold band with a mere chip of diamond up and down her finger. "Will's having a really hard time in the hospital. He can't smoke in there, and he usually dips when he's in places where he can't smoke. They won't let him do that, either. Or drink. Not that he's an alcoholic. He just wants a drink to get him through not having tobacco."

The ready excuse about drinking, defending Will before he'd even been criticized, reminded Mae of how she'd been with Mack. Covering up his behavior to others while hurt and frustrated by it herself.

"Anyway," Montana said, "Misty told me you can cure people. That you cured this man who smoked a lot and he didn't even want to quit. Could you go with me to see Will? Fix him?"

"I don't know that *fix* is the right word. Does Will want me to help?"

"I talked to him about you. I'm pretty sure he does."

"Wouldn't he rather have one of the medicine people?"

"No, see, that's the thing. You go to a medicine man, he doesn't just cure you. It's complicated. You have to do a lot of talking, and ceremonies, and there are things you need to do to get ready be-

207

fore and to follow up after. Will's not into that. He's not traditional. And he's not patient."

Mae shook her head. "If he thinks he'll get fast results, I can't promise that. I mean, I won't have elaborate ceremonies or need to talk a lot, but usually what I do as a healer is more like a nudge than a miracle. What happened with Niall quitting smoking wasn't normal."

"That's okay. We won't tell anyone if it doesn't work. Or if it does, actually." Montana glanced around as if someone could be eavesdropping, though there was clearly no one around. "That's why it's a secret. If he quits everything, he wants people to think he did it himself."

With that attitude, he didn't sound spiritual at all, let alone not traditional. Nonetheless, if he was motivated, he could change his habits while he was young, before he was coughing like Niall was. Before he got cancer or emphysema. Before he turned into a drunk like Mack. "When does he want me to come?"

Montana took her phone from her pocket and texted. "Right away."

The parade was still in full swing, with a middle school marching band followed by the dancing Zuni firefighters. Mae crouched beside Jamie and told him she was leaving for a healing client, her face in the crinkly cloud of his hair so she could make herself heard over the drums and horns.

Jamie drew back and gave her the baby seal look. "This is our weekend together, and you're going off to take care of fucking *Will Baca*?"

His voice was so strong she could hear him easily over the band, while she had barely been able to hear Montana over her mother's amplified country music. Jamie couldn't have made out Will's name. He had to be guessing.

"You don't know who the client is, sugar."

He stood and walked toward the back of the crowd. Except for the Tootsie Pop, he fit the cliché of "a face like thunder." Mae followed him. Standing a few feet behind the last row of parade-watchers, Jamie glared at her. "Who in bloody hell else is Montana going to want healed? Her worthless boyfriend fell off a bull."

"And you've fallen off a few rocks in your life. You've nearly died. You've had broken bones and surgeries. I should think you'd have a little more empathy for something that traumatic."

"So it *is* Will."

"It's confidential. He doesn't want anyone to know."

"Then he should get one of the medicine men. I know they're mostly doing the ceremonies, but Lonnie's free. Or Bessie Yahnaki. Why you?"

"I'm not an Apache medicine person. That's why. He's not traditional."

Jamie took the sucker out of his mouth and got it stuck in his goatee. "Fuck." He turned away and stamped his foot. "Bloody fucking hell."

Mae tried not to laugh. He was so angry with her, and now even angrier with himself for this bizarre little accident. She wanted to respect his feelings but it was simply too funny, and she began to giggle uncontrollably.

"I left my water bottle in the van. I need to—ah, *fuck.*" Jamie held his hands over the absurd appendage attached to his chin and faced Mae again. "Will's a wanker. He's—Jeezus. Are you listening?"

"I am." Mae wiped the tears of laughter from her face. "I'm sorry." She suppressed the next explosion of hilarity as best she could.

"I know you don't like him, but that video was trivial. It's not a big deal compared to what he's been through."

"It's not just the fucking video. There's something wrong with him. Like he just *needs* to be bad. He thought Mel was more fun 'cause she was Zak's girlfriend, and that drinking and smoking were more fun 'cause he was underage."

"A lot of kids think like that. They get a kick out of breaking rules."

"Nah. He was worse than that. He'd steal stuff for the hell of it. Didn't need a thing—the Bacas are better off than anybody on the rez—but he'd take stuff. One time he and Mel and I were walking to the store to get sodas, and we passed this truck parked at the gas pumps with groceries in the back. Will stole a carton of orange juice from one of the bags. Bloody wanker acted like that juice was the best thing he'd ever tasted, just for being stolen, y'know? Mel was stoned, so she was laughing at him, like 'I can't believe you just did that.' But he thought he'd *impressed* her, y'know? He'd light up a reefer and dare her to smoke it with him in public, in broad daylight. I was scared they'd get caught and she'd get arrested, but he didn't care. He's like a psychopath, y'know?"

Mae lost the urge to laugh. This was not funny anymore, even with Jamie hiding his afflicted beard. "You're saying Will doesn't have a conscience?"

"Never acted like he did."

The prospect of healing someone so deeply flawed was troubling. Will probably only expected help with his addictions, not his entire character, but if he lost those bad habits and didn't change, what would happen? She would need to reach him deeply.

Ezra trotted up with a bottle of water and a wet paper towel and handed them to Jamie. "Peanut butter works really good for getting candy out of your hair, but warm water's good, too. This one's been in my sister's car all day."

"Thanks, mate." Jamie calmed noticeably and began to soak his beard. "How'd you notice?"

"You're you. I asked Grandma and she said to come for lunch and a shower after the parade. You need to give me a grocery list so Mom can shop for what you're cooking."

Mae thanked Ezra and added, "I'll be late for lunch. Maybe two or three hours. Should I still come?"

"Of course. You're on Indian time here. Things start when everybody's ready and finish when everybody's done."

"Great. I'll call Jamie for directions when I'm on my way."

Jamie gave Mae a tired little smile, all the fire gone out of him. "Can't kiss you—too sticky. Drive safe. Catcha."

She watched him walk back to the parade with the boy, drained but peaceful. An Ezra effect, or an end to their argument? All three of the Chino sisters had now asked for her help, and all three times Jamie hadn't liked it.

As Mae and Montana entered the hospital room, Will Baca pressed a button on his bed to elevate his head and shoulders. A boy Mae recognized from the race sat in the chair next to the bed, a teenager with short thick hair that flopped onto his forehead, and a pretty, almost girlish face, contrasting with his hard wiry body. Both men were small, no more than five-foot-six, and Will might once have been as sweet faced as his little brother, but his nose was slightly crooked with a bump in the middle and a scar ran from his upper lip to his left nostril. His hands were scarred, too, and rough, lying on the white sheet, the right one restless, the left one lifeless at the end of a cast that wrapped the arm. On that hand, his fine-boned fingers had thin horizontal scars below the second knuckle like they'd been sliced by a knife. His eyes were glazed and tired.

"This her?"

Montana nodded. "Mae Martin. Yes."

"Good. Refugio, wait outside, head off Mom and Dad if they get here." The boy rose and Montana started to take his place, but Will shook his head. "You, too. This is private."

She looked hurt but followed his brother out and closed the door.

Will fixed his weary eyes on Mae. "All right. Let's get this over with. Do the thing."

She reached into her purse and wrapped her hand around the velvet pouch of crystals. Will had made it sound like she was going to pull a kid's loose tooth. He needed to understand there was substance to her work, even if she wasn't doing a long, complex ceremony. "I know you want this to be simple. But can we take a minute so I can be sure I know what you need?" She put the crystals on the bedside table and rested her hands on the bed rail.

"Clean me out. Get rid of everything." Will turned his head toward the window. "Your life really does pass before your eyes. *Slowly*. I watched a whole damned movie while that bull was trying to kill me. And it was a bad one."

A man who both dipped and smoked had a serious tobacco habit, but that wouldn't make his life a bad movie. Mae knew he didn't want the long talk a medicine man would ask of him, but it helped her as a healer to know the scope of the problem. Will sounded as though he might have a conscience after all, or at least some regrets. "I've been told you use a lot of tobacco and that you drink. Is that everything? Or do you need some other stuff cleaned out?"

"Weed. Women." Will glanced at the door. "Gambling." His right hand bunched up a fistful of the sheet. "Done a few other things I'd rather not say."

"More than your brother knows about? Or Montana?"

He nodded. "I never killed anyone, nothing like that. Just stupid stuff. Debts. You know how it is."

She didn't, but took a guess at some kind of theft, maybe lifting from easy targets the way he had as a kid, or stealing from a girlfriend's purse. He'd said women were one of his problems. If he was cheating on Montana and had gambling debts, he could easily have done something to make the bad movie.

Mae waited for more, but Will seemed to have said all he was willing to share. She began sorting through her crystals, choosing ametrine to promote transformation, ruby and garnet to help with both change and stability, and Apache tear for healing old wounds. Amethyst would boost her intuitive powers and also ease Will's addictions.

Will peered at her hands. "What are you doing?"

She held them open so he could see. "I'm gonna put some crystals on your body. They help me channel the healing. You may feel some emotions, or you might feel heat or light, or have images in your head. I had one lady bust out laughing while I healed her. That's all normal. Just lie still and let it happen. Okay?"

"Fine. As long as it's quick and no religion."

"No religion. I promise that."

Mae laid the red stones on his lower belly, put the black Apache tear stone in his right palm, the ametrine on his diaphragm, and added another—leafy green tree agate—on his heart, to aid his renewal and letting go. Holding the amethyst, she took time to clear her thoughts and calm her body and breath, and then rested her hand on Will's head. She sensed he was ready. Her work would be to loosen the memories or energy scars that clung to the drugs, the gambling, the old way of life.

While she sought the root of the problem, she hoped to send energy to remove it without having to see it, but the tunnel that signaled a psychic journey overtook her vision. It swirled her through a layer of colors, then fog and darkness, bringing her awareness to a rocky clearing in deep but spacious pine woods.

Will, aged thirteen or so, with a girl Mae recognized as a young Melody, sat on a broad stone outcropping that formed a shelf in the steep slope, sharing a joint and a bottle of wine. Sunlight dappled the rock and threw bright spots on their hair and limbs. Lowing cows sounded not far away. Melody stood, wobbling, and tossed the wine bottle into a plastic barrel on which someone had drawn a planet earth with its tongue hanging out over the hand-lettered words, *Save Our Mother*. Below this, a badly drawn cartoon of Smokey Bear with a doobie between his lips bore the caption, *Put it Out*.

"I feel like I'm slo—oow." Melody giggled, imitating the cows.

She lost her balance, landing in Will's lap. He flopped backward and they laughed harder, rolling into each other's arms and kissing.

The tunnel moved Mae's vision through flash images of Will in bars, at rodeos, in hotels, always drinking or smoking tobacco or weed, or tucking a dip behind his lip. Will at casinos playing slots. The visions slowed finally at a cluster of bland apartments with flat treeless lawns. Will was young, his nose straight, his lip unscarred. He parked a dented pickup with a camper shell, got out and looked around, then grabbed two six-packs from the passenger seat and strolled to one of the apartments, whistling. Balancing both six-packs in one arm, he rang the bell.

Melody, a little heavier but still a beauty, opened the door. "God, it's good to see you. I'm so glad you got in touch. I've been bored out of my mind here."

"Zak won't let you get in any trouble," Will said with a laugh, setting the beer on the coffee table. "That's your problem."

They hugged. Melody said, "He gets *himself* in trouble trying to keep me out of it. The sober guy starting a fight at a party because somebody got me to play beer pong. It'd be funny, except his commander doesn't think so."

"Hell—that *is* funny. But I guess we'd better not play beer pong."

The vision blurred. Melody and Will lounged on couch cushions on the living room floor, and he was rolling a joint. Most of the beer cans on the coffee table were still in their six-pack rings, but two were open, and a couple more lay crushed and empty. The door opened, and Zak, in army fatigues, froze, then slammed the door shut.

"What the hell?" He strode across the room and hauled Will to his feet. "My wife has been trying to get clean and you *dare* show your sorry ass? I told you to stay away—"

"I'm not fucking her, for crissakes, we—"

"You would be once you got her drunk enough." Still holding Will by the shoulders, Zak kicked one of the six-packs across the room. "This could kill her. Do you understand?" He shook Will, shouting in his face. "Kill her."

"She had *one* beer—"

"She can't stop at one." Zak pushed Will to the floor, pinning him down. "But you don't give a shit as long as you can get her drunk and shove your dick in her. I'm trying to save her life and you don't care if you kill her. I should kill *you*."

Melody screamed. Will tried to buck free, but Zak struck a blow to Will's face that snapped his head back. Blood poured from the smaller man's nose. Melody begged Zak to stop.

Someone banged on the door. A woman's voice called, "What's going on? Melody? Are you all right?"

Zak struck again and Will went slack. The neighbor opened the door.

Mae pulled back from the vision, barely able to keep her trance. Any more of this story would be too much. It was already too much. But the Sight had showed her the wounds, the places in Will's heart that needed healing. Mae wanted to think about Zak and Melody, but she focused on Will again, quieting her reaction, and the tunnel retook her.

When it opened, she saw him in a Jeep parked on a dirt access road behind a strip mall. The angle of the light and shadows suggested late afternoon or early evening. The back door of one of the shops was open. Will got out, scanned the area, and made a phone call. A few seconds later, a large blue parrot flew out the door in a burst of flapping as if someone had given it a liftoff and landed at his feet.

Startled, Mae lost the vision and became aware of the faint hum of the lights, the sound of voices in the corridor. She needed to finish the healing before her analytical mind or her emotions took over and she lost her trance completely. Drawing on whatever source the healing power came from, she asked it to reach Will's stuck and broken places. She moved her hands over the crystals she'd placed on him, holding the connection until she sensed a vibration at each location and a kind of shifting, like muscles relaxing at a subtle level, soul muscles ceasing to grip and grasp.

Will exhaled with a groan. Mae brought her hands to his feet, then back to his head, closing the healing. She waited until she felt peace, and let go.

"Okay, Will. I'm done. You may want to be quiet for a while. Just relax and let the change soak in."

He nodded and lay still. Mae used snow quartz to cleanse herself of his energy traces and put the crystals she'd used into the separate pouch for those that needed rebalancing in sunlight or salt water.

After tapping softly on the door, Refugio opened it a crack. "I heard you talking. Are you done? Can we come in?"

Will opened his eyes and tipped his head to the right to indicate his bedside table. "Yeah. I need you to pay her."

Mae started to object. "I didn't expect—"

"And I didn't either. I changed my mind."

Refugio opened the drawer and took out a battered wallet. His brother said, "Give her what's in it."

The boy extracted a twenty and offered it to Mae. It wasn't much for her effort, time, and gas, but it was more than she suspected Will could spare. His injury reminded her of when Jamie had been hurt and couldn't play his instruments. She pushed the money away. "I have a special rate for cowboys who can't ride."

"But what about partners in the Baca Ranch who come home to roost?"

Refugio sounded skeptical. "Seriously, bro? You're gonna stay for real this time?"

Will gave his injured arm a rueful look. "What do you think?"

Refugio handed Mae the twenty and put the wallet back. "Mom and Dad will need some convincing."

"Call 'em for me, would you?" Will said. "We'll convince them."

Montana rushed toward his bed, tears in her eyes, arms reaching out to him. Will held up his hand, shook his head, and let the hand fall. "Sit down. Let me rest a minute. Then ..." He looked at Refugio and back at Montana. "We need to be alone, babe. And talk."

Chapter Seventeen

The hour alone on Mae's return trip to Mescalero gave her a chance to think. She had driven herself to the hospital rather than riding with Montana, so Will's fiancée could stay with him. Mae doubted the couple's time together was going to be as joyous as Montana had hoped. More likely, their talk was going to be a hard one.

Part of what Mae had healed had to do with Melody. The first vision might have shown the root of Will's troubles. Early substance use was all it took for some kids to end up with problems. He might have romanticized his bad habits, too. Having his relationship with Melody entangled with them gave the addictions an extra layer of power.

There was nothing romantic about how things had turned out, though. Zak's fight with Will must have been the last straw that led to his other-than-honorable discharge. Elaine's claim that Zak had been trying to be honorable made sense now. He'd been out of control, but no doubt in his version of the story he'd been a hero.

For once, Mae couldn't judge him. She understood his rage. In what turned out to be the final month of her first marriage, she'd seen Mack with an old girlfriend staggering out of the bar at the hotel where Mae worked as a front desk clerk, and heading not to the parking lot but down a corridor of rooms. Risking her job, she had followed and screamed at them, telling Mack not to come home. Though she hadn't hit him or the girl, she'd felt like it, felt like grabbing something and throwing it at them. If she hadn't been in that bare corridor without even a potted plant in sight, she might have. She'd been lucky not to get fired. Zak had been in the wrong—but Mae got it.

Disturbing as the fight was, it was less surprising than the final vision. The fight hadn't come out of nowhere. Mae knew about Melody's relationship with Will, her alcohol and drug problems, and Zak's discharge. Jamie had warned her that Will liked to break rules for the hell of it, so drinking and getting high with his married ex-girlfriend fit her expectations of his character. But she didn't have any context for Will and the parrot.

Had he by sheer chance been behind the exotic bird store when the parrots flew out? It was unlikely, and yet it was equally hard to believe that Shelli had *sent* them to him. Jamie believed that someone had found the birds and kept them. What were the odds that Will had found them and sold them? He was, according to Jamie, both a reckless risk-taker and a casual thief.

Mae couldn't ask Will for the rest of the story—or tell anyone what she'd learned. This was like what a priest heard in confession or the confidences shared in a psychologist's office. Private. Even more so, because in her case, the client didn't know what he'd revealed.

When she reached Mescalero, she called Jamie for directions to Bessie Yahnaki's house, and then took a winding country road past evergreen forests and open pastures. The view reminded her of her vision of Will and Melody in the woods. Had the healing triggered Will's memories of the same events? Or had he already seen them in his "bad movie"? Mae regretted knowing so much about Will and Zak, and yet she wished she'd stayed focused to see more of the parrot incident. No—if she'd seen more, she would be even more tempted to share it with Jamie, and she couldn't. Will didn't even want the healing itself talked about.

She pulled in at a double-wide trailer in a grassy hollow with a creek running through it. The place gave her a peaceful feeling. Maybe she and Jamie would finally have a pleasant time together here. Something to make up for the way the weekend had gone so far.

A sturdy, broad-faced woman, her gray hair hanging down her back in a single long braid, stood watering the vegetable garden that took up nearly a third of the yard. She wore a floral dress and sensible shoes, and leaned on a three-pronged aluminum cane. Bessie reminded Mae of her Granma Rhoda-Sue Jackson, the folk healer. She'd loved to work in her garden, dressed the same way, and had the same sturdy build, soft and old-womanly but strong.

There were several cars in the driveway in addition to Stan and Addie's red Fusion hybrid and Jamie's van. Mae guessed the older vehicle with handicapped plates was Bessie's, and the rest had to belong to her relatives.

Under the shade of a small deck, a fat brown mutt and a shaggy black-and-white one barely lifted their heads. As Mae climbed out of her car and approached, the brown dog gave a small, whispery woof, and both dozed again. Bessie lowered the hose and made her way to the side of the trailer to turn it off. A smile lifting her full cheeks and deepening the crow's-feet lines around her eyes, she reached out and took Mae's hand. "Bernadette speaks highly of you."

Mae felt as if Bessie could see through her. The medicine woman was warm and relaxed, not at all challenging, yet the sensation was powerful, and Mae felt self-conscious as she spoke. "And of you."

Jamie came bouncing out the door. "Ready for tomatoes." His hair was restrained by a blue bandana tied into a tight little cap. Combined with his gold-toothed smile, the effect was oddly fierce and piratical. "You're not late for lunch, love. It's taken that long. Had to get people here, get food, shower ..."

He started down the steps at a jog, then stopped abruptly as if his left hip had caused him a jolt of pain and changed to a walk. With only a faint hesitation, he passed the sleeping dogs, taking an arc around their lair.

"Not bad," Bessie said. "My lazy dogs don't scare you anymore?"

Jamie let out his breath and slipped his arm around Mae. "Been working on it." He kissed her ear. "Sorry I was grouchy earlier. Everything go all right?"

"Yeah, thanks." Was it going to be that easy? No fight to finish up? "Do we need to pick tomatoes?"

"Yeah. One for everyone."

Bessie listed people by name rather than counting, picking tomatoes and handing them to Mae and Jamie, one fruit per name. As an only child of parents who had left each other and their roots, Mae wasn't used to such large clans and gatherings. She had barely gotten the names of half of Bernadette's family down, and now she would have to learn the Yahnakis as well. Jamie gave Mae most of the tomatoes and juggled a few while Bessie walked ahead of them to the house.

Ezra's mother, whom Bessie introduced as her daughter-in-law Cheryl, opened the door, letting them into the packed and noisy living room. After depositing tomatoes in the kitchen, Jamie escorted Mae to the bathroom, showing her where he'd hung her clean clothes on the back of the door and where he'd put her lotions and deodorant on a shelf, then hugged her and drew back, toying with her hands. She'd hardly needed the tour, but she suspected he needed to make up for being angry with her over helping Will. To be the good boyfriend who thought of everything, and for her to notice.

She stroked his cheek. "Thanks, sugar."

"Does my beard look funny?"

"Hmm. Kinda." It was a little scraggly, as if he'd torn a few hairs in his impatience to get free of the candy. "It won't show if you braid it."

He laughed. "Don't let me have any more lollipops. You get along all right with Will?"

"I think so." She tripped over the urge to tell him Will might have stolen the parrots. "But I shouldn't talk about it. It's private. Let me get cleaned up, okay? You've got a lunch to finish cooking."

"Yeah. Sorry." He kissed her and left, closing the door.

The hot water refreshed her body, but her mind wouldn't unwind. She wished she *could* tell someone about her visions. Could she talk with Bessie, one healer to another? No. She didn't have Will's permission. And certainly not Zak's. What she really needed to ask Bessie was how to stop seeing what she didn't want to know. How to heal people without her psychic gift intruding.

When Mae returned to the living room after her shower, she saw little chance of an opening to get to know Bessie at all, let alone ask questions about healing. Cheryl introduced her to everyone, another inundation of new names and faces. None of the guests drank alcohol, but they were as lively as if they did. The kitchen adjoined the living room directly, with people crowded at the kitchen table while others ate from plates in their laps. Off and on during the meal, Jamie wandered around with a bowl of salad, talking and joking while adding servings to plates, and then made a circuit with a tray of bean burritos slathered in green chile, offering second helpings of these as well. He circled with the cornbread last. Mae liked how easily he mingled with people he hadn't seen for two years, and admired how he'd managed a meal that would be healthy for all the diabetics Ezra had mentioned. Where *was* Ezra?

She finished eating and took her plate to the kitchen. Jamie squeezed her bottom on his way to the oven, dancing a little. He slipped a pair of oven mitts on and extracted two sticky-looking brown pies. "Peanut butter and dark chocolate. Sweetened with brown rice syrup." He sounded proud of this. "They need to cool a minute. Want coffee?"

"Thanks, yes. Have you seen Ezra?"

"Out back. Having a shy spell."

Mae couldn't blame him. She was ready to have a shy spell herself, and went out to join the boy.

Ezra sat alone at a picnic table in the backyard, absorbed in creating a piece of beadwork, a half-eaten lunch beside him. Without looking up from his work, he took a bite of salad, made a face, and added another bead.

"Hey." Mae sat across from him. "Don't you like vegetables?"

"I do. But the dressing is funny. Don't tell Jamie."

It was balsamic vinaigrette. Mae wouldn't have liked it when she was twelve, either. "Can I see what you're making?"

He laid the small rectangle of beadwork on the table, a geometric design that reminded her of a sunrise over a mountain. "It's for a hatband for my father. The pattern will repeat a lot. He's got a big head."

This was said seriously; Mae didn't think Ezra was making fun of his father's large head. "It's beautiful."

The boy resumed beading, took a bite of cornbread, and glanced at Mae. "Jamie said you went to see to Will Baca."

Mae drew in a breath. "He shouldn't have told you."

"It's okay. He only told me and Grandma. He was mad at you for doing it and he needed to talk."

Of course. Jamie had to talk to sort out his feelings. He'd made a mistake in mentioning what Will wanted kept private, but in a way Mae was glad of it. Now she *could* talk with Bessie about the healing.

The back door opened and Bessie started down the steps. Ezra popped to his feet and helped her, though she had adequate assistance from her cane. She sat beside him, told him to finish his lunch and go in so she could talk with Mae. The dogs ambled around the house and lay under the table near Bessie's feet.

"Can I stay if I'm quiet?" Ezra asked. "I want to learn from what you teach her."

"All right," Bessie said. "But you'll need to go in and get us some coffee when it's ready. And a little piece of that pie."

Bessie folded her hands on the table. She spoke to Mae without looking at her, attentive yet focused inward. "I understand you helped one of our people."

"I tried."

Jamie opened the kitchen window and announced that coffee was ready. Ezra rose and went inside.

Bessie spoke softly. "Is Jamie doing well now? He seems happy."

There was no simple answer to that question, but Bessie had to know that if she knew Jamie. "He's working on it."

"Stan mentioned he's got a gift, too. And that it came out just this summer."

"He doesn't like using it."

"Jamie's a late bloomer for a healer and a seer. It's a lot for him to handle."

"I know. The only way he uses his gift is ..." Mae hoped the truth wouldn't make Jamie sound silly. She respected his efforts to cope with an unwanted ability. "He practices on his cat."

"Good." Bessie nodded. "Beginners should be careful." She finally looked straight at Mae.

Does she mean me, too?

Ezra returned, carrying an old red metal tray bearing three mugs of black coffee, three forks, and three small plates with wedges of pie. Ezra served his grandmother first, served Mae next, and then set pie and coffee at his own place and sat to resume his beadwork, head bowed.

"Thank you," Mae said. "You're a good host."

He ducked his head further.

"He's a good boy." Bessie gazed at her grandson's hands. "He's been a traditional dancer since he could walk. He speaks our language. Knows all our traditions."

Mae said to the boy, "You're lucky. My grandmother was a healer, but she didn't get to teach me. I lost her when I was a little younger than you."

He nodded, barely glancing at her. Mae took a sip of coffee and wondered if what she said had been wrong. It had sounded sort of *poor me*, and she hadn't meant it to. Rather, she'd meant to acknowledge the reason Bessie had been telling her about Ezra's training—the contrast.

"One of the medicine men is teaching Ezra," Bessie said. "He's a forecaster. He's better than the weather channel." Her eyes twinkled. She patted his arm and rested her hand there, her face growing serious. "He dreams things that are coming."

He dipped into a plastic box for a new bead and threaded it, his thick fingers precise and agile. "She knows."

Bessie drank her coffee and studied him. "When you dreamed that thing that happened, you didn't talk to me about it."

He shook his head and added another bead. "I told Zak."

"Could he help you understand it?"

"No."

Bessie said to Mae, "I help him with the meanings sometimes. So does his teacher. He'll learn to dream on purpose, with time. To answer questions. It's a strong gift. But it's not easy having it. It can make you seem special, maybe impress people you look up to, and that's tempting. It's not what the gift is for, though."

Ezra bit his lip and nodded. Bessie let the silence sit. She turned toward Mae. "You said your grandmother didn't teach you. Who did?"

"Nobody, really." Mae took a nibble of pie, found the flavor peculiar, and washed it down with coffee to get rid of the taste. "I had one lesson. Mostly I learned from books. Bernadette helped me choose what to read and made me practice, so I had some guidance but not a teacher. And once in a while, I feel my Granma's spirit helping me."

Ezra squirmed. "I wouldn't want a dead person talking to me."

"I don't mind," Mae reassured him. "It's not scary or anything."

Bessie said, "White people have different ideas about the dead. They say their names. Keep all their things. They don't get ghost sickness."

The boy frowned, poked at his salad, gave up and took a bite of pie. "Why not?"

"The spirit world is all the same place, but we use different routes through it."

In the quiet that followed, Bessie ate pie and drank coffee, watching as Ezra wove beads into the hatband. He slid his work in progress around for Mae to look at again. He had added a row of sky-blue beads on either side of the abstract sunrise. She studied it, told him she liked it, and he took it back.

Bessie spoke to her. "You ran in the race and watched the parade. You went to the hospital and now you're back here already. That was quick for a healing."

"What I do *is* pretty quick. That's why Will wanted me."

"Is that a good reason?"

Of course not. Mae blushed. "Most people ask me to help them for other reasons than being fast."

"I'm sure they do. But we're talking about *this* person. Do you think you helped him?"

"I might have, yes. But I have visions sometimes while I'm finding the root of a problem, and I saw a whole lot of his past. I saw him do something wrong. I wanted to ask you about this. I only aim to heal the person, but I end up seeing some of their problems even if I don't want to."

"Does that happen a lot?"

"Maybe half the time. I can't tell what to expect when I start."

Bessie took a moment. "So you can't stop these visions."

"No, ma'am. I mean, Bessie." Mae couldn't remember when she'd last felt this inadequate. "I guess I'm not as ready to heal people as I thought. What would you have done if Will asked you to help him?"

"I would talk with him a long time first. Pray with him. Be sure he was ready to make peace with people he'd done wrong to. That he had a plan for his life. We'd do that while he was still getting well in his body. Then, when he was able, I'd have him build the sweat house himself and we'd do the ceremony. We might do two or three sweats if he had a lot of problems. A lot of places where he'd been hurt and had hurt people."

Mae thought of all the effort Jamie put into healing himself, and how long a process it was. Bessie's ideas of healing were equally demanding. Mae had let Will be lazy. "I wonder if I really helped him or just made him feel good."

"I'm sure you helped." Bessie reached down and fondled a dog, provoking a deep canine sigh from under the table. "But you might have healed him backwards. He feels good now, but he's still going to have to do all that work if he wants to keep feeling good. He didn't get out of it."

"Do you mean he'll deal with these things I learned about him?"

"He'll have to. You see things like that, you stir them up. Maybe that's why you have those visions. Truth doesn't want you to stop it. It wants you to stir it up."

"Like my dreams," Ezra said. "It's like ..." He glanced at his grandmother, hesitating.

"Go ahead, Ezra. Let me see if you understand."

"Mae sees things people need to deal with in their past or that people need to know from the past. And I see things people need to know in the future. It's like ..." He looked down at his beads, one finger stirring them in the little plastic box, and pulled out a black bead. "Like ... Sorry." He dropped the bead and chose a blue one. "I had it. I can't explain it."

Mae said, "I think you meant, it's like the truth wants to show up. Whether anybody invites it or not."

Bessie nodded. "The spirits use you. You're not supposed to stop those visions, any more than Ezra should try to stop his dreams."

Mae thought of the visions she had on purpose. Were spirits still using her then, or was she on her own? Truth could hurt people, in small ways like her telling Jamie she didn't like camping, or in big ways like the talk Will must have had with Montana, but people couldn't heal without it. Relationships couldn't, either. Painful or not, truth wanted to be known.

Chapter Eighteen

In the evening at the ceremonial grounds, as the Ga'an and the clowns began their initial silent ritual, Jamie trailed Mae along the front row of the bleachers to join Bernadette and her family. He'd wanted to stay down by the arbor with his parents and Bessie to watch the beginning of the ceremony, but Mae had preferred to be with Bernadette. The relationship book had warned Jamie against arguing about little things. His discomfort around Zak wasn't exactly a little thing, but he'd fucked up earlier with a trivial fuss. Mae had looked at him funny when he'd had two pieces of pie at lunch. On their way to their cars, he'd accused her of silent nagging. A stupid fight. The look had been because she hadn't liked the pie. He owed her one less argument.

Most of the Pena-Fatty-Tsilnothos family watched the ceremony in reverent silence. Zak, however, was hunched over his phone texting, and Melody was tending to Dean, who was having a meltdown, while Deanna lay on her back on the bench talking to herself and kicking her legs. Bernadette scooted closer to her oldest niece, making room between herself and Zak. Mae took the spot offered, and Jamie ended up side by side with Zak, who ignored his greeting. Jamie's toes clenched and wriggled. He couldn't leave things this way between them.

"Jeezus. Be a fucking adult, will you?" he whispered. "We're too old for this not-speaking crap."

Zak stood and walked a few feet away, focused on his text chat. Jamie stifled an exasperated noise.

The line of dancers faced each of the four directions in turn, moving around the fire. At each quadrant's stop, the clown ran to the end of the line and brought back dirt that he placed on the lead dancer's foot. Sacred dirt? Jamie had never known what it meant, but he loved the gesture, that handful of earth. It seemed like an act of completion and grounding, and made him imagine taking Zak aside and placing an offering of dirt on his foot. *Now can we talk?*

Accompanied by a silent row of drummers holding their instruments without playing them, the dancers moved toward the big tipi and did a similar ritual around it but without the blessing of dirt. Facing the tipi in a line, the dancers made soft, eerie hooting noises when they raised their lightning sticks. It usually sent a charge into Jamie, something that woke up an extraordinary energy in him, but he'd been in and out of shadows all day, and the magical sounds felt darkly alarming tonight.

"Shit." Zak jammed his phone into his pocket, and hurried down the steps from the bleachers with heavy, slamming footfalls. Melody watched but didn't stir, hugging Dean in her lap. She had finally gotten the little boy to calm down. Jamie caught her eye and raised an eyebrow. She nodded, and Jamie followed Zak.

He caught up with him easily. Zak had stopped for the Ga'an dancers on their fourth approach to the big tipi, out in the modern-world part of the grounds. The line of massively crowned, black-painted men angled between Orville Geronimo's booth and the big tipi and repeated their ritual. Zak kept his distance, his shoulders tense, his rapt gaze occasionally broken by restless looks toward the vending area. *Torn. He'd rather stay.* The message couldn't have been fire or rescue work. If it had been, Zak would have gone around the other way and run. No long conversation—and no inner conflict.

When the dancers and the drummers moved back into the arena, Zak shot Jamie a warning look and loped away. Jamie's hip felt like he was slamming bone on bone as he went after him. "Mel wants to know—"

Zak stopped. "Are you her messenger?" Noise from the bounce house and the chatter of passersby blurred his words. "She's got a phone. She can call me."

"Don't think you noticed—she's got her hands full with Dean." Zak glared and folded his arms.

"What's so bloody awful about talking to me?" The depth of Jamie's hurt ambushed him. To his embarrassment, his voice cracked. "I haven't done anything to you."

Zak threw up his hands. "You and Mae have to stay out of my business. Can you do that? Can you stop following me around?"

"Can you stop acting like a fucking criminal? I only asked where you're going."

"I told you." Zak stepped closer and lowered his voice. Though quieter, he was no less angry, his words the hissing escape of a substance under pressure. "It's something Mel can't know about. If I tell you, you'll tell her. Then she'll tell her sisters." He winced as if this idea had struck him painfully. "*Shit.*" He glanced toward the vending area, then back at Jamie. "I've got enough to deal with as it is."

Reno stepped out of his father's booth and approached Zak, speaking in Apache. Zak answered and then disappeared down a side aisle, the one where David and Shelli were located. Reno returned to the booth, took down a small painting with a *sold* sign on it and slid it into a box. Orville was talking with a customer, but broke off to ask his son something. Reno replied and poured packing peanuts into the box from a plastic bag. Jamie felt that he'd stepped into the middle of a quiet explosion.

Reno's little brothers strolled up, carrying trash bags and picker-uppers. Lifting their bags to show how full were—about halfway—they waved at Orville,

He shook his head. "No money yet. They have to be full."

The boys wandered off toward the entrance, scanning the ground, chasing down a blown-away napkin. Jamie started down the aisle Zak had taken and encountered Letitia coming from it. She smiled as they almost collided.

"Have you thought any more about that picture? I'd really like to shoot you."

"With a camera, I hope."

"Of course. Unless you do something to deserve the other." Letitia gave him a wink and crossed to Orville's booth.

Jamie knew she'd been joking, but she'd been warning him, too. She might not aim a gun at him, but like Zak, she wanted him to back off.

Reno sealed the box with the painting in it and offered to carry it to her car. She accepted as if she were surprised at his kindness, gushing a little too strongly. Another tangent of that subtle explosion, another trail from whatever piece of fireworks had gone off. She didn't need help with that little box. *They're up to something.*

Trying not to seem nosy, Jamie approached David and Shelli's booth with as little show of concern as he could. Zak was leaning on their counter, talking softly while David rearranged the pottery display. Shelli sat in a camp chair with a shawl over her shoulders almost hiding baby Star nursing at her breast. No sign of any haste or worry, but Zak's posture and near-whispering suggested secrecy. He drew back abruptly as David grinned and waved Jamie over. "Haven't seen you much. How's your weekend going?"

Jamie answered with "Mmm" and a right-left shrug. He juggled imaginary balls, dropped one and watched it roll away, and then dropped the rest. "Yours?"

"Excellent. We sold some of our best pieces. I *love* tourists."

David had moved all the inexpensive items to the table at the back of the booth and was in the process of setting the more expensive ones prominently at the front. He arranged a double vase and a swooping bowl of Shelli's golden micaceous ware on either side of one of his exquisitely painted little pots featuring a hummingbird in black and brown on a white background.

"You like that?" David asked. Zak frowned at him and gave a tiny shake of his head. David continued, unaffected. "Hummingbirds are for good luck."

"I could use some." Jamie glanced pointedly at Zak. "Been a fucked-up couple of days. Why are they lucky?"

"I don't know. Just a tradition."

Shelli said, "I read in some bird article about how they can do all sorts of things other birds can't. Not just hovering." Deftly slipping the shawl over her bosom, she lifted her baby to a burping position over a small towel on her shoulder. "Did you know they can fly *backwards*?"

"That's weird. Do they ever land?"

"They perch." Shelli stood and patted Star, who responded with a burp of milky drizzle. "But they can't walk. Their feet are underdeveloped."

Weirder still. David placed a parrot pot next to the hummingbird pot, reminding Jamie of Placido's fate, and oddly, of the bird's agile gray feet walking up his arm to his shoulder.

Shelli asked, "Can you take Star while I button up?"

David took his daughter and held her at eye level, making silly faces and noises at her. While Shelli turned her back and adjusted her clothes, Jamie rotated the parrot pot and found an identical bird on the other side. He felt Zak's eyes on him. Jamie turned the pot over and read the price. "Jeezus. I should get this. Cheaper than a real parrot."

The joke made him sad and he set the pot down. Zak shot a questioning look at Shelli. She made a small gesture with her fingers, spreading them as if smoothing something down just above the counter, like she was urging him to calm down and act like there wasn't a problem.

What *was* the problem? Why was Zak still standing there? What had he been telling them? *Can't I just ask them?*

Zak's phone beeped. A second later, David's made a quacking sound. At the end of the aisle, Jamie saw one of the young Geronimo brothers—without his trash bag—tearing toward Orville's booth, arms and legs pumping, shouting, "Uncle Lonnie! Uncle Lonnie! You need to help Montana!"

Zak bolted in the direction the boy had come from, toward the front gate.

"Who's Montana?" David asked, sliding his phone from his pocket and glancing at it.

"His wife's sister. Think I'd better go with him." The boy had asked for a medicine man, not an EMT. This could be an emotional crisis. Zak wasn't very good with those, and Lonnie would be slow to arrive. Jamie jogged painfully after Zak.

At the entrance gate, two BIA cops in reflective vests, one male and one female, held Montana by the arms. She was crying and reeked so strongly of alcohol that the smell hit Jamie from over a foot away. She wailed, "That witch. I have to see that fucking witch."

Zak told the cops, "Let me take her home. I know what to do."

"No. I want to hit her." Montana struggled and then retched, sobbing and vomiting at the same time.

The male cop said, "You'd better go with him. We can arrest you for drunk and disorderly if you don't."

She curled over, spewing a stinking stream of liquid, practically hanging from her captors' hands. "I need to see that fucking witch."

Jamie knelt, avoiding the puddle of vomited booze. The bandana he'd used to contain his hair while cooking lunch was still in his back pocket. *Never using this again.* He mopped her mouth and chin. She recoiled at first, but the touch silenced her for a moment, and she looked confused.

"Better?" he asked. "Lucky you didn't get any on your clothes."

She nodded and took a deep breath. He stood, and she straightened up, mumbling, "Why are you nice? Your girlfriend's a witch."

Fuck. This was about Mae?

"Let me take you home," Zak said. "Then I'll take care of the witch for you."

"She's not a fucking witch," Jamie said. "Jeezus. We need to talk her out of that."

Lonnie arrived and held a brief exchange in Apache with the female cop. Zak asked a question and Lonnie answered. Montana whined, "What's everybody saying?"

Lonnie said, "That you shouldn't come to a sacred place in your condition, Montana Chino. You know better. Now, let Zak and Jamie help you or you'll go to jail."

"*You're* supposed to help me."

"I will. Tomorrow. When you're sober. You come see me at my camper."

"I need to see the witch."

"I'll talk to her for you. What do you want me to tell her?"

A crowd of rowdy teenagers approached the gate. The male cop nodded to Zak and they switched off so fluidly that Montana didn't seem to notice Zak was now grasping her arm.

"That she killed me." Montana began crying again, and tried to twist her left hand out of the female cop's grasp. Her engagement ring was bloody. "She killed me."

Her hand wasn't injured. The blood was on the stone. Jamie had a feeling that she'd used it to cut herself. He pointed it out to Zak, who said he'd check her over when they got to his house.

Lonnie asked Zak to make sure Montana woke up early and came to see him, and that she wasn't alone during the night. He agreed, and the female cop handed the drunken woman's left arm to Jamie. Montana sagged and struggled.

"I can handle her on my own," Zak said. "Carry her if I have to."

Lonnie raised an eyebrow. "All the way to your house? She's a sturdy girl. And a fighter. Jamie understands her, I think. Let him help you."

Zak hesitated, then nodded, and he and Jamie guided their charge down the hill. Montana alternated between attempts to get away and sudden collapses into tears. They passed Reno and Letitia, standing by the back of her SUV. She'd parked it on the side of the road above the parking lot where vendors had been set up during the daylight hours. Without stopping, Zak exchanged a few words in Apache with Reno. Jamie made out one English word, *Misty*. Maybe this time they weren't using their language to hide secrets. Just bringing a sister in to help.

As they progressed through the crowded parking lot, Montana began to drag her feet. "I wanna lie down."

"You can lie down in bed," Zak grumbled.

She sniffled. "Lie down and *die*."

"No wonder Lonnie said you understood her."

"All too bloody well." Jamie slid his arm around Montana's waist as she tried to drop to her knees. She whimpered in protest as he supported her. "Shh. I know you want to lie down. But *I* don't want you lying in the dirt, all right?"

She tried one more drop, and Zak added his arm around her. "We should carry her. You know how to make a seat?"

"Nah. Seen pictures of it. Never done it."

Zak directed Jamie and they linked hands under Montana's thighs with her arms draped over their necks, forming a kind of chair for her. As they hoisted her and began walking, she suddenly laughed through her tears. "I'm a queen."

"You sure are," Zak said. "Cleopatra, Queen of Denial."

"That's a song." She began to sing it, a country song about denying the obvious truth that a man was cheating. After a few lines, she broke down in tears again.

Jamie hands were sweating and starting to slip and he had to grip Zak's harder.

Zak winced. "Christ, Pudge. Is that because of Tana's ass or are you always that hot and sweaty?"

"Nah. It's you. All the years I've known you, mate, to think we never held hands 'til now."

Zak laughed, with an expression as if he'd surprised himself. Montana bellowed, "It's not funny. I wanna *die*."

"Holy shit." Zak stopped so suddenly Jamie nearly lost his grip. "You almost *did* die."

A dirty white subcompact sat with its nose smashed into the back of a larger vehicle. A sparkly blue van with smoked rear windows.

"Jeezus. Bloody fucking hell. Couldn't you have hit a fucking tree?"

Zak started to laugh again and took a breath. "Sorry. Drunk driving isn't funny." He cracked up. "That's your van?"

"Just bought it for my tour. Can we put her down for second? I need to—"

"No, we can't put her down for a second. Your van's not going anywhere. But Tana could do anything, if she was really crazy enough to cut herself. How'd you figure that, anyway?"

"Been there. Not all those scars are from accidents."

Zak looked into Jamie's eyes. "Christ. You never told me."

Jamie didn't know why he'd finally shared it now. It had just spilled out.

Montana began to writhe and wail. Her bearers picked up their pace and her large breasts, conspicuously at eye level, bounced with their steps. There were dark red spots on the jiggling part of her T-shirt. Montana had ground her tiny diamond into the flesh over her heart.

Misty's Harley roared into the driveway as Zak and Jamie guided Montana up the steps, too fatigued to carry her any further. The youngest Chino sister ran to catch up with them.

"What in the world? Tana never drinks. This is crazy."

"Tell me about it." Zak aimed Montana toward the gilder. Jamie sat with her and held her while Zak unlocked the door. "Where's your mother? Reno said you were at her place. Is she coming?"

"Come on. When has she ever had a Saturday night off? She's got a gig in Ruidoso at nine. I was getting my monthly ten minutes of Mom time."

Montana curled against Jamie and whispered, "It's all her fault."

"Your mum's fault?"

"Melody."

Zak shook his head. "First it was Mae, now it's Melody. Next thing it'll be me. Or you. Let's hope she passes out before she hates all of us."

He explained to Misty about Montana's cuts, and that she'd need to clean her up and make sure they didn't get infected, and then asked her to help him rearrange a few things. "We need to put the kids in together and put one of their beds in the living room so you can keep an eye on your sister tonight."

"Sure. I'll take care of her. But why can't Jamie move furniture?" Zak opened the door and gestured for her to go in ahead of him without answering. She started in, then paused, glancing back at Jamie with a frown. "Seriously, Zak. Shouldn't I stay with Tana and Jamie lift stuff?"

Jamie's hurt exploded. "I'm not allowed in the fucking house."

With a heavy sigh, Zak put a hand on Misty's back. "Go on. I'll be with you in a second." She went in. He stood in the doorframe, arms crossed. "She'll be asking me questions all night. You could have just said your back hurt. Or kept your mouth shut. And you wonder why I won't trust you." He turned and closed the door.

Fuck. Just when their friendship had been mending.

Jamie began to rock the glider and stopped. For Montana, things were already spinning. He could feel it with her, the sickening drunken rotation that wouldn't stop, and the bottomless pit of loss, the crazed blind urge to take it out on herself. He hugged her and she wept, softly now, tears he shared with her.

The border between them was shifting. The healing energy leaking. He hadn't meant to do it, but he'd been moved and it happened like it had with Ezra. It was stronger this time, and if Jamie didn't stop it the inner door would open, and he would see and feel her whole soul. Closing that door was hard, too hard for a night like this.

Feeling guilty, he pulled himself in a little. Lonnie would help her more and do a better job of it. He rubbed Montana's shoulder. "You want to talk?"

She raised her head, leaving a puddle of tears and snot on his shirt. "I can't."

"Hurts too much?"

Montana nodded.

"Guess Will broke up with you."

Whimpering like a wounded animal, she dropped her head and clung to him again. Affirmation, as if he'd needed it. No point in asking more questions. Mae had healed Will. It must have moved him to come clean. Maybe to confess he'd never loved Montana, but had always kept that place in his heart for Melody—who had never loved him, just used him for fun and to get back at Zak. The old dead-end soap opera, still playing.

Jamie hugged Montana tighter, letting her weep. Her loss soaked into his heart with her tears soaking into his shirt. Loss of love. Nothing worse in the world. No world left after it happened.

*****

Mae stood with the crowd behind the drummers, wondering when Jamie would be back. She felt as though more than an hour must have passed and she was starting to worry, but she didn't want to miss him by going off to look for him. That could make *him* worry.

The black-painted Ga'an dancers exited and a new group of drummers settled along the benches. A line of men reloaded the fire with logs, each approaching the blaze, tossing his burden, and filing out the far end of the arena. Another group of dancers entered, painted bright green with yellow symbols like a row of mountains on their backs and chests. As the new song started, the dancers slapped their lightning sticks against their leather-kilted legs. The night sky was crawling with rags of gray clouds, blazing with stars and distant lightning. Songs came from in front of and behind her with equal strength, the rattles and gentle chanting of the medicine men in the big tipi and the more vigorous drumming and singing of the men on the benches. The Ga'an dancers sprang and swayed in front of the fire, the clowns echoing their movements.

Jamie loved this more than any other part of the ceremonies. Where was he? Feeling it would be rude to use her phone in this sacred space, Mae eased her way through the people packed between the big tipi and the drummers' benches. A few phones lit up occasionally among the community members watching from the bleachers and the circle of lawn chairs. Maybe it would be all right to call from there.

Earlier, Pearl's husband had arrived with chairs, and the family had moved down closer to the dancing. Mae noticed Melody tucking a blanket over the twins in their stroller, empty seats all around her except for Pearl's sons and husband. Many of the Apache women, wrapped in shawls, had formed a curved line around the perimeter of the dance area and sidestepped in a tight formation, shoulders subtly turning side to side, feet keeping the rhythm. Most wore jeans and sneakers below their wraps, a few were in military uniforms, and others wore full traditional regalia. Bernadette and her female relatives passed in a cluster, shoulder to shoulder.

Mae made her way to Melody's side and took one of the empty seats. "Hey. Have you heard from Zak? I was gonna call Jamie, but I thought maybe you knew what was up."

Melody shrugged. "Call him. I have no idea."

"I see a few people on phones, but is it bad manners to call from here?"

"Kind of, yeah. Not that it's ever stopped Zak. He's so *traditional* and *spiritual* and then he sits here texting."

Mae didn't know what to make of Melody's attitude. She sounded bitter or cynical. "You got something against traditional and spiritual? Or Zak texting?"

"The whole Zak thing. I don't speak Apache. My dad's Navajo—or so Mom says. I grew up on the road with her band until I was old enough for school. Mom and the drummer were the only Apaches I knew until I was five. I've been trying to be more into the culture for Zak, but I'll never be where he is. Or where he says he is. It's like, I could always try harder, but it's okay if he doesn't because he's already perfect."

Another group of dancing women passed, blocking Mae's view of the Ga'an dancers. No wonder Melody wasn't among them. Not only sore legs from the race, but a break from meeting Zak's expectations.

"I saw Refugio Baca," Melody said. "Will's little brother. He said Will's quit drinking, smoking—everything. He even wants to quit rodeo and come home to be a *real* cowboy on the Baca ranch."

Mae did her best to act surprised. "Wow. That's great."

"Getting sober is. But coming home? He broke up with Montana. It'll make her miserable to have him around. And he'll be bored out of his mind. Start riding the damned free-range cows. He's come home to rest after some injuries and pulled that line before, but he never really planned to stay and his parents didn't want him to. He's not reliable. So why try it again now? A grown man wants to live with his parents? He must have money troubles."

He did. And there could be another reason. Though Melody had joked about her unattractiveness and Zak's jealousy, Will might not care about her weight, and he'd never cared about her relationship with Zak. In fact, Jamie had said Will was all the more attracted to her *because* she was taken. Mae said, "Maybe he won't stick around. Once he gets some things straightened out."

"I wouldn't mind if he stayed a while. Once I lose some weight, I could ride some Baca horses again."

I hope you really mean horses and not Will. The images of the fight lit up in Mae's mind. Melody should know better than to play with fire that way. "And make Zak jealous?"

"Will's my friend. I can choose my friends. I let you and Jamie in the house, didn't I? Zak doesn't get to run my life, even if it drives him crazy. Serves him right if it does. Running around with that photographer."

This is not a healthy relationship. And Melody knew it. She didn't believe in them.

Mae excused herself to go call Jamie, but as soon as she reached the vending area, one of Orville's younger sons, carrying a trash bag and picker-upper, approached her. "Uncle Lonnie wants to talk with you. It's really important. He's in the booth"

Before going in, Mae double-checked with Orville that it was okay, then went behind the counter to sit with Lonnie.

"My nephew has no helpers besides me right now," the old man said, "so I'll make this short. Montana Chino is drunk and she says you're a witch. Do you know how bad this is in Apache culture?"

Stunned, Mae froze for a moment before she could answer. How could this happen to her again? This was like the gossip back in Tylerton, North Carolina—only worse. "Yes, Bernadette told me. It's really evil. Scary."

"Orville says you healed his friend, Niall. And I know when I'm in the presence of a witch. You're not one. So why does Montana say this about you?"

"I don't know." Mae clenched her fists. She tried to hide her rising anger, but her voice shook. "I didn't do anything bad. She asked me to help someone."

"She asked *you*?"

"For the other person. Yes."

Lonnie watched a group of noisy, laughing women arriving at the booth. Mae had the feeling he wasn't really looking at them but into his thoughts. He finally spoke. "Be careful. She's a very dissatisfied customer."

He stood, and Mae followed suit, assuming she had been dismissed. "Thanks for letting me know." She took a step to leave, then paused. "Where is she?"

"Zak and Jamie took her to Zak's house. You shouldn't go there tonight. I'll see her in the morning. You can't talk sense into a drunk."

Mae paced up and down the main aisle of the vending area while she called Jamie. Were people looking at her strangely? How many of them had heard what Montana said? Did they know who was being called a witch, or not? He didn't answer. She left a message for him to call her and returned to the arena to take her place beside Melody again. Leaving out the witch part, afraid to have it overheard, Mae summed up the rest of what Lonnie had said.

Melody rocked the stroller back and forth as Deanna began to wake. The little girl closed her eyes again. "Tana can't bear life without drama. Will's out of the picture, so now *she's* drunk and crazy. At least her mess got Zak talking to Jamie."

"I wonder if he let him in the house."

"I doubt it."

They watched the ceremony without talking for a while.

Startled by the sound of slurping through a straw, Mae looked around to see Jamie standing behind her and Melody with a large cup of soda. "Hey, sugar. I missed you."

He took his hat off, shook his hair as if something had landed on him, and jammed the hat back on. His eyes had a hot, distracted look, avoiding meeting hers. He'd changed his shirt, not to a sweatshirt for the cold evening but another big loud Aloha shirt, wrinkled from being in his pack.

"Sit down. What's going on? How's Montana?"

Jamie sucked on the soda again. Caffeine and sugar at night—a bad idea for an insomniac, but those were his go-to fixes when he was stressed. He finished the drink with massive suction through ice and crushed the paper cup, squirting the remaining ice out as the lid came loose. "She's a fucking lunatic."

Someone behind him asked him to sit down and stop swearing. He squeezed between Mae's chair and the one beside her and dropped into it. One hand clutched the crushed cup, while the one closer to her clenched around a wad of fabric, his fingers prodding and kneading the cloth. Mae placed her hand on his and whispered, "What's the matter? Is it what she said about me?"

Jamie shook his head and took an unsteady breath. "She got snot on my shirt." He paused. Mae was sure this wasn't the issue and waited for more. "Zak and Misty had her sort of under control, and

he wouldn't let me in so ... I went back to the tent to change and ..."
He slid his hand away from hers, bringing his thumb to his mouth,
biting his knuckle and scrunching his eyes shut. "Jeezus."

Mae started to take his hand down and then noticed what he
was holding. Dull green synthetic fabric. A piece of his tent.

Chapter Nineteen

Mae wanted to ask what had happened, but Jamie needed to calm down first. He huddled with his arms wrapped around himself, shivering, his breath fast and uneven. She put her arm over his shoulders and rubbed him gently. He gazed fixedly at the dancers, and after a while she felt him grow steadier, though he still shivered now and then.

She whispered, "We need to get some warmer clothes on you, sugar."

"Can't. She trashed 'em."

First a witch rumor, now this? Mae stood, excusing herself and Jamie to Melody. "We need to go."

"Jeezus, no, I need to be here."

"I can't stay." Mae walked off. She didn't trust herself not to lose her temper and spoil the ceremonies for others.

Jamie didn't follow her right away. She waited by the big tipi. A passing family spoke among themselves, casting glances at her. She had no idea if their words in Apache said, *is that the witch?* or something else.

Jamie finally joined her. "Why in bloody hell do we have to leave?"

"I'm too pissed off to sit there. I need to know what Montana did to our stuff."

"It's all in the van." He jammed his hands in his pockets. "I took care of it. You don't have to do anything."

"Wait—she vandalized your tent and our clothes and you cleaned it up? That was a crime. You got rid of the evidence?"

"I'm not prosecuting her. Fuck. She hit my van, too— She'll have to pay for it, and that's enough." He sighed. "Her heart's broken, y'know? She went off the deep end."

246

Jamie wandered away. Mae caught up with him. "When most people get their hearts broken, they just cry. I can't believe you're taking her side after she cut up your tent and our clothes."

"She didn't cut up our clothes. Dumped the food out and ground it into everything. But she didn't fuck with my roo or the sleeping bag. Lantern's okay, too. It's not as bad as it could have been. Sad about my tent, though. Got this big hole in it. We'd freeze in there tonight and if it rains—" He shrugged. "Got a tent repair kit at home, but I didn't think I'd need it."

"Forget repairing it. She needs to buy you a new one."

"No." He recoiled, giving her a shocked and wounded look. "It's *my tent*. I can save it."

"Fine. You love your tent. You feel sorry for Montana. But she was drunk and destructive and she shouldn't get away with it. You know what she said about me?"

"Yeah. That was bad. She owes you an apology for that."

"And she owes you more than that. I hope someone saw her at the campground."

"Nah. No one around except this one couple. They came out of their camper when I was packing the tent up and asked why I was leaving early. Told 'em what happened. They didn't hear a thing. Said they'd been taking a nap, but they might have been making a little noise of their own, y'know? And it doesn't matter. Tana's been through enough. She doesn't need to be punished."

"And it looks like she won't be." Mae took his hand. Jamie was too kind. She thought he was wrong, but it wasn't the worst fault a man could have. "Did she admit she cut up your tent?"

"Nah. Haven't seen her since I found it. But who else would have done it?"

They went out the gate and down the hill to the parking lot, where they moved their luggage, which gave off a smell of chocolate and apple-cinnamon muffins, to Mae's car. Seeing the damage to the van made Mae angry with Montana again. Driving drunk. At least she would get some consequences for that. Mae took a picture of the car with its front end in the back of the van, making sure to get the license plate in the shot in case Jamie relented on this, too.

They decided to look for a motel with a vacancy sign in Ruidoso rather than drive all the way to T or C, since Jamie still had to deal with Montana and the collision in the morning. Between Mae's student budget and Jamie's touchscreen aversion, neither of them had a smartphone to look up the hotels, but Mae didn't mind the drive, even though the odds of finding a vacancy were low on a holiday weekend. The other choices had been to move their sleeping bag into his parents' tent, or to impose on friends who had limited space to put them up. The prospect of privacy and a proper shower and bathroom was worth the hunt for a vacancy sign, and she preferred to be where an enraged, intoxicated woman with a knife was less likely to find her.

Mae glanced over at Jamie as she drove. He had tipped the passenger seat back and closed his eyes. His long silence worried her. She squeezed his hand and then let go to steer the curves of the mountain road. "It's so weird having you all quiet like this. What are you thinking?"

"I'm not."

"Not thinking?"

"Nah. Just ... mud. It's all mud." He twisted the tent scrap and then flattened it on the dashboard in front of him as if he was ironing it. "Can't believe she did this."

"And it's not even you she's mad at. That knife might have been meant for me rather than the tent."

"Jeezus." Jamie's eyes widened and he sat up straight. "Bloody hell." He slapped the fabric onto his knee. "It wasn't her."

"What? Who else was crazy enough and a carrying a knife?"

"Just hit me—Tana didn't *have* a knife. I felt more of her than I wanted to carrying her to Zak's house and she didn't have a knife on her anywhere. She cut herself with her ring. And she said she wanted to *hit* you. Didn't come bawling to the gate wanting to *kill* you. And—she was crying and yelling and puking, but the people in the camper *didn't hear anything*, and—fuck—look at this." He held up the piece of his tent. "It's neat. The fucking thing is almost *square*."

Mae didn't take her eyes off the road to look. She got his point. It was a bizarre way to do the damage. So deliberate and calm. A drunk couldn't have done it. Mae should have felt more relief that Montana didn't have a knife and want to kill her, and that Jamie had pulled out of his inner mud, but there was a shadow to his revelation. "Do you think someone wanted us to leave? Someone who knew which tent was yours? Look at what they did. Made sure we had nowhere to sleep and no clean clothes. It was kinda planned, wasn't it?"

Jamie slumped, squeezed his eyes shut, and shook his head. "*No.*"

"I didn't say it was any of your friends, sugar. Zak was with you. I was thinking maybe someone heard what Montana called me and wanted to drive me off. Did she say my name? Describe me? Say I was your girlfriend? We stick out in a crowd."

"Yeah. She said, 'Your girlfriend's a witch.'"

"So the person who cut up the tent could have been sending me a message."

Jamie's shoulder twitched. "Or making it easy for me to sew it back up."

He turned away and rested his head against the window. Silence. Back in the mud.

Mae slowed down inside the Ruidoso village limits and scanned the signs on chain motels on Route 70. No vacancies. Jamie mumbled a reminder to turn left on Sudderth Drive.

The main drag of the town had plenty of mom and pop motels, all full. The Alpine Lodge caught her attention. No vacancy, but a woman in jeans and a light hooded jacket was putting luggage into an SUV. Mae pulled in at the art gallery across the street. It was closed for the night, a good spot to park and wait to see if the vacancy sign lit up.

"What are you doing?" Jamie asked.

"I think someone's checking out."

"Go over and ask."

"I don't want to act like a vulture."

He got out, took her suitcase from the back seat, and slung his backpack on. "Have to, so we can grab it. If they're checking out this late, it can't be rented yet. You pay the whole day if you stay past eleven in the morning. Owners should love getting paid for the night twice."

There was no light on in the office. Unlike the chains, this small motel didn't appear to have a front desk open twenty-four-seven. The owners might answer a bell, though. Mae got out and locked her car.

While they were waiting to cross the four lanes of traffic, a light drizzle began to fall. Mae turned back to the car for her umbrella and noticed another car in an unlit area of the art gallery's L-shaped lot, as far from the sidewalk as it could be parked. It had a duct-taped back window and a rear bumper that looked like more stickers than car. Even in the shadows, its amateurish bright turquoise paint job glowed. The Rabbit.

Why was Reno here? Mae got her umbrella and rejoined Jamie. He put his hand on her arm and guided her down the street. "Don't want her to see us."

Mae looked back at the Alpine Lodge. The woman had either gone back in the motel or inside her vehicle. "I thought you were good with being vultures."

"It's Letitia. Didn't recognize her. She had that hood up. Look at the license plate."

A brief gap in traffic let Mae glimpse the NMOFNM vanity plate. "Is Reno with her?"

"He was earlier tonight—'round the time Montana showed up."

"His car's here. Like he's hiding it or hiding that he's with her."

"Come on." Jamie stopped, locked his arm with Mae's, shot a glance both ways, and bolted into the busy street, pulling her along. Cars honked.

They paused on the center line—there wasn't a median—and Mae demanded, "What are you doing? Why—"

Jamie hauled her into another dash between cars. He was grinning when they reached the sidewalk, having obviously enjoyed the little adventure. A full recovery from his gloom because he'd risked getting hit? *I will never understand him.* "We're hiding," he said. "While we figure out what to do. They can't see us as well if we're on this side."

"They. So Reno is there?"

"Dunno. But we can find out. This beats you doing psychic stuff, right?"

Mae wasn't sure she followed Jamie's logic. Maybe what he was doing felt less wrong rather than more effective. "How can we see them if they can't see us? Are you gonna hide in the bushes at the motel?"

"Could. I *am* quiet."

"Sugar, even if we don't make a sound, we are the two least invisible people in the world."

Jamie's shoulders wriggled in his one-two shrug. He guided Mae up close to the buildings they passed. The Alpine Lodge was set back from the street with a crowded parking lot and two small patches of lawn featuring benches and garden gnomes under slender pine trees. The nearest end of the motel was two-story with a chalet-style roof, perhaps the owners' residence above the office, while the rest of the building was a one-story strip motel with a long screened-in porch for a corridor along the front, which guests had to traverse to reach an exit. He led her to the building's street-facing side on the chalet-style end, snug up against it, and cupped his hand to his ear. Of course. They didn't have to see or be seen, just listen.

A door closed. Over traffic they wouldn't hear steps along the porch-like corridor, but Mae guessed people had walked down it when another door shut, and steps sounded across the parking lot, one set hard-heeled, the other set slapping. Flip-flops. A car door opened and closed.

"Thanks." Letitia said. "That saved me a few trips."

Silence. Reno must have replied too softly to hear, or with a gesture or an expression. Letitia spoke again. "Is there any way I can possibly talk you into a few more?"

Silence again.

"All right. I do respect your reasons, you know. I'll be in touch."

The flip-flops started across the parking lot toward the street. Letitia said, "Drive safely in that thing."

The flip-flops continued, and soon Reno's slender figure crossed the street. Mae wondered if he recognized her car. He might have seen it the day they talked outside of Passion Pie in T or C, but he hadn't seen her get in it, and it was small, gray, and ordinary, a forgettable car. He didn't pause but walked straight to the Rabbit.

Jamie drew Mae along the back of the motel to a service road between the building and a steep cliff of red dirt, lit by a single light on a utility building at the end of it.

"Have you been here before?" she asked. "Do you know what you're doing?"

"Nah. Winging it. Thought we could watch her light go out from back here and then come around the front when she's leaving and surprise her. Ask her what's up."

"Sugar, Zak and Reno aren't telling the people closest to them. I don't think your charm is gonna get very far. And we don't know her. She could be dangerous, carry a gun—"

"Tight as her clothes are? She couldn't hide a penny."

"That hoodie's not tight."

"She likes me. She's a fan. Worst thing that could happen, she tells me to mind my own bizzo." He stopped walking abruptly, shoved a hand under his hat and grabbed his hair, grimacing. "Fuck. We can't ask her. She'd tell Zak and he'd hate me even more." He blew out a breath, dropping his hand to his side. "Guess we let her go and tell the managers we want the room."

"She could have packed the car but plan to leave in the morning."

"She wouldn't leave whatever they're selling in her car overnight."

"If that's what they were packing. I wonder what she wanted Reno to do a few more of."

"Jeezus." Jamie shuddered. "Hope that little lizard isn't posing naked."

"Reno's not bad looking. Some women could like him." Nude shots did seem a bit of stretch, though. He didn't look very strong, and a man without muscle wouldn't make much of a calendar model. "She couldn't be having affairs with both of them, could she?"

"Zak wouldn't cheat on Mel. He loves her."

He could have fooled me.

The center room of the motel darkened. Only one other room had been lit, at the far end of the corridor, and its lights remained on. Fireworks shot off in the distance, spinning green and red arcs accompanied by a whistling noise. Jamie nodded toward the other end of the dirt road. They passed the utility building and came out among the pine trees near a gazebo with screened windows. Letitia was starting her SUV.

Jamie squeezed Mae's hand. "We've got a room, love."

Letitia might have checked out, or she might be going out to buy something she needed for her trip but planning to leave in the morning. The lit room could be hers, and she could be coming back to it. "We'd better make sure that was her room that went dark and not someone going out to watch the fireworks."

The corridor was empty and quiet. Even the room with a light on was silent. Jamie counted off doors under his breath and tapped on the one in the middle. No answer. It wasn't a modern key-card door, but had a knob like a private residence. He tried turning it and it opened. "Bloody hell. She didn't lock it."

He switched on the light. The bed was made, with dents in the bedspread where suitcases had lain on its taut surface. Two keys with large turquoise tags lay on the table. He walked in and set their luggage down. "Wonder if the sheets are clean or if they leave 'em until you check out."

At least they had found the right room, but Mae couldn't quite believe that Jamie had opened the door and walked in. Feeling like a trespasser, she followed him and closed the door. "I don't think they're gonna have anyone at work to clean it at this time of night. And we still don't know if she actually checked out."

"Sure she did. Motels get your card number when you check in. You leave without stopping by the desk, it gets charged. This place look to you like she's coming back?"

Along with the keys, a sealed envelope lay on the table with the notation on it, *For Housekeeping*. "No. But ... this feels weird. We should see if we can wake up the manager—"

"Nah. Second thoughts about that. No one to clean it, they might not rent it again. Might kick us out. And then what? It's paid for, right? We can sleep here."

Jamie prowled the room, checking drawers, peeling the covers back and even looking under the mattress cover. He bent down and sniffed the pillows. "Fuck. *Perfume.*" He went to the closet and brought out two extra pillows. "Clean!" He tossed and caught them. "We can sleep on top of the top sheet, use these. Won't be *too* bad. I sort of know her and she's not, y'know, *unhygienic*. Don't like having a TV in the bedroom, though. Big screen looking at you." He opened the refrigerator and the microwave, frowned at their insides, then disappeared into the bathroom, probably to smell the towels and look for hair in the drain. "Heard about some study, think it was done in Italy—people who had TVs in their bedrooms had less sex. Or worse sex. Something."

He insisted that Mae relax while he cleaned the bathroom with a used washcloth and a dab of the motel's shampoo. While he cleaned, he narrated what he was doing and rambled through his stream of consciousness about showers, towels, and whatever else popped into his head. Mae sat at the table and in spite of the odd circumstances began to feel some relief. His chatter was reassuring, a sign that he had recovered from his emotional mud-state. She would have a shower and a normal toilet. A queen-sized bed in which to get a little space from Jamie's excess body heat. Room to stand up.

He washed a few small items of laundry in the sink and took them to the gazebo to hang out to dry, over her objections to having her panties and bra out there. "Breeze," he said. "They'll dry in an hour, no one'll notice 'em."

While he was out on this errand, she called Melody, Bernadette, and Jamie's parents, leaving messages to let them know she and Jamie had gone to a motel and probably wouldn't be back at the ceremonies tonight. None of them answered, but she hadn't expected them to.

Jamie returned, dancing. "There's a Jacuzzi in the gazebo. And a lot of clean towels." This seemed to delight him as much as the Jacuzzi. "Come on, we can get in it and watch the fireworks."

"Get in it in what? We don't have bathing suits."

"Our grundies. Hang 'em up with the other stuff after. Could go in the nuddy, but who knows whose arse has been in that tub?" He took her by both hands and pulled her to her feet and kissed her. "Ready?"

She returned the kiss and hugged him. They should have been at the Apache ceremonies with friends, but instead here they were in someone else's motel room—and he was working hard to make it nice for her, being romantic and attentive, taking care of her, rescuing their weekend as well as he could. "I'm ready."

The gazebo roof blocked a portion of their view of the distant fireworks display, and the low skyline of the town cut off another part, but in the pine-fringed gap, the explosions sparkled. Mae rested her head on the edge of the tub while one of the jets massaged her back and another soothed her feet. Jamie laid his arm over her shoulders and snuggled, rubbing his foot along her calf. "This all right, then?"

"It's strange, but yeah, it's nice."

He sighed, squirming a little. "Guess you like it better than the tent."

"I do, but I'm sorry it got ruined. I can't imagine anyone you know being mean enough to do that."

"Could picture Tana doing it drunk, but the only person I can think of who's really mean enough is Will and he's in the hospital.

Somebody must've channeled him." A sudden hah-snort-hah laugh escaped him. "Jeezus. *I* fucking channeled him. I *stole* the room."

"You kinda did. But you didn't really steal it. It was more like we found it. Like finding money on the street."

Jamie's free hand fidgeted with the room key on the shelf beside the hot tub. He ignored a spectacular whizzing eruption of white fireworks. "Like whoever found Placido."

Will had found the blue parrot. Maybe Placido, too. Had that encounter been by chance, like nabbing the room, or had there been a plan? Random bits of ideas began to click together. A plan would mean Will knew Shelli. David knew Zak. David and Shelli lived near Santa Fe, Letitia's home. "Where does Will live when he's not on the rodeo circuit?"

"Dunno. Not around here."

"Could he live in Santa Fe?"

"Mm. Reckon. Sort of pricey for him, though." Jamie leaned forward into a stretch and resettled himself. "Never ran into him, either."

"Would you? I don't think y'all would hang out in the same places."

"What—can't see me in a cowboy bar? Drinking cheap piss and listening to country music?"

"Not really." Would David and Shelli run into Will? Did they go to cowboy bars? They had a baby, so they probably didn't go out at all, and Will didn't seem the type to shop at Whole Foods or the exotic bird store. They could have met at some Indian event, a powwow close to Santa Fe. Mae couldn't picture Will browsing through pottery and jewelry, though, from what little she knew of him. Letitia would, however. She might shop at Whole Foods, too. Maybe she was the connection. She'd been taking pictures at the rodeo. If she liked to photograph cowboys, and he lived in Santa Fe, it was possible they'd met.

Jamie broke in on her thoughts. "Why'd you ask about Will?"

"I was wondering if he knew Letitia. If he modeled for her or something."

The fireworks show sent a starburst of red, white, and blue into the sky. Jamie watched until it faded, then said, "You can find out anything you want about Letitia. We're sleeping on her sheets."

Mae's first reaction was *why didn't I think of that*? Her second was amazement that Jamie had. "Sugar, I never thought you'd—"

"Wasn't saying I *wanted* you to do it. Just came out. Shouldn't have mentioned it."

"No, you should have. It was important." When she went to sleep with questions in her mind while in contact with a source of possible answers, her dreams could be taken over by psychic journeys. It was the worst way to pick up psychic information—no control and no real sleep. "If I don't do the journey on purpose while I'm awake, and I'm wondering about all this, I'll probably do it by accident, like I did sleeping in your sweatshirt once."

"Then stop wondering about it. This wasn't supposed to be what our weekend was about, y'know."

"I know. And it's not. But Misty and Melody will ask me again. Sooner or later they'll give me Reno's or Zak's things to work with. Those guys won't talk. You hope they will, and it would be better if they did, but they won't. They don't have healthy relationships."

Jamie met Mae's eyes. "I don't like this, y'know."

"I know. But at least Letitia's not your friend."

"Fuck. Get it over with, then." Jamie slid low in the tub, scowling, then added with a hopeful, apologetic smile. "Come back and soak when you're done?"

"I will."

Parting with a kiss, she returned to the room wrapped in a towel, swapped her wet underclothes for her shorts and tank top, and looked for something of Letitia's that he might have overlooked in his cleanliness inspection. A dropped earring, something less intimate than the sheets. Mae didn't want to pick up images of Letitia's sex life, especially if it involved Zak or Reno.

She found nothing useful. The bed would have to do. She sat cross-legged on it with the covers pulled back. From her collection of crystals she chose amethyst, turquoise, and clear quartz and started to slow her breath and clear her mind.

A green square on one of the chairs snagged her attention. The piece of Jamie's tent. Could she use it to find out who had cut it? If the vandal had been the last person to handle it, maybe, but now she would get flooded with Jamie. Too bad. The tent itself was the only witness to what had been done to it.

She closed her eyes and refocused on her breath, the crystals, and the energy traces from Letitia. *How is she part of Zak and Reno's secret?* The woman's energy was easy to sense, and the tunnel took Mae's mind quickly.

The vision that opened from it showed Reno and Letitia leaving the gate of the ceremonial grounds. Her SUV was parked nearby on the slope of the road. She put a small flat box inside it and they leaned on the vehicle.

"Are you sure she's coming?" Letitia asked.

"Will said she was. She's calling him and crying and yelling at him every twenty minutes or so, drunker every time."

Letitia crossed her booted ankles and looked at her watch. "We could wait all night for a drunk to show up, though. She could run off the road, pass out, change her mind ..."

"I need to know if she understood what he told her. If she remembers it now."

"I can't believe he really did that. Will, having an attack of honesty."

A woman's voice, bellowing curse words, approached. Reno shook his head. "This is sad. She doesn't usually drink. I don't know if she ever has before."

Montana stumbled up the slope. Reno rushed to her and caught her. "Tana. What's the matter?"

"Will." She let out a small howl. "He's not gonna marry me."

"I'm sorry." Reno stood close, his hold on her firm. "Did he say why?"

"I ... He wanted a healer. I brought him what's-her-name. The red-haired woman. So he could quit smoking. Like how your dad's friend quit smoking. And now he wants to quit rodeo, too—and *me*," Montana sobbed. "She fucked up. He's quitting *everything*."

Reno eased his grip on her arm. "Everything. Is that all he said?"

A family group approached, groaning about how hard it was to walk up the hill and how out of shape they were. Montana said, "He told me he was coming clean—"

The out of shape family drew close. Letitia gave Reno an alarmed look, and he cut in, "And this was right after she *healed* him?"

"Yes." She gasped and sniffed. "Coming *clean*."

"So he could break off with you."

"He said he had someone else." Montana's words faded into a wail.

More pedestrians converged from both directions. Letitia cleared her throat and gave Reno another urgent glare. He brought Montana to lean on the SUV with them, and she slid down to sit in the dirt. He sat with her, saying, "It's Melody."

"Melody?" Montana's jaw dropped and her eyes filled. "He still loves *her*?"

"Maybe not until today. But you saw this red-haired lady give Melody her running medal. They're friends. Mae is a witch, Tana, not a healer. She can put stuff in people's heads. She made Dad's friend quit smoking when he didn't even want to. She put all this stuff in Will's head for Melody. She witched him for her."

"Mae's a witch?" Montana leaned on Reno's shoulder and struggled to her feet. "She made him do that?" She swung her fist to punch an imaginary person in front of her and nearly toppled. "I'm gonna hit her."

"I don't blame you. I would if I were you." Reno stood. "It's all her fault."

Montana lurched toward the gate, and Letitia sputtered a stifled laugh. "That was the most ridiculous story I ever heard."

"No, it wasn't. It was bad." Reno gazed after Montana, who was yelling and weeping as she pushed past the other people approaching the gate. "I don't like to talk about witches. I couldn't think of anything else, though. To keep her mind off the rest of us."

"It should do. And should get Mae out of here."

Reno shook his head. "That won't matter, if she got anything from Will. If she even touched him she could know."

"Is she really that good? I've met some psychics in Santa Fe and they're hardly that perceptive. They have to be trying, too."

"Then we have to keep her from trying." He turned away, closed his eyes and folded his hands, bowing his head over them as if in prayer, except that he bit his nails. "I wish this was over. I just wish this was over."

Letitia took her phone from her bag and tapped out a message. "It will be." She lifted and smoothed out his ponytail, running her hand down the length of it, and laid his hair on his back again. "You're almost done."

Jamie opened the door and broke into Mae's trance. Wearing a towel and dragging his clothes, he leaned on the table and then pitched onto the foot of the bed. "Sorry." He sounded breathless. "Light-headed. Think I stayed in too long."

Disoriented from the psychic journey, she looked down at him as he lay wet and dripping on the heaped-up bedspread. She put her hand on his chest. "I think you did." His heart was pounding. "Hot water makes your blood pressure drop."

"But it feels like it's high. Like I'm having a heart attack. Fuck. Fuck. Fuck. I'm having a panic attack. Sorry. Shoot me."

He closed his eyes, placed his hands on his belly, and began his breathing exercises. Between rounds of breathing, he muttered an occasional "Fuck. Sorry. Shoot me," but gradually calmed down.

Mae stroked his forehead and gave in to an urge to touch his long eyelashes.

Jamie opened his eyes. "What'd you find out? Is it bad?"

Which parts did he need to know right now? Mae didn't want to upset him while he was still getting his heart to slow down. Her anger boiled when she thought of the people walking past while Reno told Montana that the red-haired lady was a witch. That part could wait until morning, though.

Mae smoothed Jamie's hair, not sure what to say. Reno had cool nerves, pretending to Montana that he didn't know what Will had told her so he could check what she remembered. And then improvising the lie about Mae. He'd regretted it, and perhaps everything he was involved in, but unlike Will, he was seeing it through. No—Will was still in it, too. He'd called Reno and warned him that he'd told Montana something.

Jamie nudged her. "Did you see who hurt my tent?"

"No. I saw Letitia and Reno talking. Will is part of whatever they're into. Reno and Letitia think I might have found out when I healed him."

"But you didn't. Or did you?"

"Nothing that clears it up. I still have no idea."

Chapter Twenty

Way too fucking early. Jamie could tell without opening his eyes. The light wasn't bright yet. His phone was sounding its Mozart ringtone from the upper right-hand corner of the bed, reminding him he had to get up and deal with Montana and his van, when he wanted to stay in bed with Mae as long as possible, making up for every miserable minute they'd had this weekend.

She rolled over, gave him a perky, wide-awake kiss and bounced out of bed to begin dressing. To his dismay, she had gone to sleep at ten o'clock the night before. *Ten o'clock*. Rather than subject her to his restlessness, Jamie had borrowed her car and gone back to the ceremonies until midnight to stand behind the drummers. The music and dancing had done him good, but now he groped for his phone and mumbled an incoherent syllable into it, exhausted.

Melody's warm contralto voice came through. "Tana's gone to see Lonnie. I told her you'd meet her at his camper. Be nice to her. She feels like shit."

"Bet she does. She remember anything?"

"Zak had to tell her she hit your van. She says the only thing she remembers is that Will dumped her."

He thanked Melody, wound up the call, and relayed Montana's memory status to Mae.

"Blackouts are funny." Mae pulled her tank top over her head. "My first husband used to have some holes in what he'd done, but he'd remember other stuff from the same night. I used to wonder if he was lying about what he forgot."

"Tana's honest. She wouldn't have made that up."

Mae, fully dressed already, bent down to lace up her shoes. Jamie had brought her clean clothes in from the gazebo when he'd come back from the ceremonies. He should have hidden them to

263

get her to stay in bed naked longer. She looked literally ready to run. "You're not vey cuddly this morning," he said.

She sat beside him and combed her fingers through his hair, taking out a few tangles. "I've got a lot to do today, and so do you. I'm gonna go home and do laundry, get all that food out of our clothes. And I need to see how Niall is doing. I want to do a little research, too. And you have to get your van to a body shop. See your insurance people. I hope they'll take care of it on a Sunday."

Jamie forced himself to sit up. "And then what? What if I can't get any of that crap done today? You're coming back, aren't you?"

"I didn't tell you this last night. Reno told Montana that I put some kind of spell on Will to make him break off with her so Melody could have him back. He said I was a witch. Would people believe it if they overheard him? He described me, talked about me giving Melody my medal after the race. And there were a lot of people walking by."

"Fuck." Jamie got up and began to dress. "Yeah, that could stick. Not because it's Reno, but the Geronimo credibility could rub off on him."

"Does that mean Orville or Lonnie could defend me?"

"Nah. Doesn't work like that. Witch talk is all ... scary. Underground. You don't have open conversations about it."

"Then Reno is one self-centered, inconsiderate ass. Was he that desperate to make me leave?" Her movements brisk and forceful, Mae picked up the package of hotel coffee and tore it open. "Reckon this is better than nothing."

"Is it one of those *pads*? Little round pad?"

Mae put it in the coffee maker and carried the carafe to the bathroom and filled it. "You got something against 'em?"

"Yeah. Coffee's dead. Ground like five hundred years ago. And Lonnie has fucking *instant*. I need *real* coffee."

Mae returned to the bedroom and poured the water into the coffeemaker's reservoir. "We got worse problems than bad coffee. Thanks to Reno, this vacation is over. I'd better not come back."

Bloody hell. Could anything else go wrong?

After Mae dropped him off at the campground, Jamie watched her drive away and then walked past his former campsite, the empty space where he'd been so excited setting up the tent, so hopeful for a romantic getaway with Mae and a reunion with his friends. The contrast with how things had turned out hit him hard. His parents' tent was quiet. Envious of their peace, he fought back the urge to disturb it and unload his troubles.

Reaching the medicine man's camper, Jamie knocked on the door and Lonnie called to him to come in.

The old man stood at the narrow stove, frying eggs and bacon, filling the air with what was to Jamie a sickening smell. He lingered in the doorway, looking in at the half-sized appliances and Lonnie's stooped, skinny frame. The view made him feel like a giant. A sick, tired giant.

Montana, sitting on the narrow, wedged-in bench at the table, jerked nervously at the sight of him, spilling weak coffee-like liquid from her mug. Her eyes were red and she was wearing a T-shirt that was obviously Melody's, too big even for Montana's endowments.

"I don't suppose you'd like some coffee?" Lonnie asked with a twinkle.

"Nah. Might eat it out of the jar, though."

"You might have to. I don't have food you'd eat."

Lonnie put cold white bread on a plate and took a stick of butter from a sloshing cooler. He had a gas stove, but no electric hookup for his toaster or refrigerator. Buttering the bread tore it, but he did it patiently. He served the eggs and bacon onto the same plate, except for two strips of bacon, which he put on a smaller plate and delivered to Montana before bringing his breakfast to the table. He sat across from her, indicating that Jamie should join them. Jamie took the place beside Montana, and Lonnie closed his eyes and said a prayer in Apache.

"Now," he said to his guests, "you two need to talk."

Montana nibbled a slice of bacon, avoiding Jamie's eyes. "I'm really, really sorry I hit your van. I shouldn't have been driving."

"Yeah," Jamie said, "you shouldn't have. Lucky you lived, the shape you were in. But your insurance'll take care of the van."

"It won't." Her voice shrank and she dropped her hands to her lap.

"What?"

"I don't have any."

"You don't have fucking *car insurance*?"

Lonnie tapped the table in front of Jamie softly. Jamie tried to rein himself in, but he was rattled. "Jeezus. I've heard of not having health insurance—"

The old man gave him a look, sipped his coffee and cut his egg into tiny pieces, dipping his bread in the yolk. The thick lenses of his glasses were spattered with grease. Jamie wanted to take them off and clean them for him, but it probably bothered Jamie more to look *at* them than it did Lonnie to look *through* them.

For some reason, this minor annoyance took the edge off the big one. Jamie unclenched his fists, rippling his fingers. "All right. No insurance. So, what's the plan?"

"That's better," Lonnie said. "Listen to her."

Montana slid him a grateful yet uneasy glance, then talked down at her plate. "Will owes me money." She crumbled the bacon, placed a piece in her mouth, and chewed it. "I helped him with his bills, but then I ran out for paying mine. He didn't pay me back yet. When he does, I'll repay you what it costs to fix your van."

"You think bloody fucking Will Baca is going to pay you back?" Jamie stood abruptly, and his thighs collided with the edge of the table. "Ow. Fuck." He strode to the open door and the fresh air. "His *ex*-girlfriend—"

"He has money coming. It should be a lot, seriously. I can't tell you where he's getting it, but—"

Jamie spun to face her. "You bloody well can. My van is worth more than Will Baca's word. You expect me to settle for this? Some secret source of money I may never see?" He caught a disapproving look from the medicine man. "Wait. Did you tell Lonnie?"

She nodded.

Jamie stared at the presumably wise old man.

Lonnie said, "Think about it. From your heart."

"My heart says I've been fucked."

Jamie stepped outside and sank onto the foldout steps, shivering in the morning chill. A raven croaked in a nearby tree and traffic rumbled past on Route 70. Lonnie wanted him to be compassionate. If he let himself, he would feel Tana's pain. The poverty, the loss of love, the desperate need to be rescued. He'd been through it all himself, and not that long ago. It was the fact that Will was behind Tana's problems that outraged him.

He could claim the damage on his insurance, though he'd have to pay a deductible and his rate might go up. Since he wasn't buying a parrot, he had the money to cover it. However, she seemed to think he could pay cash for the whole repair and not claim it and wait for her to pay him back. It might make her feel as if she had her life in order and that she'd taken care of things. Psychologically, it would do her good, but then Jamie would be taking the money from the big dark secret. *If* she ever got any.

Montana came out to sit beside him. "I don't remember much from last night, but I do remember how you held me when I was crying. It's like a light in the fog. You were so kind."

"People crying get to me. So, don't cry now, all right?"

She half-laughed. "I won't." She twisted the hem of her shirt and sighed. "I wanted to apologize for what I said about Mae. Lonnie told me I said it. I don't know how I got that idea."

"You remember talking to Reno last night?"

Montana squeezed the twisted wad of shirt and shook her head. "What's he got to do with it?"

Jamie recalled his own words on the Geronimo credibility. "Mm. Nothing. Just asking if you saw him. Don't suppose you remember anything related to my tent?" He was sure she hadn't vandalized it, and yet he had to double-check.

"No." A look of alarm crossed her face. "Did I do something to it? Did I puke in it?"

"Nah. Somebody cut it up."

"That's awful. I was crazy, but I wasn't that crazy. And I wasn't mad at you." She sighed and got to her feet. "I feel awful about the van. Can I pay you back when Will pays me?"

Jamie took his hat off, shook his hair, and put the hat back on. "Feel like I'd be receiving stolen goods or something."

"It's nothing that bad. No one's getting hurt. And Will has no other way to get the money. He can't ride for a long time and his parents flat-out told him not to come home. They said he's pulled the prodigal son act one too many times. He's got no choice. So, neither do I."

Not long ago Jamie had been injured, unable to play his instruments. It had sent him off the deep end. Unable to do rodeos, Will had to be going crazy as well as broke. And Letitia had that foolish divorce settlement. Struggling to hold onto land and horses wasn't the same as being penniless, but having to give up animals she loved would be heartbreaking. And Montana was innocent of anything other than falling for a wanker.

"Lonnie knows where the money's coming from?"

Montana nodded. "He won't tell you."

"Didn't think he would. Just spinning the moral compass. He's north, y'know?" Jamie closed his eyes and let the needle spin in his heart. It came to rest on an answer, a decision, but it vibrated with uncertainty. "How about you repay my deductible? That's all the money I'll be out. Take your time, though. I'll be in touch."

Montana thanked him with a kiss on the cheek.

When she'd gone, Jamie went back inside, lingering near the open door for bacon-free air. "You believe Will's going to pay her?"

Lonnie looked up from his breakfast and took a sip of coffee. "I believe that he *said* he would."

Silence except for the clink of Lonnie's fork against his plate. Jamie leaned against the wall, not sure what to say next. Lonnie finished his last bite and dabbed his mouth with a napkin. "Come in. Sit down. Tell me what happened to your tent, and why you asked Montana about Reno. She's hungover. She didn't pay attention. But I did."

Jamie squeezed into the little bench and met Lonnie's bacon-spattered lenses more than his eyes. "Would you mind if I cleaned your glasses for you?"

Lonnie took them off and wiped them on his shirt, then laid them on the table. His eyes were sharp and intense without the thick, smudged lenses. "Why did you ask about my great-nephew?"

With some reluctance, Jamie shared what Mae had learned in her psychic journey, feeling obligated to explain about the motel room and the way Mae worked as a psychic as well as what Reno had said. Lonnie remained silent for a moment, and then asked about the tent. Jamie described its fate and the peculiar details of the neatly and silently executed damage.

Lonnie asked, "You were at Zak's house long enough for this to happen?"

"Reckon."

Lonnie put his glasses back on, squinted, then took them off, went to the sink and washed them. "What do you think made someone cut up your tent?"

Jamie took a deep breath. He didn't want to think about this. "They wanted us to leave. Could have been someone who heard what Reno said about Mae, but ... it could have been, y'know, someone who's in on his secret. They're afraid Mae will find out."

Lonnie nodded. "That's a scary power she has, if you have a lot of secrets." He dried his glasses on a paper towel, held them up to the light, and put them back on. "I think you can figure out who damaged your tent."

The idea had been lurking at the edge of Jamie's mind ever since he'd noticed how neat the hole was, but he'd refused to let it in. Reno and Letitia had been with Montana and then gone to the motel. Zak had been with Jamie. That left Shelli and David, one to watch the booth while the other went to the campground.

The thought made his insides churn, and the smells of bacon and eggs and the congealing traces of them on Lonnie's plate made it worse. He took the dishes to the sink and ran water over them. Meat grease floated on the plate now. Jamie walked to the doorway to watch the campground begin to stir and let the fresh air wash over him. He had thought he'd made peace with his friends' secret. They claimed it wasn't hurting anyone, but it was driving them to do hurtful things.

His back to Lonnie, he said, "You know what they're hiding. I won't ask you what it is. But is it really okay with you?"

Water ran and stopped, followed by the squish of a soapy sponge. Lonnie was washing his dishes. "I never said it was."

Jamie turned to look at the old man. "You told me to think from my heart."

"About Montana, yes. And you did. That was good." Lonnie rinsed a plate, set it aside, and scrubbed the next. "It's not the same as liking how Will gets her the money. However, I'm a practical man. I look at the balance of things, not the absolutes." He finished the second plate and began washing mugs. "I can't uncook this stew they've made. I'm a medicine man, not a policeman. If any of them comes to me, I can help that way. Bring them back into harmony. Into *gozho*." Lonnie rinsed the mugs and placed them on the drain board. "And that's all I can do. All I should do."

Why hadn't Jamie and Mae seen this? It seemed so obvious now. His wavering inner compass needle found true north and settled. "I hope Reno turns to you. And Zak. I'm worried about him. You did a lot for Tana. She was scared to talk to me, but she actually seemed at peace with Will, y'know? Ready to move on, forgive him."

The old man got to work on cleaning the frying pan. "I only finished what you started last night. That light in the fog."

"Wasn't trying." Jamie fiddled with the door latch, clicking it back and forth. "Just leaked, y'know?"

"You need to be readier with that gift. Not just leak. You need to go back to your teachers."

"I'll think about it. After my tour."

"Why put it off?"

"Only got a month to get ready, and I have to get the van fixed."

Lonnie ran water over the pan and then dried it and the dishes, putting them in the cabinets one by one. "Your teachers are in Santa Fe?"

Jamie nodded, and Lonnie continued, "Will you need your van to see them?"

"Nah." Jamie had his Fiesta and his bike. His shoulders wriggled. "But I'll be busy."

"One of our medicine men is a professional musician. Writes songs, plays the guitar, performs all over the country. He was on our tribal council when he was younger. A busy man. Bessie Yahnaki went to college. She was a social worker *and* a healer. I was in the Navy before you knew me. I was a medic. Your girlfriend has her job and goes to school, but she's still a healer."

"Thought you said she was driving around without a map."

"I did. She needs to study more, too." Lonnie stopped tidying and looked at Jamie. "You both do. But she's answered the call. You can make excuses, but the spirits may not listen to them. Your own power may not listen."

Chapter Twenty-One

Mae got home in time to throw the laundry in the wash before meeting Niall for lunch. When she'd let him know she was back, he'd been surprised, but then invited her to Passion Pie to meet Daphne Brady. Mae had suggested they exercise on the way. As they walked the riverside path through the Rotary Park, Niall adjusted his ball cap lower over his eyes, squinting in the glare of the sun on the Rio Grande. "I can't believe I'm taking a frickin' walk."

"Isn't it nice, though, breathing the fresh air?"

He stopped and sat on one of the yellow metal picnic benches. "I'll breathe better if I sit."

Something rustled in the brush along the bank. Snake? They were shy and Mae didn't get to see them very often. She peered into the weeds. A red-winged blackbird fluttered up to a branch. "You still think about smoking?"

"Not so much the smoking as ..." Niall leaned on the table, chin in hand, index finger over his lips. "I miss the part of me that smoked. You wouldn't know what that's like. You never had a bad habit in your life. You and Marty. If you'd ever had a bad attachment, you'd understand."

"I had a first husband."

Niall hacked out a sound that passed for a laugh.

"I'm serious. I've had a man habit. Straight from high school boyfriend to break-up to new boyfriend to marrying him to divorce to new boyfriend to marrying him ... This year being single is some kind of record. I even went seven months without a date."

"You like being single?"

"Yes and no. I like being in a relationship but ..." Despite the reason for her departure from Mescalero, getting home had felt wonderful. "I like having my own place, too. My own space."

"Better make sure Jamie knows that. He doesn't need to be alone like a normal person." Niall coughed, hawked, and stood to spit into the trash can. "Christ. Crap keeps coming out. I want to stick a frickin' vacuum down my bronchioles. Those cilia have got nearly forty years of garbage to sweep out. Good thing Marty used to be a baseball player. He's used to seeing people spit." He hawked and expectorated again, and they resumed their walk. "Hell. I should stop bellyaching. I may sound like I'm dying, but you probably saved my life."

"You know Daddy thinks you're smoking again?"

"I did buy a pack."

"Niall! Why?"

"Can't explain it. I was in the Family Dollar at the checkout and I was so used to asking for my brand I just did it. They're in the glove compartment in the Beetle."

"You should get rid of them. Misty's sister Melody used to drink and she won't get near alcohol. Her husband gave a party and she kicked everybody out for bringing it."

"But I bet she didn't have an involuntary spiritual experience when she quit."

"No. Just a lot of hard work."

Niall gazed at the mountains across the river. "Maybe I'm tempting myself. Making myself have to work."

They left the park and turned up Foch Street, passing a dusty trailer park and chain-link fencing half-hidden in the prickly flesh of cow's tongue cacti. Mae caught herself getting slightly ahead and stopped to let Niall catch up.

"You heading back to the reservation tonight?" he asked, slightly out of breath.

Mae stood still, letting him rest. "No. I'm kinda sad about that. I made a good friend there—Melody—and I wanted to spend more time with Bernadette, too, and see all of the ceremonies. But Reno started this rumor that I'm a witch, and that's really evil to Apaches. It might be why somebody tore up Jamie's tent."

"*Reno Geronimo* said *that* about *you*?" Niall's head jutted forward even more than usual. "Damn. That's not like him."

"There's a story behind it. Reno and some other people are up to something they want to keep secret, something serious, and having a psychic around made them nervous. I think he said it to drive me off."

"That wasn't too bright. You both live here."

"I don't think Reno's used to lying and hiding things."

"Any idea what he's hiding?" Mae shook her head. Niall sighed. "I like Reno. He's a talented kid. I don't want him to screw his life up."

"I think he's already done it."

Niall stopped to pick up a quarter off the sidewalk. "Maine quarter. Believe that? What are the odds? Like you picking up a North Carolina." He put it in his pocket. "So where were we? Before Reno?"

"Not going back to Mescalero tonight." They crossed Broadway and continued uphill toward Main Street. Out of habit, Mae crossed to the far side for shade from a building's awning. Niall gave her a twisted look, probably objecting to the extra steps. "Jamie called. He's still there, but he wants to come here. He needs to get his van to a repair place though, and if he wakes up in Santa Fe he'll get it there sooner. I pointed that out, but he's had a pretty rough day—rough weekend, really, when it was supposed to be fun—"

"And what does Mae want? She who loves her own space?"

"I ..." Mae hadn't let this need surface until now. "I want a night off. I feel bad about asking for it, but he's ... he's ..."

Niall exhaled a laugh through his nose. "He's Jamie. You don't have to explain. One of my favorite people in the world, but sometimes you just have to put him outside."

Mae imagined a restless, blond-furred, dark-eyed cat climbing the curtains and Niall picking it up and sending it out the door. "It'd be hard to do it tonight, though. This was supposed be the fourth night of our four-day weekend."

"Be careful. Once you step in quicksand, you're not getting out."

"Jamie's not quicksand."

"You make someone happy doing what you don't want to do, that's quicksand."

"But I'm not doing things I don't want to do with Jamie."

"You went camping."

"But I told him I didn't like it—finally—and he took it okay. Sort of. Just a little fight."

The shade came to an end, and Mae crossed again, to an antique shop's awning. Niall coughed. "Shade to shade. It's like walking with a frickin' lizard."

"If you were as white as I am, you'd do this too. I get all the sun I can handle while I'm running. Anyway," she gave him a gentle nudge, "I like making you walk a little extra."

"Trying to distract me. We were talking about Jamie. Mark my words. You cut short his nice long weekend, I bet you my magical Maine quarter, you'll have more drama than Shakespeare. But if you don't do it, he won't know how you feel."

"You're kind of exaggerating."

"Am I? I've known him a lot longer than you have." Niall flipped the quarter and slapped it down it on the back of his hand. "Call it."

"Heads."

He lifted his top hand. "Some psychic you are. Tails. Typhoon Jamie coming up."

The coffee shop was busy when they arrived. Niall brought her to an art-topped table in the center and introduced her to Daphne

Brady, who rose and shook Mae's hand with a firm, assertive grip. The lawyer wore a tight-fitting sleeveless blouse and a short, equally tight skirt. She was thin to the point of emaciation, that old-smoker look like Niall had, only worse. Her skin was the loose-fitting garment that her clothes were not. Cascades of wrinkles bagged on her shoulders, arms, neck, and knees, as well as her face. *She needs some muscle to fill that skin.* Mrs. Brady's stick-straight hair, a faded graying blonde, was clipped in a low ponytail with a big sparkly barrette, a jarringly youthful touch.

They exchanged a few pleasantries, sat down, and then Daphne said, "Niall says you don't have your own place to practice yet. Mind if we do the healing work in my office? It's a long way to our house out in Arrey, and it'll be quieter without Chuck and the dogs."

"That would be fine."

"Wednesday night? Six o'clock?"

"Perfect."

Misty delivered an iced coffee and a pastry to Daphne. Mae was surprised to see her. "You didn't take the whole four days off?"

"Just two. I'm only working lunches, though, and I'll go back at night. It's a fun ride on the bike."

To her relief, Mae didn't sense that Misty had heard the witch rumor or that she blamed Mae for Will's rejection of Montana—a good thing. Misty had been the only supporter of that relationship. "How's Montana this morning?"

"Hungover. But nowhere near as upset as I thought she'd be. Can you meet me when I get off at three?"

"Sure." Mae had promised Misty information about Reno's secret activities and hadn't been able to learn anything yet. Maybe Misty had something of Reno's Mae could use. "Meet you here?"

Misty nodded.

Niall glanced at a note Daphne slid toward him. "What's that?"

"The code we'll use. You asked Florencia to install ... you know. Chuck's putting it in later this week."

Misty stepped back a little. Decent of her, with something private going on. Niall folded the note and tucked it into his shirt pocket. "Should I shred it and swallow it after I memorize it?"

"Something like that, yes. Florencia thinks the whole expense is ridiculous, that she'll be dead by the time Chuck gets around to installing it. And she doesn't want the studio opened before she dies—but we can work around that. Or Chuck says he can."

Niall asked Mae what she wanted to eat and followed Misty back to the counter to order and pay. Daphne bit into her pastry and wiped frosting off her mouth. "I'm so ready for something to finally work. Especially after watching what Florencia is going through. I've tried the patch, gum, hypnosis, cold turkey, and I still missed my cigs and went back to them. Every time."

Niall's healing had left him disoriented. He was normally so cranky Mae couldn't tell if he was having withdrawal symptoms or just being himself, but he certainly wasn't at ease with his experience. She didn't want Daphne to be so unprepared. "Maybe if you do a few things to get ready, like making a list of the reasons you want to quit, it'll go better." *And maybe I won't see your unfinished business.*

Daphne studied her nails. "I'd love to spend my smoking money on a manicure. I hate the nicotine stains." She looked up. "But what I really want is to go dancing with Chuck and not get tired."

"I bet he'll be happy about that."

"He sure will. Back when we were in law school, he almost didn't ask me out on our first date because I smoked. He's always said it's my only fault, and I've said it's the only one he doesn't have." She drank her coffee. "Just kidding. He's the love of my life. Pain in the ass, but the love of my life."

I know that feeling. "If y'all were in school together, you must be the same age." Daphne looked older, but she probably wasn't. "How come he retired and you didn't?"

"Prostate cancer. Scared him into wanting to have more fun. He's been in remission for three years now, but he never wanted to go back to work after that."

Niall returned to sit with them, bringing coffee for himself and handing Mae an iced tea.

"Florencia's the opposite of Chuck," Daphne said. "Having cancer makes her want to work more. She can't do much, but when she's feeling up to it she sketches."

Niall took a long slow drink. "It's what makes her feel alive. I need to bring her some colored pencils. She wouldn't want to go out in black and white."

Mae had an image of David's intricate black-and-white art, his weaving-lightning pot. She asked, "Does she ever talk about making up with her family?"

"No," Niall replied. "They're still banned and so is Reno."

Daphne pulled a chunk of her pastry off. "Florencia wants to die on her own terms, according to *her* idea of going in peace. That means that if people pissed her off or hurt her, they don't get to stress her out in her final hours by crying and asking for forgiveness." She popped the bite into her mouth and chewed. "I told her we should play Sinatra at her funeral. 'I did it my way.' "

Niall half-laughed, rubbing his eyes behind his glasses. "What funeral? Why bother? Who's left in her life to come to it?"

A promising cluster of dark clouds huddled west of town while Mae hung out her laundry in the side yard next to the carport, trying to get up the nerve to tell Jamie not to come tonight. The storm gave her a reason to put it off. She needed to get the clothes up quickly so they'd have the hour or so it would take them to dry. Voices drifted to her from the backyard, where Niall was working on the deck project with help from Mae's neighbor Kenny.

Hanging the fire-danger shirt brought her back to the night Jamie had vanished from the tent, the night of Zak's party. She realized now that it wasn't Zak's shirt—he wore his clothes skin tight and it had fit loosely on Jamie—and that it was more than a firefighter joke. Either Zak had given it to Melody as a way of warning her off any smoldering passion for her old flame Will, or she'd chosen it as a comment on Zak's jealousy. Either way, it was a reminder of what a mess their relationship was, a kind of warning label. *If you don't communicate, you could end up like this couple.*

The wind blew a few puffy strands of plastic packing material over the fence at the end of the property past the laundry shed. They skittered through the carport and Mae ran to catch them, popped them, and brought them inside to the trash.

Her phone was ringing. She checked the caller ID. Jamie. And she hadn't figured out what to say to him yet

"Had an idea," he said. "Lonnie wanted me to go back to my teachers and I didn't want to, but he's usually right, so I called Fiona and she's doing a three-day workshop next month. Sort of intermediate training, but she said we could handle it."

"It does sound good, but I have my young'uns in August."

"They can come up to Santa Fe with you. I want to meet them. Spend some time with them."

"You will, but I can't be in a workshop for three days while they're here."

"I already signed us up. There weren't a lot of spaces left."

"Did you pay for it already?"

Silence, then—half-pleading, half-joking, "It was cheaper than a parrot ..."

Stop charming me. Mae wanted to argue on principle. This was another surprise. But she'd read Fiona McCloud's book on energy healing and had wanted to study with her. Jamie had finally hit on a surprise Mae wanted. He understood her better than she'd given him credit for. "Thank you, sugar. I'll see if Daddy can come up with me and do something with the girls during the day. That was generous."

"Nah. Selfish. I'd be scared shitless going by myself. I don't like getting better at this crap."

Reassuring him that it wouldn't be scary with his teacher there, Mae went back outside and tucked the phone against her ear to resume hanging laundry.

A piercing squeal drowned out Jamie's next words, followed by small fussing voices and another squeal. "Sorry. Dean and Deanna. I'm at the powwow with Mel. Trying to get up the nerve to talk to David."

I know how you feel. As thoughtful as Jamie had been with this latest surprise, she found it even harder to ask for a night on her own, though she still needed it. "Talk about what?"

"The tent. Think he's the one who hurt it. Dunno how to mention it. Thought I'd just tell it like a story, y'know? Tell him how upset I was. Normal stuff I'd share with a mate. See how he reacts."

"If he's a good liar, he won't react much at all." Mae clipped Jamie's parrot-print shirt to the line. "I have another idea. What if you got someone to buy some inexpensive thing he made? Then I could find out for you. He can't know who all your friends are."

"Nah. He's already thought of that. He was taking all his cheap stuff off the counter last night. Don't want you doing the psychic stuff with him anyway. I just wanted to know about the tent. And

Placido. Not this whole big secret about the money—we have to drop that."

Mae moved the phone to her other ear, hunched her shoulder up to hold it, and hung the next item of clothing. "I can't drop it if Misty and Melody don't want to."

"Yeah, you can—" Dean or Deanna made another nerve-rattling noise. "Seriously, love. You'll do more harm than good if you dig it all up and try to stop them."

"*Harm?* I'm trying to prevent it. I'm gonna see Misty in a few hours and I hope she'll have something of Reno's I can use. She needs to know the truth before she marries him."

"Let them sort it out for themselves. I'll explain more tonight. Gotta go. Hopi rain dancers are coming on. Catcha."

"Hang on a second. If you're not taking your van to your mechanics in Santa Fe tonight, why don't you stay for the ceremonies? No one thinks you're a witch. You could share your parents' tent."

"Nah. Rather be with you. I've seen the final morning a lot. It's nice, but it starts really fucking early."

Mae stalled for time. Telling Jamie *no* hadn't gotten any easier. "What am I missing?"

"The girls run down the arena and back. Really beautiful. After that there's a giveaway. Families drive pickups in and toss truck-loads of stuff to everyone. Fruit, paper towels, laundry baskets. Things that won't break if you pitch 'em into a crowd. The tipi comes down. And then the medicine men bless you if you want. They pray and mark your face with something. Think it's ashes from the fire that was in the tipi."

"This is when the girls have healing power?"

"Yeah. They have a lot of power that morning." He sighed. "Wish Reno hadn't said that about you. If anyone believed it and saw you there, it'd be bad."

"I'm sure that's why he said it." Mae felt her jaw clench. She had to get off the Reno track and back to un-inviting Jamie. "But I could use a good night's rest—"

"Yeah, it'll be nice to be in your bed, won't it? I'll give you a backrub. Foot massage." The noisy twins began chanting a *did-not-did-too* argument with no admonishment from Melody. Mae could tell by the fading of their voices that Jamie had moved away. "Love this dance. Girls have this fringe over their eyes like the way rain looks when it's just a thin band of it. I can leave when they're done. It should rain then. They're good at that. Be at your place in about three hours."

"I'm meeting with Misty then, remember?"

"No worries. I'll do some grocery shopping or something. Hooroo, love. Catcha."

Mae put her phone in her pocket and watched the clouds piling up. She hadn't told him no. Hadn't even known how to try.

A fringe of gray rain stroked the mountains, in harmony with the Hopi dancers she was missing. She pulled Jamie's old *Don't Worry, Be Hopi* sweatshirt from the laundry basket. The tent vandal had ground a lot of chocolate into it, and some stains lingered. The shirt was probably like the tent and the roo, though. He couldn't throw it out. And she didn't want him to. He'd loaned it to her the chilly evening in Santa Fe when they'd first met, when he'd first started both charming her and sticking to her.

Mae brought her laptop with her to the coffee shop, arriving a little early. She still hadn't done the research she'd wanted to, and this way if she found something of interest, she could show it to Misty. The café was almost empty, with only a few people drinking coffee and working quietly on computers. Mae had her choice of tables and selected the one with the lizard in the desert painted on it. The reptile was appealingly realistic, with a subtle orange-and-brown checkerboard look to its skin. The artist had gotten the shades of orange just right, how it was brighter at the mid-back and shoulders and faded out toward the tail.

Enough lizard-gazing. She bought an iced tea and began her first inquiry. She was curious to explore David and Shelli's web site, and Letitia Westover-Brown's. Also, she wondered if Will Baca had taken the embarrassing video of Jamie off his Facebook page. Since David was a tent-slashing suspect, she started with him.

The MVP pueblo pots site featured his and Shelli's most impressive pieces. No earrings or little cats. The "about" link stated the pueblos the couple came from and mentioned that David was the nephew of the well-known Acoma painter Florencia Mirabal. A late relative of Shelli's who had been the governor of Pojoaque Pueblo also earned a few proud lines. Did the potters like to ride coattails?

The photography on the home page was excellent and the marketing simple: a list of events at which the couple would be selling their work. They didn't take online orders, and the page under the link for Shops and Galleries said *under construction*. David and Shelli had obviously been deterring her from a purchase, not encouraging her. They might even have taken down their retail information temporarily.

Mae bookmarked the site and looked up Letitia. Her home page featured a striking black-and-white portrait of a bare-chested man riding a racing bike, his lean, sculpted body gleaming with sweat. The heading *Notable Men of New Mexico: Portraits and Calendars by Letitia Westover-Brown* floated above him. In the text below, he was identified as the winner of the Tour of the Gila the previous year. A sidebar described the photographer's appreciation of the beauty and vitality of her male subjects, and how she drew her inspiration from artists as diverse as Michelangelo and Delmas

Howe. *Howe.* He'd painted the cowboy angel in Florencia's collection. Mae looked up at his tabletop displayed on the wall, an entanglement of male arms. As far as she could tell, it never came down to take its turn as an eating surface the way the others did.

Letitia and Florencia both liked the same artist—but then, he was famous. The coincidence probably didn't mean anything.

Mae clicked on the Calendars link and found a list of Letitia's annual productions. *Howe-dy Pardner,* a tribute to Delmas Howe's cowboys, featured real cowboys posed like the paintings. It wasn't risqué, not the sort of thing Lonnie and Orville had been joking about. The cowboys were sexy, but they had their clothes on. The next title was more suggestive, another cowboy calendar called *Wild Riders.* The one listed as the bestseller was *Smokin' Bare: New Mexico's Hottest Firefighters.* Was Zak going to be in it? Mae clicked on the title. A new tab opened, showing a muscular man wearing nothing but Smokey Bear's brown hat and holding a massive hose in a strategic location. He gave the viewer a mischievous grin.

Misty stopped by Mae's table. "You need a refill— Whoa, what are you looking at?"

"Letitia Westover-Brown's web site. The photographer that was hanging out with Zak and Reno."

"You think they're—? No. No way."

"You don't think Zak would pose with his hose? He seems vain enough."

"Can you imagine what that would do to his image with those kids he coaches? And Reno is *not* calendar material. I love him, but undress him and he looks like a twelve-year-old."

Mae felt her face redden. She didn't want to think about Reno undressed, but Misty was right. David Mirabal was even further out of the picture. "I was just looking to see what kind of connection they all might have."

"You don't need to." Misty glanced back at the counter. A customer stood there smiling at her, poised with his cup, asking for a refill. "I'll be back in a second. You want a refill on your tea?"

"Thanks. Yes."

Mae switched to Facebook. She'd finally given in to pressure from friends in Virginia and gotten a Facebook account, which she used about once a week for staying in touch with them. Her search for Will Baca brought up his fan page as a rodeo pro, filled with pictures of him holding trophies and riding bulls, and videos of Will in action. It wasn't the page Melody had looked at. Mae tried again and found his personal page, but all it showed was the header and Will's name, age, and place of birth. The rest was blank.

When Misty delivered her tea, Mae asked, "Could Will have taken *everything* off his Facebook page?"

"He never put Montana's picture up to have to take it down."

"I didn't mean that." But it said a lot about him. "I can't see *any* pictures."

Misty looked at the screen. "You don't do Facebook much, do you? He's got it set private, so only his friends can see his personal stuff."

"Jamie told me that Letitia was looking at Will's page and this video he took of Jamie. That means she's Facebook friends with Will?"

"Why not? If he's on her naked cowboy calendar. But you don't have do all this Nancy Drew online stuff. What I was starting to tell you is—" Misty lowered her voice. "All you need is the table. Reno painted that lizard."

Chapter Twenty-Two

Wind-driven rain began to patter against the windows, followed by thunder and lightning. Mae thought about her laundry she'd forgotten on the line, but let the concern go as the patrons of Passion Pie Café cheered the rain and shared their hopes that the storm would last a while. Misty turned the sign on the door around, indicating the place was closed, and began sweeping. A man in the kitchen started singing along with the classic jazz ballad that was playing. No one rushed to leave but took their time to finish cookies and coffee and final emails. Mae didn't feel conspicuous lingering, especially with the downpour. She felt like she'd won. Reno had driven her out of Mescalero, and she'd ended up doing exactly what he'd tried to prevent.

He'd probably thought he was safe with his art on a café table. In a busy public place, it would be hard for her to concentrate, and a lot of people had eaten on his work since he'd painted it. Mae hoped his energy traces would still be strong, though. She turned off her laptop and phone, then got the crystals from her purse, discreetly cupping several clear quartz points in her hand. To strengthen her receptivity, she also put one on Reno's signature, which she'd discovered between two long slender toes of the lizard's left rear foot, "Reno" up the inside of one toe, "Geronimo" down the next.

Mae turned to face the wall, laid one hand over the crystal on the signature and closed her eyes. *What's Reno hiding?*

Her vision rolled and swirled through a tunnel, coming out in a room that had to be Florencia's studio at the back of her house, though Mae had only seen it from the outside with its blinds closed. The view through the windows at the far end showed the detached carport, while the rest faced the steep bluff across the narrow street behind the house. The artist stood in front of a large sheet of paper attached to an easel, sketching. Her thick, short hair was dyed fuchsia, matching the frames of her glasses, and her full figure looked firm, healthy, and strong. Several small canvases with what appeared to be drafts of the work she had in mind stood around her, images of a narrow rocky staircase like a crevasse in a mesa.

Reno sat on a wooden stool watching her, his heels hooked on a rung. They were silent together, yet strangely intense.

"Don't put it off," he said. "It could be just a cyst. You need to find out."

"I already know what it is." She drew carefully, slowly, studying each stroke. "I can *feel* it."

"People survive breast cancer now. More than they die of it. I looked it up. It's not like pancreatic cancer. My mom never had a chance. You do."

"You know what happens to your arm and chest muscles if they cut your boob off?" Florencia paused in her work. "I'm right-handed. It's my right breast."

"So what? You can recover from surgery, even if it takes a while. But you won't paint anything if you're dead." Reno kicked the rung and looked down at his feet. "I'll love you with one breast. I'll love you while you heal. Or I'll love you with a scar where they take out a lump. Whatever happens, I'll love you. Please. See a doctor."

She walked over, looked into his sad, serious face, and touched his upper lip with her charcoal stick, drawing a moustache before he could pull away. He looked wounded, but she burst out laughing and said, "I should go ahead and die of this so you can get on with your life. With a nice Apache girl your own age."

Reno glared at her, swiped at his mouth, and walked out. Florencia's mood changed suddenly, like an actor dropping a role backstage. She bit her lip and pressed her fist to her chest, tears brimming in her eyes.

Mae ended the vision and sat staring at the lizard. Around her, the café had emptied. The only person left in the room was Misty, still sweeping. The vision was going to be hard to share with her. She couldn't be expecting this to be Reno's secret.

What had Florencia been grieving? The potential loss of her breast, the feared effect of her treatment on her painting, or the affection she had turned away? Maybe all of it.

Reno's declaration of love had come across as discouraged, spoken from a distance, avoiding eye contact. Florencia might have rejected him more than once. Mae had a hard time picturing the artists as a couple, and not only because of their age difference. Their personalities were a mismatch.

Had Florencia returned his feelings at all? Had they been lovers and broken off, or had he been a friend she could neither let go of nor love in return? Mae had felt that way about Jamie once. The situation had torn her until she'd had a change of heart. Florencia might have struggled even more if she'd loved Reno but turned him down, believing he should be with that girl his own age. A young artist falling in love with his older mentor sounded romantic—until it actually happened. What Mae had seen looked sad and hopeless.

The only thing that made her wonder if they had been lovers was the hair. Florencia hadn't chopped her chemo-thinned hair off and dyed it fuchsia. That had been her look before treatment, and yet there had been long black hairs on some of her clothes Mae had packed. Either Florencia hadn't had her sweaters cleaned since before she did her crazy hair color, or she'd been very close to someone with hair like Reno's.

Mae put the quartz points in the pouch for stones that needed rebalancing and used snow quartz to clear her aura of Reno's energy. Misty emptied her dust pan into the trash and gave Mae a curious look. "Well?"

"I didn't find out how he's getting money. I saw something else."

Loud rapping on the door interrupted them. Jamie stood in the rain, holding his hat from blowing off his head, his floral-print Aloha shirt flapping in the wind. On the street outside sat his dented van. Misty made a face and walked over to point at the *closed* sign. He made the same face back at her, and she unlocked the door.

"Sorry." He stepped in, took off his hat and shook the rain from his hair, then said to Mae, "Couldn't get hold of you, love."

"I turned my phone off so I could concentrate on something."

"But—" He frowned, sounding utterly bewildered. "You knew I'd call."

"I thought you were going grocery shopping while I talked with Misty."

"Yeah, but then I didn't have a key—where d'you keep your spare?—to go in and see what we needed. And then it started pouring and I thought about you getting wet and I remembered you were meeting Misty and must be here, so—" He took a breath after his nonstop recitation. "I'm here to give you a ride. And we can shop."

"Thanks for thinking of it, but I need to talk with Misty. Can you wait in your van for a few minutes?"

"No, it's okay," Misty said, "Call me later. Jamie's being so thoughtful. So *not-Reno*."

"We need to talk about Reno. Stop by my house before you leave for Mescalero." Mae wasn't letting anything get in the way of sharing her vision. Misty would be on her Harley as soon as the rain stopped, and the last time Mae had seen the girl ride while angry with Reno, she'd been reckless. How she'd react to the news that he'd been at least interested in his father's ex-wife, his mentor, Mae couldn't imagine—break the sound barrier?—but surely she'd give his ring back without needing to know where he got the money to buy it. "It's the green converted trailer on Marr, next to that old warehouse. Come over as soon as you finish closing up here."

While Jamie drove to Bullock's grocery, rambling about possible recipes, Mae watched the storm and half-listened, letting him become like the sound of the rain. The puddles were filling up nicely at the intersections, the sign of a good storm. He slowed the van and plowed through the water. "Italian, y'think? You like pesto? It's good on whole wheat noodles. Or how about zucchini lasagna? I'm in sort of a pasta mood."

I'm not in a Jamie mood. She felt guilty about that. The Chino sisters' relationships made her feel she was being ungrateful. Jamie was considerate, communicative, sensitive—everything Zak, Will, and Reno were not. And she loved him. How could she not be in the mood for him? Niall, fond as he was of Jamie, had encouraged her to stand her ground for going slowly in the relationship. She'd tried a few times over the weekend, but Jamie didn't seem to grasp the idea. *He doesn't need to be alone like a normal person.* He wouldn't understand unless she said it outright. Anyone who thought a couple could spend four nights in a tiny tent didn't need his own space.

The thought of the tent made her put off the uncomfortable discussion. "Did you talk to David?"

"Yeah." Jamie steered into the parking lot behind the store. "It's weird. It was like I thought—they had only their expensive stuff out. Said it was some marketing experiment. Attracting serious buyers. At a fucking powwow?"

They dashed through the rain to the back door of the store and into a hallway with bulletin boards and a stand full of flyers. Mae asked, "How did he react about the tent?"

Jamie took off his hat and shook his hair again, tapped the hat against his leg a few times, and put it back on. "It was weird. He was holding Star and rocking her while I told him what happened, and then he looks up at me and says, 'I'm sure it looks bad to you now, but everything's going to be all right.' Real gentle, like he cares—and like he *knows* something."

"Did you ask what he meant?"

"Couldn't. He was like this *oracle*. And then some people came up and started looking at pots and David gave Shelli the baby and he says it again, 'Everything's going to be all right,' and starts his sales pitch for the high-end pots."

Everything's going to be all right. Could David know that? Jamie had told the tent story to check his friend's reaction, but had no doubt been genuine in his dismay. David might have wanted to make Jamie feel better, or he might have found a clever way to cut off the topic. Maybe both. Mae squeezed Jamie's hand, not sure what to say.

They started shopping, Jamie swinging a green plastic basket and musing over the merits of various fruits—in season or out of season, local or imported—and how he craved apples even though "they're out of season and probably came from New Zealand and—that almost *rhymed*."

"Just get what you want." Mae tried to hurry him so she could get home to meet Misty. "I like everything."

"You know blueberries are good for your brain? Read that somewhere." He put a package in the basket and then examined several varieties of apples, reading the little sticky tags on them.

Mae's phone rang. Misty.

"Where are you? I'm at your place."

"You're done already?"

"Yep. Wash the tables, close the cash register. It doesn't take long."

"I'll be right there." Mae's house was only three blocks away. She ended the call. "I'm gonna run and see Misty."

"You'll get wet. Let me drive you."

"I won't melt. Finish the shopping." She opened her wallet and offered him some money, but he drew his head back as if the cash smelled bad. "I'm paying for dinner," she said. "I don't want you buying everything. You already paid for that workshop."

"Doesn't matter, does it?"

"It will if we don't pay attention. I don't want to get unequal."

"Bloody hell, we're already fucking *unequal*."

"Lower your voice, sugar." Further up the produce aisle, Chuck Brady was examining tomatillos. He glanced at Mae, raised an eyebrow, and went back to choosing vegetables. "People can hear you cussing."

"Right." Jamie whispered. "There you go. See? Bloody fucking unequal."

"I am not having a fight with you in this grocery store." But she felt like it. He'd started one over nothing—the practical, common-sense sharing of expenses. What would have happened if she'd asked for a night alone? Niall had been right about Typhoon Jamie. It didn't take much to stir up a storm. "I'll see you at the house."

Mae pushed the money into his front pocket and strode toward the front door. Chuck gave her another eyebrow lift as she passed. She wanted to stop like some seeker at the feet of the guru and beg him to tell her the secret of healthy relationships. Chuck and Daphne had been together through good times and hard times, illness and aging, and they adored each other. Surely he knew the key to making things work. But Mae had to go talk to a Chino sister, one of the all-star experts in unhealthy relationships. She gave Chuck what she felt might be a desperate look, her hands palms-up in the universal signal of frustration, and hurried past.

As she approached the front door, she heard his resonant voice. "You must be Mae's boyfriend. Chuck Brady, retired."

And Jamie's lighter but equally resonant voice, a tad shaky. "Um—yeah. Jamie Ellerbee." A pause. "Retired what?"

The automatic door slid open and Mae darted out into the storm. *Thank you, Chuck.* Maybe Jamie could sit at the feet of the master.

Mae and Misty sat in the old metal chairs on the front porch, and Mae shared her vision. When she finished, the young Apache woman curled over with her forearms on her thighs, fists pressed together, head down, and stayed there. Not crying, just silent.

"Misty? Are you okay?"

"Shit! What do you *think*?" she exploded, standing and kicking the chair into the railing. "What was the matter with that woman?"

"With—" Mae almost said her name. "With *her*? What do you mean? She turned him down. She told him to be with—with you, I assume."

"And flirted with him while she did it. And kept him hanging on and hanging on. For what? Her *ego.* How could he not worship her? A great artist. His teacher. She should have drawn a line in the sand. But she used him. Middle-aged woman gets young man to love her."

Mae should have seen that aspect of the story, but she'd been too stunned to analyze it right away, and then Jamie had showed up. Misty was at least half-right. Florencia should have nipped that crush in the bud. "I'm sorry that's what I found out. I was hoping I'd learn where he's been getting his money. You still need to know. Has he got stuff he keeps at your place?"

Misty shook her head. "He took it. Not that he ever had much—just a toothbrush."

"What about gifts? Did he give you any of his art? I can go back to the Pie and try with the table again tomorrow, but someone could be sitting at it, or it could sell. I'd like something I can use at home."

"He gave me my ring. And my skateboard. That's about it."

"Not much use to me unless he uses it a lot."

"Reno? Ride a board? He thinks it's too dangerous." She leaned on the railing and reached a hand out into the drizzle. "Rain's slowing down. I should get going."

"Drive safely. Don't speed." *And get a helmet.*

"Where's the fun in that?" Misty started down the steps. "You sound like Zak. Except he always adds, 'Get a helmet.'" She strode down the driveway and into the street and was quickly out of sight.

Mae sounded like *Zak*? No—only when he was giving good advice. He'd probably answered some EMT calls for injured or dead bikers. People like Misty who took risks for the fun of it. She hadn't listened to him. Maybe someone should point out to the wannabe dentist that she could get her teeth knocked out. She was stubborn, though. She saw only *poor Reno* being used by Florencia, not Reno being disloyal. If Mae found out he was in some illegal scheme, would Misty still make an excuse for him and marry him, or would that carry more weight than a crush on his mentor?

Jamie's van rolled into the driveway, passing under the mesquite tree near the street with a scratching of thorny branches along the roof. He pulled up by the steps and got out, bags dangling from his arms. "Sorry about all the plastic. My cloth bags are in the Fiesta." He climbed the steps, and Mae opened the door and took a couple of bags from him. He continued, "You know they banned the plastic ones in Santa Fe? It's weird to even see 'em. City's trying to exterminate the state flower—plastic bag snagged on a cactus. But they're actually useful, like for cleaning Gasser's litterbox, so can you remind me to take them with me?"

"Sure."

They took their shoes off on their way in, and then unpacked the groceries, Jamie singing snatches of various songs. When he started to put the bags under her sink, she took them and stuffed them into one of his sandals by the front door. "So you won't forget."

"Already did."

Had he also forgotten they'd been arguing? It lingered in the back of her mind, unresolved, but Jamie seemed unaware of it. He washed an apple after peeling its sticker off and offered it to Mae. She thanked him and bit into it while he rinsed another, working far too long at the adhesive residue. Obsessing. Maybe he did remember. Mae asked, "Did you like Chuck Brady?"

"Yeah. Nice bloke." Jamie rolled the last bit of gumminess off. "Jeezus. You'd think a sign that says they're Fujis would be enough. Every apple doesn't need a fucking name tag. Let's go outside. Look for the rainbow." He put his arm around her waist, leading her in a hip-to-hip stroll down the hall to the back door in her bedroom.

The rainbow hadn't arrived yet. Rain was still falling in patches and streaks over Turtleback Mountain as blue sky began to break through the clouds overhead. Apple in his mouth, Jamie swiped at the top step with his hand. "Not bad." He sat, chomping on the fruit. "Sit on my lap if you don't like getting your bum wet."

"No thanks." That was something petite women did, not Mae. She sat beside him. "I like to see you when I talk to you. And I feel like we didn't finish—"

"Fighting?"

"Sorting things out."

"Same thing. Chuck could tell we were having a fight." Jamie spun his apple by its stem, first one way and then the other, watching the bitten place twirl by. "Gave me some advice."

Good. "What'd he say?"

Jamie snort-laughed. "The woman is always right." He spun the apple again. Mae wanted to tell him to stop. Any second, it was going to fall off its stem and roll down the steps into the dirt and then he would be back in the kitchen fussing over little sticky labels again. Jamie said, "I told him that was our whole fucking problem."

"I'm not always right."

"But you act like it. This bothering you?" He indicated the spinning apple.

"Yes."

He stopped and took a bite, talking through it. "You can tell me about stuff like that. I'm not kicking myself when I say this. I know I can be irritating."

Mae almost protested his self-assessment, but it was true. "A little bit. Sometimes." She bumped him softly with her shoulder. "See, I'm letting you be right."

He flashed a smile so sweet it caught her by surprise, a smile that grew broader and brighter like the light from between the clouds and crinkled little lines around his eyes. When he was radiant and open like that, his warmth could sweep away everything that got on her nerves and make her fall in love all over again.

"Love it when you look at me like that." His smile faded, and he grew serious. "Like you see me and not just what's wrong with me. That's something special about you, y'know? About Zak and Mel, too. Seeing *me*." He took a bite of the apple and looked down at his feet. "Sorry I got pissed off in the store. It was *me* seeing something wrong with me. Not you. You were treating me like a normal bloke and I was ... dunno ... had two fucking panic attacks in the past two days ... feeling like I'm not good enough and like you wouldn't let me make it up to you by paying for stuff. I'm sorry. I miss my book—it was helping—I forget so fast. Got the attention span of a flea."

Mae rubbed his back. He was hot, even hotter than normal, often a sign of some emotional storm brewing. "You okay, sugar?

He surprised her by turning to lie on his back across the top step, pulling her on top of him and nuzzling her neck. Their apples tumbled to the ground with soft thuds.

"Did we need to talk more or are we—"

His kiss answered her question. He slid his hand under her tank top and unhooked her bra.

"We should go inside," she said. "There's gaps in the fence. And Niall might come back to work on the deck."

"After the rainbow." Jamie kissed her again and traced the line of her cheek and jaw with one finger. His eyes were huge and black, swallowing her in their depths. "Have I told you how much I love you today?"

The enormity of his love, the naked vulnerability of it, left her at a loss for words. *Yes* would be trivial. *I love you too*, barely adequate. She managed a small nod and tucked her fingers under the broad lateral muscles of his back.

"I miss you so much when I'm not with you." He twisted a strand of her hair around his finger. "Think about you all the time."

"You don't need to *miss* me, sugar. We're still connected when we're not together."

"I don't do well alone, though." He turned his head to the side and stared at Turtleback Mountain. "Feel like something bad will happen."

Mae sat up and stroked her hand over his chest. There was no way she could ask for a night on her own now. His heart was beating too fast and hard for just lying there. The urge to use her healing gift to calm him swept through her, but she sent her love through her hand instead. It should be enough.

It wasn't.

"You feel like something bad will happen to us?"

"Nah." He pushed himself upright. "Just bad stuff in general. Think about death a lot. Mum and Dad getting old. Stuff like that."

"Getting old is good. I mean, it beats the alternative. When I healed Niall, Daddy thanked me for more years with him. He was always so afraid he'd lose him early."

Jamie's hand squeezed hers hard. "Let's live a long time, all right? Both of us."

He means together. She liked to think they would last, but she couldn't make promises after dating for less than two months. Unable to choose the right words, she squeezed his hand back.

Jamie sang a new tune Mae hadn't heard before. She knew it was his. He often created songs that had only one or two lines, with variations on the mood and the melody. This one had a hymn-like quality, soaring and simple.

"*We'll live forever, love lasts forever ...*"

With each exploration of the line, his voice grew stronger, vibrating every atom in her body like a powerful light passing through her.

"Look. Look!" Jamie broke off his song, sprang to his feet, and jumped up and down. "Look!"

Mae looked. A double rainbow over the Turtle. "Oh my god. That's so beautiful."

"It's a sign. Remember our first double rainbow?"

It had been in Santa Fe, when she'd known him for less than twenty-four hours and didn't know what to think of him yet. The rainbow had made him insanely happy then, too.

He swept her into his arms and kissed her, danced her down the steps and twirled her, then dipped her back as if they were ballroom dancing. "*We'll live forever, love lasts forever...*"

Chapter Twenty-Three

A touch on Mae's shoulder woke her, followed by a velvety-soft kiss on each eyebrow. The room was dark except for the night light she'd put in for the nights Jamie stayed over. He touched the tip of her nose with one finger. "The hot spring is full and the wine is poured. The stars are waiting for you."

Exhausted, Mae groaned. "What time is it?"

"Time for love." He wrapped his arms around her and squeezed. "Get up. Get wet."

"In the middle of the night?"

"I couldn't sleep, so I thought the hot spring would help, but then I thought, what if you woke up and I was out having a soak without you? Be weird. So, I'm being romantic instead." Wrestling her gently, Jamie licked her ear, made a deep humming sound against her neck, and then blew on it with closed lips, making a fart noise.

"Yeah, that poot sound was really romantic."

He repeated it and licked her ear again. "Play with me, love. Life is good."

Mae wanted to sink back into her dreams, but it wasn't an option. She could reject another well-intentioned surprise and start an argument, or give in. Either way, she wouldn't get any sleep. Too drowsy to fight, she surrendered and rose. He opened the door beside the head of the bed, and they stepped out into the night.

Mae never went out to the hot spring without a bathing suit because of the gaps between the boards in the backyard fence. She descended to ground level in haste, the wind slapping her bare skin. Jamie followed.

Most of the clouds had blown away, revealing a crescent moon. Its light gleamed on a bottle of wine and two glasses on a small table next to the big metal tub. Towels were draped identically on a pair of lawn chairs. Mae followed the red flagstones leading to the tub, stepping over a stake and a string where Niall had marked out the eventual dimensions of the deck, and lowered herself into the hot water. "Thanks sugar. This *is* romantic."

Jamie got in with her. He caressed her back and hips in a tentative sensual inquiry, kissed her, and let go to sink deeper in the water. "Thanks for brushing my hair, by the way."

When his insomnia had become distressingly conspicuous, she'd gotten his brush from his backpack and done the one thing she knew could calm him down. "Did you sleep after that or just relax?"

"Both. It was bliss. Think I was out for at least an hour before I got squirmy again." He wriggled, stretched, and took her hand and kissed it. "You're good to me. You let me be myself. No complaints. Can't tell you how much that means."

She thought of the complaints she hadn't spoken and leaned her head back against the rim of the tub to gaze at the stars salting the sky. What was she going to do with him? It wasn't as if he did anything wrong. No man had ever treated her better. She loved him. And yet he wore her out.

"Forgot." Jamie stood, sloshing the water, waded over to the table, and handed her a glass of wine. His body looked good wet and naked in the moonlight, as if his extra weight somehow blended better into the whole of his form. "Cheers." He picked up his wine and took a sip. "This all right? Had to run up to the big box place while you were sleeping."

"It's fine—yes. Thank you. But don't drink much in the hot water. It'll make you woozy."

"Don't want me to drown?" He held his glass above the water and slid under the surface, exhaling bubbles for a longer time than seemed humanly possible, then let the air cease a while before he emerged. "Sorry. You don't like death jokes, do you?" He drank and leaned back.

"I don't think you killing yourself is ever gonna be funny. How can you treat it so lightly?"

"Dunno." He rubbed his foot against her ankle, then curled his toes over hers in a strangely agile clasp. After toe-squeezing her other foot, he met her eyes. "Don't think about doing it anymore. Now I think the way normal people think about dying, I guess—not that I'd know what normal people think. But I never used to imagine getting old. Might be why I like the idea of a parrot. He can grow old with me. Fuck. That was pathetic. I mean, he's a *pet* that'll grow old with me. Jeezus. He was for you. *You're* going to grow old with me." He paused, drank, and twisted to put his glass on the table. "Aren't you?"

"Can't we take things one day at a time?"

"Not much commitment there." He crossed his leg over hers and jostled her. "That the best you can do?"

"I love you. You know that. I want you in my life. But I've been married twice. It's ..." She took a sip of wine, feeling Jamie's baby seal eyes on her. What she was going to say might hurt him, but sooner or later they would have to talk about this. "It's not very appealing, to be honest. I don't think marriage is romantic anymore. *This* is romantic. What we're doing right now. Marriage is ... It's something that goes wrong."

"Bloody hell, *everything* goes wrong. Doesn't stop people from living."

Jamie turned over in a seal-like move that became like a floating yoga pose as he hung by his arms from the rim of the tub in a little backbend and stared at the metal in front of his face. It was a strange form of sulking, but she knew him well enough to recognize the mood swing.

"Sugar, if you'd stop pressuring me, we'd *be* living. Having the moment together. Romantic. Just like you want."

He dropped under the surface and exhaled for a while, sustained another bubble-less silence, and emerged in his backbend again. "Doesn't work. It's not ... not *permanent*." He turned over to sit beside her once more. "I know it's fucked up, but I can't help it. I think I could lose you. And you're my soul mate."

"How could you *lose* me?"

His shoulders wriggled. "Dunno. You're still in classes with the Greek."

She had dated a college classmate, a man of Greek origin, before she finally fell in love with Jamie. "I am *not* interested in Stamos."

"But I annoy you."

"Not that much."

"You sure?"

She set her wine on the table and turned so she could face him. "Okay. You sleep funny. And fuss over stuff. And your cat annoys me. But that doesn't mean you could lose me. It might make it hard to *live* with you, but not hard to *love* you."

"See, that's the thing. Not living together. We're three hours apart—"

"And you're going to be on the road for how long? Three months. Being apart goes with your work, sugar."

"Jeezus. I could change that. Just do local gigs." He sighed. "It's not like I can do something else for a living—I *hated* teaching, I'd get depressed again if I had to do that—but I can figure something out."

"I didn't ask you to. You need to be successful."

"You *want* me gone for three months?"

"I didn't say that."

He picked up his wine, drained it, and set the glass down with a punctuating thump. "You could at least move to Santa Fe. Transfer to UNM, take the Rail Runner to classes—"

"I like it where I am. And I get free tuition because Daddy works there, remember? Maybe I could move to Santa Fe after I graduate." Mae snuggled closer. "That'd be a good place to do fitness work and healing work."

Jamie's face softened, and his voice came out in a whisper. "You think we could start a family then?"

How had he read *that* into moving to the same city in three years? He looked so entranced, so touched and awed, his heart bared to her in his eyes. She didn't want to hurt him and yet she didn't want to do what Will had done to Montana—string him along for years without ever tying the knot. "I don't know if I can tell you that. I'll be thirty-one by then and I didn't say we were getting married."

"Bloody hell. My sister's thirty-three and she's trying to have another kid. It's not fucking *old*."

"Did you hear the last part, sugar?" How could she want to hold him while she said this? She restrained the urge. It would only make it harder for both of them. "If you want to get married and have kids, it's not fair for me to ask you to wait and see if I'm ready—because I don't know if and when I will be. Oh, god, I hate to say this, because I love you, but ... maybe we should—"

"No." The word was crisp and hard, not his usual drawling *nah*. "You don't get to break up with me. We're soul mates." His voice shook as he stood and climbed out of the tub. "I'll wait." He leaned over, hands on his thighs, and took a deep, loud breath.

"You okay, sugar?"

"Yeah." He stepped over a pile of lumber and flopped onto the chaise longue. "Just dizzy. You're right about drinking. Jeezus. Heat got to me."

Mae climbed out of the tub and walked over to him. "I thought you were having a panic attack."

"Nah. Just too hot. Think there's steam rising from my skin."

That was something that should happen in a cartoon of him, the way he could get angry in a flash and then the mood would evaporate just as quickly. She fetched the towels, put one under his head as a pillow and wrapped herself in the other, not sure if she was relieved or frustrated that his dizzy spell had broken off their discussion. "I don't think hot soaks agree with you. The tub at the Alpine Lodge got to you, too, and you weren't even drinking."

"You have to hate it that I'm always having a problem. Gets old, doesn't it?"

She sat on the edge of the chaise and placed her hand on his heart. Stress-fast, but not panic-pounding. "Reckon it gets old for you."

He wove his long, slender fingers through hers, holding her gaze. "Not a direct answer, love."

She sighed. "I love you. I get tired of going without sleep, that's all."

"That's all?" He brightened. "You weren't actually seriously trying to break up with me?"

Those eyes. That *look*. She ducked her head and studied their hands. "I don't *want* to. I was giving you the option. So you could find someone who's ready to settle down and start a family. But I wasn't trying very hard."

"Good. Then stop trying." He drew her down beside him. "I don't want to find *someone*. You think I'd be happy with just *some-one*? I love *you*."

*****

Listening to the erratic roar of the window air conditioner, Jamie lay holding Mae while she slept—or pretended to sleep—in her

pitch-dark bedroom. After having bothered her so much, he'd conceded on the night light and let her have what she liked: suffocating, claustrophobic darkness. He hoped he was holding still
enough that she was genuinely sleeping and that he was keeping
her company, not annoying her. The terrible, soul-ripping offer that
she'd made had shaken him so deeply he couldn't bear to let go of
her.

"I'm sorry," she whispered, "but you're so hot, right up against
me. I need a little space."

Jamie sighed. He needed his cat. Gasser would let Jamie hold
him, sparing Mae. He kissed her, missing her lips in the dark and
finding her chin instead. "No worries." He felt around on the floor
for his pants and took them outside with him so he could see to put
them on.

As soon as he closed the door, a giant bat flew over the back
fence.

"Bloody hell!"

"Jamie?"

The creature drifted to the ground, becoming a piece of wind-
blown trash. "Sorry. Go back to sleep."

Jamie drew his jeans on and dodged the thorny little weeds in
the dirt to reach the former bat. It was a rectangle of black cloth,
light and cheap and stiff, about the size of a window, with bits of
masking tape stuck to its edges. Strange. He looked up. Another
piece blew past and snagged on the towering sunflowers in Kenny
and Frank's back yard.

He peered through one of the spaces between the wide red
boards at the section of the fence that bordered the alley. The view
showed a dumpster and the garden of the spa across the alley. The
dumpster lid was closed, so that wasn't the source of the cloth.

But T or C had a lot of these little dumpsters, several per
alley for trash and for recycling, instead of curbside pickup. Some-

where, a lid was open. Jamie considered going out and finding it and putting anything that had blown out back in it, but his shoes were near the front door and it was locked. He would have to go through the bedroom to get them and that would wake Mae yet again, and he couldn't go prowling around unpaved alleys barefoot. He needed Ezra to give him another sacred-earth-anti-litter speech before he'd do that.

Due to the dumpster system, Mae didn't have an outdoor trash can, so Jamie anchored the cloth with one of Niall's pieces of lumber and lay in the chaise longue again. A real bat, backlit by the stars, crossed the sky. Mistaking the cloth for a scary giant bat would have been funny if he wasn't so worried about bothering Mae.

He had to face up to what she had said, and yet it wasn't safe to contemplate. Too much risk to his hard-won semblance of partial sanity. How could she think he would want to break up with her so he could start a family sooner? Did she imagine he could be happy with someone who wasn't her? Or, for that matter, that anyone else could be happy with him?

He hoped Mae *was* happy with him. To make her happy was what he wanted most. The only time he was sure he succeeded was when they made love, those moments that filled his soul when he brought her to ecstasy. It was spiritual, the connection they had then. And when they danced, he knew he made her happy, too—it was almost as good as sex. But when it came to all the practical, everyday-life parts of the relationship, he kept falling short.

Could he call Zak and ask for the book back? He hadn't formally given it to him, though he'd meant to offer. What if Zak and Mel were reading it, though? *Golden Love*. He liked the idea of his friends reaching their fiftieth anniversary. Jamie felt in his pocket for his phone. Calling Zak felt like a good idea—a mate he could bounce things off of, someone who would joke and lighten his mood. When they'd helped Montana to the house, Zak had thawed toward Jamie, though he wouldn't let him in. That had hurt, but they were still friends.

Zak would be asleep, though, if he wasn't out on a rescue call. The phone would wake Melody, too, and she needed her rest from her rambunctious children. Like Mae needed rest from Jamie. At this hour, he had to face it: there was no one to talk to. At least the wine was still sitting on the table by the hot spring. Not the best way to unwind, but better than nothing.

Jamie rose to fill a glass and noticed movement at the gate that led in from a path to the driveway. The latch was lifting so slowly that it didn't make a sound. He stared. The gate began to creep open. No one with good intentions would sneak like that. It eased open another inch. Jamie had to warn the intruder off without scaring Mae. With silent steps, he made his way toward the gate, taking a gulp of wine on the way, and slid his hand through the opening to grab the wrist on the other side. The owner of the wrist froze but didn't make a sound.

Jamie was the one doing the surprising and the situation felt so disturbing he wanted to shout *bloody fucking hell*. He had some stranger's wrist in his hand in the middle of the night, someone who was so cool about trespassing that he didn't react.

No—not he. *She.* This was a small wrist, and the forearm had no perceptible hair on it. This didn't make Jamie less nervous. He had met some dangerous women in his life. Faking courage, he whispered, "Whatever you were doing, don't even think about it again. I won't be as nice to you next time."

He let go, and the woman moved away slowly, crunching mesquite pods and gravel underfoot. Something rustled—a sound like a paper grocery bag. Jamie closed the gate. He didn't want them to see each other. It was safer if they couldn't recognize each other on the street in case this would-be thief was angry or vengeful.

What was he thinking? She would know him. She'd heard his voice and seen his hand, and he had to be the only black Australian in town. What would she say or do, if anything, to the man who'd caught her? Maybe nothing. She might be ashamed. A woman with a bag alone on the street after midnight could be homeless. No. If you were homeless, you stayed under the radar. You didn't sneak into the yard of a house with two vehicles in the driveway.

Jamie returned to the chaise longue. He wanted to get in bed with Mae, but that would wake her even if he didn't talk, and though dawn was creeping into the sky it might be too early even for her.

The neighbors Frank and Kenny, the dedicated yogis, were in their backyard chanting in Sanskrit. Jamie closed his eyes and rested in the soft, soothing early light, the birdsong, and their clear, untrained voices, liquid words he recognized yet didn't understand. *Have to get to Santa Fe in time for yoga.*

Mae woke him with a kiss not long after he fell asleep. She was dressed in workout clothes and smelled of sunscreen. "I wanted to make sure I said goodbye in case you're gone when I come back. Me and Daddy are practicing the whole triathlon up at Elephant Butte. What time do you have to be in Santa Fe?"

"Dunno. Need to call a body shop. Think I've got Dr. G at one ... Fuck. Yoga's at eleven. I have to get up *now*."

"I hope you tell your doctor you slept funny. Weren't you working on a sleep schedule?"

"Weren't you working on not acting like my mum?"

This could turn into a fight or a joke. It teetered in between. Jamie offered his best smile. Mae smoothed his hair and kissed him again. "Sorry. Lock up when you leave. And drive safely."

"Yes, *Mum*."

Jamie figured he had an hour to do something to make up for the shortcomings of the night. He hadn't remembered to tell Mae about the person trying to sneak into the yard, and he had to leave her something uplifting, not just a note about that. Something to make her smile when she came home. First, he needed to wake up. But Mae was out of coffee, and when he headed for the shower, a baby lizard lurked in the bathroom, transparent and frail with enormous eyes.

How in bloody hell had that gotten in? Not that Mae would mind. She would think it was *cute*. Jamie caught it in his bare hands, cringing at the touch of its weird little feet. He pushed the screen door open with his elbow and crouched on the bottom step of the porch to release the creature. It scurried under the trailer, no doubt planning to come right back in. If Jamie was handy, he would fix whatever gap allowed it entry. Handy, though, he wasn't. Niall would have to take care of the problem and Jamie would have to do something else to be of service.

The laundry was still on the line. Bringing it in would be a small favor, but better than nothing.

Before Jamie could look for the clothes basket, a lanky young man with a blond ponytail strolled up the driveway. He had a long nose, a large mouth, and bright blue eyes, a goofy cartoon of a face but so cheerful it was pleasant. Frank, one of the neighbors. "On my way for coffee. Care to join me?"

Coffee took precedence over laundry.

Walking to Main Street, they passed a row of murals on the back of a building, scenes of the river and the mountains, with animals and birds in floating visionary images above the semi-abstract landscapes. The murals reminded Jamie of one of Orville's paintings, an image of an eagle in the palm of a hand, like a view through a keyhole. "Did Reno's dad paint those?"

Frank nodded. "Yeah. I used to stop and watch sometimes when he was working on them, and he was a fun guy. He'd talk with me, crack jokes—they're so different you wouldn't think they were related."

"Yeah. Reno never took after Orville except for the art."

When they arrived at the coffee shop, Jamie felt as though they'd somehow conjured Reno by talking about him. The young man should have been at the final blessing and the giveaway, but he was talking with the café's owner, a tall, handsome brunette. She asked Reno, "Are you sure you won't reconsider? It still might sell. Some take a while."

"No thank you." His voice was flat and his face haggard with dark circles under his eyes. "Its time is up."

He lifted the only empty table, tried to turn with it, and smacked its legs into the coffee table. A couple seated on the couch grabbed their drinks as they sloshed onto an open newspaper. Reno put the table down and walked backwards, dragging it toward the door. Customers interrupted meals and conversations, scooting chairs out of his way. The owner called out, "Reno—wait. The base is ours. You can't take the whole thing."

He kept moving, though he was clearly struggling. "The painting is mine. And I need it back."

Jamie stepped up behind him and put his hands on Reno's slender shoulders. "Hold on, mate. We'll help you in a minute."

Frank eased the table from Reno's grasp and returned it to its place. The owner thanked him, then approached Reno, speaking quietly. "You can have it back, but we need to get the drill, take all the hardware off, and attach another painting to the base, and we're busy right now." A long line was forming at the counter. "Can you come back at three?"

"I'll get tools. I'll do it myself."

"Please, at least wait until after the rush." She gave Jamie a look that he read as *talk some sense into him* and went to assist the barista.

Jamie gave Reno a side-hug. "Have some coffee with us."

The young man drew away. "I'd like to do it now."

Frank joined the line. "I thought you had today off. What's the rush?"

Instead of answering, Reno left. Jamie expected him run off to get tools, but the young artist dropped onto the bench on the street, the hunched shape of his narrow back visible through the window.

"Get me anything vegan and a giant coffee, would you? Got to see what's wrong with him." Jamie handed Frank some cash and went out to sit with Reno.

"Why aren't you getting your tools? Don't have any?"

"A hammer and a screwdriver."

Jamie snort-laughed. "You're as bad as I am. Think I can find a drill in the shed at Mae's place. But you should wait, let the people here help you later. Right now, customers need to eat on that table."

"I can't wait." Reno stood. "Mae's place is just behind Frank and Kenny's, isn't it?"

"Sit down. I shouldn't have mentioned it. Those are Niall's tools, and he's picky about his stuff."

Reno glanced back and forth, then reached for the café door again. "I need it now."

"Mate, it's not a fucking emergency." Jamie took hold of his wrist to stop him from making another scene. His delicate, smooth-skinned wrist.

Bloody hell. That hand at the gate last night hadn't been feminine. It had been Reno's—and he knew who had caught him. Jamie had an image of Reno as the creepy little baby lizard that had squeezed its way into Mae's house. What had he wanted? And what had he been carrying? There'd been that rustling sound like a paper bag. A bag of black cloth? He could have been trying to get the piece that blew away because it was in Mae's yard.

Desperate to hide his secret, he'd called her a witch to get rid of her, and then he'd come back to T or C in the middle of the night. Because he was suddenly worried about her using the tabletop? Because he had to finish some strange task with black fabric? "Okay, maybe to you it *is* an emergency. You're scared Mae'll find out what you're hiding."

Reno yanked his hand away. "I'm not scared and I'm not hiding anything."

"Right, and you're not lying either." At Reno's look of alarm, Jamie softened his tone. "Sit down. I'm not out to get you." Like a half-wild animal being offered food, Reno seated himself as far away as he could get, watching and waiting. Jamie spoke the way he would to a frightened creature. "I don't need to know what it is. Mae doesn't need to know. But Misty does. Talk to her. She'll stop asking Mae to find out."

"I don't know what you're talking about."

"Yeah, you do. And it's making you act crazy. Trying to drag the whole bloody table out on the street. You can't handle having a secret."

Reno pressed his lips in over his teeth, blinked, and looked away.

Jamie said, "Mae's out triathlon training at the lake. You've got time. I'll tell her you took the painting home already. I'll buy her some coffee and bake for her. She won't need to come to the café today, and you can come back and get your painting at three like the lady asked you to. Now go home and call your girlfriend."

No response. *Stubborn little bastard.*

Chuck Brady approached, clad in his usual tie-dye with the slogan "Truth or Consequences, New Mexico: We're all here because we're not all there" amid the orange and yellow swirls. "Howdy-howdy, gentlemen. Top of the morning. Or bottom of the evening, depending on how long you've been up." He stopped by the bench and said to Reno, "You still have a key to Florencia's place?"

The young artist winced slightly. "She asked for it back."

"Just double-checking. I thought she might have. Is there anything you need to get, anything you left at her place?"

Reno shook his head and looked down at his hands, clicking his thumbnails back and forth against each other. "Why did you ask?"

"I'm installing an alarm system today. I'd hate to have you mistaken for a burglar."

Reno almost laughed, a nervous breathy sound. Chuck clapped him on the shoulder. "I know it's rough, losing her. Hang in there. Maybe Flo will speak to you yet. There's still time."

"You have no idea what you're talking about." Reno pulled back from Chuck. "And don't say her name to me again." He strode down the street.

The retired lawyer's rosy face grew even pinker as he called after him, "I'm sorry."

Reno paused at the corner, but he didn't look back.

Chuck opened the door to the café, and Jamie followed him in. "The name thing," Jamie said. "It's not just that he's upset about her. It's a taboo, in case she's died already, so he won't get ghost sickness. The name calls back the ghost."

"Thank you. I'll try to be careful."

Frank was sitting at Reno's lizard table, drinking coffee and eating a muffin. The same disappointingly modest breakfast awaited Jamie. He took a seat and slurped his long overdue coffee.

"Is Reno okay?" Frank asked. "He's normally so quiet, that was weird."

Jamie wriggled his shoulders, not sure what to say. He hadn't expected himself to try to protect Reno the way he had. "He's a weird kid."

Chuck paused before joining the line at the counter and detoured to their table. "I didn't realize you knew him,"

"Yeah. Since he was five." Jamie pictured Reno at that age, watching ants or drawing and coloring, his attention span ten times longer than teenaged Jamie's. They'd seemed to be total opposites at first, but the more Jamie was around the quiet little boy the more he sensed they were alike. Socially awkward creative misfits. However, Reno couldn't blunder his way out of loneliness the way Jamie could. Misty had been the only person to get through to him. "He'll be okay if he can sort things out with Misty."

"A good idea." Chuck clapped his hands together. "Love conquers all." He patted Jamie's shoulder and added meaningfully, "As long as the woman is always right."

After breakfast, Jamie returned to Mae's house, relieved that she hadn't come home before he'd done anything for her. He took care of her laundry, then left a note in case she got back while he was shopping. *Had coffee at Passion Pie. Saw Reno taking his tabletop out.* It fell short of the truth, but it wasn't quite a lie, either. Jamie didn't like it, but then he didn't like any of his options in dealing with his friends' secrets.

He bought groceries, including plenty of coffee. He'd told Reno he would make sure Mae didn't need to go to the café. To bake for her, he had to correct some deficiencies in her kitchen. He went to the thrift shop for cookie sheets and glass mixing bowls and got interested in a slow cooker, a cast iron frying pan, muffin tins, certain types of spatulas, and other things Mae lacked as well.

As he placed the final items on the sales counter, he noticed a woman with long gray hair pulling the cushions off a bright, overstuffed couch and peering under them.

"Think they take the money out before they sell it," he said.

She smiled. "I'm looking for crumbs and dog hair, actually."

"F—" Jamie had rejected a spatula because of the crusted remains of fried eggs. "That'd be disgusting."

"That's why I look."

The furniture was in good shape, better than average thrift shop material. Jamie removed the final cushion, and the woman poked into the crevices of the sofa. He put the pillows back while she did the same examination of a matching easy chair. Running her hand into the corners of the bare chair seat, she frowned and drew something out. She grimaced at it and dropped the thing onto the scuffed floorboards. Jamie bent to pick it up, expecting some bit of normal couch crap—a cracker or a penny—but it was a delicate green hair-like feather. An Eclectus parrot feather.

Chapter Twenty-Four

Mae set her barefoot shoes by the door and put her water bottle in the kitchen. She was long overdue for a shower and clean clothes, having lingered over brunch with her father after their triathlon practice, talking about sports and training. The kitchen was hot and smelled both sweet and spicy, a trace of Jamie's presence. She turned the air conditioner up and sank onto the living room couch to read the note that lay on the coffee table. The letters, written in his sprawling, sloping script, were scrambled in most of the words, and some of the Ps faced the wrong way, but she was used to his writing and could translate.

Had coffee at Passion Pie. Saw Reno taking his tabletop out. Mae wished she'd gone back to try with it again, but she hadn't thought he'd be back from Mescalero yet. She resumed reading.

Got you a slow cooker, few other kitchen things at the thrift store. Cheap, all right? No fussing. I didn't spend much money. Lentil soup. Mmmm. Good thing Jamie hadn't been there. She hadn't even seen the crockpot on the counter. *Cookies!!!* She hadn't noticed those, either, just the heat. A quick trip to the kitchen revealed a plastic tub full of oatmeal cookies with raisins forming hearts and smiley faces. *Laundry put away. Wear those black ones more often. Want to take them off you, slow. Feather is from furniture in thrift shop. Has to be from an Eclectus parrot. Like Placido. Nothing else has those little fur feathers. Be weird if someone here had him, but could you check and see? Just in case? You can tell it's him if he can talk like me. Need to know he's okay. Thanks. Love ya love ya love ya! JEJE.*

A tiny green thing that she never would have thought was a feather lay on the table, anchored by a pebble. Jamie had been attached to the parrot and would recognize its peculiar plumage. She pictured him in the exotic bird store, petting and talking to Placido. Knowing Jamie, he'd probably fallen in love at first sight.

The odds of the feather being Placido's were low, but there was no harm in trying to find out. Or was there? A parrot might not have much of a private life, but the people it lived with did. Maybe she shouldn't do this.

No. Maybe she should. The odds weren't so low after all. Will had found—or stolen—the hyacinth macaw. The birds had vanished together. Will had been engaged to the third Chino sister. He had a T or C connection. He could have sold the birds to someone here.

Before doing the journey, though, she had to get cleaned up and changed. In her bedroom, she found that Jamie had not only put away the laundry but organized her closet. He'd folded so meticulously that her panties fit squarely into the corners of the drawer, with the black satin ones on top. In the bathroom, the towels hung in tri-folds, evenly spaced on the rack. Jamie wasn't normally this neat, but he could obsess on anything if he was anxious or eager to please. No doubt, he'd been both and had stayed so long that he must have missed his yoga class. Mae wished he'd gone to it. He needed it more than she needed soup *and* cookies *and* new kitchen equipment or perfectly folded panties. For any normal boyfriend, one generous act would have been enough. This much domestic effort carried some baggage, love coated with a layer of neurosis, that little buzz she always sensed around Jamie, his personal cloud of emotional gnats.

She showered, dressed, and called to thank him. He didn't pick up. She left a message, stumbling around the topic of his doing too much.

Voices in the backyard drew her attention. Niall and Kenny, working on the deck. She should see if they needed anything before she started the psychic search for the parrot.

Kenny, a short, muscular young man with dark curly hair and multiple piercings, was kneeling in the dirt holding a measuring tape while Niall stood on a ladder holding the other end, making a mark on the house. Mae asked if they needed anything to eat or drink, but they were set.

She noticed a piece of black cloth stuck under a board. "What's that for?"

"No idea. It's not mine." Niall let go of the measuring tape and climbed down the ladder. "Must be trash that blew in."

Kenny said, "The same stuff blew into our yard. We had to shake it off the sunflowers before we could throw it away. It was weird. It looked like someone had been blacking out windows."

Mae picked up the fabric. The shape did suggest a window, and bits of masking tape stuck to it. She used heavy curtains to make her room dark at night, but *taping* the windows dark didn't make sense. "Why would anyone do that? You'd have to take it down to let the light in, or you'd have to turn on the lights if you left it up."

"Idiot's attempt at a darkroom?" Niall shrugged. "Who knows?"

Mae wadded it up to take it in to the trash and said she would let them get on with their work. As she put her hand to the doorknob, Niall said, "Hold on. You've got a back gate now. Check it out. You can go straight out to the dumpsters."

"And to visit your neighbors," Kenny added.

The portion of fence that bordered on the alley now sported black iron hinges, a latch, and a chain she could use to lock it from the inside. Mae had wanted such a gate since she'd moved in. She thanked them, used the gate, got rid of the cloth, and went back into the house to be met once more by the view inside her hyper-organized closet.

She understood what was behind Jamie's efforts to please her—the whirlpool of anxious good intentions and inner chaos that led him to waste his morning this way—and it made her want to hug him and reassure him that he didn't have to try so hard.

But until he believed he was worthy and whole, nothing she could say or do would change anything. He would be like this.

Mae imagined herself complaining to the Chino sisters. *He's too considerate, too generous, and too eager to make a commitment.* And what, they would ask, is wrong with that? She wouldn't have an answer except that she wished he could relax.

She sat cross-legged on the living room floor, holding the green feather, a quartz crystal, and her grandmother's amethyst. After a short meditation to settle her mind, she set the question for her journey. *Is this Placido's feather?*

The tunnel took her slowly and twisted as she moved through it, as if her energy was being pulled two ways, before her vision opened in a long room with many windows and a view of a street bordered by a red dirt bluff. Florencia's studio.

A green parrot sidestepped back and forth on the perch in his cage, talking to himself in a voice that was sweeter than she had imagined parrot voices to be. The bird cocked his head to the side and said, "Hello." He tried it several times, and then seemed to answer an expected question. "Good. Good." He flapped and resettled. "Parrot. Green parrot." Perhaps this was a conversation he'd had that day, or he was practicing his words, like an actor going over lines. *Hello. How are you? Good. And what are you? I'm a parrot, a green parrot.* "Ma-a-a-ate. G'day mate." He looked around and cocked his head. "Ma-a-a-ate. G'day mate."

Surprise almost broke Mae's concentration. The feather really had come from Jamie's favorite parrot.

She renewed her focus into the vision. A small canvas sat on an easel at the far end of the studio, dots of some dark substance outlining the shapes that might become a painting. Colored sketches on paper, versions of the same work, were taped to the wall with masking tape. One was the exact size of the canvas and punctured with tiny holes along every line, a picture of a bright pink parrot against a background of blue and red corn. Mae's first reaction was that she didn't like it, followed by an inner voice that sounded like Niall's saying, *That's because you don't know much about art.*

The parrot spoke a few more words, a little more loudly. Was he lonely? Did he want attention?

Reno and Florencia came in. She looked as frail as when Mae had met her. Reno held her arm, steadying her.

"G'day," said the parrot.

"What the hell?" Florencia asked.

The parrot spoke again in his small sweet voice. "Pretty lady."

She glared at Reno. "Is this a joke?"

"No." He guided her to the stool in front of her canvas. "It's a gift."

"I don't remember asking for a parrot."

"But you've been so depressed since Violet died. I feel like you've given up. You need a new bird to love and take care of."

"I miss her. But I'm not depressed."

"You act like it. You never go out anymore. You stopped your treatments. It's like you quit on yourself." Reno walked over to the cage. "You'll love him. He'll be good company." He opened it slowly and urged the bird to step up onto his forearm. "You'll feel like trying again." Reno stood over her, petting the parrot's breast, and whispered to it, "Talk to her, introduce yourself."

The bird climbed his arm and ducked into Reno's hair.

"What were you thinking?" Florencia snapped. "He'll live to be fifty or sixty."

"You'll have thirty or forty years with him when you get well. You could live to be ninety."

"No. I didn't stop treatments because *I've* given up. My doctors have. I'm dying."

Reno's eyes widened. "What?"

"I didn't tell you everything. I waited too long. By the time I got diagnosed, it was already spreading. It's in my liver and my bones now. The most any more treatments could give me would be an extra month or two of sick, miserable life. I'd rather feel a little better and try to finish this painting. It's going to be my last."

"I'm sorry. How ... how long do you have?"

"Not long." Florencia turned away from him. "Take the bird back to the store. I'd be stupid to let him get attached to me. How could you even afford a parrot?"

Reno reached one hand to gather the parrot from his shoulder and sheltered the bird against his chest. Placido squawked, as if Reno had not handled him well. "I sold some paintings."

"*Paintings?*" She faced him again. "How many? You sell one every other month if you're lucky, for two hundred bucks that go straight into the Rabbit. Hell, *I* paid for that damn car's last repairs. Where in the world did you get the money?"

"I ... I had help buying him." He moved the bird onto his forearm again. Placido struggled to get a good perch. "I got a discount."

"You couldn't afford even a half-price parrot. Did I pay for my own bird? Should I see if anything's missing?"

"No. How can you say that?" Reno tried to adjust his arm position, but the bird only worked harder to balance on it. "I got a really good price. Your nephew's wife works in a parrot store."

"That greedy little vulture?"

"She's not—"

"She is. They all are." Florencia's eyes flashed with anger. "I told you not to have anything to do with them."

"But they helped me get you a parrot."

"Because they want to get into my will." A long silence. When Florencia spoke again, her tone was flat and resigned. "And that's all you want, too, isn't it? A *parrot*. You didn't think I'd live thirty or forty years. Look at me. You knew, didn't you?"

"No—I ... I want you to live. I love you."

"When was the last time you said that? Or showed it?" Florencia stood and smacked her palm on the stool, punctuating her words with the sound. Placido flapped off Reno's arm, flashing the patches of red and blue under his wings, and Mae's vision followed him out of the studio. He landed on the chair in the living room, tail fanned, body quivering. "Get out." Florencia's voice shook. "And catch that damned bird and take it with you. Don't even think about coming back."

The vision faded as questions flooded into Mae's mind. She took her crystals to rebalance in salt water in the kitchen and sat at the table, the feather cupped in her palm. After she'd rested and cleared her head, she might need to try another journey with it. What she'd seen bewildered and disturbed her.

When she'd thought Reno was in love with his teacher, that had been troubling enough, but pretending to love her would be worse.

Why did Florencia call Shelli a greedy little vulture? Had they met? Had Reno put Will and Shelli up to stealing the parrots? If so, why hadn't he given the hyacinth as a gift?

Florencia had implied that Reno not only wanted to get in her will, but that he might have used her money or sold something of hers to buy the parrot. It was probably only a petty comment, rubbing in his poverty and how much she paid for, but maybe not. Did his secret involve stealing from her?

Taking cash from her purse wouldn't involve other people, though. As poor as her health was, she had to be on pain meds and quite likely medical marijuana. Could Reno have stolen and sold some of the drugs? He had the opportunity. Mae couldn't see Zak getting involved, though, and Reno could only have accessed a small amount.

Mae was still lost in thought when her phone rang. *Jamie.* Her message had asked him to call her back, and he would want to know about Placido. After some affectionate small talk, she gave him a short version of what she'd found out. "I wonder if Reno kept him. If that was what he was hiding from Misty."

"Nah. Placido likes to talk. And Reno doesn't. Don't think he's the type to want a parrot. And he'd have left him alone all weekend and you don't do that to parrots."

"He came back early."

"Not early enough for a bird. Jeezus—early bird. Didn't mean that. Sorry—drifting. He came back to do some weird thing with black fabric last night. And to get that tabletop. He doesn't want you fucking with his secrets, y'know?"

"Black fabric? There was some in my yard, and in Frank and Kenny's yard."

"Yeah. Scared the crap out of me. Thought it was a giant bat."

"I wish you'd told me about it. Kenny and I both threw it away. If it was Reno's, I could have found something out."

"Nah. Shouldn't have mentioned it. My brain's a few steps behind my mouth. We need to let go of all that. I was going to explain yesterday, but, y'know how my mind works ... I forgot. But now I remembered. The thing is—they need the money. And they're not hurting anyone."

Mae listened to Jamie's explanation of Montana's financial needs. He didn't care anymore that she had gotten drunk and hit his van, only that she was broke because Will owed her money.

"I'm sorry she let that happen," Mae said. "But you've got no proof they're not hurting anyone. I worry about Misty marrying into this mess."

"You want to *stop* them from getting *married*? Jeezus. Projecting your issues or something?"

"And you're not projecting *your* issues?"

"Bloody hell. Of course I am. I know what it's like to be that poor."

"I was talking about Reno and Misty getting married. Even if they love each other, it doesn't mean they should. Not yet. There's something so sneaky about that black fabric—Reno blacking out his windows, like he didn't want anyone to know he was home."

A long silence.

"Jamie?"

"Don't think he was home. He was carrying that stuff from somewhere else. Dropped the bag or lost a few pieces. That's the only way he—Jeezus. I wasn't going to tell you this." Jamie described the hand at the gate. "He knew it had blown into your yard. So he wasn't at home."

"He'd been blacking out windows somewhere else?"

The first place she thought of was Florencia's house, which was three and a half blocks up Foch Street from Reno's place on Austin. He lived one block east of Foch. Mae's place on Marr, the next block down, was just two buildings to the west of Foch. On the west side of Austin, a small parking lot connected with the alley between Austin and Marr. He could have been on his way home and done as Jamie said, dropping the bag or losing some fabric to the wind. If he'd chased it, he'd have seen it blow over her fence.

Why hadn't Reno stopped at the first dumpster he came to, though, behind one of the businesses on Main or Broadway? She tried to imagine what would make it hard to toss a paper bag into a dumpster. If she carried several bags out, she had to put them down to lift the lid. Reno might have had his hands full of something he didn't want to set down.

She didn't like where this was leading her. "If he had a key to his teacher's house—"

"Nah. Chuck asked him at the coffee place and Reno said she'd wanted it back."

"That's not the same as saying he gave it to her, or that he didn't copy it. What if he's been stealing stuff there?" Not drugs but art. The paintings and sculptures in Florencia's living room were too big to steal without a truck or a van, but the pieces in her bedroom were small. The back of the house faced a bluff and her neighbors were away, but the front overlooked Main Street, where even in the middle of the night in July, there was an occasional passerby. He'd have needed to darken those windows. "Letitia's probably got art connections. She might know who'd buy it."

"Don't see how Zak or Will is connected, or David and Shelli. And Reno's teacher just went into hospice. He couldn't have stolen anything until now."

Mack had stolen money from Mae on a regular basis, claiming it wasn't theft since they were married. She'd endured it until she fell out of love with him. If Florencia had loved Reno, she might have let him steal from her, too. "He could have slipped some small stuff out while she was sick."

"Can't see it. He had to be close to her, y'know? Studying with her all that time."

"He's not honest with other people he's close to. He lies to his daddy and to Misty. He's been keeping her out of his place for months. He tells her it's his housekeeping, but I bet it's not that bad. Nothing he'd be ashamed of."

"Mm. Reckon. He was never a messy kid."

Mae rose and began ladling the soup into containers for the freezer. "So you know he's lying."

"Doesn't mean he's stealing. Or that we should try to stop whatever he *is* doing. Or that we can. Lonnie said it's like a stew. We can't uncook it. It's been made."

"But the marriage hasn't."

"Jeezus. You and marriage. Good thing I'm at Dr. G's office. Heading in as we speak. I need therapy after I talk to you."

"Sugar—"

"I know, I know, I need therapy because I'm fucked up." He snort-laughed. "It was a joke."

"Not one of your best."

"Sorry. No worries, all right, love? I'm a work in progress."

They wound up the call. Mae tried to reassure herself, but the conversation left her tense. It felt unfinished. Not because of his clumsy joke, but because of his defense of his friends. It was well-meaning but short-sighted. She finished putting the soup away and washed the crockpot, thinking about Lonnie's analogy. Maybe Reno's activities were a stew that couldn't be uncooked, but Misty still needed to know about them.

Mae dried her crystals, went back to the living room, and sat on the floor to journey with the feather again. She left her intention wide open this time. Maybe she would learn where the parrot was. Maybe she would learn more about Reno and Shelli and Will, how and why they had stolen the bird.

Her vision opened in an art gallery. Traditional Southwestern landscapes hung on the walls and classic pueblo pots filled the glass shelves. Shelli and a petite woman who had the same deep-set eyes and oddly indented nose as David were talking with a tall white woman of about fifty. Placido or another Eclectus perched on Shelli's shoulder.

The Anglo woman said, "I was hoping for something by Florencia Mirabal." Her stiff platinum hair and crisp, preppy-casual clothes suggested money and non-New Mexico origins. So did her accent—old South. Richmond, if Mae had to guess.

"We carry her nephew's work." The woman who looked like David's relative was as hard as he was soft, not an ounce of fat on her body. The only thing about her that flowed was her hair, long and abundant, barely starting to gray. "As far as selling *her* work ..."

"I thought you'd be expecting me. I'm Dorothy Clemens. Letitia Westover-Brown sent me."

Shelli and the gallery proprietor exchanged glances. "I need to go in and clean the parrots' cages anyway," Shelli said. "I can show her what we've got."

"Thank you." The small woman shook hands with the visitor. Her manner was warm, but it was the practiced warmth of a tour guide or a salesperson. "I'm Kathy Chavez-Mirabal. I was married to Florencia's brother. We do have a very special legacy here. It belongs to my son—my husband gave it to him when we separated. I hope you'll understand how we feel about selling any of it."

Shelli took a key from a desk drawer and unlocked a room at the back of the gallery. Another parrot's squawks greeted her as she brought the visitor in and closed the door behind them. "Do you mind if I let the other one out? They expect it around now. It's their playtime together."

Ms. Clemens hesitated, looking back and forth at the two parrots. A hyacinth macaw stared at her from its cage. It was the biggest parrot Mae had ever seen, and its huge eyes, rimmed with bright yellow skin, made it appear to be staring. It made a shrill whistling noise followed by a series of beeps. The green parrot replied "G'day" with an Aussie accent and then said "Pretty lady," sounding like Shelli.

The visitor beamed. "Does he think I'm pretty? How nice. He is, too. But that blue one is ... I don't know. Its beak looks dangerous."

"That's Violet." Shelli opened the macaw's cage. "Her beak is powerful, but she doesn't bite. She's a sweet bird. Florencia's very sick and had to give her up. Violet was with her for thirty years. It was hard for both of you, wasn't it, Violet?"

The blue parrot walked onto Shelli's forearm and whistled again. Placido flew to a perch and said, "Kiss."

"He uses that word for everything. Preening, hugging, kissing," Shelli explained while she cuddled the macaw to her chest and then kissed her on the head. "Violet can come over for a kiss in a minute. First she has to show the lady her picture."

She carried the bird—which Mae was sure had to be the stolen hyacinth—over to a wooden case where a set of framed photographs was displayed and set her there.

Family pictures, portraying Florencia from childhood up through her teenage years and young adulthood, showed her with severe-looking people who had to be her brother and her parents. She often stood slightly apart from them and made a subtle mockery of the portrait with a pose like a fashion model or the hint of a funny face. The only photograph in which she didn't appear to be distancing herself showed Florencia, young and pretty, arm in arm with a youthful Orville Geronimo, a huge blue parrot on her shoulder. The presumed Violet opened her massive gray beak and said, "Me." *Shelli must have been working on that.* The bird didn't seem to be much of a talker.

"Well, she's a smart thing, isn't she?" Ms. Clemens said. "I hope she's well trained with all this valuable art around."

The blue parrot flew to the perch in the middle of the room, where Placido snuggled up to preen her. "She is. They both are."

"You look a little like Florencia. Are you a relative?"

"No. It's the hair. You see a pueblo Indian woman with blue hair, it makes you think she looks like Florencia. I'm married to her nephew. I did the hair as a tribute, for getting the family back together. I wanted her to know how much I admired her, when we finally met."

Ms. Clemens walked around, peering closely at every display. The secret locked room was like a shrine to Florencia. The walls were hung with what must have been her childhood drawings and her adolescent works, as well as some more mature paintings.

After a circuit of the room, the art shopper returned to the photo display, studied it again, then read aloud from a framed letter near the picture of the real Violet. " 'Dear Severus. As far as I'm concerned you can keep anything I left behind. I wasn't that good an artist yet and you'd be a fool to sell any of it. I don't think enough of that crap to want to sell it myself. Florencia.' Goodness. She was hard on herself. The work she left behind—if that's what you've got here—isn't crap at all. Even her childhood drawings are fascinating. Was this written when she married Orville Geronimo?"

"No, she wrote it the year she divorced him and moved to Truth or Consequences, but the paintings she was referring to date to the years before she married him. Teenaged works. Things she did on her college vacations when she was in Acoma. My father-in-law and his parents had hoped she might come back to the pueblo when she got divorced. But you seem to know her biography, so you know there was something of a rift in the family."

"Yes, yes." The customer gave a dismissive sniff. "Does that letter mean you have some of her college work?"

The birds flew between her and Shelli, heading to a corner full of parrot toys, where they began a game of tug-of-war with a piece of sisal.

"Not her favorite pieces, but yes, quite a few. She was very productive during her summer breaks. The family ended up with things she didn't like enough to take back to school with her." Shelli walked to a series of portraits of pueblo clowns. "This is early college work. You can see elements of her future style, but it's closer to realism." Mae liked them better than what she'd seen in Florencia's studio in her other vision. Shelli moved on to some O'Keefe-like rock formation studies. "These were done a couple of years later. You can see that these also aren't quite the full-fledged Florencia Mirabal style, but there are stronger hints of her future in them."

"Would it be a problem for you if you ever sold any of them?"

"Letitia should have explained that. She knows what this archive means to us."

"She made me think you might make an exception for a serious collector."

Shelli sighed and picked up Placido, who had lost the tug-of-war with the giant macaw. She gave him a soft hug and let him climb to her shoulder. "My husband's aunt never expressly told her brother *not* to sell them, but she implied she'd prefer he didn't. And we don't want to diminish the collection too much. It's an important record of her development, and it's a family treasure, too. We've been working on a reconciliation with her—Kathy and David and I. She still won't speak to Severus, though, so it's private until we can work things out. But anyway, we hope to eventually get a museum set up, so once in a while we do sell one to help fund that project. We don't publicize the sales. I'm sure you can appreciate why we'd rather people didn't think we had a lot to sell. We need to keep the majority."

"You mean there are more?"

"Yes. We rotate the display."

Ms. Clemens circled the room again and paused in front of a pair of paintings. Both showed the exact same scene, a stone stairway winding between steep rock walls. The perspective was slightly distorted, suggesting multiple parts of the twisting path seen from different angles. A shadow of someone's legs and a foot lifted to take a step fell on the stairs, but no human figure was shown. One version of the painting was in shades of yellow, brown, and gold, the other in shades of blue. Shelli brought Placido up and asked him, "What color?"

"Yellow," said the parrot. "Blue."

"What a smart little fella," the Southern woman cooed. "He knows his colors."

"Of course he does," Shelli said, scratching Placido's cheek. "He was raised in an art gallery. We're parrot people, the whole family. That's why Florencia asked us to take Violet."

"Blue," said Placido. "Yellow."

"I think he likes those paintings. He has good taste. That's so interesting that she did two views of the same place like that."

"Well, those were her student years," Shelli replied. "She was still exploring her style."

"I think I'd like to buy the pair of them."

Shelli frowned. "Both?"

"Yes. That's what *makes* them—two studies of the old path to the mesa. I want both."

Shelli opened the door to the main gallery and asked, "Are you free, Kathy?"

Her mother-in-law answered, "In a minute. Just let me finish with this sale."

Shelli closed the door again, sent Placido to play with the hyacinth, picked up a plastic bucket and put on a pair of household gloves. "Excuse my doing this, but I need to clean my babies' cages while they're out and about. She'll take care of the sale shortly. Please, be discreet about where you got the paintings. We aren't showing this room to just anyone, not until we get the museum open."

The customer agreed so readily, she seemed to have expected the secrecy. Letitia must have prepared her.

Mae closed the vision. Was this where the money was coming from? If Florencia hadn't wanted her youthful works sold or displayed, there was some reason for secrecy, at least while she was alive.

The family hadn't reconciled with her, though, not even the partial reconnection Shelli had implied. Maybe they had tried and failed with the gift of Placido, but they'd had a plan B, something to make them seem to have succeeded. Passing off the stolen hyacinth as Violet made the effort look calculating. Shelli must have thought it was worth the risk of losing her job to provide such convincing "proof" of the artist's reconnection with her family and support for the gallery.

Why was it so important? Perhaps they'd wanted Florencia to fund the museum or donate additional works. No, there'd be no money in that, and it would have required a genuine end to the feud. Had she given some paintings to Reno and then he'd turned around and sold them? That wouldn't be something he'd hide in his trailer though, or in Zak's toolshed. He would only hide them if he'd stolen them.

Chapter Twenty-Five

Mae called Niall, hoping he would know if anything was missing.

He answered his phone with a few coughs, listened to her question, and waited a moment before replying. "I don't see how he could have taken any paintings. He'd have had to do it right under her nose, and she didn't keep much of her of work around. Once it was finished, it was sold, or on display in Rio Bravo. There should be something in the studio—she dropped a hint she'd left something in progress—but she doesn't want that opened yet."

"There was a lot of art in her bedroom. None of those paintings were hers?"

"A few small ones, I think. Old things she didn't want to sell."

"That's exactly what I think he'd be stealing. I found out there's a gallery that has a lot of things she left with her brother, and I think Reno might be adding more and selling them. Do you mind if we take a look? See if those early works are still there?"

"All right. But I think they will be."

A brisk walk brought Mae to Florencia's house in a few minutes, not much longer than it took Niall to drive. He was just getting out of his car when she arrived.

As soon as they stepped through the front door, a steady beeping sounded. He punched a code into a keypad on the wall and the noise stopped. Florencia's living room looked like a gallery now, with the furniture gone and only the art remaining. Mae noticed things she'd overlooked earlier, when she'd been stunned by the cowboy angel's overpowering presence. Complex fields of lifelike flowers hung on either side of the winged, blue-eyed man. Another one of Niall's sculptures, a disturbingly accurate junk-metal cockroach, crouched where the coffee table had been.

"Everything's okay here." Niall led the way down the hall. "I didn't go in her bedroom much. No real reason to. I hope I can tell if things are missing."

Mae opened the blinds in the empty room and tried to remember what the art had looked like. She'd been so busy with clothes and bedding and so worried about how Niall was coping, she hadn't paid much attention to anything else, but she sensed that paintings might have been rearranged. Niall studied them a long time.

"Are hers missing?" Mae asked.

"Not as far as I can tell. Reno's are gone for sure, though. His gifts to Florencia. But I can't remember if they were here when we cleaned out or not. She could have made him take them back."

Mae's neatly assembled mental jigsaw puzzle fell into a jumble. "Did she have anything she didn't hang up? Does this house have an attic?"

"Ayeh. Never been up there." Niall led the way back into the hallway, and squinted at the door of a pull-down stairway in the ceiling. "Help yourself."

Mae tugged on the handle, and the stairway unfolded with a creak. She climbed up. If there were other old paintings and sketches Florencia didn't want to sell, she might have thought so little of them she'd stored them here. After all, in her estimation, the ones she'd left with her brother had been "crap."

The only light came from two small windows at either end of the low-roofed space. A large bird cage sat near the stairs. A few quilts in dust-covered plastic zipper bags and a stack of equally dusty shoe boxes were the only other objects in the space. Mae imagined Reno offering to put the cage up here for Florencia and discovering paintings, which he later removed. Could he have handled the cage enough to leave a trace of his energy? There was only a slim chance, but it was worth a shot.

The attic was stiflingly hot, so Mae brought the cage downstairs and explained to Niall what she wanted to do. She'd brought her crystals, hoping for an opportunity.

"Go for it," he said. "I hope you find out you're wrong, though. I'll go commune with the Cowboy Angel. Let me know when you're done."

Mae sat on the bedroom floor with the cage and a clear quartz point, seeking traces of Reno. Nothing came to her but Florencia in her living room, removing a weak, trembling Violet from the cage. The bird wrapped her claws around Florencia's wrist, but the artist had to prop the macaw against her bosom to keep her upright. She whispered to her, petting her neck, "My poor, poor baby. Don't be scared," and then shouted, "Reno. Drop everything. Violet's sick. I have to get her to the vet."

Mae let go of the vision. The strong energy of that moment overrode anything else that had ever happened with the cage. She left it in the bedroom and joined Niall in his contemplation of Howe's blue-eyed cowboy.

He gestured to the painting with his chin. "Your father tells me I was this good-looking once upon a time."

"I guess you were, then. He wouldn't lie to you."

"Did you find out anything about Reno?"

"No, and there's not much in the attic. Stuff looks like it hasn't been touched for years. I don't know if that's all there is because she didn't store much, or because things are missing."

"I'm not going to upset Flo by asking about it. But Daphne should know if there's supposed to be anything valuable up there—as long as Flo remembered to tell her. I'm sure she's got an inventory for her estate."

"Could you ask her?"

"Remind me later. I need to think about it. I'm not sure I'm ready to accuse Reno yet. You done here now?"

"I guess." There was nothing left in the house with which to do a psychic journey other than Florencia's art and her collection. The odds of learning about Reno through them were low, and the chances Mae would intrude on their creators high. All traces of Reno were gone. Or were they? "He wouldn't have taken Violet's memorial when he took his paintings, would he?"

"I should hope not. That bird meant the world to Florencia. Violet outlasted all the people in her life. I've known her for twelve years. She had her parrot a lot longer than that. And she loved what Reno did to remember her by."

"I'd like to see it."

They left the house and crossed what passed for a yard, a patch of dirt spiked with prickly-stemmed wildflowers on the opposite side from where they'd parked the day they came to pack. A bright blue Mustang crouched under the detached carport. Mae had never realized the vehicle was there. Looking up the cliff from Main Street, she'd seen only the poles and roof above it. "What a sweet car. I bet she had fun driving it."

"She did. Fast enough to scare the bejesus out of you. If Reno hadn't messed up, she probably would have left it to him. He could use it."

Florencia's will. If Reno expected to be in it, would he have stolen from her? If he needed the money now, he might have, or if he was in doubt about being an heir.

They reached the end of the yard. In the shade of an elm tree overhanging a neighbor's fence stood a small stack of stones "Is *that* Violet's memorial? Rocks?"

"No, damn it." Niall scowled. "There was more. Her favorite piece Reno ever painted. Beautiful little triptych on wood. I know she'll never come here to look at it again, but if he's the one that took it, that's heartless. It meant so much to her, she wanted to be buried with it."

"You think she still wants to, being that mad at him?"

"She does. It's as close as she can get to being buried with Violet."

Niall locked up the house and offered Mae a ride, but she declined and began walking toward home. Though she was feeling the effects of the morning's workout, she needed to move in order to think, and she had a lot to think about.

There was no way to give Jamie the good news without the bad. Placido was safe and in good hands, but when she told him where the parrot was, he would know that his friends had lied to him and stolen the birds. Telling Jamie about the gallery would mean telling him she'd learned more about the money-making secret, too, when he'd wanted her to leave it alone.

She doubted she could. If Reno had stolen paintings, Florencia didn't need them back or need the money, and yet there was that sense of violation, like when Niall discovered the art was missing from the parrot's little grave.

Uncertain what to do and who to tell, Mae asked herself who had the most at stake. Who had the most urgent need to know what she knew? The answer came without doubt: Misty. Mae paused before turning left on Marr and texted her. *Learned more about Reno. Can I meet you somewhere?*

Misty replied. *I'm at his place. Fixing the Rabbit.*

Is he there?

Inside. Sleeping. Come on over.

As Mae approached the old trailer, Misty looked up from the Rabbit's engine, wiping her hands on a rag, and began to put tools away in a dented metal toolbox. She wore tight black shorts and a hot pink tank top, a matching pink baseball cap, and hot pink socks with her athletic shoes. A skateboard lay wheels-up in the dirt of the yard. Misty chomped on gum, blew a bubble and popped it. "I guess you know Reno took his tabletop home."

"Yeah. But I found another way." Mae glanced at the windows. The blinds were down, and the window air conditioner was running. Reno probably wouldn't wake up or hear them, but she didn't want to take any chances. "Can we take a walk?"

"Not far. I'm not quite done yet." Leaving the car's hood up, Misty dropped her rag on the toolbox and put one foot on her board to flip it over. She rode it slowly down Austin toward the river while Mae walked beside her.

Mae said, "Reno was getting rid of pieces of black fabric in the middle of last night. Stuff that was cut like he'd been blacking out windows."

Misty put a foot down and stopped. "That liar." Her eyes flashed. "Do you know what he told me? He said he was staying at his dad's place, and that he'd see me at the final ceremony in the morning. When I didn't see him, I called and he said he'd been there at sunrise and left early. Blacking out windows—are you sure?"

"Pretty sure. I'm guessing he was at his teacher's house."

"That's crazy. He spent the night in her house? Until you told me about her flirting with him, I could have sworn she got on his nerves, and that he only put up with her for the lessons and because she was his dad's ex-wife. He complained about her. She had all these *rules*, like he wasn't allowed to talk about her family or her whole life before she married Orville." Misty kicked her board ahead of her, watching it roll away, and they resumed walking. "I wonder who he's been lying to, her or me? He's even acting like he cares about her now. When I got back to Mescalero yesterday, he asked me if I'd heard anything about her—he knows I hear everything at work. So I told him about her still wanting to draw and Niall getting her some colored pencils, and that I thought Daphne and Chuck were putting an alarm in her house. I said it was weird that they'd bother, because it sounded like she's about to die." Misty caught up with her board and began to glide on it. "He kept asking for more, like did they say anything else, *anything else*? What else he did expect—did he think she would tell her lawyer that she loved him? What in hell is going on?"

"I'm not sure yet." Mae didn't want to accuse Reno of stealing paintings without proof. "The memorial he did for Violet is missing. He might have taken it."

"He was scared of Violet. And now he wants a souvenir of her?"

"I doubt it. He's just trying to keep me from doing any psychic work with his things. But I did some anyway." Mae explained about Jamie finding the feather in the thrift shop and Reno trying to give Florencia a new parrot.

Misty stopped abruptly in front of a mural-painted trailer, her eyes blazing. "What a hypocrite. He gave her a *parrot*?"

"Not quite. She didn't want it."

The stood silently for a moment, Misty rocking her board back and forth with one foot, Mae gazing at the images on the trailer—a pueblo double vase, a deer, smoke rising from a fire or a smudge stick, a parrot, and a poem in blue paint and uneven lettering.

One line of the verse made Mae think of Jamie every time she saw it. *Those who have moved our souls to dance ...*

She asked Misty, with a nod toward the poem. "You feel that way about Reno?"

"I wish I did. But honestly? No. I love him, but he's never been any fun."

"God. Y'all are *doomed*." Though Mae was no expert on choosing a mate, at least both of her ex-husbands had been people she could joke and play with, and Jamie, for all his neuroses, could be full of joy as well. "A good relationship takes more than having fun—but you have to actually be happy together some of the time."

"Does Jamie make you happy?"

"Yes." Mae thought of his dancing, his lovemaking, his awe at the double rainbow, his deep love and kind heart—and then the soup, the laundry, the cookies with hearts and smiles, the camping trip, and the parrot. "He tries." That sounded wrong, as if she wanted more from him. "I mean, sometimes he tries too hard."

"And that's a *problem*?"

"Kind of. I guess that sounds crazy to you. But I look at you and your sisters and I think y'all put up with way too much and that looks crazy to me. Reno lies to you and hides things from you, Will probably never planned to marry Montana, and Zak's hiding stuff too, and he practically ignores his kids."

"Of course he does. You ever wonder *why*? Some people say they look like his grandmother—that they got the Pena genes—but a lot of people say they look like Will. There's even a rumor going around that you're a witch and you put a spell on Will for Melody so he'd dump Tana and come back to her. I could just smack the shit out of the person that started it. That was the meanest thing anyone could have said—for you, for Mel, for Tana, for Zak, for Will—everyone. Who would say something like that?"

"Reno."

"*What*?"

Mae described her vision of Reno and Letitia. "He wanted to drive me away so I wouldn't learn their secrets."

Fists clenched, jaw tight, Misty glared down at the pavement. "Serves him right that you still found out."

"I didn't—not all of it, not yet."

"It doesn't matter. It's enough for me."

Misty turned her board back toward Reno's house and pushed off hard, flying down the street. Mae followed from a distance. Misty charged up the steps and beat on the door of the trailer. "Reno Geronimo! Get your lying ass out here!"

No answer. She pounded again. He opened the door, blinking and frowning, pushing his hair out of his face.

"How dare you say Melody—" Misty lost control, her words turning into a cross between a scream and a growl. "Watch this, you worthless piece of shit."

She yanked her ring off and flung it into the Rabbit's engine, where it vanished with a ping and a rattle, and then jumped off the steps, grabbed her toolbox, and shot away on her skateboard. Mae wanted to applaud. The Chino sisters might be crazy-loyal to their men, but they were even more loyal to each other.

Reno descended the steps in slow motion and leaned on the rim of the Rabbit's open engine compartment. Unsure what to say or whether she should speak at all, Mae paused at the end of the driveway. Jamie would have known what to do even if it was clumsy—he wouldn't hesitate to reach out.

"Reno." Mae kept her voice soft. "Are you all right?"

He slammed the hood down and glared at her. "What do you think?"

"I'm sorry she hurt you."

"No, you're not. Or you wouldn't have made it happen."

"*I* made it happen?" Anger rushed in, burning away Mae's concern for him. "You gonna tell people I put a spell on Misty to make her dump you? I told her the truth when you wouldn't. And the only person to blame for that is you."

Reno strode toward her. "What *truth*? You don't know anything. What bullshit are you making up about me?"

She didn't know if he'd stolen from Florencia, or how he'd acquired a stolen parrot. She didn't know if he'd had an affair with his teacher or only tried to. What mattered to Misty, though, was the witch rumor, and of that Mae was certain. "I told her the bullshit you'd made up about me."

His mouth opened, then shut. Reno turned abruptly and rushed into his house, taking his phone from his pocket.

The next day as Mae was leaving for a personal training session, she drove past Reno's trailer and noticed the Rabbit was gone. He had all the window blinds pulled up—something no one did in T or C in the summer—and the screen door flapped in the breeze, banging against the building. That had to be annoying the neighbors. She parked and climbed the steps to shut the door. Through the nearest window, she saw an empty room. Bare walls. No furniture. Reno had moved out.

Mae got back in her car and before she backed out called Niall to tell him what she'd seen. Gossip had already reached him. Reno had apparently cleared out in the middle of the night. No one had seen who helped him or knew where he'd gone. A tow truck had claimed the Rabbit first thing in the morning. Niall had already called Orville, who knew nothing of his son's whereabouts.

Mae drove to Las Cruces, relieved to be done with Reno, but at the same time doubting that she was, and feeling a trifle worried and guilty, though his problems *were* his own fault.

A few hours of work at the college fitness center allowed her to forget about him for a while. It felt good to help people and be confident she was really helping them. No ambiguity. No conflict.

When she got home, ready to enjoy some quiet time alone, Jamie's green Fiesta was parked in her carport, its back hatch crammed with his instruments, and he was sitting on her porch, reading a paperback. He looked up with a radiant smile. "Surprise."

She'd had only one night alone and needed more. Hadn't he understood what she'd told him? "Jamie—"

He laughed so hard he dropped his book, and she had to forgive him. When she climbed the steps and saw the enormous blob of orange fur in his lap, she thought she might have forgiven him too soon. Jamie rose, clutching the cat to his chest, and freed one arm to hug Mae. "Got a couple of gigs in Cruces. Thought I'd stop by on my way."

Mae gave him a quick kiss and slipped out of his embrace to unlock the door, glad he'd cut her off before she'd scolded him for crowding her. "You almost missed me. I just got back from Las Cruces."

Jamie followed her inside. "Guess you wouldn't want to go down for my show tonight, then. How about tomorrow?"

"I can't. I've got a healing client tomorrow evening."

"You're doing a healing *before* you take the workshop?" Jamie put his cat down and closed the door. They took off their shoes, following Niall's rules about the flawless bamboo floors. "Shouldn't you tell her to wait?"

"She's really eager to quit smoking. I'm not asking her to wait 'til August."

"Mm. Yeah. Reckon. Just wanted the time with you, y'know?" Jamie wrapped his arms around her and nuzzled her ear. "Only a few weeks and then I'll be on the road for months."

"This is time together, sugar. It doesn't have to be every day."

"I know. But I thought I'd try anyway. It's not like I'm asking you to go *camping*." He rocked her in the hug, then drew back enough to meet her eyes. "Speaking of that—did I tell you I fixed my tent? Took a while, but it survived. I know you're not going to sleep in it, but it's one thing I saved from the whole fucked-up weekend."

"I'm glad you could patch it." She took his hand and led him to sit with her on the couch. There was a lot she still hadn't told him about his friends and their secrets. "We need to talk."

"Did I do something?"

"No. It's about Reno. And Shelli and David."

Gasser, the cat, waddled over and began to meow. Jamie lifted him into his lap and bent over to murmur a few endearments into his fur. "Is it bad?"

"Yes and no. I found out where Placido is," she said. "He's okay. He's in an art gallery with the hyacinth macaw."

"Fuck me dead." Jamie looked up. "Reno gave him to a gallery? Wonder if they'd sell him."

"Sugar, he's stolen. He's not theirs to sell. And ... David's mother runs the gallery."

"David's mum? But that means—that means ..."

"I know. Shelli lied to you. They both did."

"Fuck." Jamie sank lower into the couch. "I thought they *liked* me."

"I'm sure they do, but that doesn't make them honest." Mae described the back room and the hyacinth passing as Violet. "Letitia sends people to see that collection and to buy part of it. I think Reno's been stealing from his teacher so they can have more to sell and still have their museum."

"You don't *know* that. Whole thing could be legit. Anyway, I asked you to leave that stuff alone. Will owes Tana, remember? We can't leave her hanging."

"It's all connected. I couldn't help it. And I didn't agree to stop trying. I'm done with psychic work for Misty, but not because you told me to stop. She broke up with Reno, and he left town."

"Jeezus." Jamie straightened up again, staring at her. "*No.* You shouldn't have done that. They needed to work it out."

"I didn't break them up." An uneasy image filled her mind, a boxing ring with the Chino sisters in one corner and Mae as their coach, and Reno, Zak and Will in the other corner, with Jamie giving ice and a towel to a pummeled, fallen Reno. "It was a messed-up relationship to start with. She dumped him when I told her what he said about me."

Jamie stood and paced, carrying Gasser like a teddy bear. "Yeah. Guess he deserved it for that." He rubbed his chin on the cat's head. "Weird. I was pissed off at Reno for saying that, but now I'm worried about him, too. Is that fucked up?"

"Not really. You've known him a long time."

"Did he go home? He needs to be with people."

"No. Orville doesn't know where he is. But I don't think he's alone. Somebody had to have helped him move out."

"Heartbreak. Guess he's trying to start over somewhere else."

"Or hiding his secret. He took the memorial he made for Violet off her grave."

"Jeezus." Jamie put the cat down and drifted into the kitchen. "Mind if I make coffee?"

Mae assured him it was fine and joined him. She got mugs from a cupboard. Jamie filled the coffee maker and measured beans into the grinder. Mae had the odd thought that this was one thing they agreed on perfectly. Black coffee, no sugar, freshly ground.

Over the whir of the grinder, Jamie said, "He's got to be scared. Does Misty still want you to find out what he's hiding?"

Mae sat at the table. "I don't think she cares anymore."

"Good." He dumped the coffee into a filter, put it in place, and turned the machine on. "I hope that means you won't go fucking around with Zak's stuff this weekend."

"If Melody asks me to see what he's up to, I'm not gonna say no. She still thinks he's fooling around with Letitia."

Jamie sat across from her, his gaze intense and pleading. "I hope he's not. But Zak's my mate, y'know? He should be able to trust me. And that means he needs to be able to trust you, too."

Avoiding Jamie's baby seal eyes, Mae toyed with the lid on the tub of cookies, peeling it up slowly. It would have been easier to argue with him if he yelled at her. How had she ever gotten up the strength to try to break up with him? To tell him so many things he didn't want to hear? She was going to have to get better at this or she'd qualify as a Chino sister. The cookies seemed to stare at her with their heart-shapes and raisin smiley faces, reminding of her of everything she loved about Jamie that also drove her crazy—his stubborn, blind, generous, misguided good intentions.

His loyalty to Zak touched her. She'd had a cheating first husband, though. Jamie might not understand, but if she had to choose between what he wanted and what Melody wanted, she would have to side with Zak's wife.

Mae finally looked at Jamie. His expression hadn't changed. She squeezed his hand. "Maybe she won't ask me."

His smile was a sunburst of relief. "Yeah. That'd be best. Maybe she won't."

Chapter Twenty-Six

On Wednesday evening, Mae walked to her appointment with Daphne Brady in an optimistic mood. After all the conflict and stress about using her gift as a psychic, working as a healer would feel good, the way her fitness work did. She found the lawyer waiting outside the red-and-white one-story building, smoking. Mae reached out to shake hands. "You ready? That your last one?"

"It sure is." Daphne dropped her cigarette into a flower pot full of gravel and other butts. Her grip was ferocious. "The last one." She led Mae inside to a reception area. "Not very mystical, is it? Niall said you did the trick on him in front of the Ellis building."

"It wasn't meant to be a trick—"

"I meant you did the thing that finally worked. Not that you tricked him." She perched her bony backside on the edge of a desk near the receptionist's name plate. Mae examined the room. Two red leatherette chairs, a coffee table displaying the Sierra County Artists' Directory, New Mexico Magazine, and a wildlife newsletter. The floor was bare hardwood. "Normally," *when I'm not having some random effect in a parking lot,* "I like to have healing clients lie down. They're more relaxed. I can get a better feel for their energy, too." Lying on the hard floor, this skinny woman wouldn't be relaxed.

"So it *is* more like a ceremony. Good. Smoking is a ritual. I'd like to banish it with a counter-ritual."

The insight surprised Mae, but it pleased her. "Do you have a couch in your office? Or a rug?"

"No. You really need a proper healing room for your business, don't you?"

The phone in the back office rang. Daphne excused herself to answer it. Mae sat in one of the leatherette chairs and looked out the window. Main Street was almost deserted. Summer. If Mae had a room like she'd had in Virginia Beach before she'd moved out West, she could do moderately well in the fall and winter. But that was when school asked the most of her. A healing business would have to wait until graduation, and then she might be moving to Santa Fe, if she and Jamie were still together. She hoped they would be, but it was too soon to know.

"I'm sorry." Daphne walked in with a handful of papers. "I need to go over this. Alan Pacheco, the art critic and painter—I don't know if you've heard of him—"

"I have. I know him."

"So you know what Florencia asked him to write, then?"

"Something like an obituary only longer, and then something else for an exhibit she wants him to organize after she dies. A biography, too, I think."

"Yes. He just emailed me the memorial article. He was trying to get it finished in time for her to approve it. I said I'd go over it first, tell him if I see anything she wouldn't like, and then I'll read it to her."

"Should we reschedule your healing? I know you wanted that to be your last cigarette ..."

"I did." Daphne looked down at her nails. "But I didn't get my manicure yet. I was even thinking of getting a massage and doing a hot spring soak. A total cleansing to get ready. I haven't had time."

She's better at thinking up healing rituals than I am. "Do you need another day or so?"

"I may need the rest of Florencia's life." Daphne sank into the other chair and looked down at the papers. "Could you take a look at this, too? Niall says, and I use his terms, that you don't know 'jack-shit about art.' I'm sure you know a little more than that, but Florencia would want people who aren't experts or scholars to find her interesting when she's gone. You're not acquainted with her, are you?"

"I met her once for around five minutes. And I helped Niall clear her house out," *and had a couple of psychic visions of her,* "so I kinda know her in a weird way."

"Believe me, that doesn't count as knowing her. She's a character. I want to see if Alan gets that across as well as her art."

When the lawyer had finished reading, Mae took her turn.

Florencia Mirabal will be remembered as a ground-breaking Native artist and honored as one of the most influential women painters of recent decades, though she never wanted to be categorized as either. She made a point of defying popular expectations of American Indians and of women.

She was known for her flamboyant persona and her caustic wit as well as her refusal to conform. In a series of self-portraits, the face she showed the world was framed by neon colors. In the first she had hot pink hair, matching glasses and a necklace of pink stones. In the next, her hair, glasses, and jewelry were neon green. In the third and best known picture, her color scheme was cobalt blue, matching her hyacinth macaw who perched beside her. The hairstyles were different, and her face a little older in each image. This was her look over time, an expression of her character, not a stunt. In each portrait, she grinned as if something hilarious had just happened or made a face at her audience.

Mirabal's rebellious streak carried her away from her native Acoma personally, emotionally, and aesthetically. Her marriage to Mescalero Apache artist Orville Geronimo while they were students at the Institute for American Indian Art was the beginning of a break with her family. The rift between Mirabal and her Acoma relatives widened when she divorced Geronimo and moved to Truth or Consequences rather than back to the pueblo.

In an interview in Native Peoples *in 1995, when asked why she never returned home, she said, "My parents were difficult people. It's always expected that daughters take care of parents, but I wasn't about to give up my life for them. They were some of the last people to live full-time up on the mesa, with no electricity, no running water. Living there was like camping with people who drove me crazy."* Mae almost laughed out loud. She understood too well. And she understood about difficult parents, too. Her mother hadn't spoken to her for over a year. *"They never supported me emotionally or in any of my choices. It's heresy to say this, because Indians honor their elders, but not all families can meet the ideal. I have no regrets, but my brother never forgave me."*

Despite her thirty-year absence from her homeland, it haunted her paintings. She often painted the ancient path from the mesa and the symbols of her culture, though in her own way. The blue and yellow pair of paintings in Mae's vision of the gallery must have portrayed the path Alan was talking about. *Not in the artistic tradition of Acoma, with its fine geometry and precise details, but in modern imagery, influenced more by Fritz Scholder than her ancestors."*

Mae read more about Mirabal's art, but the discussion was over her head, full of additional references to artists she'd never heard of. The article concluded with a few final notes.

T or C friends say that Art Hop nights will be duller without her. Friends. That was a gracious stretch, making the word plural. Acquaintances, maybe, but Niall was her only friend. *She is survived by her brother Severus Mirabal and her nephew David. Both declined to be interviewed.*

"You done?" Daphne asked, when Mae looked up from the papers.

"Yeah. It makes me wish I'd known her when she was healthy. She might have been fun."

"Fun but challenging. It takes someone as thick-skinned as Niall to really put up with her. Or someone like me who's getting paid."

"Orville loved her. I think he still likes her. But he's got to be the most cheerful guy I've ever met. Maybe he could get along with anybody."

"You know Orville, too? Not bad for someone who knows jack-shit about art. Orville does still care about her. He's been to visit her. With an old medicine man. He brought her some strange music she really likes."

"The old man did?"

"Yes. Healing music with drums and didgeridoo and all different kinds of flutes. It's hard to describe—it sounds Indian, Aboriginal, and almost classical at the same time, and this man's voice chanting—it's got to be the most beautiful voice I've ever heard. I'd ask you to use it while you heal me except it makes me see her hospice room."

"That's okay. I don't think I'd concentrate too well. That's got to be my boyfriend's music."

"Jamie? The guy Chuck met in Bullock's? He writes that kind of music?"

"Yeah. I know he seems a little ... wound up, but he's got a spiritual side. He hasn't recorded any healing music for a while, but he still volunteers at the UNM hospital in Albuquerque. They have an Arts in Medicine program and he does some music for patients there."

"He has a gift for it. It's really helping Florencia. Please tell him how much she appreciates his music."

"I will. I wish I'd known earlier. He was in Las Cruces all day today. He could have come to play for her."

"Do you think he'd make another trip to come sing for her?"

"I think so. I can't speak for him, of course, but he's very kind. He likes to help people."

"Thank you." Daphne looked down at the papers. "I'd better get back to work on this. Did the story interest you? Make you want to get to know her art?"

"It made me want to see those self-portraits. And it made her interesting. I felt for her, with that family. But it's funny—I mean, ironic. From what I know about her, she's kind of like them herself. Difficult. And won't forgive people."

"You're referring to Reno?"

"No. I was thinking about her nephew. Did he do anything, or is she mad at him just for being her brother's kid?"

"As far as I know, it's for being her brother's kid. She'll want him and Severus cut from the article. But how did Alan do with the rest?"

"I couldn't follow most of the art stuff. I think the other people who don't know jack-shit about art will like it better if the paper or the magazine runs a picture with it, maybe Florencia with blue hair making a funny face. If that's how she wants to be remembered."

"She probably does." The lawyer smiled. "Thanks. I'd better call her now. We'll reschedule my healing." They stood and Daphne gave Mae another crushing handshake. "I don't know when."

Mae pictured Daphne smoking again after her commitment to quit. If she didn't do it now, she might lose the courage, with all the stress surrounding Florencia's impending death. Especially if Niall decided to talk to the lawyer about Reno's possible thefts. "Let's do it later tonight."

"But I haven't had my massage and—"

"What if you could book one at seven? Get one at the Charles and schedule the rooftop hot spring at eight. I bet they have space in their schedule this time of year. And I could do the healing in the water."

"Does it have to be tonight? I'll pay you for your time if that's a problem—"

"That's not why I'm pushing you. It's because I know what it's like to chicken out on something hard and I don't want you to."

"You—chicken?"

"Sometimes, yeah." Mae had known within six months that her first marriage was a mistake, but it had taken her two years to end it. "Use the courage while you've got it."

Daphne took her cigarettes from her purse, looked at them, nodded, and handed them to Mae. "Tonight it is. Call the Charles for me and I'll call Florencia."

With the darkening blue sky above, the rooftop enclosure was serene, and so was Daphne, fresh from her massage. Since the lawyer was so well prepared, Mae hoped the healing would be one of the clear and simple ones. The bathing suit she'd loaned her client bagged and rippled on her bony frame, but Daphne somehow looked healthier already. Mae got in the water with her, took a moment to prepare her mind, and then let her intuition and the crystal she held to Daphne's heart guide her.

At first she sensed Daphne's inner body as tangled lines of light and sent energy through the crystals to bring them into order. A vision emerged. A haggard Florencia was sitting in the lawyer's office, wearing her beaded cap, fuchsia-framed glasses, and a dress that fit her as badly as Mae's suit fit Daphne. "Yes, I'm sure, and yes, I'm *compos mentis.*"

"I'm not worried about your *compos mentis*, Flo. I just want you to calm down. If you're angry while you make this decision—"

"If I don't do it, I'll stay angry until I die."

Daphne moved her hands to her keyboard. She spoke slowly, her tone level. "You're sure?"

"I'm sure. Reno's out. Make it simple. Niall and no one but Niall. He can give it to museums, he can sell it, I don't care. But it all goes to Niall."

The vision faded. Mae had seen the last lingering stressor that Daphne was afraid would make her smoke. She refocused into the crystals and the healing energy of the water. The lines of light untangled into a glow that grew brighter as the process completed itself.

It was only when Mae was walking home that she let herself think about Reno. He had been in Florencia's will and blown it. Money. The Mustang. Maybe the house. She pictured him bringing the parrot into the studio through the back door, setting up the surprise. Why had he done it?

The gift might have been meant to make Florencia happy, but according to Misty Florencia had imposed rules on Reno, including a ban on talking about her family. Misty had also said that Reno complained about his teacher and about Violet. Was his affection for Florencia a fraud? Had he been a "vulture," hoping to inherit? If so, he deserved her rejection, but if he'd loved her, she'd hurt herself as well as him when she sent him away.

*****

Jamie's phone rang as he was maneuvering his instruments into the Fiesta after his show. It was a complicated process to get them all to fit, making him think of his injured van, hoping it came back looking new again. He closed the hatchback and answered the call. Mae—at this time of night? She was probably half-asleep, and yet she was thinking of him. A feeling like warm butterscotch bathed him.

After he let loose a flood of endearments and asked about her day, she told him about Lonnie giving Florencia the music.

"I asked Niall if she'd like to have you sing to her and she would. It's getting hard for her to draw anymore, so she's really unhappy. The music helps her a lot. Maybe when you come down to see me next week, we could go to Las Cruces and you could do that."

The warm gooey feeling hardened into dread. Jamie had witnessed the death of a friend as a small child and had been present when another friend passed not long ago. He'd been shaken, emotionally and spiritually, and still had nightmares about the childhood trauma. Mae should have known better than to ask him to do this. "I play for people who need something to soothe them after surgery or during chemo. Not while they're *dying*. Sorry, love, but I can't do that. See someone die—y'know—I get fucked up. It's hard to get my head right again."

"You don't have to be there the moment she passes. Just help her get peaceful."

Jamie paused. Mae meant well. She wanted to help, and asking him to play for the dying woman was the way she could do it. "That what you want?"

"Don't do it for me, sugar. If it's too much, it's okay. She's got the CDs Lonnie brought her."

If it's too much. He was sure she hadn't meant it the way it sounded, but her words made him feel small and cowardly. "Nah. Not the same as a live voice. I'll do it. No worries."

"Thank you, sugar. You're a sweetheart."

When she said goodnight, Jamie closed his eyes and pressed the phone to his heart, bringing her voice back in his mind. It was so good to hear her sound like she *admired* him. Saw him as the man he wanted to be. Could be. *Would* be.

Chapter Twenty-Seven

Saturday afternoon, Mae heard a knock and a cheerful holler at her front door while she was on the phone with Jamie. She broke into his random ramblings. "Sorry—I gotta go now, sugar. Melody's here for her first training session."

"Give her a hug for me. And don't—"

"Don't start on that. It's up to me and her. I love you."

"Love ya, too. But don't do it."

They had managed not to argue for several days. Jamie had fretted over their prolonged time apart, but with his performances in Santa Fe and Albuquerque Thursday through Saturday and her plans for Art Hop with Melody, it hadn't been practical to get together. She'd thought the break was healthy for their relationship and he had worried that it wasn't, but they hadn't actually fought about it. Mae said goodbye, uneasy that they'd almost broken their truce. There were lightweight fights with Jamie, and there were big ones. This had the potential for becoming a big one.

She let Melody in, reminded her to take her shoes off, and hugged her. "That was from Jamie." Melody, wearing shiny black Lycra pants and a Mescalero five K T-shirt, was dripping sweat from her walk. "Great outfit. Zak seen you in it?"

"Not yet," Melody grunted as she stooped to untie her sneakers. "He couldn't come this weekend. His crew is getting ready to go out on a fire." Mae got her friend a glass of water. Melody thanked her and gulped it down. "He was all paranoid about me seeing you this weekend without him. Not that he'd say so, but he watched me pack. He even helped me—and if you know Zak, that's not normal."

Mae went to her spare room and brought out an exercise ball and a mat. "Did you ever find out what he's hiding from you?"

"Of course not. I ask him and he just throws Will at me." Mae set the equipment down. Melody watched the ball roll to a stop. "That thing looks like my stomach." She lay on the mat and looked at it sideways. "That's what Zak sees, lying beside me. I don't know how he could think Will wants me." She sighed, attempted a crunch, and lay back down. "I can't do that. My fat gets in the way."

"It's not a great exercise anyway, not with your bad back." Mae sat on the ball. "I think we should talk before your workout."

"About my back?

"Yes, but I'd concentrate better if we got Zak out of the way first."

Melody propped up on her elbows. "Do you know something I don't?"

"Not about him, no. And Jamie's dead set against me helping you find out. He just told me not to—again. I kinda get it. It would be better if you two could talk. But can you?"

"Not really. We've been reading Jamie's book. It has all these notes and highlights in it like he was studying for a test, which is really cute. We take turns reading it out loud in bed and do Jamie imitations. It cracks us up, but it's totally useless. Real people don't do *communication exercises*. They fight."

"They sure do."

"But you don't have *real* fights. Just Jamie fussing."

Mae shook her head. "No, we have real fights, too. He wants to move our relationship way too fast, and I want to go slow. I almost broke off with him for that."

"You can't break up with him." Melody sat up, her tone urgent and her face creased with worry. "He'll wait for you to be ready. I know he's weird and he's a pain in the ass, but he loves you so much."

"I know." Mae rocked the ball and looked down at her feet. "We may work that stuff out. I hope so. But that's not all we've argued about. I told you my second marriage ended partly because of what I do as a psychic. I thought Jamie was gonna be the guy who understood. But he doesn't like the same thing Hubert didn't: that I can find out the truth when people are hiding it." She sought Melody's gaze. "He wants me to leave Zak's secrets alone no matter what Zak's up to—and not because he thinks what I do is wrong the way Hubert did—but because I'd be doing it to Zak."

"But you'd be doing it for me." Melody turned over onto her hands and knees and pushed up to standing. "Jamie would *have* to understand that. I want you to do it. I planned to bring something of Zak's for you to work with, but since I couldn't, I brought something else. I left it outside." She headed to the door. "I've had it up to here with Zak lying. If he's cheating, I'm gone."

"You'd leave him? You wouldn't give him a second chance?"

"Come on. You almost broke up with Jamie for a lot less." Melody went out to the porch, brought a plastic grocery sack inside, and set it on the coffee table. "Did you give your first husband a second chance?"

"I did. I shouldn't have, but that's because he was an alcoholic. Sorry—I didn't mean that the way it sounded. You got sober. He didn't."

Melody lowered herself to the couch and fiddled with the bag. Her voice was quiet and strained. "It goes together. I quit cheating when I quit drinking. I would never, *ever* do that in my right mind. Those kids *are* his. But Zak can't see that. He can't let it go. And now he's punishing me, making me think he's fooling around. If it's just an act, I get it. But if it's real—I don't deserve it."

"Last weekend you sounded like you thought you did."

"I've won a race since I said that." She gave Mae half a smile that quickly faded, and resumed fidgeting with the bag. "And Misty broke up with Reno, and *she's* happy. Will dumped Montana and *she's* holding up. I helped her clean his stuff out of her trailer on my way here, while I didn't have the kids to deal with, and she was glad to get rid of it. She didn't cry once. If they're that strong—and you are, with two divorces—I can be."

"I'm sure you can." Their eyes met. "But I hope I find out that he's faithful to you. And I hope I *can* find out. Whose stuff did you bring me, if you couldn't bring something of Zak's?"

"Will's. I got the idea to grab it while I was cleaning at Tana's place."

"That might not work."

"Sure it could. He's part of their secret and he was at Zak's party. Since Zak doesn't give that kind of party and he doesn't like Will and the guy from the pottery booth was there, the party had to be a cover-up for them having a meeting. You could find out about all of them this way."

Mae picked up the bag from the table. It was full of empty tobacco tins and cigarette packs. She recoiled and Melody laughed. "I figured you'd think it was disgusting. That's why I left it on the porch."

"What's disgusting is that all this was lying around your sister's place."

"That's the Chino sisters' housekeeping." Melody let out a whoop of laughter. "You saw my place before you and Jamie cleaned it."

"Yeah." *That was a wreck.* "You know, if I see the party, I might find out about their meeting, but I wouldn't see Zak and Letitia alone."

"You could see how he acts around her when I'm not there. I almost called Will to ask him if he saw anything, but knowing him, he'd have made something up to make trouble for Zak, and he was too drunk to remember, anyway."

Mae put down the bag of Will's tobacco trash. All of these packages had ridden in his pocket. There would be a lot of his energy in any one of them. And yet she hesitated. He was her client. She felt she owed him a respect she didn't owe Reno, who had called her a witch and betrayed people left and right. Will had wanted to clean up his act. But he hadn't done so completely, if he was still part of this secret, and it was hurting Melody. Her marriage was suffering. She had to know what Zak was hiding. "Okay. I don't promise results, but I'll give it a try."

After Melody's workout, she left, and Mae prepared for a psychic journey. The indirect route she had to take might be for the best, less intrusive, since she was unlikely to witness anything too private between Zak and Letitia. She sat on the floor holding one of the empty tobacco tins, chose her crystals, and set the question to focus her search. *What does Will know about Letitia? What has he seen that would tell me about her and Zak?*

The tunnel took her vision to a half-dirt, half-paved parking lot between a row of adobe buildings and a strip mall. Will, smoking a cigarette, paced around his jeep. It was parked in front of a shop whose sign read *The Exotic Aviary*. A sign in the window advertised a sale on bird supplies. He glanced in the window, squinting against the glare on the glass.

"Shit." He took another drag and ground out his cigarette. "She needs more animals like she needs a hole in her head. "

He entered a room displaying bird cages, food, and toys, and books with various parrots on the covers. On the other side of a glass wall was a room full of cages with an open space in the middle, where smoothed branches had been turned into perches. Shelli held up a small, crested, rose-colored bird on her wrist and waved at Will with her free hand. He scowled. She smiled in return, gently passing the bird to Letitia, and the two women spoke softly.

Will walked to the door of the bird room. "I thought we came here for the sale on bird food."

Letitia sidled up, petting the cockatoo. "I know, Willie, but I am *so* tempted. Peaches would love to have a little friend, wouldn't she?"

Will shrugged. "It's your money, darling." She practically danced back to Shelli. "Or mine," he added under his breath. "I'd better win at the slots."

Startled, Mae lost her focus. The last thing she'd expected to find was that Will's other woman was Letitia. It would be ironic if she was cheating on him with Zak, but it would fit Zak's agenda perfectly if he wanted to punish both Melody and Will. He didn't know, though. He would have told Montana, to get Will out of her life sooner.

Mae had learned nothing about Zak. Still, the fact that Will and Letitia knew their way around this bird store made his finding—or stealing—the parrots less strange. How did it lead up to the parrots in the gallery, though? Mae refocused, and broadened her questions, seeking anything in Will's past that would tell her about Reno and Zak or Kathy Chavez-Mirabal's gallery.

When her vision emerged from the tunnel, she saw Will smoking in a parking lot again. She recognized this one, situated between the side of a long white building with red and green trim and a stand of scrubby trees. He was outside Rio Bravo Fine Art in T or C. Relaxed, enjoying his smoke, Will leaned against the passenger door of a white pickup decorated with paintings of mountains. On the door panel a nighthawk flew under a moon that lit the peaks, while on the side of the bed an eagle soared under the sun.

David Mirabal pulled up in a dusty gray van and got out. Shelli remained inside, primping in the rearview mirror. Kathy, in the back seat, leaned forward to talk to her.

Mae guessed she was seeing the past. David's belly was a bit smaller and his braids a little shorter. He walked around the painted truck, jingling his keys. "That's amazing. It looks like Orville Geronimo's work. On a *truck*."

Will started to speak when his younger brother Refugio came out of the gallery and jogged toward him. "You'd better go in, bro'. She wants to show off her model."

"Shit." Will pushed off the truck. "I hate these gallery parties. Everybody sober and over fifty."

Shelli got out of the van. She was a little slimmer, too, and her hair was longer and pure black. Kathy followed, carrying two small white boxes tied with gold cord, a parrot feather stuck in the bowknot of each one.

As the five of them walked toward the front of the gallery, Will said, "I'm Will Baca. Mescalero Apache. Wildman Will to rodeo fans. And this is my little brother Refugio. Owner of the truck."

The group paused for Kathy, David, and Shelli to shake hands with the brothers and introduce themselves by name and tribe. David said, "That's some great art you're driving around. I could swear it looks like Orville Geronimo did it."

"No," Refugio said. "His son. My parents gave me the truck for my sixteenth birthday and had Reno paint it. He was only a senior in high school, so it was a lot cheaper than having his dad do it."

Will grinned. "For my sixteenth birthday I got grounded. Or did I get arrested? You remember?"

"No. You were always in so much trouble, it's one big blur."

"That's the truth." They resumed their progress. "Reno gonna be here tonight?"

"Yeah. He's in there with that lady Tish wants to talk to." Refugio spoke to the Mirabal family. "She's in line to see this artist, Florencia Mirabal. Are you guys related?"

"Yes," Kathy said cautiously. "We're here to see her, too."

"She's got a parrot on a *leash*. And I think she's got Reno on a leash, too. He just stands there like she told him to *stay*." Refugio imitated someone giving a dog a command. "I haven't had a chance to say more than hello to him."

"When you do," Will said, "watch your tongue about Tish. He'd tell Misty. And Montana doesn't need to know what she doesn't need to know."

"You got me trained, bro'. I'm on my leash."

They reached the gallery door. Shelli asked Will, "You've got two girlfriends?"

"Why not?" He took a final puff and put out his cigarette. "I'm not married. And I like to live dangerously. I can have as many girl-friends as I want."

Shelli gave Will a crooked smile, shaking her head. David put his arm around her and kissed her on the cheek. "One woman is enough for me."

They followed the Baca brothers inside. Refugio led the way through the front room, where quilts and other fiber art were dis-played, past shelves of pottery, and through a large room with ab-stract paintings on the wall where a cluster of people stood talking around a table full of drinks and snacks. The group proceeded up a short flight of stairs, through a hallway hung with small paintings, and into a gallery space displaying much larger works, including the Cowboy Angel. Florencia stood in front of it with Letitia, Reno, and several people Mae recognized as T or C residents, though she didn't know their names. Reno wore small, dark-framed glasses that made him look even more serious than usual. Mae thought the man standing next to him might be the gallery owner, someone she'd seen with Niall on other Art Hop nights.

Letitia beamed at Will and reached out to him, pulling him closer. "This is Will. I've done some wonderful portraits of him."

Florencia, healthy looking and strong, her hair and glasses frames rainbow-colored, had Violet on her shoulder. The bird wore a dainty harness and her owner held the leash, but Violet seemed disinclined to fly away. Turning one huge yellow-rimmed eye to regard Will, she whistled like a construction worker eyeing a pretty woman. Florencia laughed. "If Delmas ever does a cowboy devil, you should model."

Will drew back, looking at the angel man. "Me? That's gay art."

"I bet women like him, too." Refugio gave him a light punch in the arm. "It's the Baca curse, bro. Pretty boys." He added in a whisper, "I think she's flirting with you."

Letitia gave the brothers a warning look and smiled at Florencia. "I was wondering if you could introduce me to Mr. Howe. I know how much you like my work, and I was thinking of doing a new calendar, with his permission. I'd call it Howe-dy, Pardner—a tribute. Real cowboys posing like his paintings."

Florencia sipped her drink, then addressed the people circled around her. "I suppose he should let Letitia do it. It would be her chance to move out of *pornography*."

Letitia's jaw dropped. "I don't do pornography. I do art photography."

Florencia let out a guffaw. "No. It's *good* pornography, mind you, but it's not *art*." She spoke aside to Reno, but loudly enough for others to hear. "That naked cowboy calendar in my bathroom? She did that."

Reno looked at his feet. The other people regarded Letitia, their expressions a mixture of embarrassment and amusement, and then moved away, one man wishing her luck with a suggestion of doubt in his tone. She gazed after them, her hands opening and then clenching, her lips parted for words that never came out.

Kathy, David, and Shelli closed in, approaching Florencia. Shelli cooed to Violet, telling the bird how beautiful she was. Florencia stepped back, her shoulders braced, her eyes narrowed, one hand going to her bird's breast.

"Flo, please. Don't look at us like that," Kathy said. "I know Severus was awful the last time we met, but I divorced him years ago. We should get past that."

"And what prompted this sudden warmth from my estranged family?"

David said, "Our family is about to grow," and gave Shelli a glowing look. "It seemed like the right time to include you in it."

They handed Florencia the gift boxes, having to offer twice before she accepted them.

"Hold this." She handed Reno one of the boxes and held the other up for Violet to snip the knot. David gasped as the massive beak touched the package. "Don't be silly," Florencia snapped and opened the box. "She's not going to hurt anything."

Will shook his head, muttering "bitch" under his breath, and wandered behind her with Refugio to look at the Cowboy Angel. It had a *sold* tag beside it. Will peered at the price and whistled through his teeth. "Holy shit. Who in hell bought that? I've never had that much spare cash in my life."

"I bought it." Florencia turned to him. "And I'm sorry Letitia doesn't pay you well for hanging on my bathroom wall. Maybe you should get a real job."

"She doesn't have to pay me. She's a nice woman and I'd work for her for free. And for your information, *ma'am*," he took a sarcastic little bow, "I'm a real cowboy. Not just a model. And I'm damned glad my picture can't see you naked in your bathroom or it'd jump off the wall and flush itself."

Letitia exclaimed and the Mirabal family looked stunned, while Refugio stifled a snort of laughter. Florencia took it all in, then faced her relatives. "Now that's what I call an honest man. Unlike you sycophantic coattail riders." She handed the gift boxes back to David and Shelli. "Nice try."

Kathy protested, "Flo. We're not kissing up to you. This is sincere. I have a gallery now. I'd like to show the early works you left in Acoma, if you'd allow that. Make you part of our circle. We want you to have a family. Meet your grandniece or nephew in eight months."

"You want to show the world that crap I painted when I was Reno's age? I was flailing around like he is now, trying to find my style. You don't want me as family. You want to bait people into your gallery to buy your son's and your daughter-in-law's pottery. If you really wanted me in your circle, you wouldn't have waited until it was so *useful* to include me."

Florencia strode away and stopped at the door to the hall, giving Reno a commanding look. He said, "In a minute. I want to catch up with Refugio. I haven't seen him for ages."

"He can come with us."

"In a minute."

Reno watched her leave. He shoved his hands in his pockets and his shoulders hunched in. "I'm sorry she was so rude. She's had a bad day."

"And so she took it out on people who were trying to be nice to her?" Will asked.

"She's taking it out on everybody."

"Including you?"

Reno nodded.

"What are you to her, anyway? Her toy boy?"

The young artist sighed. He looked at the Mirabal family, at the Baca brothers, and then at the floor. "Dad asked her to teach me as a favor to him. I liked her a lot at first."

"A lot?" Will elbowed him. "I gave her a hard time, but she's not bad-looking for her age."

Reno turned partially away. "She's my father's ex-wife. It would have been weird."

"She must have acted really different at first, if you liked her," Shelli said. "She doesn't deserve that lovely macaw. I thought she was awful. Not just to us. To ..." She turned to Letitia. "I didn't get your name." Letitia gave it, and Shelli continued. "Calling your work pornography. Kathy has one of your calendars in her office—the firefighters—and it's fun, it's not obscene."

"Thank you. Florencia doesn't actually think it is, either. She's a big fan of my calendars, but whenever we meet she puts me down. It's her idea of a joke. I was planning to talk to the owner here about showing my portraits, and she blew it for me. It's been hard to get a gallery show in Santa Fe, so I thought I'd try T or C."

Shelli gave her a sympathetic look. "If Kathy didn't have a gallery, we'd just be doing powwows and feasts."

"I'm sorry I don't carry photography." Kathy sounded more angry than apologetic. "Or I'd offer to show your work, and we could invite Florencia and make her eat her words. But my gallery is exclusively pueblo art."

"I was hoping you'd say Indian art." Reno pushed his glasses up. "It's hard to get a break. Florencia's gotten so controlling, I was going to stop studying with her. But I couldn't do it. I still need the lessons. And the connections."

"Lessons?" David said. "Your work on Refugio's truck looks pretty polished."

"It looks like Dad's work, though. And Florencia says my own style is too generic. That you could hang it in a motel."

"You do great nature scenes," Refugio assured him. "I really like your paintings. More than that abstract stuff downstairs. When you paint a mountain, it looks like a mountain."

Kathy asked for his business card and gave him hers. "I know Florencia expects you now, but stay in touch. And when she turns you loose for the evening, give me a call. We may still be in town. Having dinner with Letitia and the Baca brothers, if they're free to join us."

Reno fingered her card. "I'm Apache. You only sell pueblo art."

"We could still have a drink."

Will led the way toward the exit. "Reno and Refugio aren't old enough to drink. I'll have to have their drinks for them."

Mae chose to break into the vision. She'd learned more about Will than she wanted to but nothing about Zak, and she didn't have much mental energy left for another journey. It was frustrating.

Taking a break to renew herself, she went out to sit on the back steps. The heat was intense in the tiny wedge of shade cast by the house, and the chaos of the deck in progress made the setting less serene than usual, but Niall and Kenny were taking the weekend off from the job, and she still had the view of Turtleback Mountain. The sleeping turtle shape on its rocky crest gave her a peaceful feeling. She set her crystals in the sun instead of salt water this time, and let the light do its work on them while she sorted out her thoughts.

Florencia's reaction to Kathy's reconciliation attempt had made sense, rude though it had been. Kathy's timing looked more commercial than affectionate, motivated by promoting her business and David and Shelli's careers. Perhaps they'd also been ready to welcome Florencia back into the family—until they met her.

The artist reminded Mae of a dog that had been kicked. Defensive, vigilant, habitually attacking. People couldn't get close to her, unless, like Niall, they understood. She was lonely. Fragile, even, under that surface. She'd cried after she rejected Reno's declaration of love.

Good thing she had turned him down, though. He had lost interest after an initial crush or liking. After that, he'd been forcing himself to pretend he still cared. What had made him endure such a suffocating connection for two years? Maybe a combination of needing her teaching, guilt when she got sick, and greed.

What would a rare early painting by a famous artist sell for? Mae had heard astronomical prices on the news when some great work of art sold at auction. Florencia's paintings wouldn't fetch billions, but they were valuable enough that Reno would only have needed to steal a few.

There might be enough money for everyone. Kathy only showed the back room of the gallery to people Letitia sent. The photographer could get a fee for the referrals. Will might get something for his help with the parrot theft. Violet was famous, due to her presence in her owner's blue self-portrait, but her recent death might not be well known. The hyacinth in the gallery was lending authenticity to Kathy's claims of a partial reconciliation.

The pieces of the puzzle were coming together, but Zak didn't fit into it. What could have dragged him in? Letitia?

Mae stood and stretched, walked around the yard until she felt she could concentrate again, then sat and picked up the crystals and the tobacco tin and closed her eyes. *I need to see Will with Zak. See all of them together. See what happened at that party.*

Her vision passed through the tunnel slowly and emerged in Zak's kitchen. Will set a six-pack on the counter and yanked a beer from it. "Where is everybody? Let's get this party rolling."

Zak, standing with arms folded over his chest, glared at him. "It's not a party. We need to talk and I need you with your head on straight."

Will drank and tipped his head sideways. "Straight as it gets."

"I'm serious. You could be in trouble. This kid who's a seer had a dream about you."

Will brought his head back to neutral, his eyebrows lifted.

Someone knocked on the back door. Zak turned to open it. "I'll tell you later. So stay sober until we're through."

David entered with his infant daughter in a plastic carrier.

"You brought your baby?" Will exclaimed.

David sat at the table and lifted Star up to his chest, talking nonsense to her, then propped her in his lap so she could gaze with wide-eyed babbling delight at the other men. "Why not? She can't talk yet."

"Ha. Good one." Will took a drink and offered David a beer. The potter shook his head.

"Where's Shelli?" Zak asked. He went to a back window and looked out. "I told you I want all of you here."

"She's watching the booth. I thought of asking the people next to us to help out, but she's such a good salesperson I'd rather have her handle it." David smiled. "People like to buy from a pretty girl."

"Is that baby a girl?" Will asked. His tone implied that Star was not pretty.

David took no notice, bending over her and smoothing her spiky hair. "Sure is. My little girl. Her name is Star."

"Well ..." Will gulped his beer. "The *name's* pretty. But she looks like you."

David remained blissfully unaware of any insult to his child. "Looks like both of us. She's got the Pojoaque eyebrows." He ran his finger along them, "And the Kewa nose."

"Kewa? Oh. Santo Domingo. Wait—I thought you were from Acoma."

"Mom's from Kewa. Why do you think she has the gallery there?"

"Will doesn't think much." Zak took a bottle of iced tea from the refrigerator and opened it. "If he thinks at all."

"I *think*," Will said. "Like, I think David's kid looks like David. Hey—Mirabal—who do you think Zak's kids look like?"

Zak slammed his tea bottle onto the counter. "Are you drunk already?"

Will cackled. "Loosened up."

David frowned, cuddling Star. "You'd better not drink too much. We've got decisions to make."

Zak took his phone out and texted. "I've made the decision. What I need is to hear you all agree with me." At the sound of a car pulling up in the driveway, he jerked his head and put his phone away. "Shit. I know Reno's walking. Letitia wouldn't drive up, would she?"

"She's not stupid," Will said.

Zak dashed into the living room, then back to the kitchen. "Melody's home early. Get out, *now*. Tell the others—damn—"

"What the hell?" Will asked. "I'd like to see Mel. What's the big deal?"

Zak clenched his fists, and the cowboy pretended to be terrified, then scurried to the back door with a laugh. While David tucked Star into her carrier, Will paused with one foot out the door and asked Zak, "What about that kid's dream?"

"You're riding a bull and get sucked up its asshole and come out as shit."

The two men stared at each other, then Will walked down the back steps in the dark, lighting a cigarette and muttering, "Talk about assholes." He looked back. "Damn. I forgot my beer."

A moment later David came up beside him, slow and calm, the handle of the baby carrier over his arm. Star began to babble. "Hush," David whispered to her, then told Will, "Don't worry. We'll work everything out."

Mae's vision shifted through the tunnel again, bringing her back into the house. It was crowded and noisy. Will was sliding up and down the hallway in his socks in a drunken attempt at dancing, shouting along with the rap music that was playing. The vision blurred. He was on the porch, laughing with a group of other smokers. Another blur. Letitia was sending him out of the kitchen with a playful tap on his cheek, telling him to "sit down and forget about it." Reno, Zak, and David stood in a tight cluster, talking. She joined them, and Will shrugged and stumbled to the living room, beer in hand.

He'd been too drunk to be part of the meeting.

Mae let the vision go and cleared her energy field with snow quartz, then set the crystals on the steps to rebalance in the sun again. The conflict between Will and Zak was so strong, why had Zak agreed to part of this? Had they needed him for something? What did he bring to the scheme that the others didn't? David, Shelli, Reno, and Letitia had art connections. Will was Letitia's lover. He had a devious mind and no qualms about theft. But Zak? What did he get out of this or put into it? Did they simply need a good leader?

No. He couldn't lead Will. In fact, if there was any situation in which Zak lost his cool, it was one that involved the cowboy. He'd been so disgusted with Will, he hadn't told him Ezra's dream. That choice must haunt Zak now. Mae wished she hadn't seen him make it, but it confirmed that Zak wasn't in control of the group, though he might have tried to be.

Letitia wasn't likely to be the leader, either. She had come across as impulsive and irresponsible, falling in love with a second rose cockatoo when she'd gone to buy food for the first. Reno and David both had cooler heads, and so did Shelli. Kathy, though, had the strongest motive for starting the plot. Did she even know Zak?

Mae went inside and called Melody with what little she'd learned about Zak. It wasn't much more than Melody had already guessed. He had the party to cover up a meeting. Mae left out his failure to warn Will about Ezra's dream, not wanting to bring up the reason.

Melody had the same reaction Mae had to the news about Will and Letitia. "I bet Zak's after her to punish both of us."

"I thought that at first, but Will doesn't act like he suspects it. And if Zak knew Letitia was Will's girlfriend, don't you think he'd have told Montana?"

"Yeah." Melody sighed. "So what *is* he up to? Can you try and find out through Will one more time?"

Mae put the tobacco tin back in the bag and stuffed it in the trash can. "No. I'm sorry. I'm done with Will." She owed it to him as her client to honor what was left of his privacy. "I already saw too much of his business."

"Then how can I find out?"

Mae's temper frayed. She felt as if she'd been taking exams. Psychic work took mental effort, took more energy than Melody seemed to realize. "I don't know. I need a break."

Chapter Twenty-Eight

When Mae headed out in the evening to meet Melody for Art Hop, she still had no idea how to help her. Neither a bike ride nor a few hours of watching baseball had given her any moments of inspiration.

Lorilee Chino and the Cowboy Indians were playing at one of the galleries on Main. When Mae arrived, the doors were open, letting the country band's music pour out to the street, the singer's mellow alto crooning over guitars and drums, amplified too much for the size of the space. A small crowd had gathered at the counter where food and drink were being served, and a few people stood around the perimeter of the room, sipping from plastic cups and looking at the art.

Melody, clad in a bright blue dress and matching high heels, looked like she'd recovered from both her disappointment and her workout as she danced across the room, partnered by a white-haired man wearing a sequined necktie over his T-shirt. Relieved, Mae joined the group at the counter, got some lemonade, and watched the dancers. Chuck and Daphne Brady flowed with the effortless grace of life-long dance partners.

Is that me and Jamie in thirty years?

Misty left off twirling with a small blonde child to greet Mae. "Everybody's talking about Reno leaving." She grinned. "They miss the Rabbit." Implying that no one, including Misty, missed Reno.

"Are you *that* over him?"

"I feel like Melody will when she's lost a hundred and thirty pounds. Check out this art. Is this a cool exhibit or what?"

They explored the display. It included a collection of chaotic abstracts; a group of chairs strung with rope, lace, leather, and beads; and a series of paintings featuring smooth-skinned gray aliens crawling in and out of canyons in the desert. Bewildered,

Mae said, "Maybe I'm missing something, but this is all just weird to me. Who would buy any of it? Sorry to bring up Reno, but he's never had a show and his work is better than this."

"No, it's not." Misty paused in front of the last alien scene. The creatures were putting a ladder into a crevice between rocks. "This is way cooler. I wouldn't mind meeting these little guys for real. Take a ride with them. Then put 'em on my Harley."

"You've gotta be kidding. They're *creepy*." Misty's tastes had to be affected by her feelings. "I can't see why this stuff is in a gallery and Reno's isn't. What does he do with all his paintings?"

"He has his phone number in the Sierra County Artists' directory. He meets people—well, he did while he lived here—and shows them his work by appointment."

"When they'd never seen his art before except for that table in the café?"

"He used to charm people he waited on. There are all those Apache-themed images around here, and *ooh,* their waiter is this young, undiscovered *Apache artist!* He said tourists would eat that up."

Mae imagined him timing his rare but radiant smile for the end of his pitch, winning tourists' hearts. He could have done it if he had to, she supposed, but he struck her as too withdrawn to muster the effort. "Did he make money that way?"

"You know..." Misty tilted her head with a slight frown. "He used to tell me he didn't and that the only stuff he could sell was small and cheap. But once he stopped inviting me in, it was a different story. Then he claimed he was so busy, he'd let his place go to hell—that it was even worse than mine." She tossed her hair and breathed out a sound of contempt. "Which was more than a little unbelievable."

Melody, her shoes in one hand and a glass of lemonade in the other, joined them. "What are you two talking about?"

Misty answered. "Reno lying. Pretending he was painting all the time and selling his work."

"Pretending?" Melody sipped her drink. "That's the whole reason he moved here. He might have lied about how much he made from his art, but that's all Reno cares about. Drawing and painting."

Mae flashed back to her vision of the encounter in Rio Bravo. Reno lacked the personality and the drive to be much of a salesman, and he seemed discouraged about his abilities. He might not have struggled for success if he thought he would make enough money with Kathy's scheme. But even if he hadn't tried hard to sell his art, it had to have gone somewhere. He couldn't have hoarded it all in his trailer, and there had to be a lot of it after two years as Florencia's student. This was the kid whose father had tried to *pay* him to go out and play like a normal child, and instead Reno had kept on drawing, trying to copy the dollar.

Copy the dollar.

"Oh my god." Mae grabbed the Chino sisters by the arms. "I just figured out the big secret." They stared at her, then drew in closer as Mae released her grasp on them and spoke more softly. She trusted the loud music would keep the conversation private. "Reno's been forging his teacher's work. That's why he didn't have anything to show and didn't let Misty in his place. He must have been shipping the paintings out to this gallery that has some of her early works. Her sister-in-law's place. They say they don't want to sell the family archive, and then they sell Reno's fakes as if they're reluctantly parting with some treasure."

"Are you sure?" Melody asked. "Reno's good, but could he really fool people?"

"He can paint like Orville, can't he? I think he could imitate her style. He's not copying any particular painting, and he's passing it off as stuff she did when she was his age."

Misty wrinkled her nose. "And that's how he paid for my ring? I hope it's still stuck in the Rabbit."

Melody said, "I don't see how they pulled Zak into it. He doesn't have any art connections. And he's Mister Clean."

Mae took a guess. "That could be why they brought him in—as a middleman. They wouldn't want a trail that led back to Reno. Zak could have done the shipping, or maybe he'd meet someone who'd take the paintings to the gallery. No one would ever suspect him."

"Except his wife, because he's such a bad liar." Melody finished her lemonade in a gulp as if it were liquor. "He probably got dragged into it by that woman."

"Maybe he got involved in it for Reno."

Misty rolled her eyes. "Boring little weenie Reno getting Saint Zak to do something bad?"

Melody clenched her jaw. "Shit. Will could have blackmailed him into helping." She glanced at Mae. "I'm not going to tell you what it is, but Zak's done something he's ashamed of—and it was because of me. Will's not proud of it, either. They never talk about it. But if he threatened that he would tell ..."

Mae nodded, hoping her expression didn't suggest that she knew what Zak had done.

"I hate to see Zak get in trouble," Melody said. "He's always been the one saving me. She gave a choked laugh. "I used to call him my guardian asshole."

"His part in it might be over," Mae said. "As far as I know, they're still selling forgeries, but Reno wasn't going to paint any more. After he found out his teacher was in hospice, something must have gotten to him."

"I hope they stopped in time so they don't get caught."

"No kidding," Misty said. "Even Reno doesn't deserve that."

Melody sounded nervous. "Maybe they'll be okay if we don't tell anybody."

"Of course they will." Misty hugged her. "We're the only people that know." She turned to Mae and squeezed her shoulder. "Thanks for figuring it out. Everything should be all right now, as long as it's just between us."

Stunned, Mae couldn't respond. Did the sisters expect her to promise silence? They seemed to think she had agreed, but she didn't yet know if she could she do it.

The song ended, and Lorilee reminded the audience, "My daughter Misty will be fire dancing on Broadway at eight." A smile lit up her face. "And I have another beautiful and talented daughter here tonight. I hope she'll come up and do a song with me. Melody?"

The talented daughter gaped at her mother and leaned on Mae for balance while she jammed her shoes on. "I haven't sung in public for years. I'll probably pee in my pants."

"You'll be great. Jamie told me what a good voice you have. He'd be so happy to know you're using it."

Misty added, "So would Zak. Even if he'd never say so."

While Melody conferred with the band, Misty followed her and began shooting video.

Mae turned away from the crowd, pretending to be absorbed in the creepy aliens, taking a moment to think. It was disorienting that Melody was now on the same side as Jamie, wanting to protect Zak, though of course her switch made sense. Crazy as their marriage was, she loved him. Loved him so much she'd made an excuse for his part in a crime.

Could Will have blackmailed Zak into dealing in forged art? He had lived so honorably since his discharge, the truth about it might not hurt him as much as Melody imagined. Getting caught in the forgery scheme would be worse. It wasn't an act of passion, and it wasn't in defense of his marriage or Melody's sobriety. It was for money. Someone, perhaps Letitia, might have tempted Zak, not forced him.

A gallery employee putting a *sold* sign next to one of the alien pictures distracted Mae from her thoughts. A tall, stooped man with a big moustache was shaking hands with a slender woman in a white dress. Both of them were beaming as he thanked her and told her how glad he was someone appreciated his imagery. The woman bubbled with questions about the meaning of his work and his sources of inspiration.

Mae suddenly grasped the depth of Reno's betrayal. How would the mustachioed man feel if someone started forging his creepy critters? It wasn't just the money from the sale that he would lose, but his *vision* would be stolen. Forgery would be a kind of spiritual trespass. And how would the buyer feel if someone sold her a fake in a few years, after she'd made this connection with the artist? No one was thinking about Florencia, or the people who bought the forgeries of her work. If Jamie knew what his friends had done, he might find it hard to continue defending them.

*****

When he got home after his Saturday night show, Jamie had the urge to call Mae and ask about Art Hop and about Melody, but instead he hand-fed Gasser a few kibbles, opened a beer and a bag of green chile pistachios, and sat at the kitchen table with his laptop. He hated typing, frustrated by the way he scrambled letters, but it was worth the hassle. Email wouldn't wake her up. Or crowd her. Jamie was proud of how well he had coped with Mae's need for space, though he still felt a pang of lonely anxiety at night. This was the longest he and Mae had been apart since they started dating. They'd seen each other daily when she'd had a job for a group of psychics in Santa Fe. Though she had stayed with Bernadette most nights, she and Jamie had gotten closer. It had felt like progress, rapid progress. Now everyone, from his parents to his friends to his therapist, told him that if she needed some space, he should let her have it.

Don't crowd her, his mother had said.

I don't crowd her.

Yes you do, love, you're like a crowd all by yourself. Trust me. You take up a lot of space.

Before writing his message to Mae, Jamie scanned the ones he'd received. Seeing one from Melody alarmed him. Had she asked Mae to find Zak's secret? Was it bad?

To his relief, the message was "The Chino sisters rock!" followed by a link to some YouTube videos. The first was of Misty and another young woman fire dancing. The second video showed Melody talking with her mother's band in an art gallery, then stepping up to the mic and easing into the country classic "Crazy." Melody was *performing.* After all these years. He turned up the volume, cherishing the way her rich contralto caressed the song. Singing transformed her, bringing out her beauty and power.

Wishing he could have been there, Jamie applauded so loudly at the end that Gasser laid his ears back and thudded down from his lap. "Sorry, mate." Jamie stooped to pet him, then called Melody. She couldn't have gone to sleep yet, not after something this exciting.

His friend answered her phone almost the second it rang. He showered her with praise, added a good word about Misty's performance, and asked, "What did Zak think of your song? Did you dedicate it to him?"

"He wasn't there. He got called for a fire."

"Too bad he didn't hear you." Jamie drank his beer, belched as quietly as possible, and ate a handful of nuts. "Everything all right with you two? Couldn't tell by your choice of song."

"It wasn't 'Your Cheating Heart.' "

"Is that good, then? I mean—I hate to ask, but did you have Mae find out what he's up to?"

"Hang on." Melody spoke aside with Misty, muffled, as if she'd covered her phone, and then came back to him. "How would you feel if someone was pirating your music?"

"Bloody hell. Where did that come from?"

"Just answer me."

"I'd be pissed. What's that got to do with Zak? *Fuck*. Is *that* what's going on?"

"No. This is a what-if. What if someone was pirating it and you were about to die any day?"

"That's gloomy. I don't like to talk about death."

"I'm serious, Pudge. I need to know what you'd feel."

Reluctantly, Jamie imagined being old and sick, close to the end, and hearing about the piracy. "Don't think I'd care. Be more pissed off at the inconsiderate idiot who told me. When you're dying, it's time to deal with big stuff. Your soul. Your family. Not crap like that. All I'd want is love. People. As long as I didn't die alone, not much else would matter."

Melody had another side conversation with Misty and came back. "Okay, you passed the quiz. Here's why I gave it to you. Mae did some psychic work for me. I know you didn't want me to ask her, but listen before you get mad. She thinks Reno's been forging his teacher's work. Not copies. Fake originals in her style. And that Zak's been helping him get them to a gallery."

"Bloody hell. Is she sure?"

"Not quite. But it explains a lot and I believe it. Having Zak as the middleman would put some distance between Reno and the gallery. Make it harder to trace. It was an awful thing to do, but I don't want them to get caught. It would be a disaster for Zak. So many people count on him and look up to him. We agreed not to tell anybody, since we think Reno's stopped doing it."

"*Mae* agreed to this?"

"She didn't argue with it."

"She takes time to think about stuff. Don't think that meant she agreed."

"Of course she would. We couldn't talk more because I had to start my song."

"Did you talk with her after?"

"No. She danced with this older guy—" Melody paused for an interruption from Misty. "Chuck Brady. And then she went to see her father and his partner at some other gallery. I guess she went home after that or did something with them. She didn't make it back for Misty's dancing."

"Fuck."

"What's wrong? You don't think she'd turn them in, do you?"

"Dunno. She's got a different horse in the race than you do. Her dad's partner is real close to Orville's first wife. If Niall wouldn't like it—and I don't think he would—and if he thought his friend wouldn't like it—fuck." Jamie chugged more beer and got up to fetch his cat. Sitting with Gasser in his lap again, he petted him and tried to calm his thoughts. "Zak could be in trouble."

"You're scaring me. How can we help him?"

"I have no fucking idea." Stealing someone's creative identity was appalling. Outside of the near-death scenario, Jamie would be outraged if it happened to him. He was disappointed in Zak, in all of them, especially Reno, but at the same time he didn't want to see their lives destroyed. He didn't want to see Niall hurt, either. "I need to talk to someone who can think."

"Thanks."

"Sorry. I meant someone calm, y'know? Logical. But it can't be Mae or my parents until I know what to do. Everyone's connected, like six degrees of Niall Kerrigan."

"Maybe you *should* talk to Mae. Find out if she told him."

"I'd wake her up. It has to be an emergency, if I call at night."

"Pudge! This is Zak's life. That's not an emergency? I'll call her if you won't."

"Sorry. You're right." Jamie suspected he would only make things worse, but so would Melody. "I'll do it. Get back to you in a bit."

Anxious, Jamie finished his beer and got up for another. Somehow, he was going to have to be his own calm person to talk to. If he wasn't going to fuck things up, he needed to know what he was talking about before he called. He returned to his laptop and googled "penalties for art forgery."

Bloody hell. No wonder they'd been so paranoid.

Where the damage caused by a person convicted of forgery amounts to more than $20,000, the defendant is guilty of a second-degree felony. (N. M. Stat. Ann. §30-16-10.) A person convicted of a second degree felony faces a possible prison sentence of up to nine years in prison, a fine of $10,000, or both. (N. M. Stat. Ann. §31-18-15.)

He found an article about copyright law and creativity. It was in legal language so hard to follow he had to read it out loud to wade through it, but he understood enough of it to worry. If Reno hadn't copied anything, he hadn't violated his teacher's copyright on her work, so a prosecutor would have to prove he had done his in-the-style-of works with intent to defraud. Obviously he had, if he'd signed her name. There were cases in which forgers had altered the work of innocent, unknown artists to pass for masters, but he would have a hard time claiming that had happened. In short, Reno was fucked.

So was Zak, and by extension so were Melody and the twins. And David's mother, David, and Shelli. What would happen to Star if both her parents went to jail? They could get caught with the stolen parrots as well as the forgery scheme if someone raided the gallery, adding a third degree felony, punishable by up to three years in prison. Would it get tacked on to the nine? Star would be a teenager by the time Shelli was free. Letitia couldn't afford the fines or the jail time, either. And if Will got caught, there went the money he owed Montana. It would go to lawyers, to fines, to restitution.

No wonder Melody had given Jamie that quiz. She wanted him to side with her and not the artist Reno had exploited. What a choice. Especially after Jamie had promised to help the dying woman go in peace.

*****

Feeling hopeless and confused, Mae kept walking long after leaving Niall and Marty at the Brady and Brady office. The law practice dealt in property and real estate, not criminal law, but Chuck and Daphne knew and had contacted people in the field, and they had a library of law books.

Mae hadn't objected to being excluded from the meeting. It could only have made her feel worse. She'd put things in motion, done what she thought was right for Florencia, but the process was more complicated than she'd imagined, with greater consequences. Going back to Art Hop was out of the question. Much as she wanted to watch Misty's fire dancing, she wasn't ready to tell Melody the turn things had taken. Instead, Mae walked up Foch from the law office, along Third Street past the library and the back of the Civic Center, and down the commercial corridor of Date Street to Ralph Edwards Park, where she paced along the river bank, hoping to calm her heart and clear her head.

Earlier in the evening while she'd danced with Chuck, she had been so worried about what to say to Niall, she'd barely been able to focus on Melody's great moment. She'd hugged Melody at the end of her song, said goodbye, and walked to Rio Bravo Fine Art to find Niall and Marty. Dreading to bring Niall such a problem, she'd tried to come up with a solution on her way, a plan to end the forgeries and get them off the market.

The Art Hop crowd had filled the front room on the street level, socializing and viewing the newest exhibit, so Niall had taken her and Marty up to the second floor where they could be more private, surrounded by Delmas Howe's blossoms and cowboys, Dave Barnett's fields of flowers, and Florencia Mirabal's Acoma scenes.

When Mae finished sharing her suspicions, Niall clenched his fists and turned to one of Florencia's paintings, an image of the ancient staircase, full of shadows and shapes that might have been people, or spirits, or splashes of rain. "Reno. Damn him. This would break her heart. And make her furious. Especially if her family is part of it. I hope you're wrong. But—" He hissed a sigh through gritted teeth. "I hate to say it—you could be right. It makes a lot more sense than stealing. Every detail fits."

Eager to relieve him a little, she offered her plan. "We can stop them, though, can't we? If we get an expert to the Chavez-Mirabal gallery to identify the fakes. Alan Pacheco would have a reason to ask to see the family's collection. He's got the Eight Northern Pueblos show this weekend, but if he could go Monday—"

"Slow down." Niall faced her. "He may know her work, but that doesn't mean he could tell a good fake from the real thing. Reno spent two years with her. His forgeries could be excellent. She might even have had him copy her work to teach him. They have you do that in art school—copy the masters. When I was in college, I had to go to museums in Boston for practice." He broke off when a lone woman appeared and began browsing, and then resumed more quietly. "We'd need to hire an authenticator. They look at brushstrokes, look at the way she layers the paint. Morellian analysis. Every artist has a signature beyond their name, if that makes sense. And there are other methods where they find hair and dust and things in the paint that help prove it's the artist's work."

Mae's hopes for a simple solution collapsed. "Seriously? Like DNA?"

Niall nodded. "I have no idea how long it takes to get an appointment or what it costs, but that's the only way you can prove what's what. There are also radioactive fingerprints that you can embed in your work, but she wouldn't have done that when she was in college. We need an authenticator."

In the silence while the woman contemplated paintings nearby, Mae studied the prices on Florencia's work—the highest in the gallery. She could see why Reno had been tempted. One Mirabal was worth more than Mae earned in a year.

These paintings were as big as the ones in Florencia's living room, around four feet high. The ones in the Chavez-Mirabal gallery had been much smaller, probably in keeping with the size of the artist's early works, and also small enough to transport easily. They might cost less, but then again Kathy might talk collectors into high prices to make her part with these *family treasures*.

How many had she already sold? Reno hadn't seemed to be rolling in wealth, but he was smart enough to hide it except for buying Misty's ring.

On top of being ignorant about authenticating art, Mae hadn't even thought about the paintings that had been sold when she'd come up with her plan. Was it even possible to authenticate them? That went beyond stopping the sales and into some sort of investigation.

When the woman left, Marty asked, "Wouldn't the authenticator need one of Reno's paintings to compare his brushstrokes with Florencia's?"

"If we want to prosecute him," Niall said.

"Prosecute?" For a second, Mae felt as if her heart had stopped. "Not just get them to stop selling?"

"Art fraud is a crime," Niall said. "If someone was forging my work, I'd take them to court. So, who has one of Reno's paintings? He never had a show, and he took them out of Florencia's house, even the memorial to Violet."

Mae had already checked with Misty. She had nothing. "He took his tabletop out of Passion Pie, and he claimed all his sales were to tourists." She thought of Refugio Baca's truck but couldn't bring herself to mention it.

Marty spoke up. "His daddy must have a ton of Reno's work. Heck, I still have a birthday card Mae drew me when she was in kindergarten. He's bound to have kept things. Of course, he might not want to help you catch Reno in a crime. Or believe he did it."

Niall winced. "I wouldn't suggest it to him unless we had proof."

They took a quiet moment as a group of visitors came in to look at the paintings. Niall spent the time texting. Who was he contacting? Authenticators? Some kind of investigator?

Although Mae understood why Niall was taking this route, she felt guilty for starting it—but if she hadn't told him her concerns, she would have felt even worse.

Two trim middle-aged men excused themselves, asking to get closer to the painting Mae was standing by, and she stepped back. She didn't recognize them as local, and they dressed more fashionably than the average T or C resident in midsummer. Even their haircuts looked expensive. They stood shoulder to shoulder, and one spoke in a confiding tone to his companion. "It might be the best time to buy, if we're going to acquire a Mirabal. I heard someone downstairs say she's terminally ill. God knows what the price will hit after she dies."

Mae had a troubling image of the whole group of scammers going through their inventory of forgeries and tallying up the potential profits from Florencia's death. Could they be that cold? Wouldn't that bother them? Reno especially would have to be disturbed by it. Even if he'd ceased to love her, he had known her well. He had probably started forging her work when she'd been healthy and not thought beyond the money and the present moment.

As the well-dressed men began to debate their choice between two paintings, Niall answered his phone, told someone he was on his way, and said in an undertone, "We'd better finish this conversation outside."

Walking toward the Brady and Brady office, Niall explained that Daphne had contacted a law school friend, a criminal lawyer who specialized in art fraud. Mae froze. "Criminal lawyer? Can't you just get them to quit?"

They were in front of the Ellis building. Niall nodded toward the old neon sign on the roof displaying the healer's name. "Mae. Would you claim you were the reincarnation of Magnolia? Try to make money off her?"

"Of course not. I'd be lying. And I'm good enough on my own. Not as good as her, but I wouldn't need to lay claim to her. Anyway, it wouldn't be fair to her spirit. Her memory."

"And that's how Reno should have thought as an artist. I don't want to distress Flo at this point in her life by telling her, especially when we haven't got proof yet, but if Reno betrayed her the way you think he did, she'd want him to pay for it. And if her family was involved, she'd want them to pay for it, too. She may die before we can sort this out, but I'll owe it to her spirit to see it through."

"Are you sure? I mean, if you don't ask her ..."

"I know her. She's not interested in last-minute forgiveness. Anyway, whatever I decide to do, Daphne says I can't let you in on it. It has to be between me and the art fraud lawyer." Niall glanced at Marty. "And your father. We don't keep anything from each other."

Marty put his arm around Mae's shoulders. "Nothing against you, baby. You know that."

"I know." Of course they couldn't include her. She had already compromised whatever steps they might take by telling her suspicions to the Chino sisters.

Mae walked with Niall and Marty in near silence the rest of the way to the law office. On her long walk that followed, her thoughts and feelings seesawed, torn between a sense of justice for Florencia and fear for what might happen to the people who had exploited her art. Will concerned Mae the most. He was her healing client, a man who had messed up but was trying to turn his life around.

They probably hadn't thought about their punishment any more clearly than she had when she'd set them up for it. What was it going to be, if they got caught? She turned toward home. The answer might not reassure her, but she had to look it up.

Her phone rang as she drew near her house. Jamie. At least he didn't know this latest development. Or had he talked to Melody?

His words rushed out. "Did you tell Niall?"

Mae took a deep breath and let it out. "I'm sorry. I had to. Reno's teacher is his friend. And Niall is family."

"You know Reno could go to jail for *nine fucking years*?"

"I was gonna look it up. Are you sure it's that bad?" Jamie tended to scramble numbers and letters. She wanted to think he'd read it wrong.

"Yeah, I'm sure. Got it right in front of me. What's Niall going to do?"

"I don't know." Mae turned in at her driveway and realized her legs were shaking as she climbed the porch steps. Was this what Jamie felt like when he had panic attacks? She dropped into a metal chair. "He's got to check it all out before he tells his friend. It could take a long time. She'll probably die before they can prove anything. But he can't tell me his plans. It's between him and some lawyer Chuck and Daphne found him."

"He's got a lawyer already? Jeezus."

Mae expected an explosion after this, but all that followed was a long silence broken once by a faint meow.

"Talk to me, sugar. Are you mad at me?"

"Yeah." Jamie sighed. Gasser squawked the way he did when he was hugged too tightly. Jamie murmured an apology. "But the stew's been cooked, y'know? Nothing left to fight about."

Nothing? If Niall got proof of forgery, he would take Reno and Kathy to court. They might testify against people like Zak who had helped them. Mae couldn't see the tension between her and Jamie over this resolving any time soon. Their relationship could be haunted by his friends' mistakes for a long time to come.

Chapter Twenty-Nine

Late the following Wednesday morning, Mae drove on I-25 South, passing sculpted pink cliffs and bright blue sky, taking Jamie to visit Florencia at the hospice in Las Cruces. He fidgeted in the passenger seat, drinking coffee and occasionally murmuring stressed-out little *unhs* and *nngs*, and toying with straps of his backpack that he kept jammed between his knees.

"Sugar, maybe you've had enough coffee. Remember what happened at the race—"

"Jeezus. There we go. Jamie-the-sick-person. I'm not having a fucking panic attack. I'm thinking about bloody fucking death."

"She might not die while you're there."

"I hope not." He took another gulp of coffee, popped the lid off his mug, and tipped it up to get the last dregs of the drink. "Niall going to be there today?"

"He should be. He spends most days on sort of a vigil now. Daddy drops him off on his way to his softball camp and picks him up later. She never liked Daddy, though, so he doesn't go in."

"She doesn't like your father? He's twice as easy to like as Niall."

"I know. But that's her. She's picky about people. I probably shouldn't go in with you. I think I made her feel sick and old when she met me. I didn't mean to, but it was how she reacted. I hope you don't mind, but you'll be okay without me."

"Yeah. No worries." Jamie tugged the straps of his pack back and forth. "I sort of figured I'd be with her alone."

Mae wanted to say she was proud of him and that he was courageous, but in the mood he was in he might think she was condescending. She reached over and rubbed his upper back. "You'll be fine. I know you'll help her a lot."

He slumped in his seat. "Maybe."

*****

Death, however peaceful, was on all sides. Jamie knew he should be fully present, coming as a healer of sorts, but his task made him anxious. He wasn't sure he was up to it, and yet he couldn't back out.

Leaving Mae waiting for him in the guest lounge, he walked down the hall with his head full of dismal images. Flashes of his endless nightmares about the death of a childhood friend. Another friend's death two winters ago. The extra weight in his pack troubled him also, the things he'd brought in addition to his flutes. Would they work for healing the dying woman or would they upset her? He almost walked past her room, stopping only because he saw Niall rise from a chair on the far side of the patient's bed and signal to him.

Ironically, the room reminded Jamie of the one where his sister had given birth to his younger nephew. Cozy, warm, with a craft-themed décor—quilts, baskets, pottery—in shades of green and blue. It had been pinker in Haley's room, but the concept was the same. Medical hidden behind homey. The room's occupant, or someone trying to amuse her, had hung what he guessed was one of Letitia's calendars. On the July page, a slim, athletic Indian man clad in nothing but a leather breechclout rode a galloping horse bareback across a field.

Jamie recognized the profile of the mountains behind him, the Sangre de Cristo range near Santa Fe, and he recognized the rider. Will Baca. It might have been taken at Letitia's place out on the far west end of West Alameda, but Jamie wasn't sure. It had been dark when he'd stopped by Sunday night to pick up the offerings. He hoped the dying woman would receive them as he intended.

She looked dried out like a mummy. A new crop of silvery hair formed a thin sheen on her head. Niall came around the bed and grasped Jamie's hand in what felt more like desperation than a handshake and then leaned down to his friend. "This is Jamie Ellerbee. Jangarrai. The fellow that does the music Lonnie gave you."

Her creaking, whispery voice was too soft for Jamie to make out the words, but Niall chuckled.

"She says you're pretty. Manly but pretty. Her words, not mine. Trust me."

Dying and flirting? But why not? Last chance. No risk of rejection. "Manly, pretty, and straight. Your lucky day." Jamie did his best to flirt back, unpacking his flute cases onto the table beside her bed, next to a small framed picture of her blue parrot. "Here to serenade you."

She offered him a papery hand. It was weak and shaky, but he could feel her trying to squeeze. He squeezed back. Her deep brown eyes grew watery, but there didn't seem to be enough moisture left in her body for tears. She glanced at Niall and then at the door.

Niall frowned. "You want me to go?"

She nodded. Jamie said, "Heard you've been just about living here. Take a break. She's in good hands."

Niall indicated the other bedside table, where a bottle of natural mouthwash sat next to a plastic dispenser full of giant swabs. "She can't swallow anymore. We swab her mouth with some of this once in a while. If she points to it, can you do that for her?"

Jamie hesitated. Could he get that close to a dying person? If she couldn't swallow, she was close, very close, to the end. "Yeah. No worries."

"She's a little out of it. She finally let them up her morphine."

The artist moved her lips. Jamie could have sworn she said, "Up my ass."

"They put it up your arse? Seriously?"

Niall tucked his friend's bedsheet around her shoulder. "Ayeh. Suppositories. She hated having that drip attached."

Jamie snort-laughed. It felt rude but he couldn't help it. Something that might have been a responding laugh rasped from her throat. She waved Niall off. He lingered, and she gestured again. He nodded and backed out, his eyes on her. Jamie opened a flute case, waited for Niall's steps to fade, then put the flute back down and closed the door.

Feeling more confident about the first offering, he took the framed black-and-white photograph out of his pack. "Brought you a present."

She frowned, pointing at him and then at herself. *From you to me?*

"Nah. It's from the naked cowboy lady. She sent you a cowboy."

The artist's eyebrows lifted and she batted her eyes in a way that made Jamie laugh, but then the sound of her struggling breath made him feel like he couldn't breathe. He covered his unease by talking while he propped the picture against the bedrail by her shoulder. "I've met her. She keeps asking to do my picture. Not that I'd want her to. But anyway, she's a nice lady. Wishes you well. I mean, as well as possible. Sorry. I'm not saying it right. Can you read what she wrote to you?"

The artist turned her head. Jamie rearranged her pillows so she could regard her gift more comfortably. It was a portrait of Will. Bare-chested, clad in skin-tight black jeans, a black hat and boots, he leaned against a fence, cigarette in hand, a series of perfect smoke rings floating above him. On his right stood a black horse. A black goat lay at his feet on his left. His lips, forming the smoke rings, suggested a kiss. The picture was signed with a dedication. Jamie read it aloud. "To Florencia Mirabal from Letitia Westover-Brown. Thank you for the inspiration. The Cowboy Devil."

It was strange to say her name after being so careful with it in case she was gone. A hint of a smile crinkled the corners of her eyes as her head moved slowly in approval, and though her breathing became more labored, she seemed to grow more alive.

She mouthed a *thank you,* gazed at the gift for a while, and then closed her eyes, her face going slack. She pointed toward her mouth and throat.

"You want the mouthwash?"

Her lips formed the word *no.*

Throat and mouth. She wanted him to sing. "Favorite song? Any requests?"

She shook her head.

A lot of sick people wanted *Ave Maria.* Not always because of religion but because of the tenderness and transcendence and the sound of a tenor singing it. He took her hand. Her eyes opened and locked with his, intense and burning, yet distant, and her speech emerged with sudden force. "I have my devil—and my angel."

Angel. Did she mean him? *Bloody hell. I'm her escort.*

He placed the other offering in the bed beside Will's picture. "One more thing, Florencia." He put her hand on it. "You need to look."

She blinked at the object, a small, colorful wooden triptych, made like three little arched doors hinged together. The center panel showed a petite dark-haired woman in a chair, her face severe and yet beautiful with deep, glowing dark eyes and thick eyebrows. She had a few colorful streaks in her hair—pink, green, and blue—and a set of beads to match them, but aside from this reference to Florencia she looked like another famous artist whose self-portraits were even better known. The woman wore a white dress, and a large blue parrot with yellow-ringed eyes perched on her shoulder. The other two panels showed the parrot in flight over a flowering jungle background, glowing like a saint or a god.

Though her own style had been different, the woman who lay dying next to this strange little work of art must have admired Frida Kahlo. Reno's imitation of the artist's style, though not exactly a forgery, was an ironic touch to the parrot's memorial.

Florencia whispered, "Violet."

"Didn't want you to go without her."

Jamie went to the other side of the bed, lowered the rail, sat beside her, and began the song.

As it ended, he realized he was curled behind her, holding her, not singing the words anymore but slowing the melody and sustaining the notes, his voice growing softer. He felt the vibration of his voice through his chest against her frail back. Her breathing became like labor, like giving birth. Then the death light came, the crack between the worlds. The door that had stayed ajar after those other deaths. She began to dissolve into the opening like pollen blowing away on a breeze. Panicked, Jamie drew back from her and sat on the edge of the bed. His breath struggled along with hers.

For the length of that song—it could have been five minutes or five hours—he'd lost his boundaries completely. Now they were back and the transition shook him. He didn't know what he'd done. How had he chosen to hold her like that?

Her breathing stopped. She wasn't hooked up to anything, no intrusive devices to signal her departure, yet he was sure she was gone. The life force had left her. *Bloody hell*. He'd abandoned her. Though he had been in the room, at the final moment he had left her to die alone. He'd thought he would be healing her with music and art, not guiding her into death. Had she gone in peace or felt his fear when he let go?

Jamie slipped the portrait and the triptych back into his pack. At least she'd had those. Had they been enough?

The door opened. Niall and a nurse came in. Jamie walked to the window. Their words blurred behind his back, mingled with a tinny ringing sound. His heart felt crowded, his lungs frantic. He knew he should leave the room but didn't trust himself. He dropped into the nearest chair, head in his hands. The last thing he saw before he blacked out was a sketchbook lying open on the broad windowsill. A colored pencil drawing of a blue macaw with a yellow-rimmed eye.

When he came to, the nurse knelt in front of him, touching his ankle in a soft, maternal gesture and offering him a plastic cup of water. She had curly red hair, darker than Mae's, and a round face with deep sun lines around her eyes and mouth. "When you feel better, we need to give Niall some time alone with her."

The room was quiet except for the hum of the air conditioner. "But she's dead."

"He needs to say goodbye."

Niall was arranging and then rearranging something on the table next to the photograph of the parrot, turning it as if his late friend might see it. Her own final drawing of the bird. The sight made Jamie want to weep. He took the cup and tried to drink, but a deep shiver made him splash water on the nurse's knee. "Sorry."

"It's okay. I know it was a lot for you to handle, but that was beautiful, what you did for her. I wish everyone could go that way."

"I couldn't do it again." His voice came out husky. He cleared his throat. "Dunno how you can work here. People dying all the time."

"I love my job. Dying people are ... I hope this doesn't sound too New Age for you ..." She looked him over. His appearance probably didn't send a very conventional message. She continued. "They're beautiful. Death is a really spiritual time, if it's handled right. You handled it right." She rose and offered him her hand.

"Your girlfriend is in the guest lounge. Can you walk if I go with you?"

Jamie drank the water and stood. He didn't want to look at the body, but he couldn't help it. The artist had died facing the calendar picture of Will Baca, but someone had turned her on her back and folded her hands on her chest. Niall finally stopped fussing with the placement of the sketchbook on the table and stepped back from it.

"That's better, Flo." The tips of his fingers grazed the dead woman's shoulder. "You have her with you. And your work."

"Are you ready?" The nurse took Jamie's elbow.

"My flutes." He'd left them on the table where Niall had placed the sketchbook. "Do you mind...? Don't think I can ..." *Get that close to her body.*

The nurse fetched them for him, and he let her guide him down the hall.

*****

Jamie's voice had spread sweetly through the entire wing of the building. Mae could have listened in peace, proud of his courage in facing his fears, awed by the beauty of his singing, but Niall didn't stop pacing and rambling. Since leaving his friend's room he'd been talking more than she thought he might have ever talked in his life.

"She sent me out. She can't bring herself to die in front of me? I want to be there."

"You will be." Mae had no idea if this was true, but she hoped it was.

Niall reached one end of the parlor-like room and turned, feeling his pocket as if still unconsciously seeking cigarettes. "I don't want her to feel alone. She was too alone. I could have been like that. Coming out in a small town back then, everyone cut me off. Seventeen, out of the closet with nowhere to go but the living room. Not even that. I could have been bitter. My cousin came to see me when I was in college, though. Apologized. Said he would talk to my parents. It made all the difference. Her brother should have reached out like that. I wonder what she'll do with her collection. No family that cares. I always told her she should give it to your college. Museum of Southern New Mexico Art, something like that. Start some scholarships with her money, too."

Niall would have a shock coming with Florencia's will. She had used her legacy to make a statement—that she valued his friendship above all else—but if he wanted those other legacies to happen, she'd left all the work in his hands. No wonder Daphne had anticipated stress with Florencia's death.

He passed Mae's chair on another lap of the room, coughing a little less violently than a few days ago. "She should have sent Reno off, told him to go to college. But she was alone. She wanted him around. I can't believe he used her like that."

"Let's not think about Reno. Think about all you did for her. She isn't really alone. You're always there for her."

"Not like family, though. Nothing's ever the same as your family. And then her family—damn them—them and Reno."

Niall continued his restless monologue until Jamie's song changed. More softly and slowly now, he chanted without words. With a look of pain, Niall held still. "Is this is it? Is she leaving? Is this what she *wanted*? Without me?" Mae got up and took his hand. He squeezed hers back. When Jamie's voice ceased abruptly, Niall bolted down the hall. A nurse in the passage changed direction and went into Florencia's room with him.

After a while, Jamie emerged with the nurse holding his arm as if she thought he might fall. His backpack hung from one shoulder. When he saw Mae, he shook free of the helping hand, attached both straps, mumbled thanks, and walked on his own. Mae met him in the doorway of the guest lounge and tried to hug him but he pulled away. She took his hand. He was hot and shaky.

"Sugar?" She stroked his hair. "Do you need to talk?"

He shook his head and walked away. The world was upside down. A talkative Niall. A silent Jamie. She urged him to sit and got him some herbal tea from the array of beverages available on a sugar-sprinkled counter.

"I'm not a fucking invalid," he grumbled as he accepted the cup.

Mae sat on the couch beside him. "Did she die while you were there?"

"Yeah. But I fucked up. I backed off."

"No, you didn't. I heard you. It was beautiful—"

"Stop trying to comfort me." He gulped the hot tea and cringed. "Jeezus. Fucking burned my mouth." And then, in that troubling way he had when it came to causing himself pain, he drank again. "I know what I did."

Mae gave up on further reassurances. When he fell into this angry kind of misery, fighting everything she said, there wasn't much she could do but give him time to get over it.

He finished the tea and stood. "Need to get out of here."

They had to pass Florencia's room on their way. Mae hesitated. The door was ajar.

"Don't go in there," Jamie said.

"I ought to let Niall know I'm leaving."

Jamie kept walking. "I'll be in the lobby."

Niall sat in the chair by the bed, holding the dead woman's hand. Mae remembered how she had felt when her grandmother had died in her sleep, taking a nap during a family visit. Crying, not wanting to let go, Mae had kissed Granma on the cheek, saying goodbye. Her face had still been warm, as if she hadn't quite left yet. Niall had to be feeling Florencia's presence in that way, too.

Mae whispered his name and he looked up. She said, "Jamie wants to go. Do you have anyone coming?"

"Chaplain."

"You want me to stay?"

"Take care of Jamie."

"I'll call Daddy. And Daphne."

"Thanks."

Mae eased the door shut. She found Jamie hovering near the exit, vibrating in a total-body fidget as if he were cold as well as anxious. He opened the door and walked at a distance from her as they crossed the parking lot. Mae wanted to be closer, but he was in his stubborn mode, part of the faulty operating system that told him he didn't need help when he did.

"You need your book back, sugar." Mae opened the car doors. "You were getting good at sharing your feelings."

He ducked into the passenger seat. "Sorry. Feel like crap."

She called Marty and Daphne before driving.

When they got back to her house, Jamie chatted in his usual way while cooking, but Mae felt like he was playing himself as a role, making potato salad and rambling about the differences between boring white potatoes and the indigenous potatoes of the Andes, the blue and purple varieties. Recipes that worked better with the colored kind. How odd they looked on a plate with blue corn.

Maybe the release of words eased his mind and heart a little. At least he was talking. But he faded out every few sentences and paused in the middle of chopping vegetables or measuring ingredients, gone somewhere inside himself.

She couldn't get him to talk about Florencia. About anything that mattered. He even went for a walk by himself, something Jamie never did. Walking on pavement hurt his hip, and he hated to be by himself. Florencia's death had overturned him in some way.

Mae was relieved when he got back and told her he wanted to go with her when Niall opened his late friend's studio. It might give Jamie closure somehow.

Giving Niall some private time to grieve, Mae called Daphne to find out when they planned to open the studio. The lawyer told her they were waiting until late on Saturday so Alan Pacheco, Florencia's biographer, could drive down from Ohkay Owingeh Pueblo after the Eight Northern Pueblos Art Show. He was teaching summer session classes and was on the board of the art show, so it was the first day he was free.

"She wanted him there," Daphne said. "Classic Flo. Staging a grand entrance after she's dead. Or a grand exit. Or both."

Mae sat beside Jamie on the couch and put her arm around him. "Did you catch that?" He usually listened to her phone calls, but he wasn't quite himself.

"Yeah. Saturday. After your race." The Dam It Man Triathlon would be in the morning. Jamie leaned back and slumped into her embrace. "I'll camp at the lake so I get a good spot to watch you. Don't want to miss you this time."

"You don't have to camp. You can stay with me Friday night."

He kissed her, a weak, dry peck. "Nah. You'll need your rest for your first triathlon. And a night in the tent'll do me good."

Mae brushed his hair back from his face and looked into his eyes. "You mean that?"

"Yeah. I'm learning." He drew a heart shape on her thigh, and then another, just barely intertwined. "I give you space, we get closer. Right? The Zen koan of love."

*****

On Saturday morning, Jamie walked along the main road through Elephant Butte Lake State Park, looking for a good spot from which to see the lake for the swimming part of the race as well as the cycling and running. The deep blue lake in the desert with rounded gray buttes jutting from the water was a place full of meaning for him. Memories of near-death, survival, and spirits. Despite the early hour, it made him feel strangely and deeply alive.

A voice called from the playground. "Jamie!"

Ezra Yahnaki stood on the highest point of a large play structure, at the top of a long twirly slide. "We can see good from up here."

Jamie climbed the child-sized stairs, wondering if the plastic platform at the top could hold both him and Ezra. "What are you doing here?"

"Zak and Refugio Baca are in the race. Zak wanted me to give it a try but I can't swim."

"I can't run. We could register as Ezra Ellerbee. I'll swim and bike, and you can run." Jamie pulled his white cowboy hat lower over his eyes, squinting into the low, bright morning sun. "Bet no one can tell the difference."

"You're goofy."

"Yeah." Jamie rubbed Ezra's brush-cut hair. "And you're my mate, so that makes you goofy. You came all the way here just to watch these blokes race?"

"No. Bernadette's boyfriend is picking me up at Misty's place later. He's taking me to Santa Fe. I always stay with Bernadette for a few weeks every summer. Or I have since I've been old enough. Zak was going to drive me all the way, but he doesn't have to now."

"Nice of him to offer, though." Especially since being around Ezra might trouble Zak. He had a conscience, and he hadn't told Will the boy's dream. "Long drive there and back. And he just got back from a fire, didn't he?"

"Yeah. I hope he's not too worn out to race well. When I thought he was bringing me, I told him he should stay over with you in Santa Fe." Ezra leaned on the railing. "Zak needs to have some fun. He's awfully serious."

"So he needs a sleepover with a mate?" Jamie snort-laughed. "Bloody hell, look who's talking. You're like a little old man sometimes."

"I am not."

"Yeah? Dare you to be silly. Right now."

Ezra frowned, a look of deep thought. "I wish I was small enough to go down that slide."

"Yeah, me too. Get my arse stuck, though. Think I could go down standing?"

"You'd fall."

"Nah. Wear my socks, glide." Jamie slipped his sandals off. His socks-and-sandals preference earned him some ribbing from people like Zak, but it kept his feet cool yet clean. "Got a great sense of balance. Fuck, I used to rock climb. I can go down a kids' slide."

"You fell and broke your bones a lot climbing."

"Yeah, but this is, what, seven feet off the ground?" Jamie backed onto the slide, holding the railing, and then turned, striking a pose like a surfer. He slid a few inches, nearly toppled off at the first curve, and dropped to sitting. Still off-balance, he tumbled sideways, but managed to catch the edge of the slide like a cartoon character going off a cliff and grabbing a tree branch. Dropping to his feet, he collected his fallen hat and looked up, expecting to find Ezra laughing at him, but the boy's face was solemn and worried.

Jamie grinned and jammed his hat back on. "I'm not hurt, mate. Lighten up. We're on project silly, remember?"

"It's not that. I dreamed that Zak fell."

"You tell him?"

"No. You know how you wake up and don't remember your dreams, and then something happens and they come back? It just came back when you fell."

Jamie climbed back up the ladder. "Jeezus. Hope he's not going to fall in this race."

"I don't know what it meant. There was other stuff, too." Ezra paused. "It got weirder. There were birds made out of dollar bills flying around and then real birds and they all flew away."

"What kind of birds—the real ones?"

"I don't remember all of them. But there was a pink parrot. That was bizarre. I don't know what it meant. I was practicing dreaming on purpose. Zak asked me to try."

"Maybe he'll know." Jamie wondered if Zak would understand the dream. The part about the parrot and the money could be good or bad. Falling down sounded definitely bad. "Dunno if he'll have his phone with him. Mae never takes hers when she runs."

"Can you call him and see?"

Zak's voice mail picked up. "Mate. Ezra just remembered his dream." Jamie handed the boy the phone. When he finished, Ezra gave it back and leaned on the railing again, rubbing his shoe against one of the posts. "I feel bad about the other dream, still. I didn't save Will."

"Wasn't your fault. You tried. I know the feeling, though. I backed out on someone I was supposed to help. While she was dying." With this reminder, a heaviness lodged in Jamie's chest, a pressure near his heart. "They teach you what to do for ghost sickness yet?"

The boy looked at Jamie. "Can you get it?"

"Sort of. Not exactly."

"I'm sorry." Ezra ducked his head again. "I helped Grandma run a sweat house—I was the fire keeper. But I'm not ready to do ceremonies myself yet."

"No worries. Just give me a few tips. Do-it-yourself healing rituals."

"Are you being silly?"

"Nah. Serious. Dead serious."

*****

Mae heard thudding steps on her right and guessed without looking that this loud-footed runner was Zak. With his heavy landing,
he might as well have been wearing his firefighting boots. How was
he going to handle seeing her? He had to know what she had done.
He caught up and stayed neck and neck with her. They were closely matched in both their weaknesses and their strengths. As much
time as they'd both lost in the swimming and cycling, neither stood
a chance to win or place, but this was the segment of the race where
they could excel. Mae wanted to outrun Zak—and he probably
wanted to outrun her.

"Enjoyed being behind you," he said, "but I couldn't stay that
slow."

In her barefoot shoes, she ran on the sandy shoulder rather
than the pavement, and as they rounded a curve, she took a hasty
sidestep to dodge a small cactus and bumped him slightly.

Before she could apologize, he asked, "Getting clumsy? Or
cheating?"

"Clumsy. I'm sorry."

So far he was treating her the way he had before he'd ceased to
trust her. Maybe he'd taken a cue from Misty and Melody. They'd
been civil to her in the past week, though no longer sociable. This
was as civil as Zak got. Mae did her best to be friendly. "Glad you
made it after that fire. How are you feeling?"

"Whipped. But I'll still kick your ass. That's the only thing better than looking at it."

She sped up. So did he. Mae asked, "Is Melody here?" She had
talked to her once since the previous Saturday, and the call had
been short and awkward.

Refugio Baca surged past them. He could burn out by pushing that hard early in the run. Or maybe not. Misty was standing on the side of the road cheering and shouting his name. If he wanted to impress her and she liked him, he might have wings.

"Are they—"

Zak passed Mae before she finished her question. Misty waved and cheered for him, too, though not the way she'd jumped up and down for Refugio. *She sure moved on in a hurry.*

Mae brought her mind back to the race. She didn't care if Refugio beat her, but Zak was on her runners-to-crush list. She put on a burst of speed. As she caught up again, he glanced at her with a startled expression.

She made a point of not sounding breathless. "What—you thought I couldn't catch you?"

"It's those barefoot shoes. I didn't hear you and then all of sudden there's this orange blaze. I thought something was on fire. Did you miss me?"

"No. I got sick of looking at your ass."

"Good one, Miss Mary-Mae." Zak dodged around another runner and pushed a short way ahead, calling back to her, "You sneaked up, but you didn't really catch me."

Was there a double meaning? In the forgery scam, she *had* caught him. It was sad that so honest a man had gotten tangled up in it. Mae hoped he wouldn't end up in jail. But she was still going to beat him. She picked up her speed.

In the end, she barely came in a stride ahead of Zak, but that was enough to end the event with a sense of success. She hadn't expected to win her first triathlon, or even to place at all, only to do her best. Marty came in first for his age group, and that made her as proud as if she'd been the winner. Jamie praised her performance and promised her the best massage of her life as soon as they got to her house.

When they arrived there, however, his mood shifted from celebratory to distressed, with no apparent trigger. He obsessed over how he parked his car. Normally, he left it in the unshaded portion of the driveway when he visited, but he insisted that she pull her car forward in the carport until its nose was buried in the bird-of-paradise shrub next to the laundry shed, and then backed his car in so the two vehicles sat tail to tail, each with its rear half in the shade. He then crawled into the back of his car and fretted over how his camping gear was packed in the hatch, adjusting things as if the tent might be uncomfortable. Mae wanted to tell him to calm down, but let him be. Pointing out his anxiety wouldn't make it go away.

She finally got him indoors and invited him to share her shower, where he remembered the promised massage. It evolved into lovemaking with a damp and eager transition to her bed. Mae could have rested afterward, contented and close, but Jamie wouldn't hold still. He burrowed under the sheet with his feet near her head and began to give her a foot rub accompanied by soft singing, his voice muffled.

Mae stroked a hand over his muscular calf and then touched the scar on his right shin from one of his climbing accidents. His long slender toes kept curling off and on. She slid a finger under them and whispered, "Sugar. You can relax."

"Nah." He tossed the sheet back and sat up. "Still have to do the death thing, y'know?"

"You don't *have* to."

"Yeah, I do. Closure. Ritual. S'posed to be healing."

Chapter Thirty

In the evening, Mae and Jamie drove up Foch in his Fiesta, crossing Broadway and Main, heading up to Florencia's house. The sunset ringed the whole sky with pink clouds against the deepening blue, as if nature were honoring the late artist with a startling display of color. Mae would have liked to walk to enjoy it more, but Jamie said his hip was hurting after falling off a slide before the race.

They encountered Zak, Ezra, Misty, and Refugio on Foch Street. Misty and Refugio were playing in the parking lot beside the Brady and Brady office, back to back, their arms locked through each other's, apparently trying to see who could haul the other up onto his or her back in some kind of crazy wrestling game, with Misty's skateboard dangerously near their feet. Mae couldn't imagine Misty and Reno roughhousing like this. Zak might not like to see another Chino sister with another Baca brother—or skateboarding without a helmet or kneepads—but in her rebound Misty might have found her match.

Zak and Ezra were carefully removing plastic bags that had caught on an enormous cactus that clung to the bluff a short way uphill on the opposite side of the street. A trash bag sat at Zak's feet, and it bulged at the bottom with the shapes of bottles.

Jamie pulled over and rolled down his window. "Good job, mates. Picking the state flower. First time I ever saw Zak clean up litter. You're a good influence, Ezra."

"It was his idea," Ezra said. He smiled shyly at Mae and then looked at the ground.

"We're showing him and Refugio the murals at the civic center." Zak bunched a shredded grocery sack up in his fist and shoved it into the trash bag. "Thought we'd clean up on the way. Are you two ready?"

"Almost." Misty swung Refugio onto her back and stepped on her skateboard, whooping with laughter. His legs kicked in the air and he whooped like a cowboy as she propelled them toward the street.

"Are you crazy?" Zak ran at them, blocking the exit from the parking lot. "On this hill?"

"Spoilsport." Misty let Refugio down, promised to show him some tricks on the ramps later, and picked up her board. She scarcely looked at Mae, offering a belated and uncomfortable hello.

Mae returned the greeting, adding, "Don't be a stranger. Please."

Misty nodded and turned away.

Jamie drove his car down the side street. He parked in the gravel drive that curved from the back steps of Florencia's house to the carport in the side yard, pulling the Fiesta up behind Niall's Beetle.

Mae and Jamie walked around to the front of the house. Marty, Niall, and Daphne were waiting on the porch with Alan, a short, solid man with long graying hair and warm dark eyes. As they went in, Daphne turned off the alarm, led the way down a short hallway, and used a second key to open the studio at the back. Marty put his arm around Niall's shoulders and gave him a squeeze before they entered.

Though the air conditioner was running, the air was stale and smelled like paint. The enclosed former porch was dark, shaded by both curtains and blinds. Daphne uncovered a few windows, admitting a spill of bright light. At the far end of the long narrow room, an unframed painting stood on an easel. After seeing Florencia's large works in Rio Bravo, Mae was struck by how small this one was, but of course—it had been the painter's last. It was all she might have felt she had time for. A semi-abstract pink parrot glared from the canvas with one round eye. On the textured white space behind it, blue corn formed a pattern like a river, and red corn the profile of mountains. It was the work Mae had seen in progress in her vision of the gift of the parrot.

For a moment they all stood still, gazing at the tableau: the painting on the easel, a tall stool in front of it, paints and brushes on a stand nearby, and preliminary versions of the final work taped to the wall. Mae thought of Daphne's analogy. The studio was like a stage set waiting for Florencia to make her entrance, and at the same time it was the empty stage after her exit.

"Before anyone moves anything," Alan said, "I need some pictures of it the way she left it."

Niall rubbed his eyes under his glasses. "Christ. It's closer to finished than she let on." When Alan had taken his shots, Niall approached the painting slowly, his cough covering a break in his voice. "Her last real work."

"You'll want to keep that," Daphne said.

"Daow." His long, nasal negation. "Museum of Contemporary Native Art should have it. It's not signed, but still ..."

"Native art?" Marty asked. "A pink parrot?"

"Like the church at Acoma," Alan said. "Corn and parrots on the walls inside. Parrots have been important to all the pueblos for centuries."

Niall nodded. "She used to say that owning Violet was the only way she was traditional."

Daphne asked, "Are you sure a museum would want something unsigned?"

Niall bent closer to the painting, studying it. "If I get an authenticator to look at it."

Mae glanced back and forth between Niall and Daphne, puzzled. "It's in her house. In her studio. You'd still have to prove it's hers?"

"Ayeh. Unsigned, I would. And it doesn't look quite finished. Not saying I doubt it's hers. But..." He straightened, rubbing his back. "I need to make some phone calls. I've got a firm lined up for the piece from the Chavez-Mirabal Gallery. I'm sure they'd love to add this to their bill." He studied the parrot a few more minutes and turned away. "Don't move it. We have to leave it where we found it." He left the room, Marty following.

"The piece from the gallery," Mae said. "Did Niall get someone to make a purchase there?"

Daphne perched on the paint-splattered stool and took a picture of the painting with her phone. "He shouldn't have mentioned that." She took another picture. "I can't believe she didn't tell me how much work she'd actually done on this."

Alan studied the painting closely. "No one's opened this room at all since she moved out?"

"No." Daphne frowned, checking something in her phone. "When Chuck installed the alarm, all he did was put a sensor over the studio door."

"No wonder it stinks." Jamie spoke for the first time. "Need some air." He opened the back door and sat on the floor with his feet out on the steps. The outside temperature was still over ninety, and the fresh air came in with a swath of heat.

Mae walked over to the painting. There was nothing that told her it was unfinished aside from the lack of a signature, but there had to be some missing final touches Niall would expect of his friend. She must have worked on it up until the last minute, when she literally couldn't paint anymore.

Niall and Marty returned and began to examine the color sketches taped to the wall, the drafts of the painting. "These are valuable, too," Niall said. "Should help a lot with authentication."

"I still can't believe you have to do that," Marty said.

"Ayeh. There've been some big finds in the art world that had to be authenticated. Craziest one was a Pollock that two women were fighting over—his last lover, his ex-wife or his wife—I can't remember who they were, but one said he'd painted it for her. The other lady said it was a fake. Authenticators couldn't agree. The thing that decided it was polar bear DNA from a rug in his house. Can you believe that?"

Alan said, "And then there was that Kahlo archive a man in Mexico claimed she'd left at his house. That never was authenticated, even though it's been exhibited in New York. Some people say it's hers, and some say it's too rough."

Niall shook his head. "That stuff didn't look much better than Reno's Kahlo to me. But I guess every artist produces some lesser stuff she doesn't want to sell."

"Reno's Kahlo?" Mae asked. This conversation was making wheels turn in her head.

"She loved Kahlo, so he did the memorial to Violet as a Kahlo-esque thing. Too bad it's missing. She really wanted to be buried with it."

"Maybe that's for the best," Marty said. "His imitation of another artist would be like burying her with a reminder he was a forger."

Everyone but Jamie stared at the unsigned painting. Mae felt a shared unease among them after the mention of Reno. Maybe Niall had another reason besides the lack of signature for getting the pink parrot authenticated. There was one missing piece of the Reno puzzle Mae hadn't solved yet. The black fabric. If he'd been blacking out windows in Florencia's house, this could be another forgery.

She told Niall, "I'll need to talk to you in a minute," and then went over to check on Jamie. She rested her hand on his shoulder. "You feeling okay, sugar?"

He sat up straighter and rubbed his head under his hat. "Yeah. Need time alone with her stuff. I'll either get rid of the ghost or make peace with it." He stood. "Too bad everyone quit smoking. I need some tobacco for a ceremony."

Mae looked at Niall. "About time you got rid of those cigarettes. That'll be a good use for 'em."

"Cigarettes and lighter in the glove box of the Bug." Niall tossed Jamie his key ring. "You turning Indian on us? Ceremonial tobacco?"

"Sort of. Ezra gave me some guidance." Jamie sorted through the keys. "And Mum's people do smoking ceremonies. Not *smoking* smoking. Y'know. Smudging. No worries, I won't do that part in here."

Leaving Jamie to his ritual, Mae went with the others to the living room. Marty drifted to the front window to look outside while Alan studied Florencia's collection. Niall and Daphne stood facing Mae. "Well?" Niall asked.

"I hate to say this, but Reno might have painted the pink parrot. Not the whole thing, but I think he came in and finished it over this sort of sketch with dots she did—"

"A cartoon," Niall said. "Sketch with dots." He shook his head. "Why would he do that?"

"I don't know. But he was doing something strange a few nights ago." She described the blow-away pieces of black fabric and his attempt to get it back from her yard. "If he knows about authentication, he might have planned this one to pass the DNA test by doing it here, maybe even wearing some of her clothes while he finished it. When I was packing her stuff to be cleaned, there was long black hair on a couple of her sweaters."

"That's not proof of anything. For crissakes, he could have hugged her. And why would he finish her work? If he thought he was inheriting, it wouldn't make her estate more valuable." Niall's hand went to his pocket as if he still smoked. "In fact, if she left something partly done and he painted the rest of it, that would ruin it."

Daphne added, "And if he was really concerned about Niall getting this painting authenticated, Reno would have been much less likely to trigger questions if he'd finished it all the way and signed it."

"But he couldn't. Ghost sickness. He has a taboo on the names of the dead."

Niall and Daphne exchanged glances and nodded.

Mae said, "He could have been in here that night finishing that painting. But the paint was fresh and he didn't want to move it yet. He might have meant to come back for it and then Chuck put the alarm in."

"It's plausible." Alan left off examining a painting. "Oils take two weeks or more to dry. But if he did what you think he did, the authenticators are going to split. Morellian analysis will say it's not hers, DNA will say it is."

Daphne folded her arms and paced away. "Damn. This could be a mess. He might have had some collector lined up who doesn't check the provenance too thoroughly. And he could have taken pictures in her studio like I did, made it look authentic." She stopped pacing and one foot started tapping. "*Mae* could authenticate it, I suppose, though no one's going to take that evidence seriously."

"Maybe Florencia really did paint it." Marty turned to face them. "She could have worked hard right up to the last minute. Like that surge you get toward the finish line in a race. It might not have been Reno."

"I hope you're right." Mae didn't like to think Reno might have ruined the last piece of Florencia's legacy. "You mind if I go check? I know it won't hold up for anyone else, but will y'all believe me?"

Niall told her to find out what she could, and Mae walked back to the studio. She hoped Jamie had finished his private ceremony. As troubled as he'd been after witnessing Florencia's death, she didn't want to interrupt him.

Finding the door closed, she listened, heard nothing, then tapped on it and waited. No answer. "Sugar? Are you okay?" Silence. He'd been having so many panic attacks lately, she couldn't help worrying, and let herself in. The back door stood open. Jamie was gone. So was the painting.

Chapter Thirty-One

Mae's first thought was that he had wandered off, forgetting to close the door, and someone had stolen the painting. Reminded of Shelli's story about the parrots flying away, Mae had an image of the pink parrot flying off the canvas and out the door to someone who happened to find it. The idea was absurd—and then it wasn't. Her original hypothesis about thefts, not forgeries, might have been right. Zak had been—a little too conveniently—right in the neighborhood.

Picking up litter? Not a very Zak-like behavior. Ezra had helped Jamie create his ceremony. Zak could have probed the boy for Jamie's plans. If he'd watched Jamie start his ritual on the far side of the yard, Zak could have made a run for it. It was a bold theft, though, and desperately risky. Would he really have done that? And wouldn't she have heard him if he came into the house? He might have taken his shoes off to be quiet, but that would have taken time.

More likely, Jamie had carried the painting out for his ceremony. Niall had said not to move it, but in his anxiety-ridden fog, Jamie didn't always listen.

The smell of smoke drew her to the side yard beyond the carport. Jamie was kneeling at Violet's grave. A thin trail of smoke rose from it. Tobacco and some type of evergreen. Had he put the painting on the rocks, in front of a fire? What if it was Florencia's work and not Reno's? Mae hurried toward Jamie.

His back to her, he stood, brushing the smoke over himself. When she saw nothing on the little cairn but a heap of smoldering plant material, she slowed down and let him finish. He rubbed his face, looked up at the sky, and then turned to her with a sad yet radiant smile. His eyes were dark and clear, his lashes wet, as if a cleansing storm had passed through.

For a second, she almost forgot the painting. Jamie had been healing himself, *alone*—and it had worked. "You're feeling a lot better now, aren't you?"

"Yeah." He sniffed loudly and looked down at the rocks. "Zak would kill me, starting a fire—what's the fire danger level now?" He scooped some dirt onto the embers and watched the smoke diminish. "This is the parrot's grave, isn't it?" Mae affirmed that it was, and Jamie added more dirt. "Thought so. Felt like the spot called her."

Mae couldn't believe Jamie had sought out a dead person. "You talked to her spirit?"

"Not *her*. Violet. Or the parrot god or something."

"The *parrot god*?"

"Yeah. Animal spirit helper. Lonnie told me I'd find one. She listened. Helped me out." He brushed his hands on his pants. "Hope Niall doesn't mind. I used all the cigarettes."

"He'd better not care. But he won't like you moving the painting. Where'd you put it?"

Jamie sniffed again. "Fuck. Wish I could cry without snot. Need a tissue." He headed for the house.

"Sugar, can you just—"

"Tell you in a minute."

After waiting more than a minute, Mae grew concerned, thinking again about Zak stealing. She began looking for the painting. What place, other than Violet's grave, would seem symbolic and important to Jamie? The yard was nothing but weedy dirt with no garden spot. She searched the front porch and the juniper shrubs along the side fence, found nothing, and sat on the back steps.

A scuffed place in the driveway caught her eye, a drag mark in the gravel next to the Beetle. Mae got up to look more closely. A couple of smaller shoved places in the gravel looked like hand marks. Had Jamie fallen? Was that what was taking him so long?

Maybe he'd hurt himself and not tended to it until now. She hadn't heard any kind of thump or tumble, but then, she'd been in the front part of the house and they'd all been talking.

He finally came out, hat in hand, with his face, shirtfront, and the ends of his hair dripping wet.

"Sugar? What were you doing?"

"Drinking from the toilet." He sat down. "Not really. Felt dizzy. Heat gets to me. Had to drink out of the faucet with my hands and just kept splashing."

"You okay now?" He nodded, and she took a seat beside him and rubbed his thigh. It was hot, with little damp spots on his jeans. "Did you fall while you were getting the tobacco?"

"Weird question. You think I pass out every chance I get?"

"No. Of course not. It just looked like someone slipped in the gravel near Niall's car."

"Wasn't me."

She should have realized that. The long, deep track suggested someone running fast and skidding. She'd taken some falls like that rounding the bases in softball, and a worse one trail running, sliding on one knee and both hands. What if Zak *had* grabbed the pink parrot?

"You've got to tell me what you did with the painting."

Jamie met her eyes. She wasn't sure what she saw in his other than the fading of the fresh, deep clarity from his ceremony.

"It needs some more time." He dragged his fingers through his hair and put his hat on. "It's where it is for a reason, all right? Let's go in." Jamie rose, fanning his wet shirt away from his body. The parrot print shirt. "I *will* pass out if I stay out here much longer. And I need to talk to Niall."

Mae stood, undecided where to go. She didn't want to accuse Zak with so little to go on, but if he'd taken the painting, he could already be driving away with it.

"You go in without me," she said. "I need to talk to Zak."

"No—you have to be with me—"

Jamie's protests faded as she sped away. There was no time to lose. She charged down Foch, crossing Main and Broadway, turned right onto Austin, and kept flying for three blocks until she reached Clancy.

Zak's Eagle and Refugio's art-embellished truck were parked in front of the motel-like one-story apartment building where Misty lived. Relieved that Zak hadn't left town, Mae slowed down to catch her breath.

On the cement front porch that blended into the sidewalk, a young Latino man sat on a bench watching two little girls play with toy horses. Mae glanced into the Eagle as she approached. The station wagon's interior had no hiding places. The large suitcase with purple flowers on it had to belong to Ezra, no doubt a hand-me-down from one of his sisters. A battered gym bag gaped open with Zak's race clothes airing out in it. Misty didn't normally leave her doors unlocked like Melody did, but she might have done so for her guests. Would Zak have brought the painting into the apartment?

When Mae knocked on Misty's door, the neighbor said, "She went off with some friends."

"Thanks. None of them came back without her, did they?"

"Not that I know of. Not by the front door."

Mae didn't want to go in uninvited. On the chance that Zak had come in through the back and was ignoring her, she opened the door and called out from the porch, "Anybody home?"

In the combined living room-kitchen, Misty's motorcycle stood by the far wall, surrounded by standard Chino sister housekeeping: dirty dishes, discarded clothes, books and magazines lying open face down. The place was silent.

As she was closing the door, thudding steps behind told her Zak was on his way, and that he'd come at a gallop. He came to a stop, glaring at her. "What the hell do you think you're doing?"

*****

Alan, Niall, Marty, and Daphne were seated along the living room floor. Jamie felt bad for keeping them—only Marty looked comfortable—and yet things had to be finished. Brought back into balance. What was that word Lonnie used? *Gozho.* Jamie doubted that he was ever in *gozho* himself, and yet he was trying to heal this whole miserable mess.

He stood facing the group, hands at his sides, fingers squirming. Going back and forth between what he thought of as the onstage and backstage parts of the healing was stressing him out. Both parts were necessary, though, the spiritual and the mundane. There were things to be done in both worlds. He scanned his audience and focused on Niall, searching for words.

Niall spoke first. "So, you've finished your ritual. Did it help?"

"Sort of. Not done yet." Jamie wished Mae would come back. He had to plunge in without her, though, and hope her absence wouldn't lead to problems. "You need to forgive Reno."

"What does that mean? Did Mae find out he painted it?"

Fuck. This was not going well. Jamie took his hat off and shook his hair. "Not yet. She ..." If only she'd come in with him. He improvised. "She went home to get her crystals. I didn't want her to miss this part of the ceremony, but she needed them."

"Forgiving Reno is part of your ceremony?"

"Yeah. He wasn't always bad to your friend, y'know? We all do stuff that hurts people, but it doesn't mean we don't love them. Don't you think, over two years with her, he made her happy more than he made her unhappy?"

Niall pushed air out between his teeth. "She liked having a young man around. But she liked a lot of young men. Had flings with six or seven that I know of. Some of them artists. And they all pissed her off in the end. But none of them forged her work. If he did that—"

"What if he didn't? Maybe he's just one more bloke who pissed her off." Jamie rubbed his beard and began to fidget with the brim of his hat. "All you know is that Reno had a fight with his teacher, and he had a secret he hid from Misty. Mae jumped to conclusions. Hate to say this, because she meant well, but the only thing she ever *saw* that he was hiding from Misty was ... something romantic. With his teacher."

"Mae never told me that."

"Didn't think she had to. She was doing the psychic work for Misty."

Niall looked up. Something across the room seemed to hold his attention. Jamie followed his gaze to the Cowboy Angel.

"I know Reno *could* have learned to paint like her," he said, "he was with her for so long. But it doesn't mean he'd be selling forgeries. Jeezus. What's more believable? Lovers' quarrel, if you ask me."

"Then what do I need to forgive him for?"

"She's gone, and they never got to make things up. I thought there could still be some healing, though, y'know? Between her and Reno."

"I'm supposed to forgive him for her, be her proxy?"

"Um ... Yeah." Jamie lowered himself to sit cross-legged facing the others, grimacing as his hip objected to the transition. "She'd be okay with that."

Niall frowned. "You sound like you've been talking to her. I thought dead people were off-limits for you."

They should have been. But Jamie wasn't off-limits for dead people. Though the late artist hadn't haunted him the way some of the deceased had, he'd felt a thread of emotion from some outside source since she'd died. Not grief, not anger, but love, sweeping like a searchlight, seeking for something lost.

"I didn't talk to her. Violet mediated. Or some bird spirit."

Only Alan met Jamie's eyes. The other three looked down. Jamie guessed they thought he was wacked but were too kind to say so. He pushed through the awkwardness of the moment. "You could forgive her family, and Reno, and anybody who ever did anything wrong to her. Just, y'know, take a moment of silence and ..."

Jamie closed his eyes and tried to draw in a feeling of forgiveness, but all he felt was embarrassment and the unmistakable sense of being stared at, until the enormous blue parrot flew across his inner vision, stately and slow. His mind fell suddenly silent. Air fanned by her wings cooled his skin.

Then his anxiety crept back in. How much time had passed? Was Act Two over? His phone vibrated in his pocket. He needed to go backstage and see if Act Three was still on.

*****

"We'd better talk inside." Zak's voice was quiet but harsh.

He pushed the door of Misty's apartment shut behind Mae and took a gunslinger stance, feet planted wide, hands on his hips. One knee of his jeans was faintly dusty. "What are you doing? Still trying to play psychic spy with my stuff?"

"I was looking for you. And the painting that went missing."

"You think I took it?" Bad liar. He forgot to ask questions or be surprised.

"Yeah, I do. I don't know where you put it, but you need to give it back or you'll get caught."

"You think I'm hiding it? You want to check my car? My pockets?" He turned and offered his ass, slapped his back pockets, and then faced her again. "Think it's under Misty's bed?"

He strode into the bedroom, flung the bedspread aside and angled the bedframe up, revealing a couple of pizza cartons—almost large enough but nowhere near clean enough to hold the stolen art—a few socks, and a pair of pink dumbbells.

"Satisfied?" He set the bed back down with a thump. She glimpsed small cuts and scrapes on the heels of his hands as he let go. "How about her closet?" He yanked the door open. The closet was empty except for an ancient vacuum cleaner and some scarves and belts dangling from hangers. Zak marched back into the living room. "Let's do the car now. Or do you need to look behind the fridge?"

"No. You can stop the drama. I already know it's not here. You came from somewhere else—from wherever you hid it."

Zak flopped onto the fake leather couch and let out a loud breath. He crossed and uncrossed his ankles, folded and unfolded his arms, then refolded them. "You really think I walked through T or C in broad daylight carrying a stolen piece of art in a garbage bag full of litter? And then managed to hide it? You're out of your mind. Anyway, you can ask Ezra where I've been. Ask Refugio and Misty. I haven't been out of their sight all day until now except to take a shit." He lifted his chin. "Go on. See it through. Ask them."

Mae felt suddenly small and uneasy. Would Zak tell her to ask for his alibi if he didn't have one? Maybe. If she didn't ask, she might be failing to call his bluff. She didn't have her phone to call Misty, though. With Jamie driving, she'd left her purse at home and brought nothing but her house key. "Are they still up at the civic center?"

"Yes. But you can ask them later. You need to be with Baldy now. And I need to head back to Mescalero."

"You came running here that fast so you could go home?"

"Why not? Maybe Mel's in the mood. It could be a hot pussy emergency."

"For you? I doubt it. I think you came for your car to pick up the painting."

"Damn. I need to straighten you out." Zak took his phone out and texted, frowned at the screen, sent another message, and put the phone away. "I don't want to do this, but I can't have you running loose thinking I'm a criminal." He rose and held the door open for Mae to go out ahead of him, then got Ezra's suitcase out of his car and put it into Misty's apartment. Then he unlocked the passenger door of the Eagle. "Get in."

After what he'd said, did he really think she would obey? "No. I need to get back to Jamie."

"So get your ass in. He wants me to drop you off."

Zak held his phone up and showed her Jamie's scrambled message: *Yes tell erh nda give ehr a ride.*

It made her brain feel spun-around. Had she been wrong about Zak? Or had Jamie gotten him to confess?

The moment she was in with her seatbelt fastened, he aimed the Eagle onto Austin Street.

She asked, "You gonna explain what's going on?"

"I thought Miss Mary-Mae the psychic detective had this all figured out. You tell me."

"Jamie wanted you to tell me."

Zak turned from Austin onto Foch, toward Florencia's house. "Nope. You go first."

Either he still didn't trust her or he was playing games.

Mae said, "I think Reno was forging his teacher's work. Selling it at the Chavez-Mirabal Gallery. Letitia was helping them get buyers, and Shelli stole a couple of parrots to make it look like the family had Violet. Like they'd made up and had approval for everything."

"And what did I do in all this?" He paused at the intersection with Broadway, waiting for a few cars to pass.

"Delivered paintings."

"But you don't know *why*."

"Because they needed a middleman and you wanted money. Or Will blackmailed you. Or because you're hot for Letitia."

"Christ. You are so wrong. None of the above." Zak proceeded across Broadway and up the hill toward Main. "I didn't even know what was going on until Reno used my shed."

"I don't believe you. You knew Letitia. I saw you with her twice before that."

"I knew her, but not what she was doing. I'd met her in December." He braked for a chihuahua trotting across the street, no owner in sight. "Mel and I were in T or C and I was heading to the lake for a run when I saw Reno's car with the hood up on that hill before the park. I stopped to help and he had seven or eight art boxes in the back." The little dog reached the sidewalk and Zak drove on. "He said he couldn't afford the insurance to ship them so he was meeting a courier from a Santa Fe gallery."

"In Elephant Butte? Why not at his place? And what gallery would send a courier to get Reno's work?"

"Hindsight is perfect. I didn't think about it at the time. He asked me to take the paintings to the courier while he waited for a tow truck, so I met Letitia in a parking lot near a trail outside the park. I asked why they were meeting there and she said she was taking pictures."

"And you believed that?"

"Why not? It was a great view. Was it supposed to occur to me that he was forging?"

They paused at the intersection with Main. Down the block to the right, near Passion Pie, was one of T or C's two post offices. Both were busy, friendly places. The UPS place on Broadway was equally conspicuous. Reno must have gotten paranoid and been covering his tracks so people wouldn't notice how much he was shipping. "So I did figure out the truth. He *was* forging his teacher's work."

"Yeah, but I'm not psychic. I had no clue."

"Seven paintings and a fishy story? You had to wonder about *something*."

"Letitia made it sound normal. And hell, she distracted me. Wanted to take my picture."

"Did you let her?"

Zak shot Mae a narrow-eyed glance and then drove across Main, following the steep part of Foch toward Florencia's back entrance. "What if I did? What's wrong with that? I won't be on a calendar. And it was a compliment. You know the last time Melody told me I looked good? The first time I put on my army uniform."

And the last time you told her she *looked good?* Mae steered her thoughts away from the distraction. "You say you didn't know what Reno was doing, but you hid things for him."

"Reno hid them. He knew the combination for the shed. He'd finished some paintings right before he came to Mescalero and he didn't know where else to put them. The paint wasn't dry so he didn't want to pack them up, and he couldn't leave them lying in the Rabbit. Orville would notice. And Letitia didn't want to get them until after dark."

"Sounds like he trusted you to go along with it."

"No. He thought I'd be too busy to go in the toolshed. But I'm the unofficial lend-a-tool guy for the vendors along the road, if they need something they didn't bring with them." Zak turned in at the street behind Florencia's house and cut off the engine, parking a good distance from the house. "So of course I went in, and I saw what he'd done."

"You know enough about art to realize he was forging his teacher's work?"

"I know Reno's art, and this wasn't his style. And he'd signed her name. He told me later that he didn't ever want to do that again. That was why he had to finish them. Anyway, I changed the combination to keep the paintings locked up. I wasn't sure if they were stolen or forged, but I knew something wasn't right. Once I got the story out of Reno, I tried to get everyone together to wrap it up. To end it before they got caught."

"Throwing that party made it look like you were part of the scam."

"I had to keep Mel out. Our house was the most private place we could meet except for one of their motel rooms, and David and Reno didn't want to go that far. They needed to get back to their families' booths."

"That doesn't explain why you brought the paintings to Letitia the next day."

"Will's accident. He called me and ..." Zak exhaled sharply, his fingers drumming the steering wheel. "He owed Montana money. Kathy was only paying him and Letitia five percent. He couldn't ride and he needed every penny."

"You did it for Will? I thought you didn't like him."

"I don't." Zak took his phone out and rubbed the edge of it. "But I owed him."

For the accident—not telling him Ezra's dream. "Did you know Letitia was his other woman?"

"Not until I was done with her." A corner of his mouth lifted. "Wish I had."

"Done with her? You *did* have an affair?"

"Christ, no. I was tempted—and don't give me that righteous look. If *you* can ever make a marriage last ten years, you'll know the feeling. Now go inside and pretend you went home to get your crystals."

"Is that where Jamie said I went?"

"Yep."

"You could have told me sooner. I don't have them."

He smirked. "Then it looks like Miss Mary-Mae has to tell a lie."

Mae got out and he drove off. She went into the studio and took a moment to process what had happened, staring at the empty easel. No wonder Zak hadn't trusted her. The Sight gave her only fragments of any story and she'd kept looking for more. Had she tried too hard? Helping Misty and Melody learn their men's secrets had felt important, though. Felt right. More right than wrong, anyway.

No doubt keeping the secret and protecting Reno had felt more right than wrong to Zak.

He had managed to dodge the question she'd gone after him to ask. Was the painting somewhere safe as part of Jamie's ceremony, or had Zak taken it to get rid of a forgery?

She walked through to the living room, where Jamie was pouring out a passionate speech. Mae sat beside him. He took her hand without breaking his flow and scooted close to sit hip to hip. He was saying, "You don't think straight when you're in that dark place, y'know? He lost love *twice*."

Daphne cut in. "We get it. You've made your point about ten times." She looked at Mae. "Did you get your crystals? Are we ready to do this?"

Jamie squeezed Mae's hand twice. A signal. She said, "Sorry I took so long. I ran into some people and got held up. I'm ready if you are."

A soft breeze rose as Jamie led them out the back door. The sun had gone down, leaving the sky a deep blue. He brought them to the carport, where he used a key on Niall's keyring to unlock the Mustang.

Inside it, the painting faced the steering wheel. From where she stood, Mae could only see the edge of the canvas. A cheap dreamcatcher with blue plastic beads and a hyacinth macaw feather hung from the rearview mirror. Juniper twigs formed a half circle on the seat in front of the painting. Tobacco was sprinkled along the dashboard. A ceremonial space. A symbolic journey.

After returning the keys to Niall with silent formality, Jamie opened the driver's door. "Had to do it here, y'know? Bet she loved this car. Put some of her soul into it."

"She did." Niall squeezed his hand around the keys then slid them into his pocket. "Violet used to ride shotgun."

Jamie gnawed on his thumb knuckle, watching as Niall took the canvas out, lifting it by its edges so it faced him. He was strangely quiet for a moment before showing it to the others. Mae sucked in her breath. Only the textured white background was complete. A few stalks of the blue corn had been filled in, none of the red corn, and the parrot was no more than a flat pink bird shape with one eye.

"Yes," Alan said. "That's more what I expected."

Daphne asked, "Are you going to tell us what you did with the other one?"

"Can't," Jamie replied. "It was part of the healing." He walked off to Violet's grave and sat in the dirt to sift through the remains of his smudging fire.

Mae looked around at the group. No one else appeared as surprised as she was. "I think I missed something."

Marty gave her a side-hug. "I can catch you up."

"Not yet." Niall said. "That can wait. I'm sure Jamie thinks this is the real one, and it should be, but I'm still going to get it authenticated. Officially with the professionals and unofficially with Mae. Have her see if the story checks out—before she hears it."

Chapter Thirty-Two

Alone in the studio, Mae approached the unfinished painting now resting on the easel. She guessed what had happened, though not all the details. Jamie had brought the painting with him from Santa Fe, and his obsessive parking and repacking had been concern for protecting and hiding it. He and Zak had arranged the swap, and Zak had made a mad dash to get the forgery, one last effort to save Reno.

There was a slim chance the young artist had lied to them about which painting was which and gotten them to exchange Florencia's final work for his unfinished fake, knowing that Niall and Daphne had expected less progress. If he'd painted it in the studio, its DNA might confuse the authenticators.

Mae was confident she could tell who'd painted it, though. If she picked up Reno's energy, it should mean he'd been the last one to work on the pink parrot. The peaceful dead left no traces, not lingering as ghosts. For all Jamie's doubts that he had helped Florencia, Mae believed the artist had died in peace and moved on. She'd had his music and time to prepare.

Though Mae could use the Sight without crystals, without them her skill was less reliable, especially under stress. She sought an image to help her focus. Lightly touching the top of the canvas, she closed her eyes, slowed her breathing, and imagined the swimming part of the triathlon. The hardest segment of the race, it had called for commitment of her whole mind and body. No distractions, just stroke, stroke, breathe. The sound of the water. The sensation of pulling herself through it. She set her intention. *Did Reno forge this painting?*

As she dropped into the imagery, the water changed to a tunnel, and she saw fragments of scenes flashing through it. Reno walking down Foch with a large flat box across both arms, a bulging

433

paper bag hanging from his arm by its handles. A handle tore, pieces of black cloth tumbled loose, and he cursed as the wind carried them off. Back to the tunnel. Reno in his place on Austin Street, packing his clothes and crying. Sounds from another room, voices, a clatter like a drawer full of cutlery being dumped out. The tunnel took her once more and then her vision settled.

Reno sat on a cot inside a very small trailer, a single room, staring at the unfinished painting, which leaned against a dresser across from him. He was thinner, as if he'd hardly eaten since she last saw him.

A door slammed and Will came in, whistling. One arm was in a sling and though he limped, he had a spring in his uneven steps. He slowed when he saw Reno. "That's morbid, dude. I didn't think I believed in ghost sickness, but you've got it. Or you will. Hanging out with a dead person's stuff." He opened the top drawer of the dresser, scooped out a stack of folded boxer briefs with his good arm, and held them against his shoulder. "Good thing I'm moving out."

"I didn't mean to drive you out."

"Don't be an idiot. You gave me an excuse. She'd've let me move into the big house years ago if I'd quit smoking and dumped Montana." He set his clothes on the cot and sat beside Reno. "Listen. You can stay here as long as you like. Tish doesn't mind. But that painting has to go."

"I know."

"Jamie's coming for it tonight."

Reno hugged himself and looked away.

Will asked, "Are you ever gonna tell us why you did this? If you don't mind my saying so, it was pretty fucked up."

No response.

"Did you just need to pull it off? Like some ego trip?"

"*No.*" The first word exploded. "She wanted to finish it and she knew she couldn't. It broke her heart. I almost did it for her, but I couldn't." Reno leaned his head in hands. "I'd dishonored her enough."

"So you painted a whole damned copy?"

Reno looked at the canvas again. "To complete her vision." His voice faded to a whisper. "I could do it when she couldn't. I actually *could.*"

Will blew out a breath and shook his head. He seemed about to speak, but gathered his clothes and left. The vision flickered. Reno was lying on the bed and staring at the ceiling when Mae saw him again. A soft tapping on the door made him stir. "What?"

Jamie glided in. "Mate. I need to take it." Reno turned his back to him and curled up. Jamie sighed. "Jeezus." He sat behind the younger man, studying him. He tugged his ponytail. No response. "Talk to me. Will says you don't eat, don't go out. You need help."

Reno shook his head.

"Go home and talk to Lonnie."

"I can't."

"Yeah, you can. He already knows." Jamie dug his wallet from his pocket and searched through it, bringing out a business card. He reached over and tucked it into Reno's hand. "Call this bloke, too. Carl Gorman. He's good. And he's Navajo. He'll understand you."

Reno rubbed his eyes and rolled over, squinting at the card. "Who is he?"

"My therapist."

Mae left the vision. Reno was in bad shape. No wonder Jamie had been willing to help Zak protect him.

She found everyone had moved out to the front porch. The air had grown cooler and the stars had come out in all their desert brilliance. Jamie lay on his back, softly singing the song he'd sung under the double rainbow.

"We'll live forever, love lasts forever ..."

Niall and Marty sat side by side on the steps, with Daphne a step below them and Alan a few feet to their right, listening.

Jamie broke off the song and sat up. "You found out it's hers, right?"

"Yes. And that Reno painted the other. The reason he did it, though—it's not what I'd guessed." Mae hesitated to share Reno's mental state. "It's messed up, but he thought he was doing something for her."

"They know. I told 'em."

"Thanks for checking." Niall got to his feet, and the others followed suit. "Let's lock this place up. Alan, can we take you out to dinner? Give you a bed for the night?"

Alan declined, saying he had to collect Ezra and bring him to Bernadette's.

Mae and Jamie said their goodbyes and walked to the back of the house hand in hand. Once they were in his car, she asked, "Do I get the whole story now? About the other painting?"

"Mm." Jamie backed the Fiesta out into the street. "If you don't tell anyone. Has to be just you, me, and Zak."

"Does Reno know?"

"Nah." He drove toward Mae's house. "Better that he doesn't. Zak told Ezra to go on without him, said he'd seen some trash he needed to get, and he ran and got the painting from me and shoved it in the bag, and he—Jeezus, hate it that he had to do it—he got rid of it. With the litter. Passed it off as a fucking pizza box."

"He threw it away?"

"Had to—to end the forgery story."

"But it's not over."

"Yeah, it is." He paused at a stop sign. "All that's left is the love story."

"Jamie." Mae turned to look him in the face. "He *was* forging, and they *weren't* lovers."

His eyes were soft and vulnerable, meeting hers briefly. "You sure?" He drove on.

Reno had denied the intimacy when Will asked about it, but Florencia had been at her worst that night. Her relationship with Reno might have been stormy—up and down, off and on—and secret, but it was possible. "No. But I do know he was forging her work. Zak told me."

"But Niall doesn't know. David and I went to the gallery last Saturday after I talked with you. Took the whole night because he wanted to keep the frames and just destroy the canvases. His mum was so upset she wouldn't help us, but she couldn't fight it. I mean, if we're saving Reno, we're saving her—can't do one without the other. Next day she sold Niall's buyer one of the genuine early works. Feel bad about him spending the money, but at least the estate can pay for it, and he got something valuable. When it gets authenticated, he won't have anything to go on for forgery."

They crossed a silent, summer-night Broadway with a three-quarter moon rising over it and continued down Foch past Austin to Marr. With Jamie's help, Zak the hero and rescuer had made sure Reno didn't get caught. It had been a close race, but this time Zak had won. And Mae was relieved that he had.

She asked, "Are you ever going to explain the first painting disappearing?"

"Nah. It wasn't Niall's, it was Reno's. So taking it wasn't illegal. And neither was painting it. He didn't sign it with her name or plan to sell it. So—no intent to defraud, right? And it's not actually a copy. It's more like the painting she didn't finish, as finished by Reno. An act of mourning. I told Niall that if you hadn't accused

Reno of forgery, he could have left his version in the studio and returned the original, too."

"If I hadn't accused him of forgery, he wouldn't have returned the original."

"I didn't mean you'd done something bad, love. He needed to almost get caught. They all did. Zak couldn't talk them into quitting when they knew he'd never turn them in. Not like his moral imperative was that persuasive, y'know?"

Jamie parked the Fiesta at Mae's house and they climbed the porch steps.

"I hope Reno will go home," he said, running a finger down her back while she unlocked the front door. "Stay with his family a while."

"I'm sure it'd help." She went to the kitchen, Jamie following, and filled two glasses of water. Mae sat at the table, sipping. Jamie guzzled, refilled his glass and stood at the counter, drinking more slowly. She said, "But it won't solve everything. The forgeries Kathy sold are still out there. That'll hang over him for the rest of his life."

"Yeah. But there's nothing we can do about it. Can't see Kathy calling the buyers and telling 'em." Jamie gazed into his glass, then took a sip. "We took care of everything we could."

Florencia's final work had come back. Reno's reputation was intact. The Chavez-Mirabal gallery was cleared of forgeries. That wasn't quite everything. "What about the parrots. Can they take them back to the store?"

Jamie made a few humming noises, and his shoulders did the telltale one-two shrug. He was avoiding something. Mae prodded him, asking again. He sighed. "They'd planned to keep Bouquet and give me Placido when David's aunt passed—if she'd kept him—and say Shelli found him at the rescue center, but that was before they knew you were psychic. So they kept 'em both. The store had the birds insured and that made Shelli feel like they were paid for. Rationalizing, I know. But I told her that sooner or later Alan's bound to mention that Violet died, so Bouquet had to leave the gallery."

"And go where? Back to the store or not?"

"Um ... The Exotic Aviary, the store where Shelli worked ... they closed. Couldn't compete with Feathered Friends. City can't support two parrot stores. So, I have two parrots."

"Oh, sugar. Did you think this through?"

"Nah. Couldn't break 'em up, though. They love each other."

"That was sweet of you, but they're a major commitment. For a lifetime. You can't just jump into it."

"Sure I can, if I know what I want." Jamie set his glass down. "There'll be some problems, but I can solve them. I just have to change the story I tell myself."

That sounded like therapy talk. Applied to spontaneous pet adoption. "Dr. Gorman teach you that?"

"Nah. My relationship book. They say you can have the life you want if you rewrite your story." He pulled a chair in front of her and sat knee to knee. "I can have parrots. Because in my new story, I don't stay depressed and kill myself and die young. I *live*. As long as they do." He took her hands. "You could change your story, too."

"I already have. A lot of times."

"I meant your love story." His eyes searched hers. "Believe in forever. Marriage. All of it."

"I don't know yet, sugar." Before he could give her the baby seal look, she drew him to his feet, kissed him, and held him tight. "But I do want my story to have you in it."

Author's Notes and Acknowledgements

Dada Café, The Exotic Aviary, and Eight Northern Pueblos Tribal College are fictitious. I made changes to a few streets and buildings in T or C and Mescalero for the purposes of the story.

The painted trailer with the poem on it on Austin Street was one of my favorite bits of T or C scenery for years. In 2015, it got a makeover with turquoise siding. I like to think the words and images are still there, hidden like rock art in a canyon to be discovered again someday.

The Mescalero fire-danger T-shirt is made by White Horse Art and Design, Mescalero, NM.

The Dam It Man Triathlon took place every summer from 2010 through 2014. I made some alterations to the route and left out some fun but distracting details, such as the high school football team being on hand to haul competitors out of the deep water and onto the dock.

All information I have included about the ceremonies in Mescalero is material the tribe shares with the general public. I hope I have portrayed the event with the respect I feel for it and which it deserves.

I would like to thank the following people and businesses:

Darlene Parker of Feathered Friends of Santa Fe for answering my questions about parrots. Any inaccuracies in my portrayal of the birds are mine.

Delmas Howe, for permission to use the Cowboy Angel in this story. A small print of that extraordinary work of art kept me company and inspired me for two years as I worked on this book.

Passion Pie Café for permission to set scenes there and for allowing me to employ Misty Chino as their barista. I am especially grateful to Jia Apple for information about the design and structure of the art-topped tables and for the idea to have the artist try to drag one out the door.

Rio Bravo Fine Art for permission to set scenes there and to have Florencia Mirabal exhibit her work there.

About the Author

Amber Foxx has worked professionally in theater, dance, fitness, yoga, and academia. She has lived in both the Southeast and the Southwest, and calls New Mexico home.

Follow:

http://amberfoxxmysteries.com

https://www.goodreads.com/author/show/7554709.Amber_Foxx

https://www.facebook.com/pages/Amber-Foxx/354071328062619

To purchase other books in the series:

https://amberfoxxmysteries.com/buy-books-retail-links

Contact:

mail@amberfoxxmysteries.com

53206696R00267

Made in the USA
Columbia, SC
14 March 2019